SAVAGE LOVE, SWEET LOVE

"Come," he said, taking her elbow, "let's go out by the water. It is cool there."

"I—I'm not warm."

Lakota smiled to himself. "You will be, Aiyana. I am told that all wedding nights get warm sooner or later."

Hypnotically, she walked with Lakota to the water's edge. She had felt a strong sense of danger earlier standing next to him, becoming his wife. She knew he had been waiting for her to say the words that would make her his. Now all she felt was extreme nervousness being alone with him.

"Come and sit with me now," Lakota said, coaxing her with the gentle tone of his voice.

He led her to the blanket and they stood over it. Then Lakota tugged at her hands and together they knelt on the square. His long, square-tipped fingers cupped her face as Lakota gazed at her for a long time. His eyes cherished every gentle angle, every soft curve. While his eyes made sweet love to her, his other hand swept down over her, memorizing every detail of her lovely body. Everywhere he touched there was a trail of flame left behind. . . .

SONYA T. PELTON

CAPTIVE CARESS

ZEBRA BOOKS
KENSINGTON PUBLISHING CORP.

ZEBRA BOOKS

are published by

Kensington Publishing Corp.
475 Park Avenue South
New York, NY 10016

First printing: November 1986

Printed in the United States of America

In loving memory of my father—

Arne August Sillanpa,

Who passed away in the Summer of '85

Forever—
Sonya Totiana

Love is strong as death. Many waters cannot quench love, neither can the floods drown it. . . .

—Solomon's Song viii, 6, 7

Love is life's end! an end, but never ending;
All joys, all sweets, all happiness, awarding;
Love is life's wealth, (never spent, but ever spending,)
More rich by giving, taking by discarding;
Love's life's reward, rewarding in rewarding;
Then from thy wretched heart fond care remove;
Ah! shouldst thou live but once love's sweets to prove,
Thou wilt not love to live, unless thou live to love.

Spenser

PART ONE

Wild Heart

SUNDANCE PROPERTY, TEXAS, 1854

I arise from dreams of thee,
And a spirit in my feet
Has led me—who knows how?
To thy chamber window, Sweet!

The Indian Serenade
—Percy Bysshe Shelley

Chapter One

Indian paintbrushes crept over hills and valleys, blazing their opulent color along lanes and roads, above and below the Colorado River, and on pasture slopes. The bluebonnets had long ago yielded their superiority to the wolf-flowers, or *conejo,* as the Mexicans call them, the blueness of the former paling and developing into podded seeds. Wild phlox, too, burned their red and pink fires out. There was only the merest ghostlike whisper of wind stirring the heights of the umbrella-shaped cottonwood where the blue-winged thrush was warbling his rapturous song.

Wearing a cool, crisply starched and ironed umber calico patterned with white starred flowers, Willow Hayes frolicked in the dew-encrusted grass with the cherubic baby that had just lately learned that crawling got her where she wanted to go faster and farther than she'd ever gone before.

Scooting along on all fours, Sarah Brandon screeched when Willow caught up with her, looming above from behind. The baby ducked her head, her red curls wisping at her ears, her pink-bow mouth drooling on her young aunt's hand splayed in the grass beside the dimpled knees.

"Silly Sarah—Aunty Willow's got you now!"

Sarah rocked back and forth like a puppy not quite willing to sit, her lips working fast, puckered, smacking, going "Mmmm-hmm-mmm . . ."

"Oooh," Willow crooned, "baby's tired. Come on, twinkle toes."

With a strength that belied her fragility, Willow scooped tiny Sarah up as she stood, tossing back the recalcitrant blond wave that had a habit of always drifting over one eye. With a thumb in her rosebud mouth, Sarah clutched her pink-and white-starred baby quilt, one that had seen better days. As usual, Talon's Cloud was loose in the yard and came over now to sniff baby Sarah's quilt before tossing his huge, velvety head and galloping back to the place where his handsome master stood squinting his scintillating green eyes against the blinding brilliance of the sun. A smile of pleasure softened his ruggedly lean, sun-bronzed face as he gazed across the greensward at the two women and the darling child. He clapped his lean hands as his horse came running toward him, and he smiled at his fortune, for the stallion had eluded everyone but him, Talon Clay Brandon. Cloud, of Arabian-mustang stock, was like a big white puppy that was left to roam the grounds of Sundance and he got into mischief just as well as a puppy.

"It's time for your morning nap." Just then Willow glanced up to see her sister walking toward them. Tanya's face was a wreath of knowing, motherly smiles. "Better be good now. Mama's coming," Willow added in a whispery tone.

"M-*mum,*" Sarah tried, squirming and reaching for her mother as she spotted her.

"She's cranky," Tanya said, holding out her arms, "and I think she's getting her first tooth."

"Mum!" Sarah cried happily when her mother took her from aunt Willow. "Wee—" Sarah began, tossing a chubby arm back at Willow. "Woo!" she finished with a bubbly gurgle, then began to hum tiredly once again.

"You wore her out, as usual," Tanya chided her sister with gentle playfulness. "But she always comes back for more, doesn't she." The mother became busy then, fussing with her little darling.

A river of pleasure ran through Willow's blood just then as she spotted Talon Clay Brandon crossing the greensward, his loose, easy stride as stealthful and graceful as an Indian's. His most outstanding feature was his hair—ivory-blond at the ends and the rest a wheat shade. Around his well-shaped head was a turquoise headband he had begun to sport of late, ornamented with a silver concho set above each ear. All he needed now was a feather, Willow thought with a furtive smile.

White Indian was what came to one's mind looking at Talon Clay.

The Indian, Little Coyote, who had befriended Talon and his friend Almanzo—better known as Dark Horse by the Comanches and Kiowas—belonged to a northern Kiowa tribe. So Little Coyote had informed Willow. It was true Talon's features were as fine as any Kiowa brave's, with the Roman outline of the head that is so frequently found in the north and is distinct from the head shape of the Comanches and Pawnees. Talon even dressed like the Plains Indians. He often wore deerskin moccasins that reached to the knees, dyed black and laced with rawhide, and at one time she'd even seen him riding along with Little Coyote, both sporting *breechclouts!*

Willow feared that any day now Talon would change his hair style for the distinctive one of the Kiowa warrior. The hair on the left side was left to grow long and was usually tied or wrapped, with a scalp lock allowed to hang down behind. On the right side it was cut short for the purpose of showing off the Kiowas' ear ornaments. So, again, Little Coyote had informed her. He himself wore his hair in a thick black braid down his back, and sometimes free and flowing. But . . . a scalp lock for Talon Clay?

Heaven forbid!

Now Willow's worshiping gaze followed Talon back to the corral where he was beginning work with a newly caught mustang; her blood began to tingle wildly just watching him from afar.

"She'll be walking soon," Tanya said as Willow kept up alongside.

Their skirt hems brushed the already drying grass as the sun gathered up strength and rose higher. The smell of fragrant wood smoke coming from the bunkhouses sweetened the air. By nightfall, everyone at Sundance would readily welcome the cool darkness that would shroud the land.

"What? Oh, yes," Willow answered her sister belatedly, the strong, amber-brown matrix of her eyes filled with lovely and mysteriously moving shadows. Sighing, she watched until Talon was out of sight, hidden from view by a blue roan and several other rugged bulks of mustangs. He was going to find his brother Ashe, no doubt, or Almanzo, or one or several of the mustangers and drovers. Like his brother Ashe, Talon was always seen in the company of men; and, always working hard, they never seemed to have time for play anymore. Willow felt as if she had ceased to exist in Talon's eyes. There had been a time when they'd shared happy hours together, but suddenly it seemed they were always serious and tense when the situation called for their being forced to be in each other's company. He appeared almost angry when he was around her.

"I see you are preoccupied," Tanya said, following Willow's interested line of vision. "I'm going to put Sarah down for her nap. Then Ashe and I are going to have some long-awaited time together. See you later, dear."

Glancing around from under her lashes, Willow knew what was coming—or who—for she'd heard the Tuckers' wagon coming up the dogwood-lined lane out front of the big house. Moving covertly beneath the gnarled arms of the ancient cottonwood, Willow watched as Hester Tucker guided the team out back and alighted from the wagon. One of the drovers walked over to stand beside their neighbor.

Hester was decked out in powder-blue gingham, from the hem of her full-circle skirts to the ruffled bodice, on up to the light and airy sun umbrella she was just in the process of snapping open as she swung it above her head. Her tawny curls, obviously coaxed with the hot iron first into tight coils at her flushed cheeks and then into swirls below her shoulders, bounced and sprang like liquid coils when she walked.

Huh! Hester Tucker did not walk! She sashayed, like the hind-end of a horse!

Disparagingly, Willow lifted a hand to her own loosely hanging tresses on down to the flow of her hair in back. Beeline straight, as if she'd pressed a flatiron meant for clothes on it. Her hair did wave sometimes, a little, if the humidity was high enough; and Miss Pekoe, Tanya's housekeeper, said that Willow was lucky to have hair that "hangs like cornsilk from an ear o' corn and been long growin', honey chile!"

Well—I have been told I do have a "pretty yeller wave" over one eyebrow, Willow remembered. She smiled then, pleasantly reminded of Zeke, one of the mustangers, who had said her hair style was see—ductive. And Talon Clay, oh, how he had frowned darkly at those fancy words! Zeke was a drover from over at the Tuckers' Saw Grass ranch, now working for her brother-in-law Ashe Brandon, having quit their neighbors' employ for lack of pay. Today, Zeke still sported the orange-purple remains of a black eye. Talon had given it to him. There'd been a minor disagreement over Talon Clay's parentage.

It is all Hester's fault. She has been spreading a rumor that Talon Clay is half-breed. Lordy, Talon Clay might resemble an Indian . . . but he surely wasn't one. Hester only wanted to stir Talon Clay's passion up again . . . always wanting to get in his plum-tight breeches!

Keeping hidden, Willow watched Talon as he came into view and paid no more attention to Hester Tucker than he did the bothersome horseflies and ever-swishing horse tails. No longer did they take their private walks together in the woods. No longer did

Talon look at Hester in that certain way.

So, Willow now wondered, had Talon become jealous that day when Zeke had complimented her? At least, she'd *thought* it had been a nice compliment to give a young woman. A bit forward, maybe, but nice anyway. Had Talon sought to deliberately provoke Zeke? Willow smiled. This could only mean that jealousy had taken hold of Talon. And Willow knew that jealousy in a man could be very fierce and formidable.

Willow chewed her lower lip. *But which came first? The black eye from Zeke's comment? Or afterward, after she had received the compliment from rugged, blue-eyed Zeke?*

Hearing the jingle of check rings, Willow pressed further beneath her ancient wooded sanctuary, then whirled about to walk to the other side of the tree. That would be Ashe returning from Granger's mercantile. Her brother-in-law. Tanya had said she wanted to be alone with him. Willow could see why . . . Ashe was a very handsome, exciting man; besides that, Tanya loved Ashe something fierce, and the feeling was mutual with Ashe.

Emerging from beneath the widespreading arms of the cottonwood, Willow stepped onto the wooded path that would lead her to the "little house," where she and her brother, Samson, lived. She'd missed him this past week. He was either getting himself into some sort of trouble or another, or someone else "into it." Maybe he would change, grow up a little while he was in New Orleans with the Rankin family.

The Rankins' plans were to bring back a relative. Not of theirs, but of Ellita Tomas's, a shirttail cousin.

Her name, they had offhandedly mentioned, was Fleurette Baudier. Rosa Rankin had told Willow that she was about Willow's own age, nineteen, only with black, black hair, and strange eyes—yellow-green, Rosa had said.

It will be nice to have a friend my own age to visit. Hester has never been a true friend to me. Lord knows, she hates me so!

Crossing the rock-constructed footbridge and climbing the mossy banks of the meandering creek, Willow topped the small incline and stood just across from the little house, gray-brown in the noon sun. It was the house type that was brought across the Appalachians into Kentucky and Tennessee; and from there the pioneers had it brought into Texas.

Willow walked closer still, until she was standing before the porch, which extended across the front, the door opening onto it. Inside, where Willow stepped now, the house resembled a log cabin. Outside, the logs had been covered up with weatherboarding.

With the gentle, caring touch of one who has come to know and love a house, Willow ran a butterfly touch of her hand over the blackened logs of the fireplace. It had been built of thin logs, which had been placed over each other to form a square and the cracks then filled with mud. A stone hearth lay beneath her feet.

Willow looked around the main room. Shelves and pegs held spare clothes and linen. Her eyes darted back to the fireplace. Even now she could hear, without even touching, the crane speak as it squeaked when Tanya used to swing a heavy pot or kettle off the fire . . . now she herself was the only one who ever used it.

Tanya lived here in the "little house" no longer. This

house had felt their father's weary steps as he returned from Sundance's fields, had heard his deep, joyous laughter, known, as if these walls had ears, his labored breathing and his last dying gasp. She and Tanya and Samson had known it too. Was it really almost two years ago that they had buried him?

This was her house now. Willow loved it here and would keep it in her gentle care for as long as she lived within its three rooms.

Feeling alone, but not in any way dejected, Willow hunkered down before the now cold hearth. Later she would prepare a meal for herself. This day, for some reason, she wanted to be alone. To reflect back over the yesterdays, the little romance she had found with Talon Clay. Besides, Tanya and Ashe needed some time together. Tanya had said this herself.

A desperate longing seized Willow and filled her insides with aching need. For months past this longing had never left her. She had seen into her heart, wondered at what had been nurtured and was growing there. She wanted, so much desired more than anything in the whole wide world, to learn to love ultimately one certain man who would love her in return.

Talon Clay.

None other would do for Willow Hayes. He was her life, her very breath. He lived inside of her, even though he was not yet a tangible part of her being. For Talon to be flesh of her flesh was her uttermost desire.

"Moon Flower."

Starting at the deep timber of voice behind her, Willow spun about, in the same motion rising from the puncheon bench. The long, craggy Indian face was familiar, and she relaxed at once, holding up her palm in greeting.

"Little Coyote." She could almost laugh at the name, which his people, the Kiowa, had given him. He was tall, over six foot, broad as mature oak, and straight as an arrow. "Come and sit. We will talk."

"Aye. I have much to tell Moon Flower this day. Secrets . . ."

"Secrets?"

Two trapped hares hung around his neck. "First, I have brought gifts for you," Little Coyote said.

"Oh!" she said with open delight. "They are very big."

"Make much stew."

"Very much," she laughed, taking the hares from Little Coyote and thanking him.

While Willow skinned and cleanly gutted the hares with swift efficiency, Little Coyote sat cross-legged on the floor watching her. He couldn't do much better, he thought, seeing her neat downsweep of the knife section the rabbits to ready them for her stewpot.

Reaching up to place a well-seasoned buckskin pouch on the table, Little Coyote said, "I have brought herbs for your kettle, Moon Flower."

Willow glanced over her shoulder. "That is very kind of you, Little Coyote. You must stay for supper." She had wanted to be alone to think, but now that Little Coyote was here she might as well enjoy the occasion.

She had not known the Indian for very long—maybe two months. He had first come to her notice when he rode into Sundance with Talon Clay, the two of them looking like brothers but for Talon's coloring. Though Talon had blond hair, his skin was turning reddish-brown from so much time in the sun. The contrast between skin and hair was stunning, the eyes holding a new startling green shade.

Little Coyote belonged to the band of Kiowas known as Kat-U-Biters. He was an important member of the tribe, known for his artistic talent. Another Indian, whom he hadn't named to her yet, had taught him how to use the paints on the walls of caves and on buffalo skins, to tell stories. One day, he said, he would bring her to meet his "friend."

Silence reigned in the little house. Many times when Little Coyote had come to visit, he preferred long silences in which he said not a word. Then all of a sudden he would begin to speak.

This was one of those silent days, she could see.

While she worked preparing the meal, allowing Little Coyote his quiet time to muse while he thought of what he was going to tell her, she flushed as the dream of the night before returned to her. Gently, Talon's fingers had cupped her face while his thumbs traced the line of her chin, her throat, the sides of her breasts . . . and then their mouths closed together in a ravenous kiss. The dream had ended so deliciously real. His lips had been so possessive. She'd been able to detect his masculine scent, too, as he bent to lift her effortlessly in his arms. Then she had been shamelessly kissing him back! She couldn't seem to get enough of him. Every part of her had yearned for his full possession! She had shamelessly flaunted herself at him. Dear Lord—that she'd ever do that while fully awake! She had waited and waited for the tumultuous fulfillment, but it had never come. With desire pulsating through her, she'd tried to pull Talon closer, but he had resisted. He had been the first to kiss her, and then he'd laughed at her, taunted her, and had become as elusive as he was in reality. Come morning, her new, highly strung emotions caused widespread damage to her nerves! What was happening to her? Feeling confused, Willow closed her eyes for a moment before opening them again. It was almost two years gone since she'd met Talon Clay, and oh! to think she'd almost let him do *that* to her when they'd been alone for a time beneath the grove of cottonwoods. She'd had no idea how dangerous a situation she had put herself into, pretending she knew all about love.

"Listen. The wind speaks," Little Coyote said gutturally and gestured with a bronzed-colored hand.

"It's just a songbird."

"It is the Wind Bird."

Willow laughed and glanced toward the open window letting in the humid summer breeze and then back at the swarthy Indian beside her. "I can hear the thrush, Little Coyote, but Moon Flower would much rather hear Little Coyote speak now. You had some secret to tell me?"

While she watched, Little Coyote reached up with his right hand, held it close to her right cheek, with the back of his hand down, his long fingers touching and slightly cupped. Willow's eyes were bright with curiosity as the Indian moved his hand in a rotary motion from the wrist.

"Sign language, Little Coyote?"

"Yes. Of the Plains tribes."

"I see. What does it mean, what you just did?"

"*Ka-I-Giv-U.* Kiowa."

Willow nodded, and bringing her hands together she cupped her knee and leaned back, her eyes expectant.

"This," she said, "is a waiting position." She smiled. "I am waiting, Little Coyote."

The young, intelligent Indian snorted. "I have been all over the Plains with my subchief, met at the big forts many white 'squaws.' You are most impatient of all." He squared his chin. "I will tell you the rest—in time."

"Who is this subchief?"

"In time."

"I might as well make supper while you take your time in telling me this great secret."

Little Coyote pressed her arm as she began to rise, urging her to remain seated. "You may prepare supper—after talk for a time."

Willow sighed, her eyes beginning to sparkle with an even greater curiosity than ever. "It must be good if you have to keep me in all this confounded suspense. You come here with a great secret and all you do is beat around the bush. Please, on with it, Little Coyote!"

All of a sudden the young Indian, perhaps in his early twenties, Willow had often thought, suddenly became very serious over what he was about to speak of. "I will tell Moon Flower first of long ago. There were many wars, one following the other." Little Coyote made many gestures while he spoke. "It was the Dakota Sioux who were driven back from the Black Hills in this war; many Osages killed many more Kiowa warriors. It was in western part of Indian Territory. More terrible wars follow, but peace came then between Mescalero Apaches and Kiowa. First, Kiowa drive Apaches into Texas from Staked Plains to Mountains west of the Pecos. Kiowas, Comanches, Apaches and Cheyenne band together long after Kiowa did this. Big war party grow like weeds south of

Sioux Country. They be beaten." Little Coyote made a descriptive picture with his hands that portrayed bad defeat and humiliation as his face drew downward, his head hung in a dejected pose. "It was by much smaller force of Sauk-Fox who did this to big war party."

Shrugging her shoulders, Willow said, "This is not a secret. You merely tell me of history, Little Coyote."

"History, yes, history first. Secret later."

Willow sighed and rested her arms upon the puncheon table, waving for him to go on. She could almost yawn at all this, but she didn't want to discourage the new friend she had only known for two months.

"Many more die of white man's disease," Little Coyote went on. "Pox, and other much worse disease take many Kiowa—"

"I know about what you are speaking of, Little Coyote," she broke in. "Cholera, brought from the east by California emigrants. I know. Our family escaped the cholera epidemic of eighteen forty-nine. Scores of Indians committed suicide in their despair over the dread disease."

Hanging his head over his open palms, Little Coyote said with much sadness, "My own family also."

"Oh, I'm sorry." Willow touched his arm. "I did not know, Little Coyote."

"It is over now. Best to forget."

"Yes—best." Willow looked up and over to the window, thinking of Talon Clay. His father had died, not long ago, as her own had. Talon never spoke of him, and she wondered if he had even mourned . . . or even cared for Pete Brandon the way a son cares for his father. Talon didn't seem to be the kind of person who needed anyone, and now she wondered if he ever had in his entire twenty-seven years. Just who'd told her Talon was that age she wasn't certain, but most likely it'd been Clem; the old man seemed to know everything about everybody residing at Sundance.

Pushing Talon reluctantly out of her thoughts for now, Willow reflected a few moments on what Little Coyote had been telling her. What he had been relating to her was the history of the Kiowas and their trek through high mountains and green hills. But why did Little Coyote want her to know all this? What purpose did the telling serve? Did he only wish her to learn more about his people, or was there something else?

She knew that the Kiowas had begun in the "Rock Mountain" area of western Montana. By the mid-1700s they had well established their council fires in the Black Hills of South Dakota. Vince Sawyer, the new blacksmith in Bastrop, had come from South Dakota, and after church on many occasions Vince had pressed on her tales of "back home" and of his vast knowledge of the home Indians and Plains Indians. The Dakotas and the Cheyenne had driven the Kiowas from the Black Hills, and in early 1800 they had migrated to the Witchita Mountains. From that stronghold the Kiowas had moved their bands ever closer to raid into Texas and Mexico. The Kiowas had come into contact with many of the Plains tribes, during their trek eastward to the Black Hills and then southwestward to the Witchita Mountains. Those that became firm allies of the Kiowas during this movement were the Wichitas, Crows, Wacos, Pueblos, Towakanis, and then, at last, the Comanches.

"Little Coyote," Willow began, smiling at her friend,

who now seemed so sad, "why have you been pressed to tell me of the history of your people? Is there a reason for all this? I see," she said at last when he kept silent, "you have just come to talk. This is the secret you have wished to tell me? Merely a game?"

"Is my friend Little Coyote in there?" a voice, well-modulated, tinged with humor, came from the doorway.

Willow felt a little disappointment at the intrusion. There could be no mistake as to who that low, velvet voice belonged to. "Almanzo. Come in." She began to rise from the bench, but again Little Coyote held her down with a gentle pressure from his hand.

The younger Indian greeted his big friend, even larger in width of shoulder and height than himself. "Nightwalker," he said, alert as the black-clothed man entered.

"I am not Nightwalker," Almanzo Rankin corrected Little Coyote. "You know who he is. I am not true Nightwalker." It came to him then that Little Coyote was playing games with him and wanted to include Willow in this, but the time for giving away their secret had not come yet.

Interest showing in her fine-featured countenance, Willow said, "Who is he then, this Nightwalker? Your father?"

"He is not my father, Miss Willow." He looked suspiciously in the direction of his friend, his dark eyes seeming to read Little Coyote's mind. "Nightwalker, the name, has come to me by mistake . . . it belongs to another." He would not say who, but he had a feeling Little Coyote had almost revealed their secret to Willow Hayes. "What has Little Coyote been telling you—*secrets?*"

"I have not told her anything, my friend," Little Coyote said, looking up at the face that was as bronze in color as his own.

Willow stared at Almanzo's hooded expression. "He would have, if you had not come along just now. Little Coyote has been telling me the history of the Kiowas and Comanches. I have a feeling he was just about to tell me the most important part of his story." She watched the man stare away in preoccupied thought. "Do *you* know what he was about to tell me?"

"Perhaps." His eyes bored right through her before turning his attention back to the younger Indian. "Come along, Little Coyote, the boss man has returned. He wishes to speak to all of the mustang hunters."

A soft snort came from Little Coyote. "The Ranger does not like me. Why would he wish to speak to me? Ashe Brandon only likes you some because you have known the white man's ways for so long. You have lived with the white men. You even smell like one."

Willow's eyes widened, going back and forth between the two Indians.

"True," Almanzo said, his fathomless dark eyes staring down into the other's face. "But my parents—who have adopted me—are Spanish. Does this make me a white man for living so long with them?"

"Damn!" Willow shot up from the bench. "You two never stop disagreeing, do you? Have your disagreement elsewhere. All I want to know is what Little Coyote was about to tell me. Otherwise," she snapped, her dainty hands cocked at her hips, "*he* is not going anywhere—boss or no boss!"

The soft muffled pad of moccasins sounded on the porch, a voice calling out, "Almanzo, you in there? The boss is looking for you." A pause. "Willow?"

Talon.

Aflame, Willow's entire body leapt to the hypnotic sound of that voice. She recovered quickly then as she took in the expressions on the two dark faces in front of her. Little Coyote had shot to his feet, his eyes moving nervously from the door to Almanzo to Willow Hayes. There was a warning light in Almanzo's eyes.

Aha, Willow thought to herself. So, Little Coyote's unrevealed secret had something to do with Talon Clay. *But what could it be?*

"We will be out in just a minute, Tal." It was Almanzo who spoke first to break the pressing silence. Turning, he warned Little Coyote, "Say not a word to Talon of the reason you came to visit Miss Willow."

Through the stretched, transparent hide of the door—so taut she was able to make out the exciting male form of Talon Clay—Willow could hear Talon becoming impatient by the sound of his shifting moccasined feet.

"What the hell's going on in there?" Another pause; then, "I'll warn you, Willow Hayes, I'm coming in!"

Just as Talon was reaching for the latch, the door was pushed out to meet his hand. A tawny eyebrow quirked at Almanzo, and then his mouth followed the action as Little Coyote stepped out from behind Almanzo. Finally Willow appeared, bringing up the rear. Closing the door behind her, she joined them on the porch.

Willow stared at Talon. He stared back, saying, "What in hell's been going on here?" Then he relaxed, smoothing it over with, "You having a party without my knowing and not being invited, Pussywillow?"

Willow blanched. He still called her *that*. It was childish, and she had come to hate it. "Yes, we were having a powwow. I am sorry I forgot to include you. Little Coyote had some, uh," she hesitated, looking to the stricken Indian, "some very interesting *tales* to tell me."

With a slow, almost imperceptible turn of his head in Little Coyote's direction, Talon drawled, "He has, huh?" He laughed, easily. "What are you fixing to do, Coyote, tell Miss Willow your life story?"

Vigorously, Little Coyote shook his head, causing his scalp lock to sway to and fro. Willow stared at Little Coyote's new hair fashion, wondering why she hadn't noticed it before now. Back and forth, Little Coyote looked between Willow and Talon Clay. He could not look Almanzo's way, however, for Dark Horse—which was Almanzo's Indian name—Dark Horse knew what Little Coyote had been up to. But Talon Clay had no idea what was going on; he only thought Little Coyote had come to flirt with Willow Hayes. He was always making eyes at Willow, though he denied this, saying she was only a friend and he enjoyed these visits with her. But Talon Clay thought differently.

Talon Clay Brandon did not yet know he was a half-breed; and Little Coyote wondered when Dark Horse would take Talon, Lakota, to see Kijika, his real father, who was camped with Chief Black Fox at the time. It was many moons to the north, and soon Little Coyote would return home to Black Fox's camp.

Eyeing Little Coyote with great suspicion now, Talon gave the Indian a firm nudge off the porch, and

Almanzo followed. The three big men began to move off down the path to the wooded creek. Little Coyote felt the steel of Lakota's arm behind the hand that steered him onward, ever closer to the very wet waters of the creek.

Still standing on the porch, her arms bent over her hips, Willow heard a loud splash, followed by enraged coughs and sputters, then some Indian utterances that sounded much like when white men brought curses down on another's head.

Willow was somewhat worried for Little Coyote and was about to go down there to check if he had drowned, when she heard deep male laughter that told her everything must be all right. Almanzo, Talon, and even Little Coyote, their voices carried like happy talking wind, carefree, with nowhere to go. Men. Free spirits.

Do they never worry like women, these young men?

Going back inside to prepare supper for one, Willow shook her head, realizing she would most likely never hear Little Coyote's secret now. Maybe she really did not want to, after all.

Later that same day, Talon Clay sat with his brother Ashe in the cool shade of the veranda, sipping chilled lemonade. The brothers were strikingly handsome, ruggedly so, each with his own particular brand of male virility and good looks. Their hair was almost the same shade of wheat, excepting that Ashe wore his shorter and Talon's had been left to grow inappropriately long—at least that was the word Tanya used. And Miss Pekoe, the black housekeeper, was always threatening Talon Clay with her scissors, laughing until tears came to her dark eyes when the good-looking lad scooted the other way.

Relaxing for the first time that day, Ashe broke the comfortable silence the brothers had shared. "Haven't seen Carl Tucker around in a long time." He grimaced and looked away from Talon's rawhide Indian getup. "Have you?"

"He must have bled to death from that shot he received in the leg," Talon said with a knowing smile.

"Never believed it was you who was rumored to have killed Tucker. By the way, are you sure you haven't seen him?"

Talon snickered. "If I had, Tucker would be six feet under right now where he belongs!"

Of course, this all came after the fact.

Stroking his chin, Ashe said, "Just what *did* happen that day when it was supposed to have been you who rode out of town after killing—supposedly killing—Carl Tucker?"

Talon heaved a sigh. "Tucker was arguing with Butch, and I decided to make myself scarce from San Antonio. Butch was feeling repentant and wanted to turn himself in, and wanted Tucker to go along with him and do the same. Of course, knowing chicken-turd Tucker, he never went, and so Tucker must have gunned Butch down in cold blood, just like he killed that innocent man whose stage we were holding up. I can thank you, my brother, Ranger, for keeping me out of jail. But that was a damn close call, I still sweat it out at night wondering how I would have fared in jail. Not very well—I'm restless and like to roam free!"

"And wild as the wind, too!" Ashe gestured to the clothes Talon Clay was wearing. "When did you take to wearing that Indian getup? I must have been looking the other way when you changed your clothes." Ashe chuckled.

With a lopsided grin, Talon softly said, "I get along much better with the Indian mustangers dressed this way when I meet up with them on the plains."

Looking down into his glass as he held it up, Ashe said, "Almanzo must think so, too. But then, he's half-Indian, isn't he?"

"He must be."

Talon laughed and Ashe smiled, looking the other way.

Chapter Two

The full moon of summer gently defined the "little house" in a velvety etching of silver. Half asleep, with the night birds making a symphony with the male cicadas outside her window, Willow's mind-memories conjured poignant sweet pictures from the not long ago past. . . .

It had been a gentle morning in springtime. An elusive butterfly had flitted past her shoulder. Then . . . he was standing there, across from her in the Sundance yard, unbelievably handsome, undeniably rugged and virile.

A smile of poignant remembrance touched Willow's softly blurred lips now. She hugged her feather-tick pillow. She hadn't realized at the time that she was staring at a Brandon man. Talon Clay Brandon. Neither had she realized how swiftly she would fall in love, irreversibly in love with him. Not until he'd come to stand before her—

"Howdy," he'd said, his voice a deep and throaty drawl, bordering on the sensuous.

Finally, like a puppet come to life, she had found the power to move and speak. "Do I know you?" She came part way out of her daze then, adding, "Am I *supposed* to?"

Oh, how his smile had changed the humdrum ordinary morning! She had felt all at once transported to paradise—golden-velvet paradise.

She had noticed how like her own hair his was. She'd reached out to finger a silken strand. His hair felt like a thread of liquid flame, and she had jerked back as if burned by it. He had stepped closer then, his nostrils flaring gently as if he had been smelling her out.

Talon Clay hadn't answered her question, but he had been speaking, words that at first did not register in a brain that was inquisitively all female. He had been doing crazy, tumultuous things to her insides. Her bones were jellies. Her lower half was fluttering like a hundred little birds banging about seeking release.

"Hello?" He'd waved a hand before her dazed face. Another devastating smile.

Finally, again most belatedly, she'd offered, "My name is Willow." She had muttered something inane next—something about the paleness of his hair.

"Howdy, Willow."

Oh Lordy! that masculine sound coming from his throat again—like a huge, sinewy cat purring in her ear.

Then he had told her there was gold dust in her hair. What had they talked about next? (She couldn't recall now, not now, not when she was half drugged with sleep.)

A grin broke out, and she could still picture it, a white grin in a boyishly handsome, sun-browned face.

Such handsomeness, with wicked green eyes to boot, was surely a sin for a young, untouched girl to behold all in one eyeful! She had been staring. She knew it. He knew it.

"What are you doing here on Sundance property?" she had asked him. Talon Clay Brandon. How could she have known back then he was a *Brandon?* Of course, he avoided her question. He had been hiding from the law at that time. She had not realized that either. Not at first.

"What are you doing here, Willow?" he asked.

"I live here." She tossed her head, telling him that she lived in the "little house" back there. Her eyes had been totally mesmerized by his handsomeness. She could not keep from staring as she asked, "You here to see Clem?"

"Yeah—that's right."

When he had seemed troubled by something all at once and had begun to step away from her, saying he had to be going, she'd felt her newfound paradise slipping away. "I—" she flushed. "I still don't know your name."

"Best you don't. So long . . . *damn.*"

Before Willow knew what was happening, his arm had snaked out to wrap around her waist. His breath came warmly against her cheek. "You better go now, Miss Willow."

A horse, huge and lathered, came pounding across the greensward, dangerously close to her, and then he was leaping aboard. With her mouth and eyes agape, she had watched him go, calling back over his shoulder, "Go away, Willow. Don't tell. . . ."

She had stood, shaking like a windswept leaf all

over. Her heart pounded like ceremonial Indian drums. He had said, "Don't tell." It had not taken her long to figure out that Talon Clay Brandon was an outlaw. He had been hiding a stolen safe that day back at Clem's bunkhouse, Talon and three other partners in crime.

Like puffs of dangerous smoke, they had vanished. Her blond stranger, gone away like mist from a wishful dream. Would she, she had wondered then, ever see him again?

Feeling more alone than ever now, Willow curled herself into a fetal position. Talon Clay, her elusive love. He was still like a wind of flame to her. Too dangerous to touch, or to love, and always just out of reach.

Willow could not know it, but not far away, across the creek and up the woody hill, Talon was prowling like a restless caged cat in the bunkhouse. Sleep would not come to him, either.

"Eyyy, *amigo,"* Almanzo Rankin rolled over to face the yellow nimbus of light stealing from the small table set between the bunks. "Are you trying to wear out the floor before it is time to get up?"

Talon did not stop his pacing. "I haven't even got *down* yet." He tossed his wide shoulders in a restless shrug.

"What?" Almanzo came to one elbow. "You have not even been to bed yet?" He glanced at the square of window, noting the position of the moon and stars. "It is morning, long after midnight."

"Think I don't know it?" Talon stopped, bent to peer

out the window, resumed his pacing.

A slow grin lifted Almanzo's swarthy face, the structure of his countenance made even more aristocratically taut and pronounced than usual. But Almanzo was not aristocratic Spanish as many thought. He was Indian. Half-breed. His deceased father, Hungry Wolf, and his people were among those northern Athapascans who had gravitated south. The Kiowa, Apache, Sioux, Arikara, and other Siouan tribes were elements of the plains population. Black Fox's people were mostly half-breeds who had broken away from the main branch of Kiowas. Only lately had Almanzo become friendly with his relatives while visting Black Fox's village.

Almanzo looked up again to watch his friend, his dark eyes going back and forth, as Talon paced. *Soon, my friend, you too will know who you truly are. It will be painful, true, but what must be done must be done . . . Lakota.*

"You are thinking of *her* again?" Almanzo said, his voice a masculine husk in the still of morning.

Talon whirled, hot gem color in his eyes. "What?" He went to stand closer to Almanzo's bunk. Slowly he asked, "What in hell did you say?"

"Garnet." Almanzo shrugged bare shoulders. "You have uttered her name often enough in your sleep. Is she someone special, this woman who walks your dreams and haunts you this way, *amigo?*"

"God!" Talon moaned and ran his fingers through his blond mane. "Oh, God . . . the bitch. I hate her. Why does she still have this hold on me? I let her go—it has been years."

"Perhaps then, truly you did not let her go? Not all

the way? Is there someone, I mean another woman who makes you think of this—ah—Garnet?"

Talon's smoldering dark green eyes were unreadable in his slim, sun-coppered face. "Not that I'm aware of. . . ." The indentation in his bottom lip was sensual, virile, as he said, lying, "No one. . . ."

"You would rather not speak of it, I see." Almanzo rolled over to his former sleep position, his back placed to Talon. "Sweet dreams, *amigo,"* he muttered, "when, and if, you get there."

His pacing coming to a halt beside the bed, Talon stared down at the undisturbed blanket covering the narrow mattress. His weight made an indentation as he finally lay down, only to stare at the splintered timber of the low ceiling. He rolled his head toward Almanzo, but found his gaze captured and held by the lantern's tiny flame instead of the sleeping man. He stared.

He went back in time . . . but not too far back. That could only create renewed pain. He only drifted back to a couple years before . . . safe . . . but really . . . how safe . . . ?

Butterfly. First came the butterfly. Then Willow Hayes. His breath caught constrictingly in his throat now as it had then, with her standing directly across from him in Sundance's back yard.

First meeting. Willow. Fragile little girl, little Pussywillow. Actually, little woman. She was more a woman now; back then she'd been just a girl. Her smile had held an angelic quality as she watched the butterfly's color fade in the summer-blue sky while it fluttered away.

Who is she? he'd wondered. He had not long to wait, he soon discovered.

Clear as a bell on Sunday morning, her voice rang out, "Sammy is in trouble again; he's got a thistle in his foot. Running barefoot, as you told him not to, sis."

Talon knew at once that Tanya Hayes was her sister. Tanya, the beautiful, earthy redhead. A tigress. She was his brother Ashe's wife now, and they had a lovely daughter, Sarah. He had heard Tanya call back as she hurried over to the edge of the woods, watching Willow bend to pick a wildflower and hold it up to her pert nose, "Are you coming?"

"I'm going to walk a bit, sis. Do you mind?"

A worried look had crossed Tanya Hayes's face, momentarily, and then vanished as quickly as it had come. "Just don't stay too long," she said to Willow. "You promised to peel those potatoes at the little house." Tanya had tossed a searching look about the grounds, as if she had detected someone's presence there on Sundance property.

As soon as Tanya Hayes left the sunshine of the mansion's back yard, Talon had found himself breaking from cover and walking toward the dainty, willowy blond. *She is too wonderful to be real,* he had thought. He kept his eyes glued to the golden-haired girl. She had frozen like a slim statue as soon as she caught sight of him. She seemed mesmerized, but unafraid of him. "Howdy," he'd said and neared her.

She was shading her nut-brown eyes from the sun, eyes that he had already seen were large and luminous, eyes that could melt the most hardened of criminal's hearts. Finally looking up into his face, she blinked as if just coming out of a trance, saying, "Do I know you?" Then, "Am I *supposed* to?"

Talon had wanted to laugh; she was so enchanting,

this mere slip of a girl, but he felt his mouth slide into a smile, automatic and friendly. She cocked her perfectly shaped head, and Lord, how his heart did somersaults in his chest . . . and he had taken in a tiny, golden-haired beauty, so bold as to note small, pointed breasts, a tiny waist. He had stared; he wondered what her age could be. Sixteen? Seventeen? Maybe younger, he could not tell for sure; she would be beautiful at any age, though. There was only one problem, if he should care to dally with her—she was innocent—that he could tell.

"Your hair is almost the same color as mine," she'd said and he'd almost jumped back when she reached out to touch his hair. Then she jerked back, as if she had been holding a red-hot branding iron.

He had been taken thoroughly aback by surprise, sure, but had found himself being irresistibly drawn to her, despite his earlier reservations, and stepped even closer to breathe in her special odor, like delicate perfume. It was as if she had been sending sweet and voluptuous signals to him.

Talon could not believe all this loveliness in one package, in one tiny slip of a female, standing right before him in the flesh. "Hello?" She had not responded, and he waved a hand in front of her staring eyes. He almost laughed aloud again as he said,"Is anybody in there?"

Pertly, she'd offered, "My name is Willow."

"Howdy, Willow." He shocked himself by his own lecherous thoughts, forgetting for a moment or two what an innocent she was; all he wanted to do was stretch out on top of Willow Hayes and make love to her, over and over, again and again. He'd caught himself before his baser emotions got hold, saying, "Miss Willow, you got gold dust in your hair."

"What are you doing here, on Sundance property?" she'd questioned.

Her eyes had traveled his dusty, trail-stained clothes and the urge to blurt out that he had grown up here . . . well, part of the time anyway . . . the urge was great to reveal himself for what he was—a Brandon man.

Looking around, Talon's green eyes lazy, hooded, he had begun, "Uh . . . just passing through, you might say." In that moment, in a fever of intense longing, he'd been reminded of another female. But she was gone now, and this sweet thing could never be the slut that Garnet Brandon née Haywood had been.

Talon had gone on, even though an ever-tightening knot of remembered desire coiled in his belly; he'd said, "What are *you* doing here, Willow?" And he had really known *what,* but still he wanted to hear it from her own lips. He had never gotten to know the Hayes family all that well, knew only that her father, Rob, had been the foreman at one time on their ranch, on Pa's ranch, better known as Sundance property. Before the Hayes family had come to stay on, there had been Garnet . . . only Garnet, for him, while she had idled and played . . . and had torn at his young foolish heart. Had he buried all his hopes and dreams with her in her grave atop the hill? And God . . . his very soul?

"I live here," Willow had said, her cheeks prettily flushed, "back there, but it's still on Sundance property." She was staring at his hair again . . . of course, she would not remember him, she had been too young at the time. He himself had not remembered *her.*

"Yeah . . . yeah, that's right." He'd stepped back, his lusty physical urges beginning to get the best of him. "I'll have to be going now, Miss Willow." Pussywillow, that's what her soft, liquid eyes reminded him of, and they were wide and vulnerable right now . . . he had to get away, and fast! For more reasons than one.

"I—" she had stammered, "I still don't know your name."

He had shaken his head to clear it. "Best you don't." Suddenly he was reminded of the butterfly; it seemed to have been born from the silky envelope of her hair and come to him and brought a part of Miss Willow along with it.

"So long. . . ." He had sworn then, for his partner in crime was just riding across the greensward toward them. What the hell . . . was he going to ride right into them? What did Carl Tucker think he was doing, trying to kill them both beneath his horse's hooves?

She was already in motion, stepping out of harm's way, his strong arm wrapping about her waist at the same time. Into her ear, he had husked, "You better go now, Miss Willow." *God, but you're lovely,* he had thought then, so close he could kiss her if he wanted to. He did want. But he did not want to frighten her or startle her any more than she was already . . . she was such an innocent, and this was not a propitious time. Would there ever be, for them? An aching hollowness had filled him. This could be the real thing . . . if only Garnet had never come into his life. And all the other women he had known: There had been too many to count.

As Carl Tucker's horse neared, Talon had leapt aboard and they had sped away. "Go away, Willow

. . . don't tell." What had she thought of his warning back then? he wondered now.

A bittersweet memory. With a lump growing in his throat, Talon sprang up in his bunk. This would never do! Without glancing back at Almanzo, Talon quit the bunkhouse, going where his heart would eventually lead him.

Willow had not been able to sleep. She had tossed and turned, finally rising from her bed while the sky was still dark and only a few stars had twinkled out.

The morning star was yet to shine as she went down on her knees to drag out her precious things from beneath the bed.

They were all there: the locket with the tiny portrait of the lovely mystery woman, and the amber gown. There was a small coffer, too, filled with shiny pins and yellow ribbons. She would make use of all of them, never knowing of the disastrous results that would ensue.

Working with her hair while studying the portrait of Garnet, she again practiced for the day when she would finally stand before Talon wearing all the woman's things, looking like the image of Garnet herself.

Tanya had said that Talon had been in love with the woman . . . if only she could make Talon love her.

Willow stood before the mirror, righting its crooked position on the wall. She looked beautiful, she thought, standing back from the mirror, again awed at her own stunning reflection. Garnet must have truly been a beautiful woman. . . .

Willow could not know that the simple but elegant

gown had come from New Orleans, an exact replica of a Parisian creation that Garnet's lover—one of many—had ordered made expressly for her in the French Quarter. And Willow could not know, either, that the woman had first seduced Talon Clay while wearing this very same pale reddish-yellow gown.

Pirouetting in front of the mirror, Willow tingled from head to slippered foot, conscious only of the gorgeous image she made.

"If only I could make Talon Clay love me, as much as he loved her." He *would* love her when he saw that she was exactly like *her*.

"I will make him forget Garnet, because she is dead and I am alive . . . alive to take her place in Talon's heart."

What did it matter if Talon did not love her for herself? She would go to any lengths only to gain his love, his fullest desire. This meant so much to her; all the world was in it. She dare not fail in this. Someday she would show him . . . but not just yet. It was just too soon.

Willow shivered and moved to the other side of the table. She lit a lamp and sat, lonely, sad, beside it.

There was light in Willow's window, and Talon moved toward it as he wondered what she was doing up so early. It was still dark out.

Often he had been drawn to the little house, in the hush of night when the moon rode high. But tonight was the closest he had come.

He should not be here, he told himself sternly, his emotions riding high. He was in a dangerous mood.

With a muttered curse, he went closer, his body compelling him in his course of action.

The more aggressive planes of his face shone in high relief. Talon looked the Indian more than ever. In shadowed countenance he could have quickly been mistaken for an Indian. With fringed buckskin shirt and tight breeches, headband, high black moccasins, he completed the imposing likeness of an Indian.

When the moon stole out from beneath the westward-scudding night clouds, however, Talon's flowing blond hair shone golden, a dead giveaway that he did not possess the usual dark shaft of Indian hair.

He was on the porch now. A board creaked noisily in the stillness, and he paused, his chest aching, and he wondered just what the hell he was doing. The straining shape of his manhood bore evidence of where his restless, haunting desires were taking him. But he was in the wrong place! He should not be here looking in on Willow, of all women, he should be in town where he could buy his release cheap. It had been so long. He could not even remember the name of the last woman he had bedded down with, let alone her face.

Unthinkingly Talon moved closer to the window and found himself bending to peer inside . . . just to make sure Willow was all right. She could be sick or something.

Lonely? Was Willow lonely? What if she was . . . he could not ease her loneliness. She did not have a man, or a lover, he was sure of that. And he was certainly not the one! He could only hurt Willow, possessed as he was by a haunting memory. All he would do would be to drag her down to hell with him, and that he didn't want, *no way*.

Willow? Talon blinked and squinted his eyes. Was that really her, dancing in a rubied yellow gown before the mirror? No . . .

Then she turned about to face the window. Talon could not believe what he was seeing. Wild drums began pounding in his blood. Was he seeing a ghost?

The corded muscles of his stomach tautened and at the same time his lips flattened in a line that was at once harsh, ugly, his eyes green shards of frosted glass above his hard cheekbones.

Everything was suddenly twisted out of place: the rough-hewn furniture in the little house, the young woman who had quit her little dance and sat now upon the puncheon bench and looked sad, forlorn; even himself, standing here where he should not be.

Really, Talon was not here anymore, not at the little house, but at the big, main house of Sundance. The house where he grew up . . . and from which *she* had sent him away, after dragging him through hell.

"Her . . ." Talon hissed, and with a chest-deep groan he closed his eyes, and a sudden breeze slapped the wind-whipped leaves of the trees against the roof of the little house.

Talon's tortured mind spun back in time. The first day they had made love she, Garnet, had been the one to seduce him, the one actually to make love to him, to show him, tutor his fumbling, groping hands and tentative lips—she had left her mark on the boy: "I reckon we'll be doin' this every day now. . . ." he had shyly said to her, and Garnet had laughed effervescently, tossing her head, "Silly boy. Oh you *innocent!* I love you. . . ." His beaming face red and wreathed in smiles, he had cried, "Do ya really?" not even caring that the man out riding the range was her husband, his father, and his mother, Martha, was dead and buried; his father would come home later to sit in the living room with Garnet and ignore his youngest son, who was so madly in love with his stepmother that he did not give a damn what any of them thought, not Pete Brandon, not his older brother, Ashe, not the old Swede, Clem, not anybody else. Not anyone. Only Garnet mattered to the boy.

Pete Brandon had remarried, almost before Martha's grave was cold. Talon could not remember that far back, but he had heard it from someone . . . Carl Tucker . . . Clem? Anyway, someone had told him: Martha, his real mother, had been captured by Indians—Kiowas banded with Comanches—and enslaved. Tortured? That he did not know for sure. The rumor had been that Martha had been used to secure the liberation of a Comanche boy. That was the gossip spread around the ranch at that time. Someone else, he could not remember who, had said back then that it was not the first time she had been taken captive. The most unbelievable tale he had heard was that his mother was in love with the brave—half-breed, some said—who had captured her. It was rumored that she had pined away and died when he did not return the third time for her.

Long ago, it all seemed worlds ago. Garnet had shown up not long afterwards, anyway, it all seemed so run together to him, the troubled young boy of back then. Garnet had first lived in the little house. She had come up to the house, after having fed the hungry ranch hands. He had thought she was so damn pretty, a bit silly and giggly, flirting all the time with Pete

Brandon. Golden-tressed, with big saucer-blue eyes. Jesus! Those eyes—how they had flirted at him, too.

And now he was tossed back in time . . . he *went* back in time. . . .

He was standing in the bedroom at Sundance again, upstairs with Garnet. Mist swirled and made the edges of the scene all fuzzed and blurred. He stared; she was the same.

"Talon!" Willow shot off the bench and stared. She looked into the eyes that probed her own. "H-How did you come in? I didn't hear you . . . what is wrong?" She eased down again.

Then she knew. He was staring as if she was a ghost. He was seeing *her,* Garnet. Willow began to tingle all over. Now she had no choice but to go on.

The time had finally come. She was not even frightened. It would be easy to seduce him into desiring her, loving her. She had waited so long, oh, much too long. Her lips were parting in unconscious invitation already.

Rising from the bench as seductively as she could imagine how it was done, she walked around the table—with a measure of grace—the amber skirt rustling provocatively to aid her in her cause.

Talon saw none of Willow's innocence, none of her underlying vulnerability. His raw green eyes flamed over her like a torch, the exposed arch of her throat as she tossed back her head. Garnet was doing it again . . . all over again . . . she had come back to him.

Suddenly the old bitterness and hurt flared in him, and angry blood drained in his veins. "Why did you send me away?" he asked her, and Willow stared uncomprehendingly, at first, and then she understood.

Outside shadows of twilight were purpling the land, and inside the lantern light was burning low, the fuel in it shrinking fast. Try as she might, Willow could not quash the feeling of fear rising in her, nor that strange heat she had felt around him before now being forced through her belly. This was what she had been yearning for, wasn't it?

Talon's arousal was plainly outlined in his taut breeches, and she gave a nervous little gasping laugh while she tried to look elsewhere. Suddenly she *was* afraid of the warm and sweet desire that spread through her body like heated honey. Never before had she felt this hot around him. What was happening? Why did he seem so different now?

"Talon—it is me, Willow."

"Garnet."

She smoothed the amber skirt with hands that shivered, cold, as a new apprehension seeped into her. This was not as she had imagined it would turn out. She didn't understand all these strange, new things that were happening to her body. Where had these feelings been last year? She had not been afraid to get close to him then at all. She had just been in love with him.

"I am not who you think," she tried again while he kept staring and clenching his hands in frustration.

Willow pouted. She did not want to be Garnet, not anymore, not if being like her could make Talon Clay look like that, like he was on fire. Dangerous, hot, hungry, that was how he looked, and she did not like it one bit. Willow did not recognize the full-blown emotion, and it frightened her. She glanced up into his face and then quickly back down, saying in a pleading tone:

"Don't you look at me like that, Talon Clay, please . . . no, stay away!"

Willow stuck out her hands as he stalked her, backing her across the room. Talon didn't hear that she made little whimpers of fright with each step she took.

"Now, you-you just stay away from me, Talon Clay Brandon. I was only . . . only kidding, funning with you."

"Fun?" Talon only blinked while perusing her bosoms.

"Yeah, fun, all over with," she laughed nervously, her hand cutting through the air with a gesture of finality.

"Why did you come back?"

Willow gulped the knot of fear down hard. "B-back?" She stared down at his hands clenched into knotted balls of muscle . . . he could hurt her real bad if he chose. Did he really hate Garnet all that much? Or was it true love that drove him like this?

"Couldn't you have stayed dead and buried?"

"Talon!" she cried out in a wild whisper. "Stop it!"

"Talon?" He looked her over with a derisive sneer. "What happened to *darling? Sweetheart and sweet thing? My love?"*

Talon caught the wrist of the hand held out to him, and at that moment he looked ugly and savage to Willow. This was not the Talon she knew!

He pushed his face up close to hers. "Are you going to send me away again? Huh? I am not the same green*horn* boy you seduced and made a wreck of, *Miss* Garnet . . . *Mrs.* Brandon—oh, I forgot you good enough, miss high-and-mighty, when I got into the sack with one woman after the other, every night since you sent me away, give or take a few days. You want to know something?" The small woman standing shivering before him shook her head in a negative gesture, fear doubled in her big brown eyes. "No? Much I care if you don't want to hear. But you will hear me just the same."

The color of her eyes did not register in Talon's bitter smoldering brain, his eyes only took in the smaller mounds of flesh that peeped shyly up from the amber-and-lace bodice of the gown he remembered so well . . . on that first night, or was it day when she seduced him? His eyes narrowed over the woman before him. Why did she seem smaller all over to him than he remembered her being? Didn't matter, he told himself shrewdly. He was with Garnet again; that was all in hell that mattered, that made sense. Nothing else was real or with substance. Not the room they were in. Not the lantern just going out with a sputter and coil of upward-rising smoke. Not the day being born in soft mauve and mote-filled gray surrounding them.

Talon saw none of this; he saw only Garnet, wearing that same damn dress, taking him back in time. If he was dreaming, he did not want to awaken just yet. Not before he had some fun with her, for old time's sake.

And Willow saw nothing but Talon Clay, the man she had loved more than life itself. His eyes were forest-green, and his whole body exuded energy and life force. He was treating her badly, and that stung, but he thought she was someone else; and how was she going to make him snap out of his trance and return to the present?

Willow knew if she did not think of something, and fast, all would be lost.

Clamping a hand over her mouth to keep from crying out, she began to back away from him again. She was caught in a web of delight and nerve-tingling fear as he advanced.

Chapter Three

Heat flooded Willow's face. She had a sensation of his size as he moved against her with gentle, insinuating motions. His tall, muscled length strained to get closer. Then, as his arms came around her, he was gentle no longer, and he kissed her with a savage hunger. His mouth was flame itself, burning a fiery trail across her lips, slanting with a devouring thoroughness that would soon dissolve the last bit of resistance she was feeling.

She tried to push him away from her. "Talon, please, not this way." It was what she had wanted, so why did she fight him now? Why was she afraid? She'd answered her own question: Not this way. This could only end in tragedy, pushing them farther away than they had ever been.

"You feel so good, woman."

Talon crushed her to his fast-beating heart, grinding his hips closer, and closer yet, his slim tan fingers stroking her bare arms. He had to assuage the savage hunger that had been smoldering in him for what seemed ages.

"Been waiting so long . . . can't wait any longer . . . got to get you out of my blood once and for all." He looked down at her, eyes glittering, only seeing Garnet. "Don't fight it, give in."

Talon had been about to say the name of the woman who had seemed forever to haunt his days and nights. Her name did not mean anything to him anymore, only her lips, her sweet womanly softness, and he only wanted to bury himself hip-deep in her.

"Talon . . ." Willow gasped in bewildered ecstasy, between his earth-shattering kisses that were leaving her so drugged and dazed. "Wake up, Talon, and see me for who . . . I truly am."

He kissed her throat and she cried out in a fearful kind of ecstasy. "I am not who I was pretending to be—at first."

Oh, how she wanted him! How was she going to stop him? She was already on fire for wanting him. But this was not right; she knew that now. She had to say her name, again, to end it before he took her by force, if it came to that. The way he felt, she knew it would be force, and that could only hurt the both of them. Afterwards he would hate himself for taking liberties with her, even though he thought she was the other woman.

His eyes glazed over with passion, beads of moisture appearing on his upper lip, his body rippling hotly against hers, Talon said jaggedly, "The bedroom . . . show me. Hear me, woman, I want you, need you now. Tell me!" he ground out at last and shook her when she just stood there staring at him.

"*No,* Talon . . ." Finally, she broke away from the

hot circle of his embrace.

Even though she had stepped back, Willow found he was beginning to shove her toward the bedroom, the first one, which was Samson's. But how could he know in his befuddlement which bedroom was her own? Did he even know when he was sane? She doubted this.

It was much gloomier in the smaller room, the floursack curtains closed against the soft encroachment of pearly dawn light. The long drapes partitioning off the rooms fell back into place after they had stepped inside, Willow devising all the while in her mind an avenue of escape. She had never wanted it to happen like this . . . no, never.

Taking her with him, affording no chance for her to escape with his fingers gripping her as if she were a life-thread he needed to hang on to, Talon fell heavily across the patchwork-quilted bedspread. He stretched out beside her and ran his hand at once beneath the amber skirt. He felt her flesh, her youthful span of strong, muscled thigh. What was this? he wondered. He had remembered Garnet as being softer, not so firm . . . what did it matter, as long as she was here with him?

Kissing didn't satisfy him any longer. And Willow, despite herself, her slender body yearned against him, forgetting for the moment that disaster could only come of this union when the sun rose up over the hill. Her heart, mind, and soul were in total chaos. They fought helplessly with her flesh. And her flesh seemed to be winning. She was blind to sense, and to reason, too.

"Let me strip you and touch you. . . ."

As he quickly bared her lower half, pushing her

skirts higher and crushing them around her waist, Willow felt the cooler air wash over her. His fingers were warm as they kneaded on the softest part of her thighs. Dizziness assailed her when his fingers grew bolder and his lips ground into hers in a rough, bruising kiss. It was a savage kiss, unlike the sweet pressure of that first kiss they had shared.

Willow wished she had the will to fight him, but now his hands were everywhere, incredibly erotic, cupping her breast, delving deeper between her legs, kneading her back, her buttocks, and Willow could feel her taut young flesh resisting him down there. He did not seem to notice at all the barring membrane, blinded as he was by the greed of lust, and now, quickly, he unfastened the front of his breeches, totally unconcerned with the woman's comfort and giving it no more thought than if he was simply relieving himself in the bushes. This was the way it had always been with him and all the women he toyed with. He had been celibate for almost a year. Today, he could wait no longer.

Then he made a mistake in the heat of the moment. He murmured the name Willow was truly getting to hate:

"Garnet . . . I want—" He got no further.

Morning light pierced the curtains and sent a shaft of roseate gold across the bed. Willow had felt his hardness probe her. "The sun is up, Talon Clay Brandon!"

Willow lurched backward, before the damage could be done. "See for yourself, you," she was steaming now, "you, you horny toad!"

The bunched and readied muscles of Talon's thighs and back relaxed, and a short, angry curse fed from his throat to his lips. The planes of his face hardened. Passion quivered along his entire lean length and then leashed in and went still.

Talon had been thinking while she continued to resist, that surely by now she must have felt him growing hard against her. And so she had! She . . . ? What she?!

Talon's gaze sought the moist eyes below and burned into them. He was utterly devastated as light stole over the young woman's face, glinting in the gold threads of her hair. He was assailed by sudden remembrance of where he really was and what he was doing, of whom he was with.

A shaft of coruscating sunlight had slashed inward like a bright flaming sword, seeming to come from the very hand of God to condemn him to hell for his evil deed.

"Sonofa . . ." For the first time in his life, Talon was totally speechless.

As if a bolt of lightning had struck near his rear, Talon leapt from the bed. Hands on hips, he stood glaring in disbelief, muttering, "I must have drunk too much of old Clem's brew last night . . . I swear I'll never touch the stuff again." He shook his head, but that did not clear it. *"You,"* he said dumbly.

Her lips were deep pink and blurred at the edges from his passionate kisses. He already knew that she possessed teeth that were white and even; he saw them again now as she looked at him like a kitten about to hiss. There was an overpowering urge to take her in his arms again; he stilled it.

It was like plunging into an icy river.

He had been so arduously aroused by Garnet's

image—her spitting image in the sluggish light of dawn—that he had not realized she was not Garnet at all. Then . . . that damn impenetrable barrier . . . that could not have been *her,* not the unscrupulous woman he had known.

"She is dead and buried," Talon fiercely murmured, and ran his fingers through the shorter hair mussed across his forehead. Sardonic and dangerous, he stared at Willow, biting out, "Just who in hell *are* you?!"

"What do you mean, Talon Clay, just what? You know who I am, you know very well—now."

"Come outside!" He spun her from the room, unconsciously slapping the curtain in her face. He dragged her out the door, down the porch steps, across the yard.

"Talon Clay Brandon, just where do you think you are going dragging me behind you? I am not a rag doll, you know!"

"Up to the house. Maybe Tanya and Ashe can fill me in. Do they know what you have been up to?"

"No!" she lied . . . well, a little bit anyway.

"I am sorry, Willow, for treating you that way. . . ."

"Thank you!"

"I want some answers!" He reached out for her other shoulder.

Willow spun away from him and dragged the back of her hand across her face. "Don't start looking for a way to get away from me," he snarled. "I want some answers!" Talon glared sideways at Willow. "And stop that sniffing! I already said I was sorry with all my heart. Damn and tarnation, girl . . . I didn't force you! Reckon I could have though, I was damn close to doing just that. But I will warn you, Willow, next time you offer yourself so freely, I will have to take you up on it!"

"I did not offer myself so—freely!" She began to race ahead of him, going in the wrong direction instead of back to the little house, where she wanted only to hide from him.

"Now—" He spun her around before reaching the creek—"where did you get that dress? Tell me that much."

Spilled sunlight dappled the piney glade, casting a soft, golden glow over them, enchanting the place where they stood captured in a huge smoky beam slanting between the juxtaposed trees filled with flickering silvery dust motes.

Willow scowled back at Talon, trying to appear just as fierce as he but failing miserably, she knew. And her hands shook, even though she kept them concealed in the folds of the dress she could not wait to get off.

"I hate this dress," she finally blurted. "Hate it, hate it, *hate it!*"

"Why don't you take it off then?" Talon folded his arms across his chest nonchalantly, suppressing a grin.

Embarrassed, she lowered her chin, and stared at his wide brown leather belt, mumbling, "Later." Then her eyes flashed up at him. "You'd like that, wouldn't you?"

Exasperated, Talon said, "All I would like is some answers, Pussywillow." He sighed and put out his hand, but she quickly reached up to bat it away.

"Don't call me that; I told you never to say that again! I'm not a *pussywillow,* that's not what I was named for—a pond weed!"

"You *are* a pussywillow," he laughed and ran his hand down her hair. Talon knew he was playing with fire; he didn't want to start something again he could not finish. "You have silky catkins, too." He smiled into her sun-spangled eyes.

"Huh!" She folded her arms across her chest, squaw fashion, not looking at him now. "Look in *Bartlett's Dictionary* if you want the true definition of a pussywillow."

He chuckled low. "Lend it to me sometime; you are the schoolteacher. You know all the answers when it comes to that stuff. Do you think a cowboy like me has a *dic-tion-ary?*"

Talon was trying to be angry with Willow, but he could not be, and suddenly he felt like a bubbling brook of laughter within and he could not understand why. He had left Willow pure, and that made him happy somehow. He pulled her haughty chin around and forced himself to breathe normally when he looked into her wide, hurt eyes. "Believe me, Willow, I would never in my life hurt you . . . I'm sorry, darling—*Jesus,* I am sorry! I just thought you were someone else, that's all." He lowered his hand. "Someone I used to care for very much. . . ." *in a twisted way,* he kept to himself.

"Do I . . . look so much like her?"

He swung his head around. "Oh Lord, yes. Especially in the hazy dawn light when shadows play tricks . . . Willow—" He took hold of her upper arms, studying her curiously. "Do you know who she is, I mean *was?* Is she related to you . . . in some way? I was so sure she—"

"*Garnet.* Why don't you just say her *name*—is it so painful? Did you love her, Talon? Did you?"

Talon knew he was trapped. "I don't want to talk about what my feelings for her were . . . okay?"

Willow stared at his hard mouth. "Why are you

taking me up to see Tanya and Ashe?"

"I told you—to get some answers. If you won't talk to me, then maybe Tanya and Ashe will fill me in. . . ."

"All Tanya told me about you and Garnet was that you were in love with her and couldn't forget her. You loved her very much."

A question hung on her lips, and he stared at her incredulously. Talon swung his head aside. "She was an older woman. I told you. . . ."

"She was married to your father . . . *how could you . . . ?*"

"How could I what?" He had grabbed her roughly, but now he let go and sighed deep within. "I'm sorry, Willow. We will talk about this sometime, but not now, okay?"

"Oh . . . when? When the bitter hurt you feel over her drives deeper and deeper and feeds on your insides, when there's nothing left in you but an empty core?"

His eyes closed. "I don't give a damn anymore . . . not about anything." His eyes flared open. "Can't you get that through your head? All I want to do is work—work my ass off!"

Willow laughed sharply. "Yes. Work. And become—an Indian!"

"What?" *Had she said Indian?*

"Never mind." She laughed bitterly. "When did you stop feeling, Talon Clay? What will make you come alive again?"

"I was not dead a while ago back there, darling, when you led me on!"

"Oh!" She cocked her hands at her hips, brown eyes blazing gold flecks. "You were the one who was trying to ravish me! Where is all your manly control, Talon

Clay Brandon?"

"Get off my back, Willow!"

"Got to you, huh?" She watched his green eyes narrow menacingly, but she didn't care. "I am not going to tell you where I got this dress." She tossed her golden head arrogantly. "I have a locket, too . . . with *her* picture in it." She saw the merest fluctuation of his eyes. "I bet you'd like to have that so you could sit and stare at her face and remember what used to be, huh, Talon Clay? I'll give it to you . . . and all her other stuff I stole from the hidden room. Did you know about that—Garnet's own little queen bee hive, her secret room behind the bookcase? Why don't you go read all her love letters and torture yourself some more?"

He drew in a harsh breath, his eyes widening in disbelief. He made to step closer, having it in mind to strangle her pretty little throat, but held himself in check. He searched her face and seemed to find something there that fascinated him, utterly bewildered him. Then he softly said, "Foolish little Pussywillow, I have already had Ashe burn them. They meant nothing to me—"

"I bet! You almost—almost s-spoiled me, all because of h-her . . . !" A smile came into his eyes and she raged at him. "All because you—you in your distorted mind—thought I was her . . . your dead mistress! Don't you tell me you don't care about Garnet any more, you ass." She whirled to go back up the hill to the "little house," throwing another taunting jab over her haughty shoulder. "You're so sick, Talon Clay, you'd even make love to her ghost!"

Talon stared after her viciously twitching behind like a starved man. He stood there beneath the deep green redolent pines for a long, long time, a strange expression haunting his luminous green eyes. He could not even breathe normally. . . . What the hell was wrong with him?

Talon figured it all out later. He rode a fresh-broken mustang over the hills, gray-green now in the depths of summer. He wore no saddle so that the mustang should get used to the feel of a man on his bare back. The saddle would come later, maybe in a few days.

As he rode he heard the fluttering of cottonwood leaves. He looked but did not really see the distant purple ranges. The sun poured down hot, but he didn't mind. He just rode on.

Talon knew now why Willow had gussied herself up like Garnet—it was getting easier for him to think and even to say the woman's name. It was because little Willow had had a crush on him for a long time now. A year, was it? Tanya had told her younger sister that he had been wildly in love with the older woman, and Ashe must have told Tanya a bit of their past history. He snorted. Ashe had been lucky to escape Garnet's lascivious clutches, but not he, and not their father, either.

The song of a stream permeated his mind and he listened for a moment. It wasn't so hard anymore to think of Garnet. She didn't mean anything to any of them here at Sundance any longer. Especially not to him. He could not guess what he would have done had he discovered that Willow and Garnet were in some way related. That had not taken a whole lot of figuring, when he had sat down and considered the past. Garnet

Haywood had come to Sundance and passed on long before the Hayes family ever came along.

Now Talon laughed away the absurdity of his boyish fancies and his love affair with the older woman. If he remembered right, he'd been so full of Garnet he couldn't think of much else but her back then. It was just one of those coincidences in life, that Willow resembled Garnet so much when she dressed herself up in the woman's clothes.

He felt an ache deep inside him. Had he really believed Willow to be Garnet? Or had he actually been aware all along, from the moment he had stepped onto the porch and taken Willow in with his disbelieving gaze? He just did not know. Or was he kidding himself?

A cord of anger tightened in Talon's neck. If they had been related . . . now that was a different story altogether. Say Willow were Garnet's daughter, for instance—he would have made no bones about ravishing the girl and walking away without a backward glance when the deed was done. Friend or no friend, he would have gotten back at Garnet through Willow, and be damned if he broke the poor girl's heart. True, he had desired Willow at one time, hell, lusted after her knowing how easy it would have been to seduce her. But he had discovered he had cared about her a little, and had not wanted to hurt her—well, he conceded with a wry smile, he had cared a whole lot then.

His desire for little Pussywillow had been strong; it used to eat away at his groin and vitals. She owned the most enchanting little face he had ever looked on. Dainty, sweet-limbed, with curves that had just been starting to fill in . . . and now? She was maturing fast, both in mind and body, was going to be a real sweet charmer . . . hell, she already was! She had proved that, for sure, and so had his lust for her body!

For the past year he had been all work and no play, most of the time working as a wild horse hunter. Squinting along the sun's rays as he rode along on the skittish *mesteno,* Talon found himself recalling other matters to mind he had thought long forgotten. Like his own mother, Martha. Why was she coming to mind so often in the past week? And the danger-riddled years following his affair, the anguished hurt, bringing him up to the time when he had become a hard-bitten desperado.

By rights, Talon knew he should have been locked behind bars, but his brother Ashe, having been a Texas Ranger and all, had saved him from the fate all outlaws dreaded. It had been so easy—all he had had to do was bring in the loot. Of course, he had fibbed a bit, saying most of the gang had been killed off, which was partly true in itself, as there weren't many of them left now from the Wild Bunch.

Then there was Carl Tucker—Talon meant to kill that sonofabitch himself, if he could catch up with Carl!

Carl, for some reckless, insane reason he couldn't understand had turned against him and had tried to kill his brother, Ashe, and kidnapped his sister-in-law. Ah, but Tanya, she was full of fire. She reminded him of a flame-haired tigress guarding her family, which there was one more of these days. Baby Sarah.

Tanya had possessed the spunk and daring to get away from Carl Tucker, and when he himself had come along to save her from the crazy bastard, Carl Tucker had popped up like slime from the bushes and shot him. It had taken all of Tanya's strength to hitch a horse up to the traces, when she was so worn out herself—and pregnant, as they all discovered later—and get him back to Sundance before he bled to death or Tucker finished him off. Reaching the yard, Tanya had been so pale and exhausted that Almanzo had swept her up and carried her inside the house and all the way up to her bedroom. Ashe had frowned after the tall Indian taking his wife into his own care . . . but that was another story, another situation back then. In time, all wounds, inside and out, had been healed.

Talon guessed his own age was nearing twenty-five or twenty-six, and Carl—so Mrs. Tucker had said one day when Talon had been living with them—Carl was close to his own age. He wasn't friendly with his neighbors anymore, and when Hester Tucker came to visit and sashay around for a roll in the hay, he made damn certain he had plenty of work to do with the mustangs or he found one of his drover friends to ride the range with. That is, if the county harlot hadn't chosen one of them as her partner in the hayloft that morning—or night—usually it made no difference to Hester. She always hung out for more; so did they. One of these days she was going to get herself knocked up, and it for sure wasn't going to be Talon who would do the deed!

Talon had a pretty strong feeling just what it was Carl Tucker wanted. He coveted Sundance, always had. He had a bad desire to join the property with the decayed Saw Grass ranch—the same burning desire his mother, Janice Ranae, had had for years. The whole damn family was greedy and covetous, as he well remembered from his early unhappy years at Saw Grass after Garnet had sent him away from his father's own beautiful Sundance property.

And now Talon had a thirst for vengeance, and he would catch up to Carl Tucker one of these days. There was even a rumor floating between the drovers and mustangers that Tucker had tried to rape Willow in the schoolhouse not too long ago . . . if Carl Tucker was not dead by now of his own evil deeds, the poor bastard would sure be dead soon enough!

Chapter Four

The little house shifted in the heat waves, and inside, Willow scowled resentfully at the now offending amber gown she had just ripped from her body.

"Ugh—I hate it. . . ."

Kicking the gown into a rumpled heap, she stood there in the little house, slim and naked, quivering angrily all over—and how she wanted to burn it, tear the damn thing into shreds. Destroy it, over and over . . . somehow!

Willow sighed in defeat. She had no heart for the deed and she wondered if she ever would. Was she always to be so cowardly when it came to making decisions? She prayed not.

Picking up the gown, she carefully folded it in half and returned it, along with all the other pretty things, beneath her bed in the flat pigskin trunk. Her fingertips brushed the locket as she was pulling her hand out.

Willow pried the tiny catch open and stared at the woman in the locket. The woman she so resembled, and even more so these days. Each time she tried on the amber gown and did her hair up like Garnet's, she seemed to become a little more a part of the mysterious female. She knew it was true, for Talon had been testimony to that!

The morning passed uneventfully. After she had walked up the hill to visit with Tanya and baby Sarah in the shaded coolness of the back yard of Sundance, Willow dressed for riding. She would visit the school and spend a little time with Pastor Cuthbert.

Dust Devil waited outside beneath the cottonwoods for her master, tied to the rail there. Willow had bridled the mustang mare, but she left the heavy saddle off today; only a light Indian blanket covered a small square of Dust Devil's back.

Willow chose a loose-fitting white shirt with a laced bodice crisscrossing in a vee down to her breasts. Its length spilled over onto a wide-hemmed Mexican-style skirt. She pulled on her old soft boots and tucked a small handgun into the deep pocket, the gun having become a constant companion ever since the incident with Carl Tucker in the schoolhouse when he had come so close to raping her. She was sure of it now—that he had not done the nasty deed to its fullest as she had lain unconscious on the floor—because she felt—well, she just had a strong woman's intuition surrounding the facts and believed she was yet unspoiled by man.

Her hand came in contact with her knife then and she lifted it up. She never forgot to bring along the Toledo steel blade Little Coyote had given her; it was an old war relic.

Willow guided Dust Devil over the earth, golden sand here, red clay there, giving herself up to the peaceful solitude and loneliness of the hills and shrubby mesquite trees surrounding her. It was a purple summer, wild, beautiful, and savage.

Dust Devil's iron-shod hoofs rang like muted bells on the stones cropping up here and there. As she continued to ride, enchanted visions filled her drowsy mind, for she had lost much sleep the night before. A soft wind tangled in her hair. A beautiful butterfly flitted past. The smell and feel of *him.* Her spirit was full of vitality, however, as she daydreamed of Talon. . . .

Willow began to nod her head, pine-green and violet-purple shadows going past her. Yellow broom flowers poked from the shaded patches where the grass was not so parched. The feel of him, the smell, his touch on her. He was wearing buckskin pants and a cotton shirt. She loved the male smell of him, like horses, leather, and a special odor all his own. Slung across his back was a bow and a quiver of arrows. Talon looked like a fearless warrior.

He had to be gentle . . . please be gentle. Feathery kisses upon her lips, upon her gently rounded breasts . . . her womanhood longed to be filled as rapturous delight spun through her like liquid fire. With total abandonment she responded to him. Wildfire consumed them both as her slender arms circled his neck and she buried her fingers in his long hair. She tugged, and pulled the braid loose. Sweet nectar flowed between them and soon, soon, man to woman, the joining of two bodies . . . her horse neighed shrilly. Horse? *What* horse?

"Oh . . ." Willow blinked through lowered lashes. Her eyes flew open, and hot and cold needles flashed throughout her nervous system.

Dark, fierce, terrible eyes stared into hers, and Willow stared back, her heart feeling like it was being battered about wildly in her chest. She trembled under the weight of her fear. *Indian!*

Nightwalker hid a smile. Surely he was not all that ferocious to look upon. Then he touched his face and he knew. It had been so long since he had painted his face in the war ritual that now, now when he had done so, he had forgotten to remove it before riding out from the reservation where he had gone to trade mustangs for supplies for Black Fox's camp. The half-breeds, the Horse Indians, had wished to see what he had looked like when he lived with the Comanches and painted his face. How the Horse Indians must be laughing at him!

How beautiful and dainty she is, Nightwalker thought to himself. With ease, he leaned over while holding his horse's mane, and among the purple sage his fingers found the nodding white flower. Righting himself, he handed the sweet maid the most exquisite flower she had ever looked upon. A delicate three-petaled blossom with a violet heart.

Mesmerized, Willow took in the fierce Indian astride the huge horse. What was this? Had she seen him before, or possibly dreamed about him? He was not so young anymore, but still handsome, and his hair was not the usual black shaft of Indian hair, but dark brown with gray streaked here and there. She tried to see into his eyes, but they appeared to be bloodshot from the paint he had applied so near his lids, and their color was not easy to discern.

"*Hu!*" he exclaimed, then wheeled his dark horse whose coat glistened when the flaming rays struck directly without the shade of any trees.

As he rode away, Willow took in minor details about the tall Indian: armbands; breechclout; copper skin; moccasins; a long-barreled rifle. What? No bow and quiver of arrows? What sort of Indian was this? Was that a knife, though, she saw gleaming at his side? It must be.

Her eyes moved to the earth-brown ribbon beyond the line of post-oaks, where she could see the San Antonio-Nacogdoches Road. She was off the main thoroughfare, and she decided there and then to get back on it!

Entering the huge, square room of the schoolhouse, Willow paused to run her hand over the back of a chair, and another, remembering the two mischievous lads, Jeffy and Billy, she had had to separate, for they had more than once disrupted a class in session. She smiled now, recalling their naughty but memorable antics. Especially the episode of the mysterious frog in Jennifer's pocket! And Shawn grinning widely as he watched.

Willow ran a trembling hand down the front of her wide-hemmed Mexican skirt, remembering with reluctance the time Carl Tucker had trapped her inside this very room and tried to ravage her.

Willow shook her head. At night, sometimes, she still had nightmares about Carl Tucker chasing her, catching up with her, and performing his ugly, demonic deed on her person. For many months after that Willow had thought she might be with child, and then her time, which had been late because of stress, had finally come. And now she was certain he had not ravaged her, and she knew deep in her heart that only one man would ever have her.

Willow felt bewildered again. She thought of the mysterious Indian she had met on the wild track, and she twirled the nodding white flower she still held in her hands. She frowned in wonder at the delicate blossom and thought, surely there was a reason for this gift, but what could it be?

She was still mulling over the Indian's mysterious presence when Pastor Cuthbert entered, accompanied by a man Willow had never seen before. From across the deep room, the man seemed at first astonished to see her there, and then as he approached he looked squarely into her marsh-brown eyes and smiled warmly.

"I thought that was your horse tied up outside," Cuthbert said, the ever-present gentle smile lighting his long face as he and the other man neared Willow. "Impatient for school to begin?" he asked and watched her look around the room with a soft smile. "Willow, I would like you to meet our new friend, Harlyn Sawyer." He turned to the tall, thin man. "Harlyn, this is Willow Hayes, our busy little schoolteacher."

As the man greeted her, Willow thought he was a little pale of countenance, but he was not insipid, not without interesting or attractive qualities. Willow suddenly realized she was still holding and twirling the flower and laid it aside on her small desk. "Hello, Mr. Sawyer. You must be related to Vince Sawyer."

"That's right, Miss Willow," he said in an easy, western drawl. "The pastor here has been tellin' me such nice things about you, miss. Must say, he didn't do you justice, though. You're much prettier than he said." He nodded his handsome head as if for emphasis.

Willow could not help but like Harlyn Sawyer at once. His amicable brown eyes reflected kindness, and something else. She was drawn to him instantly, in some strange way, noticing a certain kind of sadness lining his worried brow. She wanted to ask him what it was that was troubling him when Cuthbert spoke up.

"Mr. Sawyer lost his wife recently." He laid a gentle, consoling hand on the man's narrow shoulder. "He's here for a short visit at Vince's ranch, you see."

Willow completely missed the quick, assessing glint of lust in Sawyer's dark eyes. Had she seen it, she would have moved on without another word. As it was, Willow did not always recognize lust for what it was. She was still so young and inexperienced.

"It's not all as bad as the pastor says . . . not anymore," Harlyn Sawyer told her, his quick-changing eyes seeming to say, "not since I met you, Willow."

Willow flushed brightly, having seen the momentary adoration shining on his face and in his eyes. "I'm sorry to hear about your loss, Mr. Sawyer." For want of something else to say, since he was now studying her more closely, she invited, "Would you both care to come for dinner . . . at my house?" She sometimes hesitated to say that; after all, the little house was part of Sundance property, owned by the Brandon brothers and now Tanya, her sister.

Willow laughed softly. Harlyn made her feel pretty, womanly, something that Talon never did, usually acting as if she was a mere child, still referring to her as Pussywillow.

"I'm sorry, Willow," Pastor Cuthbert said. "I am

counseling that poor child Ellita this evening." He sighed, discounting the fact that Ellita Tomas was a gorgeous young female with the problems besetting a much older woman. "Her parents are bringing her over. It seems Miss Tomás will never get over that humiliating scene Almanzo put her through. At times, of course, I cannot blame the young man." Again he sighed, adding, "Almanzo is an old-fashioned young man, and it is ironic to find him thus, when . . . I *am* sorry. Forgive me for the gossip."

Willow's brown eyes twinkled. "I forgive you, Cuthy." She always called him that when she was funning with him; Cuthbert hadn't much time for fun and games, being the only clergyman for hundreds of miles around. "It has been a long time since you came to supper or dinner over at Sundance. You will come soon?"

"Just ask, Willow. Now, I must get over to the church and prepare for my sermon this Sabbath." He shook hands with Harlyn Sawyer and walked away, calling over his shoulder in a mock-stern voice, "See you in church this Sunday, Willow."

"Of course, pastor . . . *Cuthy.*" Then she faced Harlyn Sawyer once again, asking, "Do you have a horse?" She laughed then, feeling feminine and giddy when he drew her eyes to the green-and-black buggy parked beside the oak shading the churchyard, a shiny chestnut horse waiting with it.

"You could ride with me?" The shrewd brown eyes seemed to be begging Willow, and she at once succumbed to Mr. Sawyer's southern-gentleman charm.

Her eyes shone like amber sun. "A buggy!" She was

delighted. "I can't ever remember riding in one!" Maybe she had in California, with her mother . . . *her mother:* What had her name been? She had forgotten; it was so long ago, everything in all her nineteen years seemed so long ago. Now that Harlyn Sawyer was here to make her feel like a real lady.

"I'll tie your horse behind," Harlyn was saying, and Willow smiled, looking from him to the buggy while she walked alongside him.

Harlyn Sawyer was a once-wealthy rancher who was now losing his ranch to his dead wife's relatives. Lena Sanchez was gone now. She had left Harlyn nothing, and he had even lost his job with the Texas Emigration and Land Company. He was just about destitute and had to do something fast.

Harlyn, from his lanky height, smiled down into Willow's lively eyes. To Willow, as she looked up at the sky and into the surrounding trees before being handed up into the buggy, the sky had never appeared brighter, the leaves never greener. And the wind was blowing more sweetly by the time Willow and Harlyn Sawyer left the church and schoolhouse behind.

Talon Clay was just emerging from the forest of post-oaks bordering the San Antonio-Nacogdoches Road, when he spotted the spic-and-span green-and-black buggy coming along at a smart clip, a big and shiny Thoroughbred drawing it with a proud bearing. Through lowered lashes he watched it near the curve in the bend.

"Sweet Jesus . . ." Talon hissed through his teeth. "Ain't she a bright-eyed filly." It didn't take him a second to tell which was which, male or female; not since he had become a professional mustanger. Anyway, he had lived and breathed horses every day for . . . well, almost all his life. He had been, as they say, "born in the saddle." The danger, the thrill of adventure, and the constant change of scenery had awakened in his youth and called upon him in his manhood, all characteristic of the hard trail of a wild horse hunter.

Talon sent an irritated glance over his shoulder, angry that he had been followed into the woods again. A man could not even have the pleasure of hunting alone nowadays.

While Harlyn Sawyer watched out of the corner of his eyes, Willow Hayes twisted her long hair into a silky golden knot at the nape of her neck, saying, "Whew, Lord, but it's hot and muggy," wishing she had a bright length of ribbon to tie it in place. She released the hank and it fell back into place, streaming down her back almost to her slim hips, cornsilk straight.

"You have very nice hair, Miss Willow. Back home there are many pretty ribbons . . . in my house, and . . ." he fell silent, thinking of his wife who had left him nothing in her will. But he was not about to let Willow Hayes know just how destitute he was; it would ruin all his plans and Randy's.

"And, you were about to say?" Willow put in, "where is home, Mr. Sawyer?"

"West Texas, I—I have a ranch there," he said, not adding, "not for much longer."

Harlyn had to return there to retrieve all his belongings that were being packed into boxes by the Sanchez family . . . the bastards! They would all pay;

he planned to buy them all out. And by hook or by crook he would! He had run into a man going by the name Randy Dalton, but he felt strongly that the man had been lying and had not revealed his true identity to him. What did Harlyn care, as long as Randy lived up to his end of the bargain and lent him the huge sum of money he had promised? All Harlyn had to do was deliver to Randy what he wanted . . . Harlyn looked down at Willow again.

She really is a pretty piece, he thought, wondering how she was going to react when he asked her to come back to the *rancho,* as his wife. And, he might just do that, take her back—after Randy was done with her. Whatever it was he wanted with Willow was none of his affair, either. He just hoped Randy didn't use her all up and leave nothing for him but an empty shell of a woman.

Just then Willow's head shot up as she spied Talon Clay emerging from the stand of post-oaks. Her heart did somersaults, as was her usual reaction when he suddenly appeared out of nowhere, always out of thin air, it seemed. He always did that, popped up when she least expected him. Especially now, she did not want to see his handsome, rugged face and green eyes tearing into her soul. She loved him; she would forever, but it was hopeless, she was coming to understand. Talon did not even know she was alive, and all that mattered to him in this world was the memory of a beautiful woman, now a ghost that would continue for as long as he lived to haunt him.

Willow felt her spirits begin to lag. What was she going to do? Talon would forever and ever be a part of her . . . their souls seemed to be inseparable. If only something would happen to cause her to hate him. If only she could hate him just a little, then maybe she could begin to live.

By rights, Willow knew she should really despise him for coming close to shaming her. But that had not entirely been Talon's fault, either; she had had a part in it too, enticing him to fall in love and desire her. All that scene had done was make Talon believe she was even more the foolish virgin, pining for a love she could never win, throwing herself at him like the cheap, worldly woman Garnet must have been. How could he ever love her after that?

"Damn if he ain't a savage!" Harlyn Sawyer hissed through his straight, white teeth with the slightest part in the center. "A yellow-haired Indian, at that. What's he waitin' for, Willow?" He glanced at Willow Hayes and thought she must be overcome by the heat of the day.

"Talon Clay Brandon," was all she could manage. Her heart was doing flip-flops, was aching so bad she felt ill.

"*That's* Tal—" he bit off. "Brandon?" he revised, being careful now that Willow Hayes had turned her head to study him more closely. "I've, uh, heard of the Brandons—don't they own Sundance property?"

A glint of covetousness shone in Harlyn's eyes as he reviewed in his calculating mind what Randy Dalton had told him. The Brandon brothers had just returned to Sundance not too long ago, after having been away for some years, having gone their separate ways. Strange, the older brother had become a Texas Ranger, the younger, Talon Clay here, an outlaw. That must have been some showdown when they came together. Harlyn would like to hear the whole story someday.

"That's them," Willow said. "Talon is the youngest Brandon man."

"Has he turned savage?" Harlyn asked coyly.

"You would think so." Willow looked down at her hands so she would not have to look into Talon's eyes as they drew closer to him, in the bend of the road where he stood above on a gentle slope of hill. "Ever since he has been hanging around Almanzo Rankin, who is a half-breed, and meeting up with Comanche mustangers, he has run around dressed like a savage himself!"

Harlyn glanced at her, saying, "You sound mighty bitter, Miss Willow."

As the buggy took the bend in the road, so did Willow's eyes widen, and she felt a hurt pierce her heart like a sudden arrowhead had lodged there. Why did he always make her feel like she was in pain when he was near? The pain in her breast was so bad she could hardly draw another breath, for now, Hester Tucker, disheveled, her bodice flapping open two buttons down, had come to stand beside Talon Clay. Mesmerized, Willow watched as Hester reached out playfully for Talon's hand, but he knocked it aside . . . as if he had had enough of her charms for one day!

With sunken heart, Willow realized what had taken place in the green sanctuary they had just emerged from. Again, Willow thought with despair, again . . . Talon had taken up with Hester Tucker again. Didn't Hester know when to give up? How shameful she was! The hussy! Talon only used her as a plaything, just as he had used all the other women in his past. He had told

Willow as much, that there was nothing he had not done with a woman, that he was bad. He had warned her, "Stay away, Willow, you'll only get hurt by me."

What a juicy baggage, Harlyn was thinking to himself when the tawny-haired woman came to stand beside the White Indian.

"He *must* be an Indian," Harlyn was saying as they passed the couple standing above the road. "Did you see that savage look in his eyes when he noticed you sitting right here beside me? No? I did, and it sure did give me the spookiest feeling, I must say, Miss Willow." He looked down at her, allowing his gaze to sneak lower than her throat this time. Maybe Willow Hayes was not as full-blown as the young woman with the White Indian, or his dead wife Lena, but she sure was lovely . . . and maybe she hid more beauties than the naked eye could see beneath that blouse . . . and the long Mexican skirt.

Harlyn moistened his lips, experiencing a hard desire, knowing Willow had not brought it on that quick, but the tawny-haired one with the more healthy curves had, for sure. What did it matter; women were all the same when you turned them upside down.

"I do hope you like rabbit stew and boiled potatoes, Mr. Sawyer," Willow asked over her shoulder, reaching into the pine corner cupboard for a mixing spoon.

"Reckon I sure do, Miss Willow." He watched her walk about the kitchen, preparing the meal, and watched especially the way her softly rounded buttocks twitched when she mixed some batter for the biscuits she was making.

As Willow worked, Harlyn's eyes roved, and he sat admiring the colorful tapestries gracing the bare wood walls. "Very pretty," he said of the decorations, not having much to say about the rest of the place.

"Oh—them, thank you," she said with gentle pride in her humble dwelling.

Creativity and thriftiness, along with skilled hands, had enabled her to convert scraps of fabric into works of art. "I would not trade this place for my own antebellum home, like my sister Tanya's."

Wrinkling his nose behind her back, Harlyn said, "It's, ah, very nice, Miss Willow."

"Please," she laughed, really beginning to enjoy this gentlemanly man's presence, "just call me Willow. I'm not used to being addressed otherwise."

"You laugh, Willow, but I happen to know you're put out over something. Did it have to do with that White Indian we saw back there in the bend of the road?"

"Mr. Sawyer, I mean Harlyn, I told you that that young man is Talon Clay Brandon!" She walked over to place the sugar loaf in the center of the table.

"Gosh, I'm sorry Willow." Harlyn watched her use a nipper to cut the staple into chunks. "Reckon you can forgive me?" He flashed her a handsome, toothy grin that never failed to captivate the ladies in Nacogdoches or New Orleans, or for that matter, in New York.

But now, Harlyn thought, now there would be no more pleasure trips for him, since . . . damn, that was all in the past, and the future was a bright promise.

"There, the sugar loaf is cut." Turning back to the meal preparations, Willow shook her head, hunching her shoulder over the recalcitrant wave that always curved over one eyebrow. "You really are something else, Harlyn Sawyer, sure enough."

Watching the provocative wave of Willow's hair fall back into place, Harlyn agreed silently that he sure was something, yes ma'am. He continued to leer covertly at Willow's backside and smile charmingly whenever she turned to glance at him during their intermittantly paced conversation. He had charmed her, sure enough, with his good looks and easy southern manner, just as he had the pastor.

He was, Harlyn thought in self-satisfaction, becoming very well acquainted with Willow Hayes. But then, a man had to work damn fast nowadays; there weren't all that many pretty gals about, and he had decided to kill two birds with one stone!

Chapter Five

Willow had almost forgotten how angry and hurt she was over seeing Talon and Hester together again. She was having a delightful time, and she found Harlyn Sawyer interesting company.

Willow and Harlyn had just finished eating and Harlyn had waited patiently while she'd cleared away the dishes and put them to soak in her dishpan. With coffee cups in hand they drifted outside, where crickets sang evening-approaching songs and southward-scudding clouds filtered the melting rays of the setting sun.

Tipping his chair back against the weathered wall of the porch, Harlyn had begun to answer a question Willow had just asked him, when he looked across the yard. He froze.

The tall, disturbing savage stood there. Harlyn could think of him as nothing but a half-breed Indian, since Talon Clay Brandon looked nothing like the Anglo Whites he himself had grown up with. Actually, Harlyn's parents had been Tennesseeans. There was nothing left of his family; the Kiowas had butchered them, and Harlyn had been the only child to escape. This had all happened because his oldest brother had raped to death one meaningless filthy squaw!

"Where is your ranch located?" Willow asked Harlyn as she sipped her hot coffee.

Coming out of his trance and seeing that she had not yet noticed the White Indian, Harlyn cleared his throat, saying, "Above the Little River—actually, somewhere between Waco and Ft. Worth."

"Below the Brazos?" she said.

"Somewhere in there," Harlyn said distractedly.

Now Willow saw him, too. But she pretended not to, her eyes skimming the yard and returning swiftly back to Harlyn Sawyer. "But that is not West Texas. At least," she shrugged a dainty shoulder, hoping Talon noticed her flirtatious gesture, "my American geography book says it's not."

"Well," Harlyn began again, feeling nervous knowing he was being watched by a white savage, "suppose it's more near Clear Fork Reservation, then. You know where that is?"

"No." Willow laughed—and it was a tinkling sound that carried—throwing her golden head back and causing the provocative yellow wave to fall over one eyebrow, and she didn't brush it back with her hand this time. She said, "That's clear up by Fort Belknap, though, isn't it, Mr. Sawyer? You live very close to the Great Plains—Indian Territory!" ending with a soft exclamation and feeling her nerves shiver-wracked by those beautiful green eyes watching every move she and Harlyn made.

What was Talon thinking? she wondered. Could

he possibly be angry—even a little jealous?

He has no right! Willow thought and became angry all over again. She was enjoying herself, thoroughly, with a gentleman. Talon Clay was . . . he had become nothing but a coldblooded savage! He cared for nothing, no human at least, only those damn wild mustangs! He was meeting Hester in the woods again. She did have good reason to hate him . . . and she did . . . she *did!*

"Your friend is spying on us," Harlyn whispered, leaning forward and making it all look cozy and intimate with Willow. Carefully his eyes dipped into the vee of her blouse and then back up to her flushed face.

"What friend?" Willow asked, finding herself staring into eyes that had become almost black now. How was this—weren't Harlyn's eyes supposed to be brown?

"The savage."

"Oh—him." She pushed back, clamped her knees, and stood, saying, "Let's go inside—for dessert."

Willow picked her skirts up at the sides, in the ladylike fashion she'd seen Hester do, and feeling very foolish and fluffy-headed, she led Harlyn Sawyer inside.

Talon gritted his teeth, muscles jerking and tautening in both sides of his lean cheeks. The western dandy—he thought of the handsome stranger with Willow—just who was he and what was he doing with Willow? He'd bet the slicker didn't even know which end was up when he made love to a woman. He had better not. . . .

"Damn . . ." Talon cussed between clenched teeth, feeling frustration reign.

Talon took a slow step forward. She was so damn innocent, such a child. He clenched his hands against the well-seasoned buckskin at his flanks. He stopped himself. What was he doing? Why couldn't he bear the thought of other men touching Willow? It wasn't as if Willow was his sister, or even related to him at all, so why did he feel this sudden rush of protectiveness toward her? That handsome dude, however, was not a man to inspire Talon's liking . . . hell, let it be.

On moccasined feet he whirled about, fringed buckskin slapping his long, lean legs. *Forget it, Talon. Let her live her own life—she does not belong to you!*

"You can't be serious!" Tanya said to her sister as Willow worked industriously over her bed, sorting things out she would take with her, those she would leave behind.

When Willow chose not to answer, her older sister went on, "Why, you hardly know this man . . . what did you say his name was?"

"Harlyn Sawyer." Willow glanced up at Tanya and her velvet-brown eyes had gold fires in them. Willow was anxious and wanted nothing more than to get away from Talon. She went on, "He's a rancher." She smiled at last. "From West Texas."

"That's it?" Tanya spoke over her shoulder and went to push the curtains aside to let some of the morning breeze circulate in the room.

Waiting for her answer, Tanya absently stared out the window, until something caught her eye. Talon?

What was he doing here so early? He strode closer to the window, leading Cloud. Tanya frowned, glancing over at Willow and seeing that she was still busy with her packing.

"Well?" Tanya pressed, letting the curtains fall back into place. "Aren't you going to tell me more about this Harland?"

"Harlyn," Willow corrected.

"Harlyn." Tanya shook her head. "I just can't let my baby sister run off with some stranger and get herself married. He might be an outlaw, for all you know."

Baby sister! Willow fumed, but only said, "He might. It doesn't matter."

With her back to the window now, Tanya faced the room. Morning sun behind her captured the burnished red in her hair, creating a fiery halo all about her head and shoulders. Tanya Brandon was pretty, with an earthy sensuality about her. Though she was as bold as an adventuress, could hunt and shoot almost as well as most men, Tanya loved to putter in her antebellum home, which was a rare sight in the hill country, and she loved her husband Ashe and her baby Sarah. Tanya was content.

"Tanya," Willow said, swishing her calico skirts and moving to the trunk beneath the window, "I am not a baby, as you stated earlier. Everyone around Sundance thinks I am such a child." She looked up into the sky briefly and didn't see the man's head just below the window. "I'm not little Pussywillow anymore—can't everyone see that I am a grown woman now? *You* baby me—" she moved away from the window— "Ashe babies me, and my own *brother* laughs at me when I tell him to do something. When Samson is bad he has to be sent up to your house to be punished, he won't listen to me. He sticks his tongue out at me! I can hardly ever be alone here at the little house; someone is always seeming to be checking on me and making sure I am all right, fetching for me. I can do for myself and I can even hunt for my own supper, as well as you can, sis. You asked me to move up to the big house and close the little house because you thought I was lonesome living all by myself. I love it here, sis; but not anymore."

Into a carpetbag she tossed a chemise Tanya had given her, the bodice still too large for her bosom.

"So," Tanya began sternly, "you think you are too big for your britches—they've grown too small for you?" Tanya laughed, flicking a finger at the undergarment. "You can't even fit yourself into this yet! it doesn't look like you have worn it once since I gave it to you, an—" Tanya stepped back as Willow whirled on her, furious as a hissing yellow kitten. "Willow!!"

A low chuckle outside the window went unheard by both the women.

"That's just it, sis. You *gave* it to me, you give me so *many* pretty dresses and feminine things." Her mouth tightened as she spread the teal-blue inner folds of the skirt outward with splayed hands. "You gave me this too, but, sis, take a closer look?"

Tanya did so, and shook her head. "I don't see . . ."

"Look closely at the stitches in the bodice and look at the hem." Willow frowned when her sister laughed and shook her bright red head in mirth. "You laugh, sis, but I don't like it *one* bit! The stitches are terrible and you know it! The thread doesn't even match, and I couldn't find any blue . . . look at this, *brown* thread, how ridiculous! I—" she sniffed— "I look like a rag doll, or, or a tavern wench!"

"Tavern w-wench?" Tanya couldn't help but laugh so hard she had to grip her sides. She dried her eyes then. "Where did you ever hear that one? This is Texas!"

"I got an English novel from the Yankee peddler!"

"You what!" Tanya looked at her younger sister as if she had just popped up out of a toy box. "You mean the peddler with the nutmegs and tin pans? Him? Silas—whatever?"

"Yes! Yes!" Willow stuck her chin up with a defiant air. "The same peddler, and I traded some things for the novel and he even had a copy of the *American Spelling Book;* and four older volumes of *McGuffy's Eclectic Reader,* published in the thirties."

"What is the novel like—is it any good?" Tanya was curious to know since she had never seen one of those racy novels women in the East read.

"A man puts his hand on a woman's breast . . . here." Willow put her hand two inches below her collarbone.

"No! That's terrible," Tanya said, shocked that so many women, and maybe even some gentlemen, would be reading such intimate material. In a fast breath, Tanya said, "Where did you put it?"

Willow peered innocently at her sister. "Where did I put what, sis? The book?"

"Yes, yes."

"Why?" Willow said slowly.

"What do you think? I want to read it!" Then Tanya went still all over, looking serious once again. "You aren't really going to run away with this man, are you, Willow?"

"Yes."

"I'll find you some thread to match your dress," Tanya offered, feeling helpless at the situation.

Only a few minutes had passed since Tanya had arrived at the little house. Willow went on arranging her two small bags.

"I'll give you three new dresses, and we'll have Miss Pekoe alter them for you . . . she's very . . . good at it." Tanya stared down at her hands, then back up again. "When will we ever see you again? You are going so far away!"

"Actually, sis, it's near Fort Belknap, not so far west after all."

"Not so far! That's over one hundred miles . . . maybe more!" Tanya gaped at the bags Willow had packed to bulging. "And it's *north;* it's colder there."

"Not all that much."

"I hear it snows there twice a year sometimes, and they had an inch of snow last winter!" Again Tanya turned serious, looking worriedly at her younger sister. "What about, ah, Talon Clay?" She had forgotten about seeing him outside, walking his huge mount toward the house. He must have gone by now. "I thought you wanted to win his heart? Or have you outgrown him, like you've outgrown everything and everybody around here? Don't you want a future here? Has anyone told you that Talon is building Le Petit Sundance, that they have already set to work on the plans and chosen the site over on the eastern seven hundred of Sundance property? It's a very large parcel, Willow, and beautifully wooded, with Strawberry Creek running through it. There's a pond there, too. Sometimes I wish we could build there. . . ."

"Why don't you?"

"Willow, you sound bitter, almost jealous!"

"You've got everything, sis. Your husband adores you, worships the air above you and the ground beneath your feet."

"Talon will have his own home soon . . . I thought you wanted to become his wife . . . someday."

"Oh," Willow exclaimed, turning to face her sister and saying loudly, "Marry Talon Clay? Ugh! He is nothing but a white-faced savage, and he never dresses normally anymore! Marry him? Never!"

Just then Tanya drifted over to the window to look out. Her countenance was worried; she was hoping Talon had not been standing out there overhearing their conversation. But he had—oh no! She could see him now, just walking away leading his horse Cloud. His profile looked as if it was carved from dark stone. He was just in the process of mounting Cloud.

"I am going to become Harlyn's wife and . . . and he is a gentleman, and he makes me feel grown up," Willow continued as Tanya stared out the window. "He'll give me pretty things, not hand-me-downs . . . I am sorry, Tanya, but I want my *own* things." She looked about the room, part of the house she had always cherished. She went on spitefully, "Harlyn said we could go to New Orleans after we're married! Tanya? Did you hear?" Willow went to stand beside Tanya. "What have you been staring at out there?" Then she saw what Tanya had been looking at—Talon, just galloping Cloud out of the yard. With a sinking feeling, she turned to Tanya, "You knew he was out there, didn't you? How much did he hear, Tanya!" She gripped her sister's shoulders, her eyes smarting with wild tears. "How much?"

Tanya shrugged and looked Willow squarely in the eye. "I'm not sure . . . but I think up to when you said he was a *savage* and it would degrade you to marry him."

Willow's eyes flew wide. "Oh no!" She snatched up her skirts at the sides, galvanized to fly. "I'll have to go after him, Tanya. I didn't mean all that!"

"No!" Tanya placed a strong restraining hand on Willow's arm. "Don't you dare. Don't be foolish, Willow. Talon won't listen to your explanations—not now."

"What do you mean—not now?"

"Leave him alone for a while. Besides, what's the use, you are going away with Harlyn Sawyer and Talon Clay knows that now."

"No—he doesn't know about that."

Tanya nodded her head. "Yes. He knows why you are packing."

"Oh, sure, that's right. Everyone, right down to the drovers and mustangers, knows every move that *little* Willow makes! She can't hardly even go to the toilet by herself without someone keeping an eye out for her!" She spun about in a furious half-circle. "I am going for Talon, to tell him I was—"

"Were what, Willow? You can't take back what you said, what he overheard, Willow. He would think you were fibbing. He would only laugh in your face. Talon is very hard, despite his friendliness and easy manner toward folks. You became one of his best friends when you stopped chasing after his pants. Remember that."

"But you said he . . . you said something about me becoming his *wife.*"

"I know."

Willow looked helpless. "How can that ever be?"

"Wait around, Willow, give it more time. Talon will come around; he has to forget his hurt." She knew this; oh, how well Tanya knew this since being married to Ashe Brandon!

"Oh yes. Garnet." Willow sounded bitter. "I tried on the yellow dress the other morning. It was very early in the morning. Talon must have seen the light in my window." Her face flamed. "He must have been watching me, because all of a sudden I came out of my trance and he was standing there! But he could not even see *me* for imagining he was seeing Garnet all over again." Willow didn't notice her sister's stricken look. "H-He tried to make love to me, Tanya." She looked away. "I would have let him, too, but I was so afraid, sis. At first I wasn't, but then he got rough and he was just not the Talon I know . . . I knew. I always thought I would be able to go through with it, but when the time came I was so scared." She shook her head. "So scared."

Tanya sighed. "It was lust that frightened you, Willow. Not love. True love is never frightening, Willow. Lust steals from a person; love gives. You both want to give and give to each other, with all your heart, soul, and—body," Tanya said softly, a reminiscent look in her eyes.

Willow's own eyes were big and brown. "Oh, Tanya, I think it was all my fault!" She sat down hard on the edge of the bed, sighing, tears smarting. "I—I wanted him to desire me and I thought I could get to him if—if I looked like Garnet." Her eyes fell.

Tanya chewed her lower lip. How could she tell

Willow that she *did* look like Garnet, more so with every day that passed? After all, Garnet had been Willow's mother; her own mother, too. Maybe it was really Willow for whom Talon had been waiting all his life, not Garnet, the cheap, wordly woman who had gone after every man she could get her hands on. Tanya was ashamed that her mother had been like that, but that had been Garnet's way.

It was time that Willow knew the story.

"Willow, I have something to tell you . . . I should have done so a long time ago. But you did not want to hear any more about *her* at that time."

How could Tanya know that what she was about to reveal to Willow would have disastrous results? She wouldn't know until it was already said and done.

"What do you want to tell me?" Willow asked, eyeing her sister closely, feeling apprehension take hold of her.

"Willow." Tanya picked up Willow's dainty hand, threading her fingers through her sister's. "Garnet was . . . she was," she raced on, "she was our mother! She—"

Willow broke away and stood up violently. "I don't want to hear it!" She clamped her hands over her ears. "No!" She dropped her hands then and shook her head. "Yes, it's true, it has to be." She whirled to face Tanya squarely. "Tanya," she began slowly, "how is it that Garnet, our m-mother, came to live here before Pa and us kids? And how was it that we were not here with her? Why did she go away and leave us when Sammy and I were so small? I'm nineteen now, so I must have been a toddler when G-Garnet up and left us with Pa in California."

"I don't know the answers to all the questions, Willow. Maybe Pa was trying to find Garnet." Her eyes misted over. "But Mother—I prefer to call her by her name, Garnet—you do understand, I see. Garnet did live here at Sundance before us."

"Before us, yes," Willow echoed.

"Garnet married Brandon on the heels of Martha's burial. She, Garnet, was our real mother, Willow, sad, but so true."

"Talon even wondered about that," Willow said wistfully. "Oh God, I have to get away, Tanya! Far away . . . Talon will kill me!"

"Don't be silly, Willow—you can't just go away."

"I can, yes I can! I can't stand it a minute longer here . . . my heart is breaking, sis, can't you see!" She stomped her foot. "Oh, what a fool I've been! Why couldn't I see that she was my mother—it was so plain to see!"

"Talon Clay doesn't know," Tanya said softly.

Willow whirled on Tanya. "Don't tell him, Tanya, you're right—Talon doesn't know for sure. He will only hate me all the more . . . please?" Her eyes raced back and forth across her sister's face.

Tanya sighed, relenting, her blue eyes deeply troubled. "I promise." She stared down at the few packed bags that contained all of Willow's meager possessions. Willow was going away and there wasn't a thing Tanya or anyone else at Sundance could do about it.

Early morning mists hovered above the ground as the green-and-black buggy stopped by the little house to pick Willow up. She took one last look around. The house was closed up. It looked so lonely, Willow thought as a lump formed in her throat. Sammy would be coming home soon; he would have to move in with Tanya and Ashe, or settle back in Clem's bunkhouse . . . he was always back there anyway, with the ranch hands. She would miss him. . . . Don't start crying now, she told herself.

Harlyn smiled to her as he steered the horse around and out of the yard. Willow's return smile was weakly formed about her pinched lips. She was not going to look back . . . never look back.

"We'll come back for a visit, dear," Harlyn said.

"Sure," was all Willow said, and she looked straight ahead.

Neither of the occupants of the green-and-black buggy noticed the young man who stood at the line of trees stretching across the hill above Strawberry Creek. His dew-laced hair blew against the lavender hues of the morning sky as he stood looking down at his moccasins, which had accumulated moisture from walking through the woods and ankle-high grass. He slowly looked up. Now his fists coiled and uncoiled as his anger grew with his frustration. He gritted his white teeth and raised his fist to the air, shaking it violently, his eyes now gleaming in the sun that had just crested the horizon. He hissed, "How dare you take her from me?" As he raised his sun-gilded face to the sky, as if to howl like a lonely wolf, no other words came from his mouth.

Chapter Six

Sliding from Cloud's back, Talon strode to the bunkhouse where the door was already opening and Almanzo Rankin was stepping out. The half-breed could see the bitterness and frustration carved on Talon's darkened face. Almanzo did not speak, but only raised his hand as if to calm Talon. The slightly younger man eased by him, and Almanzo pivoted to follow him into the bunkhouse. Once inside, Talon roughly grabbed a tin cup and the large black coffeepot. Not knowing it was that hot, he grimaced with a flicker of pain, dropping it back onto the crude pot-bellied stove.

Almanzo moved into the room, saying, "Do you not think it would be wiser to use a cloth to pick it up with? I always do."

Talon sneered, a half-smile on his face. "If you think you can do any better, here." He handed Almanzo the empty coffee cup. "You fill it, then."

Almanzo moved to take it from Talon's hand as the other strode by him to sit down. Almanzo picked up a cloth and poured the steaming brew and set it on the table in front of his friend. He poured himself one then and sat down beside Talon.

"What is it, my friend, that troubles you so?"

"Women."

Almanzo's black eyebrows raised. "Ah, I see, *amigo."*

"Think so?" He swung his face aside. "Hell, you don't know the half of it!"

Almanzo tilted his chair, tossing back, "Do not take it out on me, just tell me what is wrong!"

Talon tossed the long braid over his shoulder and stood brusquely. "We have to get out of here! Where can we go?"

Almanzo rose from his chair, scraping it backwards. "I know just the place. You can tell me what is bothering you on our way there. It will take *many* moons to get there!"

They rode into Black Fox's camp with six days of dust covering them, hungry and tired. In the camp there were other half-breeds, exhibiting a large and varied array of attire. There were military blue coats and various colored shirts, and most wore headbands and black felt hats with feathers and beaded hatbands around the brim. Some wore dangerous-looking bandoleers with ammunition in them and carried rifles or army pistols slung on their hips. The women of the camp wore soft Indian buckskin or bright Mexican skirts, and some of the "full bloods" wore breechclouts, and their naked chests were strong and glistening.

After swinging down from their mounts, Talon

looked over the back of his horse, softly exclaiming, "What are we doing here?"

"Now you ask, after six days of riding." Almanzo laughed and added, "You will learn soon, *amigo*. Just follow me."

Talon felt more at ease, feeling as if a new adventure was starting for him and wondering at the same time where all this would lead.

Almanzo now strode to a half-breed dressed in a blue army half-coat. "Jim Blue-Coat, can you tell me if Nightwalker is in camp?"

Jim looked at Almanzo and then at the stranger, the "white eyes," with a narrowed gaze. Jim had seen those same eyes before, but where just now he couldn't place. His black eyes shifted to the right as he pointed to a tepee. "Over there," he said lazily.

The two men strode to the lodge Jim Blue-Coat had indicated and stepped inside, for the flap had been tied back to circulate the air inside. There, seated on a buffalo hide, his legs crossed, was Nightwalker, an impressive figure of man.

Nightwalker looked up into eyes the same shade of green as his own and a look of surprise entered his face. *Hu, the winds have brought back one that I know.*

A chill ran down Talon's back, as if icy fingers played upon his spine. Almanzo was the first to break the silence.

"Talon," Almanzo said, indicating the seated man with a wide sweep of his hand, "meet your father—Kijika."

Talon stared at both men in disbelief. "My 'father' *what?* I already have a father; his name was Pete Brandon. What is this, the father of the half-breeds?

What kind of joke—"

Nightwalker now spoke, slowly and distinctly, in English. "You are my true son, *son of my blood.* Sit, I will tell you. It is a long story."

Much later, as Talon sat quietly in stunned silence, Nightwalker placed a pounded gold medallion with the face of a flaming sun in the center about Talon's neck, calling him, "My son. You are my son. I have long ago named you and now you shall hear your real name . . . Lakota."

Over the next few days, Talon, Named-Lakota, learned much of this band of Horse Indians that were welcome in the camp of the Kat-U, the Ka-I-Giv-U, Kiowa. This was where they were now, in Black Fox's camp, for the plains peoples were typically large-game hunters, dependent for most part of their diet on buffalo and using buffalo hides and deerskin for clothing and receptacles. At this time of year they came together and hunted.

Seated around the campfires, Little Coyote and his friends related to Lakota the history and movements of Black Fox's band and those of their allies, the Comanches.

This new band of Kiowa had come into being when one of the young leaders had separated from the parent group, along with a following of brothers and sisters with their spouses and offspring. A son of the Kiowa chief Spotted Bird, Black Fox was naturally classed as Kiowa, but Spotted Bird himself was half-Comanche and had married a woman from the Siouan family of Dakota-Assiniboin. Nightwalker was Black Fox's uncle. He was also Spotted Bird's half-brother.

The Indians of the southern plains frontier had taken female slaves among Mexicans and whites, and it was a common custom to carry off and adopt children. Although it was Indian practice to grant the adopted slaves full tribal rights, the kidnapping inflamed the American frontier as few other acts had.

Martha Brandon had been one of those captives, but she had loved her half-breed captor, Nightwalker. He himself was not a full-blooded Indian. Talon, Named-Lakota, was to learn this story later. He was still in a daze, having learned that Pete Brandon had not been his real father.

For now, Lakota was learning what it was like to be with his Indian brothers. He accepted this, without question, that he was half-breed, as if he had known it all along and had just come home.

One night, after the Horse Indians had ridden far into Comancheria, the vast heart-shaped territory located in the Great Plains, Talon sat with Almanzo and Little Coyote surrounded by the dark fires of the Indian camp.

"Why do you call me 'brother'?" Named-Lakota asked Almanzo.

"It is *you* who are Nightwalker's son. For moons upon moons our white friends have thought of me as the offspring of Nightwalker. I am not. I am son of Nightwalker's brother, Hungry Wolf. Also, the old Chief Spotted Bird, dead now, was Nightwalker's brother. I will tell you more . . . cousin."

Almanzo told him that the Kiowas were a small but very warlike people, but their cousins, the Horse Indians, had come out of the mountains of Montana and roamed the Black Hills of South Dakota. Here they had collided with the terrible Dakotas, or Sioux, then moving west. The Kiowas, harasssed by Sioux on the east and Cheyennes on the west, began to drift south. Like the Comanches, they had become a wholly plains-living, bison-hunting tribe. Here was one of the most splendid big-game regions upon the earth. Between the timber on the east, the mountains on the west, and the increasingly hot, dry savannahs of the south, this series of plateaus and prairies, hills and valleys, was incredibly fertile for grazing animals.

The winters were mild, compared with those further north, and the ground was endlessly green and flowering in the spring, or after summer rains. In later summer the oceans of deep grass—buffalo, bunch, needle, and gramma—burned off; the shallow lakes dried, and the country appeared desertlike, only to flower again. The bison roamed over immense distances, following the scattered rains and the grass.

Besides buffalo, there were enormous numbers of other species: hundreds of thousands of pronghorn antelope, bounding and skittering over the grass; varieties of deer and peccary; hares, rabbits, turkeys, and squirrels. The game drew predators, wolves, coyotes, and several varieties of cat, including the cougar or mountain lion. There were elk in the high river valleys, and lurking bear as well.

Kiowas and Comanches now shared the high plains hunting grounds, and soon were riding the warpath together against their common enemies, Apaches and Spaniards.

These people possessed immense herds of horses. The Kat-U were the most skillful of riders among the

Plains Indians. They were noted for outstanding horsemanship and superb fighting ability, just like their Comanche brothers. The Kiowas, along with the Comanches had few, if any, equals among the Indians as "horse soldiers."

"Now you know why you are so good with the horses, my friend," Almanzo told the "new Indian" who had been welcomed into Black Fox's band. "Your 'brothers' possess great stamina; they are able to remain for hours at a time on horseback, and soon you too will stay on your horse for days at a time. You will learn to be skillful with the shield, bow, and lance. Many of my 'brothers' have removed their killed and wounded from the battlefield while riding at full gallop. I myself have ridden against the Apaches and have often fired from beneath the neck of my mount during battle to keep my body from being used as a target."

Named-Lakota shook his head, still puzzled over many things. "This is all like a dream, Almanzo. Tell me then, what is your Indian name?"

Almanzo chuckled, saying, "Hungry Wolf's Son Dark Horse."

"So, you are a half-breed, right? Who is your mother? Is she Indian . . . no she couldn't be."

"The woman you asked about earlier, the one with the blue eyes and black hair, she is my mother—Rain Lady. Her other half is Texican. She gave me up to her relatives when I was but a small boy. I know you have often heard me referred to as Nightwalker." He chuckled. "I, too, have often shrugged my shoulders and said, "Yes, I am Nightwalker, so as not to answer so many questions regarding this great legend." He smiled as he remembered Willow Hayes calling him Nightwalker—she must still think that was his name. Someday he would have to tell the little lady otherwise.

"Rain Lady's relatives, then, must be shirttails of the Rankins, naturally."

Almanzo laughed. "Naturally. Come," he said, rising from the earth, "let us go see what Beautiful Feet and Rain Lady have prepared for our evening meal."

Named-Lakota rubbed his hands over his well-seasoned buckskins and rose to follow his *cousin* Hungry Wolf's Son Dark Horse. "Damn," he said, "if this ain't something!"

Splashes of varied color pinks were brushed onto a misty blue canvas of sky as Willow and her betrothed traveled the Preston Road on a northwest course.

Across the vast prairie they went, heading for Cottonwood Spring where they would camp for the night. Harlyn had picked up supplies at Fort Belknap before continuing on their journey. Willow hoped he knew what he was doing. Major Neighbors had suggested they take along a Delaware Indian as guide and hunter, but Harlyn had told the major that he had stocked plenty of food in the buggy. The major had looked at that light conveyance with a dubiously raised eyebrow. Harlyn had made it before, without mishap or Indian encounter, so why not this time? But this peace that Harlyn was so confident over was not to last. . . .

"Someone has been trailing us," Harlyn said to Willow as she dozed intermittently, "maybe more than one."

"Wha-What are you saying?" Willow had been swaying sleepily in the northbound conveyance and hardly taking notice of her surroundings. She sat up straighter now.

Willow at once took notice of Harlyn's nervous trepidation, and for the first time since she had met him eight days ago she wondered what in God's name she was doing running away with this man, this mere stranger. All she had wanted to do was to run away, to get as far from Talon as she could!

For five days she had been on the road with Harlyn Sawyer, getting to know him while they rode all day at an easy pace, then camped at nightfall. All the while Harlyn had been pleasant, and never once had he made an overt move toward Willow. She liked him well enough, true, but now that she was so far from all that she knew and loved, she was beginning to have second thoughts.

Harlyn had said someone—or more than one—was trailing them. Could it be that Talon was coming after her? Harlyn had said there might be more than one following. Almanzo? And maybe even Ashe, or Little Coyote?

No, she decided, not Ashe. Her brother-in-law had not been getting along all that well with Talon. Ashe had not taken kindly to his brother's actions lately, his becoming more the savage with each day that passed.

"We won't be setting up camp just yet," Harlyn said, his tone hard and brittle. "I ain't sure, but I think we're being followed by, ah, Indians."

"I don't see any," Willow said after looking to the left and right behind them as the buggy left the road and Harlyn struck out into the prairie. The huge red ball of the setting sun sent its swordlike rays across the Little Witchita River.

"They're out there somewhere," Harlyn said, gritting his teeth. He was thinking about the young "savage" and the possessive way he had been measuring Willow Hayes the first day Harlyn had seen the White Indian.

Damn that Brandon lad with his searching green eyes. There was something about Talon Clay Brandon that gave Harlyn Sawyer the creeps, as if the younger man was after him and waiting like a huge talon-clawed hawk for the right moment to pounce on him unsuspectingly!

Harlyn pressed his lips together, wondering why Talon hadn't attacked him before this, when he was riding alone in his buggy from Sundance to Vince's. That bronze-faced lad had had plenty of opportunity.

A chill coursed along Harlyn's spine then . . . maybe the White Indian would attack him now, now that Harlyn had taken something that the other thought belonged to him: like Willow Hayes.

Now Willow was sitting at attention, her ears attuned to any sound that might mean approaching hoofbeats . . . if their company threatened to overtake them, and if they were Indians, they would strike at right angles to the buggy. Horror-filled thoughts jarred her mind as terrible visions of the strange Indian who had given her the white flower came to her. She shivered. Had the flower been a foreboding of her impending death?

From Little Coyote she had learned of the ways of the allied Comanches and the Kiowas, who banded together when they struck. Had her strange Indian belonged to the fiercer of those tribes?

Little Coyote had told her that those Indians were among the finest horsemen ever known, that they could fire a shower of arrows with deadly accuracy from the gallop. The Comanches raided by the light of the moon and galloped back to the trackless plains, sometimes with prisoners, back to the Llano Estacado, or Comancheria. These rich grounds were the preserve of the Quahadis, Antelope Band, those known as one of the fiercest of Comanche peoples. Also, he had named the Kat-U, of the Kiowa. They were known for their distant raiding, even more than the Comanches. They, like the Comanches, harried both Indians and Anglos.

Willow shivered again. And Little Coyote had said both were so fierce . . . they even took scalps!

At the thought, Willow reached up to place her straw bonnet back on her head, firmly. As if that would do any good, she thought; her thick, flowing mane of blond hair stuck out from every angle, blowing in the wind. There was no help for it.

Twilight was yielding to night as the buggy rode over a rolling country covered with groves of mesquite trees. Eerie mists were steaming across the land. The course Harlyn took was slow going, intersected by several spring branches, which were tributaries to Salt Creek, flowing through valleys blanketed with a dense coating of green vegetation.

Willow drew a languid arm over tired eyes. Even in the lavender dusk she could see that the valleys teemed with a multitude of beautiful flowers. By day the brilliant hues of the blooms must be breathtaking to behold, she thought romantically.

The aromas of the blossoms laced the misted air with a most delicate fragrant perfume, and there was an almost tangible excitement in the air, too. Willow had a feeling that something was going to happen soon, and for some strange reason she was not all that frightened at the thought.

When Harlyn finally broke the eerie silence, Willow jumped off her seat a little.

"The horse is tired."

He should be dead by now, Willow was thinking. It was cruel . . . why did Harlyn not have two horses? He was supposed to be so rich.

"We'll make our camp at the large spring up ahead," he went on, and Willow nodded in tired boredom.

It was near the head at one of the branches of the west fork of the Trinity that Harlyn Sawyer pulled the dust-coated buggy to a halt. Finally, Willow thought.

It was weary going for Willow when she had to prepare the beans and stringy beef over the measly fire Harlyn had built for her. She was beginning to think Harlyn Sawyer was lazy.

With the fire burning low so as not to attract Indians, Willow snuggled in her bedroll and stared up at the huge Texas stars. Why did everyone always say that everything was bigger in Texas? Even folks from California said the Texas sky was deeper and wider than their own.

From across the fire Harlyn's voice sounded blurred when he spoke. "Did you know that it was the horse that first gave the friggin' Indians freedom to always move about across the plains, from camp to camp?" Harlyn sipped noisily from the bottle he usually took out when night fell.

"Which Indians, Harlyn, do you speak of?" Willow asked as she braided her hair. Too excited to sleep, she had sat up and wondered what she could do in the dark to occupy herself.

He grunted.

"There are many kinds of Indians," she said, hoping he would continue the conversation.

Why, she wondered, had Talon flashed in her mind's eye just now, dressed in his savage attire? Always she thought of him when the subject of Indians was brought up. She was beginning to think of Talon as Harlyn did, as White Indian.

Harlyn burped. "The Comanches, Kiowas, Cheyennes, Crows, and Dakotas," he said, smacking his lips.

"Oh? I thought they also moved about on foot. Can't they be nomadic that way, too?" Willow tied a leather strip to the end of her braid; Harlyn looked over and seemed mesmerized by the long, fat, yellow braid of hair.

"Not completely," Harlyn said, still staring at Willow. "They live in the saddle nowadays mostly. Horses are a sign of wealth, and the more they have to trade with, the more they have of other things then, too."

"They live on the move," Willow said thoughtfully. "How exciting." But then she remembered Sundance, where she had . . . no, don't think of that now. "You know a lot about Indians, don't you Harlyn Sawyer?" She shifted to peer over the straggly burnt-orange flames. "Harlyn?" she said again.

But Harlyn had fallen fast asleep, his liquor bottle cradled against his chest.

Sleep was slow in coming for Willow that night

under the stars. In the distance she could see the lightning flashing across the sky. Though she could not see Harlyn, she knew he was still clutching the bottle tightly.

Earlier, she had noticed that Harlyn seemed to be shivering. Was he more afraid of the night than she was? She began to wonder about him again. How could she marry this man she hardly even knew? He seemed nice enough, a handsome gentleman rancher, but she had noticed that he didn't have much backbone for a man. He seemed to be afraid of his own shadow sometimes, yet prepared to lash out bravely at others—especially when he tipped that ever present whiskey bottle he carried with him in his dusty, sweat-stained coat. A breeze carried Harlyn's scent across to her. She could smell him now, and she realized that he never bent at a stream as she did to wash her face and hands. She had even removed her dress and wrung it out in the water, letting it dry overnight while she wore a fresh one to bed and then washed again in the morning.

Willow had grown up in a family of clean folk, people who bathed often, and even the Brandon brothers washed themselves regularly and always had a nice, clean, manly smell about them. Even though Talon had begun to look like a savage, he never seemed to neglect the cleanliness of his body.

In the cool night air, Willow's nipples hardened reflexively when she thought of Talon's body. She knew he was clean, for she had been near him often enough.

Willow was jostled all the next day in the wagon, and

by nightfall her bones felt as if they were ready to break. For supper that night they had fried salt pork, crusty bread, and black coffee. As it cooked, the roof of Willow's mouth formed saliva. It smelled so good she could not wait to attack the meal!

That night, camped under the stars, Willow began to really miss Talon—"White Indian," as Harlyn called him every time his name popped into their conversation during the day. She missed Sundance too, the lovely old house, and even the little house that had been home to her, though she truly did not have a place to call her own. She had just been "staying on" at Sundance. Her Pa had come to work there when she was just a little girl, and she had always loved the place.

But she had become miserable at Sundance lately. Talon would never forget Garnet—her own mother! For God's sake, he had loved her *mother!* How could she ever begin to even think about living peacefully at Sundance with that always hanging over her head? It was best for all that she was running away.

Turning over in her bedroll, Willow came to the conclusion, a most difficult one, that she had made the right move in leaving. She would become Harlyn Sawyer's wife, start a new life with him, and forget she had ever come to love the blond outlaw at Sundance property. She squeezed her eyes tight, knowing the time would come when Harlyn would want children. How was she even going to become pregnant by him when all she had dreamed of was Talon and their getting married someday and having their own little towheads to raise? How . . . in God's name, how?

Biting her lower lip, she tasted her own blood. She vowed that someday she would be strong enough and mature enough to banish Talon from her heart and mind completely.

But deep in that very same night, Talon walked her dreams again, startling her awake more than once, burning in her soul like a flame.

After breakfast the next morning, Harlyn set out on a northwest course. For six miles they crossed several small tributaries of the Trinity, which were wooded along the banks with mesquite.

Peering sideways at Harlyn, Willow noticed his eyes were bloodshot again and she knew he must have drunk some more whiskey after she had fallen asleep. Adjusting her Mexican-style skirt, Willow felt for her handgun, discovering she'd lost it somewhere!

Willow frowned. "Harlyn, have you spotted the men again you thought might have been tracking us the day before yesterday?"

He only grunted his reply, which was no reply at all. Willow decided he must be really hung-over. She would keep her silence and wait for him to speak up next. But it wasn't much fun having no one to talk to, and she was sick over losing her handgun. She was hot and hungry, but the food would have to wait; the heat she could do nothing about.

They had been rationing their food supply, Harlyn said it was running low. He had not counted on any Indians, or whoever, making them take a zigzag course to avoid being seen. She could tell Harlyn was frightened of something, and he was trying to hide their passage as best he could.

She was beginning to think Harlyn Sawyer was a coward who would never stand up and fight for her, even though he had a Kentucky rifle on the ready right beside his seat. If only she'd thought to bring along her Toledo Steel knife!

The rifle was very long, almost as tall as Harlyn. But it looked very heavy and hard to handle, Willow thought, eyeing it now and then. She did feel safer, knowing it was there. There had been some conversation between them about the rifle's capability. Though it was ungainly, the gun was immensely accurate, up to two hundred meters or more. It was most effective when shot from a rest, but it was difficult to load, Harlyn said. The rifle was fitted with a short, awkward wooden stock, and small-bored, about .32 caliber. Willow wondered how good Harlyn was with it.

Only time would tell what Harlyn was really made of, if that time should ever come. And maybe *she* would have to pick up arms to defend the both of them should Indians attack them.

"It is a beautiful, sparkling day even though it is hot and humid," she blurted, forgetting she had promised herself to let him speak first to break the long silence that had been stretched endlessly.

"I feel sick," Harlyn groaned, and Willow watched him draw up the ribbons while he leaned over the side and retched violently.

Harlyn's hair was disheveled; he appeared to have been on a ten-day drunk. Poor, handsome, Mr. Sawyer, she thought compassionately. He really was a mess, a bundle of raw nerves, and seemingly growing thinner by the day.

"If you don't stop that tippling at night, Harlyn Sawyer, you are never going to make it to your *rancho.*" There was a smile in her voice and when he looked up at her, he seemed to be glaring angrily.

"We'll both make it, *you* and I, girl."

Willow wondered at the emphasis he had made but did not dwell on it too long. Harlyn was just suffering a hangover, that was all. She looked up ahead, trying not to listen to the tiger growling of hunger in her stomach.

She wanted very much to ask Harlyn about the ranch, but every time she mentioned one word about it he would become closemouthed. He would always change the subject then.

Occasionally they passed a grove of post-oaks, and here and there a cottonwood or willow loomed majestically in a wide sweep along the banks, their proud leafy heads reflected in the clear water. Suddenly Willow felt a great thirst and asked Harlyn to halt the buggy. The horse was tired anyhow, its chestnut coat looking dull in the gloom that was descending with ominous speed.

"Reckon you're right, Willow."

Harlyn seemed to be his old self again, some color having returned to his cheeks in the last hour. "It's goin' to rain pretty soon, too." His eyes stayed on Willow as she alighted first. "The water in all these branches is clear," he said, gazing at a distant spot and frowning. "It's safe to drink . . . don't worry, Willow . . . and it's available any . . . season."

Unaware of anything odd about Harlyn's behavior, Willow knelt to the bank, leaned over on her stomach and drank with a greedy thirst. She could see clear to the bottom, and in some places it was not so shallow.

There was a predominance of dark sandstone, and in many places it cropped out or was laid bare by the action of the water.

A gray cloud scuttled overhead. The moon made a sudden eerie presence in the clear water. Willow shuddered . . . Comanches struck deep into enemy territory, two or three hundred miles or more away from camp, to kill, and sometimes to take prisoners. They would gallop back to the trackless plains, to Comancheria . . . by the light of the moon . . . Little Coyote had told her.

Now Willow froze. The hair was rising on her arms. Something whizzed by her head and not a breath of a moment later she heard a loud *thwack* in the tree beside her and an even louder, collective *"Aiee!"*

Chapter Seven

For one tumultuous moment Willow had felt an almost stunning urge strike her . . . she wanted to take up arms against the band of Indians that had attacked them! But the dark-visaged Indians surrounded her. Oh! Where was Harlyn when he was needed? She'd seen him only minutes ago, outside the buggy.

Suddenly Willow knew! Letting out a bloodcurdling scream, Harlyn had made a mad dash for the prairie; he was trying to get away, but an Indian with a long, craggy face, wearing a high-crowned sombrero and frontier clothes, captured Harlyn near a cottonwood by whipping a long *reata* about Harlyn's legs and halting his escape instantly.

All the while Willow was contemplating the rifle beside her. If only she could snatch it up! But several pairs of watchful dark eyes pinned her movements. They hadn't touched her yet, and it was mostly, she guessed, because she sat subdued . . . for the moment.

Harlyn was handed over into the custody of two warriors. He had long ago ceased his struggles. Blood ran darkly down the side of his face, evidence that the craggy-faced Indian had cuffed him on his head. She heard this long-faced Indian referred to as Nayati.

While the Indians seemed to have their full attention on their leader and Harlyn, Willow saw her chance and snatched up the rifle! She only prayed it was loaded—maybe she'd be able to scare them all off with one shot!

Leaping from the wagon armed with the rifle that was a head taller than herself, Willow made a mad dash for the nearest tree. She rested the barrel against the bole and prepared to fire—but Lord, the rifle was heavy!

"Kijika!"

Willow gasped when the huge Indian was alerted and nudged his horse into action. As the mount was whirled to face her, Willow felt that she'd seen this gorgeous beast before. The symmetry and grace of the animal caught her attention. His almost black coat glistened in the bright moon that had just come out. His great, flashing hoofs matched the perfect proportion of his legs—he was much taller and heavier than the average Spanish mustang. He was of mustang stock and perhaps Arabian, as Talon's Cloud was.

Hefting the rifle upward, Willow prepared herself to fire. Now that the weapon was in her hands, she wondered if she'd really be able to shoot . . . she'd never killed a man, only a small animal in hunting.

"D-Don't come any closer!" Willow warned the Indian leader. "If you do, it will be your last step."

"It would be foolish for you to fire," he said with soft calm as the dark mustang curvetted before her. She had daring and spunk, the yellow-hair, Kijika was thinking. But if he died by her hand, his Indian companions would be sure to slay this beauty. All he had told them before they attacked the yellow-hair and her man was that the girl must remain unharmed—he should have told them the reason why.

"No-o-o-o!" He'd moved his mount so expertly and swiftly that Willow could not think twice and they were there in front of her! "Damn you I-Indian . . . move back . . . now!"

She could shoot now and be rid of their leader. Just like that. But what would happen to Harlyn and her then? Should she chance it? Could she kill a man in cold blood?

Willow could not know that the rifle shook badly in her hands. All she could take in in that mesmerizing moment was the striking color of the Indian's eyes. As the moon struck him full in the face, she saw that they were gray-shadowed green.

It struck Willow suddenly that the Indian leader was very handsome up close, middle-aged she guessed, maybe somewhat older. It was difficult to tell, but he would be handsome at any age. By the downsweep of his black lashes, she could tell he was studying her, too. At length, he stared.

Willow studied him curiously, feeling captive in some sort of trance. She perused the bronze planes of his striking face. He had a crisp, mobile mouth, and for some unfathomable reason he again appeared oddly familiar to her.

Willow stared at him in amazement. Could this be the same handsome Indian who'd presented the white flower to her with such a gentle hand? No, this could not be the same one. The other had had his face painted boldly in savage lines and bright colors.

The Indian leader in the commanding attire dismounted slowly, with seeming caution. But all the while his stunning and laughing eyes seemed to be holding Willow hypnotized. He also seemed to be laughing at her brave actions.

Just then Harlyn loosed a painful whimper and Willow brought her rifle to the ready again, waving it from side to side as threateningly as her weakening grip would allow. "Leave him alone! Stop hitting at him!" she shouted. "One of you will die—at least one! Who shall it be? Your leader?"

The mentioned one chuckled low as he walked near her, standing not four feet away now. Willow felt his compelling eyes pierce her, and it seemed he was peering into her very soul. What eyes this man owns! she thought with admiration.

The wind murmured through the cottonwood spring like a thousand primitive voices. Some infinitesimal part of Willow's mind recognized something about this leader that was familiar to her, but the greater part rejected it, since she could think of no way that she could know him or anyone, for that matter, who was related to him!

He'd come to stand before her, tall and erect, his chest strong and muscular and proud. He had an easy and graceful gait—so like another she knew. No, this Indian could not be anything like Talon Clay!

Boldly Willow spat into the distinguishingly handsome face, "Leave Harlyn—leave my husband alone. Let him go!"

"Ah." The Indian seemed surprised as he said softly, mesmerizingly, "Husband? How can this be?" He shook his head in disbelief.

He spoke perfect English! Caught off guard, Willow lowered the rifle. She could only gape in stupefaction at the Indian. She had lied that Harlyn Sawyer was her husband—but how could this Indian possibly know that?

It was then, while she was so distracted, that Kijika reached out to gently and easily extract the rifle from her nerveless fingers.

The Indians struck camp that night upon a confluent of the Little Witchita, where it was bordered by high, abrupt, rocky bluffs. The water stood in moonstruck pools along the bed of the stream, beckoning and deceitful.

Ignoring the busy Indians, Willow sank down beside the water, and when she took a drink and spit it out, Kijika laughed to himself softly.

Aiyana—so this was his son's choice. She is very lovely and spirited, he thought. His son did not know it yet himself, but Kijika knew that his son was very much in love with Aiyana. Kijika recalled to mind the hushed conversation he and his son had had only three nights ago seated before the campfire. At length, his son had revealed the desire that burned in his soul for one very special woman. Kijika had read the jealousy in his son's eyes when he spoke of this yellow-hair and the man who had taken her away. Kijika knew that his son had not meant to speak so openly of what was hidden in the secret recesses of his heart. Only through time and much pain would they at last come together, he knew.

On soft deerskin moccasins, Kijika walked beneath

the rocky bluff and handed her his hide canteen. "Here. Drink," he said. "It is filled with clear, palatable water from the last stop. This water here is not so clear."

Daring much, Willow snatched the hide canteen from him, saying, "You mean where you viciously attacked us, don't you?" She drank greedily then, not waiting for his reply.

He spoke then. "You are lucky we did not scalp you, little flower. Aiyana, you have such lovely hair. It could have become a great prize to hang in some chief's tepee."

Gracefully wiping her mouth with the back of her hand, she asked, "What chief is that?"

He shrugged laconically. "Any chief, Aiyana."

She read kindness in his eyes, and he didn't frighten her half as much as he had at first. "What does that mean, what you call me?"

"Pretty Indian flower that blooms eternally."

Aiyana, like the three-petaled love blossom with the violet heart, the one he had presented her with when he had come upon her with his countenance painted so fiercely in the war colors of the Kat-U tribe. But she does not recognize me!

Pretty flower, he thought, you are for my son, who awaits your coming, though he does not yet know this himself. She would be brought to the nearest village, some one hundred miles away. His son was there, and he would not let Aiyana go once she was brought to his attention. And if he should let her go for some reason, it would not be for long, and his son would have her back again.

"Where are you taking us?" she wanted to know.

"North," was all he said, stroking Mah Toh's dark,

silky mane.

Looking around, Willow noticed that the ten riderless mustangs were rope-corraled, and she wondered for the first time why the Indians took so many spare horses to travel with them.

"How far north?" she asked, admiring his magnificent mount.

"Not far. First I must go to the reservation with the horses and may be detained there. They will be tamed by the Indians there and then sold to whoever comes to the reservation wanting to buy fresh mounts. Some of them trade the horses for needed items."

"Why are we traveling north?" she pressed. "Is there a camp there—where you are taking us?" She had never been to any Indian camp, and she wondered a bit fearfully what it would be like and what would happen to her and Harlyn Sawyer once they were there.

Such an inquisitive female, Kijika thought, but this is good. While she was studying the horses, he said, "You will see."

Then he strode away, both he and his mount seeming to walk ephemerally on the night wind.

Such a strange, mysterious Indian, Willow thought. But then she had never known any Indians besides Little Coyote and Almanzo Rankin, the latter being a half-breed. She had heard this leader referred to as Kijika. But was this his real name? She was intrigued by him and a little frightened at the same time. What, she wondered, would his name mean in English?

Willow soon learned that their captors were banded with the Horse Indians. There were twenty of them in all traveling with her and Harlyn. Though their leader made his home for most of the year with the nomadic camps of Kat-U and "Horse," he told her, he also brought wild mustangs to the Comanche Indian reservation, also known as Clear Fork Reservation. There the peaceable Indians broke the horses for the Texas Rangers or anyone in the West interested in purchasing a ready-made mount.

The Horse Indians' business was mainly mustanging, and they were an odd-looking bunch that wore anything ranging from Indian to frontier garb—and sometimes a garish mixture of both. Kijika rode the enormous distances with his small band at night and then hid in brushy streambeds by day, but this, he told her, was only when they were fighting with the Apaches. Otherwise, they were not a very warlike people. Why was he telling her all this, Willow wondered.

Only now, since they had taken the girl and Sawyer captive, did the Horse Indians ride tirelessly by day. Willow still did not know who their leader could be; all she had heard one of the half-breeds call him the night before was Kijika.

As the Indians had with them four extra tame mounts, Willow was allowed to ride a painted pony. Kijika called the pretty horse a "paint," an expression Willow had never before heard. The horse was all black, with the exception of a light sprinkling like snow that dotted her sleek hide. The paint's name was Istas. And though she was a beauty, with flashing eyes and hoofs, Willow missed Dust Devil, her own horse, the mustang that Talon had caught and tamed especially with her in mind—so he had said.

"Do you like Istas?" Kijika asked Willow, riding alongside her on his magnificent tall stallion.

"She is beautiful. What does her name mean in English?"

"Snow," he simply said.

Willow only nodded and looked up at the thistle-pink sky of morning, then back at the handsome older Indian. She ducked her head when he glanced her way. He was the eldest in the bunch, though by far not the weakest. In fact, Kijika appeared to be very strong.

"How are your friends treating my—husband?" As she asked this she looked straight ahead.

Their course was nearly west, she determined, but gradually they had been deflecting to southward. This puzzled her somewhat. She thought Kijika had said they were traveling north. He had not answered her question yet. And had he caught when she had faltered over the word "husband"?

Now he answered her. "As kindly as they would treat most any woman," he said with a smile in his voice.

Willow whirled on her mount to face him, but Kijika was the one now staring straight ahead. He was avoiding her deliberately, she realized, and he seemed to be mocking her silently. One thing she had to admit was that the Horse Indians had not been overly cruel to Harlyn Sawyer after Nayati had cuffed him on the side of the head. But Harlyn had whimpered and cowered like a naughty child as they held him afterward to keep him from hurting himself. As a woman might have done upon capture by Indians, Harlyn had gotten hold of a knife and tried to stab himself in the abdomen. But

Nayati had been swift to retrieve his fallen weapon and save Harlyn Sawyer from wounding himself, perhaps fatally.

After thinking over what the leader had said, Willow turned back to him. "What did you mean by that?" she snapped insolently.

Kijika smiled now and he looked all the more distinguished and handsome. "Your . . . husband whines like a child. He whimpers like a woman in distress when he is thirsty for the firewater or has the need to relieve himself—" he grinned broadly here—"and that is very often. His liking for the firewater is great. I am sorry if I offend you, but my companions like it, too. They stole the last of your husband's drink. Now he whines and cries like a suckling babe without his mother's breast. Did you know, Aiyana, your man was so thirsty for the firewater when you . . . married him?"

Even with her face reddening, Willow turned to glare at Kijika. "You do not believe Harlyn Sawyer is my husband, do you? Yes, I can read this is so in your face."

Willow did not expect an answer, nor did she receive one. At least, not yet. She watched Kijika turn back to gesture to his men, and then they were again changing course. Looking up ahead, she guessed that his purpose in deflecting southward was to avoid the numerous branches of the river she had heard referred to as the Witchita.

Willow sighed. At times, it seemed they were deviating far off their course or even going in circles like the hawks above their heads high in the sky. Soon Willow discovered the reason for the change. As they would have been taken too far from their course—which he said was north—he had them now crossing the branches at right angles.

Suddenly Willow's startled brown eyes swung around to rest on Harlyn Sawyer, and she listened to what he was saying as he shouted at the top of his lungs.

"Damn Injuns! Where we goin' now? Ow—ouch! Tarnation!"

Willow cringed and swung around to exchange a reluctant smile with Kijika. Harlyn Sawyer must really be tangled in knots inside, she thought, since the leader had shoved him none too gently into the buggy and ordered him to stay put like a naughty child while Nayati, the long-faced Indian sporting two fistfuls of hawk feathers and a Mexican hoop through one ear, rode Harlyn's horse up front pulling the buggy. The green-and-black conveyance looked as if it had gone through a war, no less. The sight was humorous to behold!

Kijika's voice came out low and ominous. "It will be too bad if this crazy man is truly your husband, Aiyana."

She saw that while Kijika said this his eyes blazed . . . across to her. A shivering of nerves passed through her. His words seemed to have carried a double meaning, but this was not what was bothering her the most. The sun had caught Kijika directly in his eyes and Willow's keen eyesight had picked up the deeply beautiful shade in them. They *were* dark green!

Kijika continued to lead them along a gradual slope of beautiful and picturesque country interspersed with mesquite glades and prairie lawns that spread out ahead for eight miles or more.

Willow could not contain her curiosity any longer and nudged Istas to catch up with Kijika. "Why do you say too bad?"

"Now you are curious, Aiyana. You could not wait any longer to hear the reason why I said those words."

A new brand of apprehension traced over her nerves as Kijika sent her a hooded look. "What do you mean?" she pressed, feeling the need to swallow hard. And she did, her nub of adam's apple bobbing. Kijika stared at her neck.

Still he said nothing. Something was wrong about what he had said, and his words seemed to have carried a double meaning.

"You will see," was all he said.

Willow could not contain the anger that had been brewing up inside of her. "All right, if you must be the mysterious Indian—then go ahead! See if I care!"

Kicking her mount past the Indian, Willow caught a glimpse of a mocking smile on his lips. Why did he have to be so consarn mysterious! The strange part was she did not feel so very frightened of him anymore, not since she had become better acquainted with him and his moods. She did not think that Kijika would harm her in any way. He did not strike her as being very dangerous, at least not where women were concerned. Although the looks he shot her at times made her shiver. For now, she seemed to be safe enough. But what about Harlyn Sawyer—what would be his fate?

The Horse Indians halted for a light repast of dried wild plums, jerky blended with ground maize, and a drink that Willow thought tasted suspicously of water sweetened with a bit of wild honey. Though it was tasty, Willow longed for a tall, cool glass of Tanya's special herbed tea that tasted like mint julep.

Kijika had not come to sit by Willow this time to share the light fare, but had wandered off by himself. She wanted to talk to somebody, so she drifted over to the buggy to seek Harlyn's company, however silent and sullen he could be at times. She had to admit she much preferred Kijika's company to Harlyn's. Still, if they were to make plans in trying to escape these Indians she had to get through to Harlyn somehow!

There was a slow, affirmative nod from Nayati who was stationed near the buggy. Willow moved as close as she could sidle to Harlyn before Nayati's hand rose to indicate that she should halt right there and go no further.

Willow sent Nayati the nastiest grimace she could manage, but this only served to make Nayati toss back his feather-decorated head while pointing at her and laughing raucously. The hoop earring danced from his lobe, striking yellow from the sunlight.

Willow had no idea what Nayati meant, but he was beginning to irritate her, and, besides, she was hot and sticky!

Her hands going to her hips, Willow faced Nayati squarely. "You think I look funny, do you? Well, just go and take a look at your own face in the water! You are not the prettiest sight, you know!"

Willow employed sign language in places where Nayati failed to understand her words, filling in until he nodded in understanding of what she wanted him to do. When Nayati bent down and saw himself, he straightened and laughed deep from the belly, saying the one English word he knew well. "Ugh-ly, *hu!*"

"You said it, feather-brain!" She laughed along with

Nayati, knowing the joke was on him.

Then she stared as he pounded his chest, saying, *"Eoyta!"* which Willow had an idea meant Nayati said he was "the greatest."

"Pooh!" she said, still laughing at him.

She went still then as he pointed at her again and chuckled, directing her to walk to the water and take a good look at her own self. Walking to the water and bending over, Willow saw her own reflection!

"My God," she gasped, slapping both reddened cheeks. "How did I get so dirty?"

Rubbing her face very hard, Willow glared while Harlyn and Nayati both laughed at her futile attempt to make her face come clean. By their looks, she had a good idea she was only making it worse!

She looked down at herself. Not only were her hands dirty, but she was travel-stained and dusty all over. Now she could even smell herself, come to think of it.

Nayati directed her gaze back to the water while rubbing his face with his hands, expressing himself in pantomime. He nodded vigorously then, and Willow caught his meaning and tossed her head.

"Of course, feather-brain," she said imperiously, "I know when to wash and when not to! I sure don't need any looney Indian ordering me around and telling me what to do!" She sniffed at the pile of hawk feathers sticking every which way from out of his head.

"Hu, Ugh-ly Aiyana!" he called the taunt after her as she stomped away.

"Oh—shut up!"

Willow stomped off up the brook in search of a private place to wash, but before long several pairs of dark eyes were peering from the bushes out at her.

"Can't a female ever hope to get any privacy around these parts?"

Removing only her worn shoes, and flinging back her long, greasy hair, she strode into the shimmering brook fully clothed and madder than a wet hen. The brook was cold, but she found it refreshing just the same.

Gritting her teeth, Willow washed herself as best she could, even snatching up her skirts, rubbing two folds vigorously together, muttering, "Might as well kill two birds with—" She whirled to put her back to the grinning bronze faces and laughing dark eyes. "Shut your face . . . dagblasted redskins!"

Willow sighed in defeat. There didn't seem to be any chance that she and Harlyn would ever be able to escape from their clutches.

Willow had no idea that at that very moment her future was being planned for her in the mesquite glade. It was where Kijika, Nightwalker, had gone to meet with the Lipan scout, Akandao, from the Llano Estacado, he who had come hastily upon receiving the message that Kijika wished to meet him at a certain point just north of the reservation.

PART TWO

Savage Moon

TEXAS PLAINS: INDIAN TERRITORY

I arise from dreams of thee
In the first sweet sleep of night—

The Indian Serenade
—Percy Bysshe Shelley

Chapter Eight

Like lambent tongues of flame, warm breezes of evening played across the earth to caress Willow gently and blow tendrils of golden hair at her forehead and ears.

But Willow did not feel the breeze; she was asleep under the stars in the camp of the Horse Indians.

Willow was dreaming. In her dream there was a warm sensation that seemed to be encircling her heart. Even though she was dreaming, she remembered everything, even down to the smallest detail. It was a hot day, and the sunswept scene would be alive in her mind and her dreams forever. . . .

It was the first time Willow had seen Talon Clay ride in on a freshly broken mustang, long-bladed knife thumping against his buckskin-clad thigh. His chest was naked and smoothly bronzed like an Indian's. She had fainted dead away!

When Willow had come awake that day, it was only to find herself staring right into the blazing green eyes of Talon Clay Brandon. She had been about to swoon again when he spoke her name ever so softly, saying in a deeper, richer tone of voice than she had ever heard him use before, "Willow, sweet pussywillow, why are you always lying flat on your back with your consciousness knocked out of you?" He laughed, a deep, breathless sound. "Even Ashe says he saw you kick up your heels in a swoon once, and you didn't come to for a long time."

Talon turned, and his handsome, sun-bronzed face was bold and keen, a reckless flash in the sunlight. Then he shifted, putting his back to the sun. "Is that you, Talon Clay?" She blinked up at him as she came part way out of her swoon, seeing the sun's rays coruscate about his head like a hot penumbra, so bright and heavenly that she couldn't even see his face and read his eyes like she wanted to. "It don't sound like you . . . don't look like you."

"It's me, darlin'."

"You're beautiful," she whispered as she felt herself being lifted and carried into the house.

"You are the one that is beautiful," he murmured as he kicked the door open, his knee-high black moccasins whispering across the carpet as he brought her to lie on the sofa in Ashe's cool study at the back of the house.

"What did you say?" she asked him, her head spinning as she chided herself for forgetting her bonnet again on this hot summer's day.

"Nothing. Just rest."

He went away, came back and she felt a cool cloth covering her forehead. "I was afraid you would not come back," she told him in a soft voice.

Willow lay there on the sofa of Spanish leather,

looking up at him, stretched out flat on her back. When he remained silent, she said, "You look so different, Talon . . . you even sound so different." She tried to reach his taut, bronzed cheek and he leaned closer, sitting on the edge of the sofa. "Did you go away to become an Indian?" Her voice was barely above a whisper.

He smiled tenderly. Her heart skipping beats every so often, Willow continued to feast her eyes on Talon. She was so aware of his bare, bronze-colored chest with the muscles that were so taut and hard. Allowing her gaze to drift downward, she saw his long, finely muscled legs encased in buckskin breeches, the kind with long fringe like the Indians wore.

Her eyes dragging back up to his head, she reached out to finger his long silken blond hair. "You look just like a savage . . . how did your hair grow so long?" Her misty eyes slipped from his hair to his eyes, eyes that were now smoldering a forest green.

"I took a scalp," he said.

She had smiled up at him dreamily, and once again caressed his golden mane. "I can hear the wind of your travels, the fleet hoof of your new white mount. You have already gone far and wide with this horse."

"You silly girl." He brought his lean face closer to hers. He had watched as her hand slid downward, coming to rest over the left side of his chest. His next words emerged as a painful, sweet whisper. "Now you are holding my heart . . . pussywillow."

Their lips had brushed in the merest touch of a kiss.

"Oh, God, Willow. . . ."

He wanted her. She knew it!

Her heart fluttering like a wild thing, she said,

"Please, Talon, just kiss me once?" Her breath rushed in and out in panting little sounds of ripening passion. "Just once . . . and never again? I promise you won't have to ever again?"

"I can't," he groaned.

She remembered his forehead pressed against hers, his lips hovering close to the tip of her nose.

"Talon, oh please, Talon!"

"Willow, I don't want to hurt you, dear heart. We just wouldn't be good for each other. I have been around. You have not." His eyes had been closed, and then they opened to sweep over her in a gentle caress. "I can't, darlin', I just can't hurt you. You don't know what I am like."

Her body had unconsciously jerked against his and she had felt her tears come. Hot and wild, they flowed down her cheeks.

"Little darlin," he murmured, putting her back against his pounding chest, and curling, he had cupped her into his body.

Both weary from many sleepless, frustrated nights, they soon fell sound asleep. Willow did not know that Talon dreamed of her.

Even now, in the camp of the Horse Indians, Willow softly sobbed and cried into the blanket, wishing she were in the arms of the one she loved and could never have.

In the camp of the Kat-U, Talon, Named-Lakota, walked in his dreams as he had once before. His feet were bare, his long dark-blond hair braided. He walked alone.

All the earth surrounding him and before him seemed full of golden halos and streaks of violet blue. There was a thick amber haze that he seemed to be breathing . . . like mist lifting from a watery meadow. He could see his exhaled breaths as if he walked in a wintry cold, streams and puffs of it before him sparkling like golden motes of the finest rare dust.

Now he was not alone. Ahead of him there was a woman.

In his recurring dream Willow stood naked, ankle-deep in a bubbling spring. So wondrously transparent was she, that the golden halos of sun seemed to shine clear through her. And her body was like a white opal catching shimmers and coruscating gleams!

Willow's gilded hair was braided Indian fashion, the glints in it flaming like strands of fire cast in bronze. Her opalescent arms stretched high above her head in ecstasy, while glistening droplets of water dripped from her fingers.

While he walked in his dream, Talon felt his body harden with manly desire. Her body was riper, her curves and face more mature, and the light of the haloed sun touched her pensive, beautiful face as she turned to look at him. Her slim arms stretched out to greet him, her winsome face an aching testimony of her boundless joy. Her feet lifted in a run, while the slow-motion drops of water sprayed into the air, and the sun grew brighter all around the glade.

With a fierce elation, Talon went to meet her. Then her eyes shadowed like haunted, elusive wraiths. Her tears sparkled silvery now, and Willow vanished before her arms could reach him!

"Willow!" Talon shot up from the buffalo robe with

a deep, wrenching sound torn from his throat.

He awoke now as he had then, again bathed in streams of erotic sweat and his hard shaft pressed insistently against the front of his breechclout. He was shocked to find that his face was wet with tears!

Talon was fast learning to speak the language of the Kiowa, and he did this very well. The Kiowas spoke a different language from the other Plains Indians. The nearest Indian language to theirs, Talon learned from Little Coyote, was Tanoan, which was spoken by the Pueblo Indians in the Southwest, but it was also related to the Shoshoni language. Still, there was no communication barrier, not for the Kiowas or other Indians of the Southern plains, for sign language was in common use.

A message had been sent to Named-Lakota that his father was on his way to the camp, and that another messenger from outside the reservation would come bearing a gift for him. Little Coyote was his interpreter—he had spoken with the Lipan Scout that had come to the camp with this message.

Bare of chest, Lakota lifted the flap of his tepee and entered with Little Coyote after the scout had gone. "What sort of gift is this to be?" he asked his friend.

Little Coyote shrugged and said gutturally, "Maybe it is a . . . woman."

"A woman?" Lakota shook his head. "I have no desire for a woman. Get this straight, Little Coyote, women have meant nothing but bad trouble for me. I have not had one for a long time."

Black eyes stared into green ones. "How long, my friend?"

Ever since I met Willow Hayes, he was about to blurt, but he kept his silence. Lakota turned aside so that Little Coyote could not see the pain in his eyes. Was this true? he wondered. He shook his head, denying to himself that she meant anything more to him than just a friend. It was only instant lust that had compelled him to look upon Willow as he had that first day in Sundance yard. He told himself now that she had only resembled Garnet, nothing else.

"How long?" Little Coyote persisted.

Lakota chuckled. "Moons that I can't even count. Now, let's hear no more about this. What is the name for woman in Comanche?"

"Comanche?"

"That's right."

"Herbi."

Lakota chuckled. "No *herbis* for me, my friend. They are all off bounds for me."

"Women do not interest my friend? You like the men that way then?" Little Coyote wiggled his eyebrows.

"Hell *no."*

Lakota poked at Little Coyote's bronze chest. "And don't be trying to fix me up with any pretty squaws either!"

Lifting the flap, Lakota strode outside into the September sunlight. Before he mounted Cloud, he spoke again to the Indian, who was just mounting his own horse. "Don't misunderstand me, Coyote," he called him for short. "Someday I might want a woman again. But that will be a long time from now."

One of the women of the camp had dyed Lakota's hair with blackberries and the bark of the black walnut. They would be riding out to meet with the Comanches who were allied with the Kat-U and planned to raid the camp where a band of Apaches were keeping some horses. Word had been sent that there were Apaches in the area not far away, and the enemy had no idea they had camped so close to the Kat-U.

They rode out then, with ten braves following, riding in the direction of the great olive-green bowl of shelf land that led down into the rock country. It was not long before they could see the long string of bobbing mustangs stretched out. There didn't appear to be any Apaches in sight—they were in for quite a surprise, these Apaches!

On the crest of the ascent, upon the summit level of three streams—the Brazos, Trinity, and Little Witchita—it was here that Willow looked out upon a most glorious panorama spread out below them.

The Indians paused to gaze out in silent awe with her, delighting in the pretty yellow-hair's pleasure of the splendorous wilds.

Willow turned her head. On the left, in the purple distance, she could see the lofty cliffs bordering the Brazos, while in front, toward the sources of the Little Witchita, were conical mounds too numerous to count. Their regular and symmetrical outlines were exhibited with stark clarity on a background of transparent cornflower-blue sky.

"This is beautiful," Willow said in breathtaking awe, a primitive sensation filling her up inside to the walls of her being.

She turned to the right, where several tributaries of the Little Witchita, embellished with feathery pine-green fringes of trees, flowed in sinuous grace among sea-green meadows. They wound through a basin of unsurpassed beauty as far to the east as the human eye could reach, almost lost in the dim purple distance.

Willow looked over her shoulder to the left, focusing on a high ridge, thinking for a moment she could see distant riders. Then she blinked and the vision was gone, only a violet haze remaining above the ridge.

The romantic scenery, plus the thrill of the exciting unknown, threaded the air, producing a most tinglingly pleasant effect upon her senses. She sighed jaggedly. A new and inexplicable feeling shook her dainty frame. Something was about to happen, something frightening and wonderful. Any day, any hour—soon.

Lakota's nerves leaped with the thrilling excitement of the chase as they descended the hill into the green basin, heading for the scattered rocks and mesquite that hid the mustangs from view now. The blanket of wind pressed at him harder and harder as Cloud fell into a long, stretching lope beside Little Coyote's mount. At these times, Cloud took on new meaning to him; the beautiful white horse was a comrade, a friend. They scaled the heights of the adventure of the chase together. This time, however, they would not only be chasing horses—but human beings! Talon, Lakota, felt the vibration of muscles, the heat of wild blood. He was one with his horse.

Now they sat motionless on their horses, and Lakota turned to Little Coyote, asking him, "How many warriors?"

"Many, I think." Little Coyote looked at his friend,

who was so different with his hair colored a dark nut shade. Lakota was very handsome as an Indian, he thought, and he would make many squaws' hearts pound with desire.

Peering into the trees, Lakota felt a sense of remorse for what he and the Kat-U were about to do. He should not be feeling this, he told himself, for Indian blood flowed in his veins. To rid himself of these unwanted emotions, he thought of the vicious Apaches who attacked defenseless whites, including women and children. There were no Indian children in this camp, he had been told. He felt a little better about what he was about to do.

One of the mustangs, tied in the Apache's rope-corral, blew noisily and stomped its foot against the stone outcroppings. Now Little Coyote lifted his feathered lance, and the Kat-U braves lifted their own lances and bows, shaking them at the sky.

"Hiyaa!" Little Coyote shouted the war cry, and then they were off in a thundering cloud of dust mingled with the bright colors of their weapons.

Lakota saw a figure leave the scattering camp and run quickly toward the line of trees. Still running Cloud, he lifted his lance and poised it for flight. He let go and when he emerged from his own dust cloud he saw that his victim lay facedown in the olive-green grass. Blood squirted from the hole in the Apache's side.

Then it was all over. The anticipated glory he had first experienced turned to ash, and for the next several minutes the Kat-U cheered and shouted savage whoops. He turned aside when several of them dismounted, starting toward the bodies with the intent of scalping the Apaches. He had no stomach for this part of the killing.

There were thirty Apaches killed in all, and forty-five mustangs captured. Suddenly Lakota saw a figure leave the concealment of rocks and brush, to run quickly in the direction of the Indian he had killed. Lakota kicked Cloud into action, thinking that if he could take one alive he could save face for not having taken a scalp.

Leaping from his horse, Lakota landed clean on top of the Indian. This one was wearing a buffalo robe. While the Kat-U watched, Lakota stripped the robe from his captive. His eyes widened in surprise then. It was a young woman, a beautiful doe-eyed Apache, and she was completely nude without the covering!

"Herbi." Lakota said the Comanche word for "woman."

Chapter Nine

By dawn the next morning the Horse Indians and their captives were already on the move.

Willow brushed the long wave of yellow hair away from her creamy cheek and slapped once again at an annoying fly. She knew she must really look a mess. Looking down at her slim arms, she saw that her skin was turning a golden shade and the ends of her hair were turning white. But she was grateful that Kijika had retrieved her bonnet for her and not let the strong wind the day before blow it away—otherwise she'd have a sunburned nose!

Her calico dress was fading from many washings in streams and strong sunlight. Allowed no privacy, watched constantly as though by so many fierce hawks guarding her every movement, the only times she found a peaceful moment or two was when she was allowed to go into the bushes. And at times there were no bushes to go into! Just rocks; and she was grateful for one thing—that they were beginning to grow bigger as they went along.

Even then, when she emerged from her outdoor toilet, she encountered one of the Indians, no matter which direction she chose after her job was finished. She believed at times the Horse Indians had eyes in back of their heads!

Oftentimes Kijika walked away from the circle of campfire and melted into the dark, sometimes returning hours later, when, on her sleepless nights, she was still awake. He moved as silently as a whisper of night wind, going and coming as stealthily as a huge, night-prowling cat. Who was he really? And where was he taking her and Harlyn Sawyer?

Soon, Willow thought, soon she would know their fate!

They had to slow down to construct a travois to cross several more of the Witchita's tributaries. The adjacent uplands were broken and rolling, olive green and raw sienna in the late summer. She had a feeling that the early part of September was already upon the land.

At the head of one of the streams, upon the summit of the bluffs, nothing could be seen toward the west but one unbroken expanse of yellow-green prairie. It spread out until it was lost in the hazy blue-violet distance.

They found an abundance of game, which enabled them to be supplied with fresh meat. The Indians liked her cooking, and she found the task pleasant when there was plenty of meat she could add to the beans and hard breadstuffs they carried with them.

Where they halted one afternoon upon the summit of a hill, there was a spring of cool, wholesome water, the first in a long time. The spring was surrounded with a luxuriant crop of dewy grass, which afforded their hungry mounts with the very best pasturage at this time of year.

Willow found she had become attached to the paint, Istas, and the horse nuzzled her hand gently whenever she came near where the mare was cropping grass or waiting for her to mount when they broke camp and rode out.

After a light repast of jerked venison and berries, they continued over the mesquite glades. Eight miles or so later, the party arrived in a broad lowland valley. A stream meandered, about twenty feet wide and two feet deep.

The leader of the Horse Indians walked over to Willow just as she was sliding off her mount's back. His virile presence startled her for just an instant. Harlyn forgotten, Willow found herself becoming attracted to the handsome Indian. Many times at night lately, she found herself walking in the cooler evening air to chill the fires that were beginning to burn in her loins.

"You ride well," Kijika said.

"You already said so." Willow turned her blond head, tearing her gaze from his implacable features.

"This is the main trunk of the Little Witchita," he said in conversational tones, his dark eyes watching her closely.

"Yes," was all she said. But she paused to peruse her surroundings before bending to take a drink. The banks were about ten feet high, skirted with elm and cottonwood.

Kijika gestured to the water with a coppery hand. "It is not bad," he said.

Willow drank. The water had a slightly brackish taste and she wiped her mouth, commenting, "It's not all that good, either!"

Kijika smiled and Willow noticed once again how very green, very dark, his compelling eyes were. She had begun to wonder about this deep-feeling man with the knowledgeable eyes. She was perplexed by him, his kindnesses to her. His face bore lines not easy to read. She sensed rather than knew he had something important in his mind, something that had to do expressly with her. Harlyn he did not bother with much. He ignored the western dandy for the most part.

Willow hardly spoke to her betrothed anymore, and somehow it pleased her not to do so. And Kijika, as he continued to study her, knew this also. It was good, he thought. She does not carry any flame within her soul for the man.

Standing apart from the camp now, atop a small hill, Kijika prayed to the heavens in a low voice edged with much pain. Martha, soon your son will become one with the flower Aiyana. You know him as Talon Clay. This lad did not really know his heart when he was not fully grown. The woman, Garnet, worldly and cheap, stole his heart and put the lad in the cruel bondage of lust. Garnet was the little flower's mother. Her cheap behavior on this earth has nothing to do with her offspring; they cannot be held at fault for her sins, for they are gentle maids. Then this loose-moraled woman took your husband from you. I think you did not care. But foolishly, my moccasins did not follow the path back to you. You belonged in name to another in the white man's way, yet your delicate heart was mine alone.

Ahh, *Kimama* Martha, I let you fly from the nest of

my arms. I was foolish, and our son was foolish also. He mistook the vain woman for the one he would someday come to love. Their love will come yet, out of much pain, much tears, just as ours did. But our son shall not be parted from his beloved, as you and I were.

I am sad to know you died of a broken heart. It was this; now I know. I felt this also as I stood before your resting place and felt your tears had moistened the earth. I loved you and you should have known of my endless love. I love you now as much as before and someday we shall walk together in the heavens. I love you even more, I believe. You had knowledge of my many wives, and I would have given all up for you, *Kimama.* Now I have none. It is so sad that this should have been the way of it while you still lived. But you live in my heart, walk in my soul. Only you are inside me, Martha Brandon.

You wanted to share your life with me. I sent you back with a child in your belly. How long you must have watched and awaited my return. You wandered far from your home then, and the Apaches took you captive. Those evil ones have suffered and died by my own hand, those that tortured you before you were sent back when the son of the Apache chief was returned from those who held him at the white settlement. It was not my people who did this evil deed against your person, as so many believe.

Your son needed you, Martha Brandon; you should have stayed at home for him. Why did you leave your peaceful wooden house and come looking for me? It is this. Now I know. You truly were my heart's flame, Martha love. This man the little one is with is not her husband. Now I must do what must be done. Tonight, when she is deep in slumber, she will be awakened to be taken to my son. Sleep now, my lady, my deepest, dearest heart, and know that your son will soon come to find his joy of life.

Apprehension tugged at Willow's nerve ends. The time was drawing near when she would at last know her fate. She felt this deep inside, and saw it in Kijika's eyes. Those green eyes spoke volumes, and she knew that whatever happened to her soon had been Kijika's doing. She only prayed that what he had in mind would not hurt her—she feared pain more than anything else.

The wind had quietened. But now it picked up, and Willow marked the quick change that had taken place in the air currents. The afternoon was veiled in a lilac haze. When day gave way to night the sky and land turned a midnight blue, and it was hard to tell where the earth and sky met.

The Horse Indians had resumed the trek downstream and gone many miles before camping. Willow was so hungry she could hear her stomach growl. No woodland could be seen now, save that which was directly along the banks of the stream. The valley was shut in by rolling raw sienna uplands, entirely void of any timber, save for mesquite.

The Indians finally struck camp, and Harlyn Sawyer watched with veiled interest from the side of his buggy as the broad-shouldered leader walked over to Willow Hayes. His dull eyes fixed upon the two of them, and he knew that Kijika was speaking softly to her again. Feeling irritated, Harlyn looked quickly away.

Harlyn stared at the dark valley below, wondering

how in the world they were going to get away from these Indians. He should have met Randy Dalton long ago and delivered Willow Hayes to the man. He needed that money bad if he was to buy out his dead wife's relatives, and all he had to do was get Willow to Randy Dalton. He hadn't said anything about dead or alive, but Harlyn had a pretty good idea what it was Dalton planned to do. The man wanted to use the blonde as bait to lure the Brandon brothers to his hideout in Badman's Cave. He was, no doubt, planning to ambush the brothers, getting for himself a pretty piece of land once the evil deed was done. There would be only one woman Dalton would have to deal with—Tanya Brandon. Then there were all those mustangers and drovers. Just what did Dalton plan to do about them? Maybe he hadn't thought that far ahead. Or maybe he thought to set a trap for them when they returned after one of their annual mustang-and-cattle drives. Damn, but he wished he had a good stiff drink just now!

Kijika went to stand beside the dainty blonde, and noting how weary she was and how her gaze lingered on the fast-shadowing valley below, he said softly, "There are timbered lands below, Aiyana. But we will not go that way."

"In the morning?" She vaguely wondered where this mysterious trek would take them next. Willow was so tired that she felt like crying.

Kijika ran his hand down her hair and felt her shiver. "We will go north once again, Aiyana." But you shall not be with us then. "Have no fear," he said aloud and turned away from her.

Before Kijika walked away, Willow noticed that

something in his dark emerald eyes wavered for a second. Something had been added to their liquid depths, but the emotion that had flickered there was lost entirely upon Willow.

Carrying her own bedroll, she moved to where the night shadows were deepest. For some inexplicable reason, she felt like crying. She stretched tired limbs inside her blankets and was grateful that sleep would soon come sweeping over her. When it finally came, she dreamed of the White Indian.

Willow was awakened abruptly when a hard hand clamped over her mouth, and a gentle pressure was applied when she squirmed. What is this, her mind screamed, was one of the Indians planning to rape her while the rest of the camp slept?

Endeavoring to free herself from the steely band that held her, Willow twisted and turned to get away. She whimpered and gnashed her teeth in frustration and fear. The dream she had been having was fleeing fast from her subconscious. In it she had been lying beneath Talon Clay and feeling him growing hard against her leg. Sweet juices had begun to flow—and then she had been rudely awakened! Now was she to be raped by someone else? If it had been Talon, and that's what it had come down to, she would have welcomed the rape—such brave thoughts!

All she could make out was a huge blur when she strained her eyes in the dark. This was a brand new form of fear she had never known before. Her heart thudded painfully and her stomach was in great turmoil. Dear Lord, don't let me be sick all over him and let him see how really frightened I am!

Renewing her struggles, Willow soon found it was futile to fight with the assailant. His strength was far greater than hers. Come morning, this Indian was going to pay for his trespass on her person when Kijika got wind of it!

Perhaps Kijika would not even care if one of his warriors had sneaked off to take her during the night. What did one white woman's deflowering matter anyway?

These were her tormenting thoughts as the rough-textured hand clamped over her mouth, and she could only utter muffled groans and tiny shrieks through his hard, long-boned fingers. Then, while she swallowed convulsively, she felt her body being clasped tight to the Indian's muscled frame. His hard body made her remember another man's body so like this one of her attacker. Maybe, she thought frantically, just maybe this Indian would soil her before Talon ever got near her again. Somehow, this thought frightened her more than anything else could have at that moment. She realized now that she could have never allowed Harlyn Sawyer to make love to her—husband or not!

"I will try not to hurt you. If you do not quit fighting me, you may get hurt and I cannot be blamed for this then. Do you understand what I am saying?"

Willow nodded, but the words he had spoken had been guttural, his English very chopped and hard to understand. Akando looked down in admiration at the dainty woman he held as gently as he could under the circumstances. The feel of her trembling against him made him feel remorse over what his friend had commissioned him to do. He must take her to the camp of the Kat-U, though he would much prefer to carry her off to his own mat in the Indian reservation. But then, he could not have time alone with her, for the others would never welcome this lovely "white-eyes," nor leave her in peace for very long.

"You will remain silent?" he asked his captive.

Willow could only nod her head. His hand slowly came away from her mouth then and Willow sucked fresh air into her lungs. But he did not release her all the way, and Willow could not know how very much Akando desired to pull her even closer—he wanted to bury himself in her!

Courage, Willow, she told herself. There may come a time when you will be able to escape them all—for it was evident he was taking her away from Kijika's camp.

She tried to see her abductor, but all he was was a dark, menacing figure. But she had the strong impression that he could see her much better than she could him. He was nothing but a mere shadow, and he had no face that she could see to calm her fear.

After being half-carried across the ground, Willow found she was being lifted onto the sturdy back of a big, stout horse. From one Indian's hands to another's; Willow was all too aware of her sorry state all of a sudden. Captive again! Was this the way of the Indians? And was this man an enemy of the Horse Indian?

Where was she being taken to? Suddenly she felt anger grip her. Just who did these Indians think they were, that they could drag their white captives from one camp to another, never sparing a thought for the one they were abducting—how cruel!

Her anger renewed, Willow tried to kick at him, but the Indian was already springing up onto the horse behind her. "Do not fight me," he ground against her ear. "I will not hurt you, Aiyana."

So, he knew the Indian name that Kijika had given her. It made her even angrier to think that one of Kijika's own men would betray the leader by taking her away for himself. How could they be so deceitful to one another?

For a foolish second Willow thought she could try screaming for help. But scream for whose help? Who was there to hear her in this savage wilderness? Swallowing painfully, Willow felt all the life in her seem to go out.

Hours drifted by slowly, and it seemed to Willow that the spotted mustang could go on forever. In the strawberry moonglow rising in the south, she could see things a little better now. She could not see her captor, of course, for he rode behind her while keeping one arm wrapped possessively about her waist. Was her fate to become a white squaw then, toiling in endless drudgery forever and ever? Dear Lord, don't let my life come to this sorry end!

The Lipan scout kicked his mount into swifter motion, and then Willow saw that other riders were detaching themselves from shadows to join with them by riding directly ahead. Escorts? Willow wondered. Was this man who held her a chief then? She gulped. Kijika had mentioned that her hair would make a pretty scalp for some Indian chief's tepee.

"No!" Willow screamed. "I will not let you take my scalp—I'll bleed to death." She wailed. "Oh, I won't be able to stand the pain. . . ."

The spotted mustang was knee-reined to a slow trot while at the same time Willow felt herself being shaken until her teeth rattled in her head. "No, no, no!" she went on, struggling for her very life, not noticing the Indian escorts that had paused in a precarious position to look back from where they had been winding their way through the canyons to the high bluffs.

"Hush, little one," Akando demanded. "It is your heart I would take. Not your scalp."

"My heart?" She twisted to look up at him with the horror draining from her eyes. "Did you say heart?" Now her heart picked up its mad tempo once again. "You don't mean to—eat it, do you?"

Akando tossed back his head, laughing so hard that his broad shoulders shook. "We are not flesh eaters, Aiyana. Whatever gave you that idea? I meant that I would have your heart joined with mine in love."

Willow fell silent, unable to think of something wise in answer to that statement!

Willow began to miss all that was familiar and dear to her as they rode, never-endingly it seemed, over the yellow-green flora and sepia earth of the rugged and untamed country. How vast and open this western wilderness was! she thought. And she prayed that her captor would soon stop for a rest. He seemed to be driven by a single-minded purpose in this flight to get her to wherever it could be he was taking her.

The *Llano* itself was an eastern-sloping high mesa, rising out of the Great Plains. Here were immense, high, flat regions, broken only by infrequent rivers such as the Colorado and the Red. Its broad plains held scattered playa lakes, and here and there rose golden sand dunes.

"Oh Lord—will we stop soon . . ." Willow did not realize she was speaking out loud until the Indian answered her.

"There," he said, reaching to point past her. "In the high rock walls. There is a camp in the valley beyond."

"That far?" Willow licked her dry lips under the sun that was fierce and yellow now. "I'm so thirsty."

Akanda at once brought around his hide-canteen and tilted it to her lips. When she began to drink greedily, he drew the canteen away from her, warning, "You must not drink the water so fast." He tilted it again and she sipped while he measured each tip toward her lips carefully this time.

Up ahead of them Willow could see the Indians entering a crevice in the rocks. When they finally took their turn and entered the rock crevice, Willow held her breath in awe. There was the Indian camp below. She brushed the back of her hand over her dust-begrimed face. In a huge corral below, Willow could see a bobbing mass of horses, their snorting and pawing reaching her on the wind, along with the fragrance of wood smoke.

One slim, rough trail led down into the golden-rimmed Indian camp. Willow was breathlessly entranced. She had not been prepared for this sight, so rugged and beautiful, so unreal in its isolation, and as wild as the towering mesa that bulged wondrously above it. As they descended the trail, Willow stared at her surroundings. The hidden camp was full of golden-red shadows reflected from the looming walls. In some places further on, the earth was purple with sage. All this was backed by a belt of tall timber. She could imagine the lonesomeness of this spot when the Indians picked up and moved on.

Degree by slow degree they descended, and the Indian gave Willow a chance to take it all in before finally releasing her into the custody of Little Coyote. Kijika, known here as Nightwalker to his friends and relatives, had made it expressly known that she was meant for his half-breed son. It was a secret, he had warned. And she was not to learn immediately who she had been abducted for. But now Akando jerked with a start as he recognized the White Indian Kijika had described to him. Surely this could not be the same young man, for this one had a dark head of hair. Yet, how could this not be Kijika's son? For there it was, on the firm bronze-colored chest, gleaming proud in the afternoon light—the pounded gold medallion with the face of a flaming sun in its center.

Willow was staring too, but not toward the gold medallion!

Chapter Ten

Wild imaginings took place in Willow's head as she stared unblinkingly at the handsome Indian that so resembled Talon Clay.

It *must* be he, she thought, looking down from the spotted mustang as her captor kneed his mount closer to where the man stood still as a bronze statue. But this could not be Talon Clay—this man had a dark head of hair!

Seeing the "gift" that was being brought into camp, Little Coyote had made himself scarce. Whatever Nightwalker was up to, Little Coyote had a strong feeling that this was not the way he had planned their meeting to come about. Nightwalker was being very secretive, and suddenly Little Coyote thought he knew the reason why. So, Nightwalker was a bit of the coward when it came to playing the matchmaker. Little Coyote chuckled to himself, deciding to lay low and watch the outcome from a safe distance.

Willow stared.

Named-Lakota stared.

They looked at each other for a long time in wary silence, thinking their own scattered thoughts, Willow wondering if this could be Talon's lost twin; Named-Lakota positive about her identity. But what was this Lipan scout doing bringing Willow Hayes into the camp? Surely, she could not be the "gift" of woman meant for him? He was angry for a moment, prepared to send her back to wherever they had abducted her from. No doubt they had captured the pretty-faced Harlyn Sawyer along with her. And just where was he now, with Nightwalker?

Suddenly a wild idea came to Lakota. It seemed Willow did not recognize him, otherwise she would have been angry enough to question him as to why she had been brought here to him this way. She would demand to be returned to that dandy so they could go on their merry way to their nuptials. What would it hurt if he had a little sport with her before he allowed her to return to Harlyn Sawyer? He wouldn't hurt her, he would never harm a hair on Willow's head, he had already promised himself that. He had come too close to ravishing the dainty virgin once before, and he wasn't about to make that mistake again!

Lakota confessed to himself that all he really wanted to do was hold Willow . . . kiss her a little. He had always enjoyed her company . . . she would never know his true identity if he played his cards right. What could it hurt?

Deciding to play the Indian to the hilt, Lakota spoke in deep, halting English, ordering Akando to take her to his lodge. With that out of the way, he returned to the freshly caught mustangs in the corral. What he didn't count on was that Willow Hayes would come face to face with his first "captive," Kachina, the beautiful Apache girl.

Kachina moved about the tepee, bored and listless. She had a stunning feline quality about her and her golden-tan skin was smooth as cream. She had a sensuous body, well-formed, and curved in all the right places.

Five, ten, maybe even fifteen of the Apaches had raped her since her capture. She could not be certain, for some of them had taken her time and time again. Kachina was sure that life held nothing for her now.

She squatted on her heels by the fire and began stirring the pot of stew she was making for the green-eyed Indian who had captured her. Surprisingly, he had not been mean or tried to rape her as the Apaches had. He really did not want Kachina in his tepee, she knew, but the others had laughed in his face when he had cast her aside upon entering the camp. She had understood their words, and to save face, he had taken her into his tepee. Only to cook and keep the place clean, he had said in front of his friends.

The sun slanted through the narrow opening in the entrance, dappling her body more golden than it already was. Kachina stood, flipping her long black braid over one shoulder. Stupid men! If only they had really searched Kachina's eyes, they would have seen her eyes were not black but blue like the night sky. Her father, chief of the Shoshoni, had said her eyes were very much like her mother's, Diana, she who had been a white woman he had loved very much. But they were both gone now, killed by the very hands of the Apaches who had taken her captive!

Kachina's jet-black hair, falling in a shining curtain to her waist usually, was braided now, full of knots and snarls. She had not taken the time to comb the tangles from her hair. What did it matter . . . life was over for her now.

Kachina heard a noise outside the tepee and turned just in time to see a white woman enter with Malina, the nasty Mexican-Indian woman with the darting black eyes. Another Indian, a man this time, entered, and he was a stranger to Kachina too. So many strangers . . . in such a short time. How long ago was it that she had been captured, her parents butchered? She could not even recall.

Hatefully, Malina pierced the lovely Apache girl with her evil black eyes. "You have company now. You will wash this white woman and dress her pretty for Named-Lakota. Do you hear, Kachina? I know you speak the English, too. If you play dumb, I will bring out the switch." Malina looked closer at Kachina, her eyes narrowing. But Kachina looked downward in a semblance of humility, not allowing the nasty woman to see deeply into her eyes.

I am not Apache! Kachina wanted to shout into the woman's face and slap the ugly smirk from her face.

Drawing herself up to her full height, Kachina became several inches taller than the older woman and glared down at her. "Go," she said softly, with the unusual air of authority Malina could not understand in a mere captive.

Willow stared from one to the other. She had not been aware of what was going on until now. She had remained speechless after looking upon the Indian with the dark hair and green eyes. She could only walk about in a passive daze. But now she was coming out of it, seeing the lovely Indian girl standing before Malina with an angry look in her dark eyes. Willow could have sworn she had caught a flash of blue, like lightning, in the young woman's eyes. Now it registered on her what they were arguing over.

"You will not tell me what to do, old woman. I shall not do your bidding!" She sent the dirty-faced blond a quick perusal. "You wash the white woman!"

"Be silent!" Akando stepped in, barring the women from each other, as it seemed they were near to blows. "You will do as the woman says. You will wash her and care for her."

Beautiful Kachina squared her shoulders. "By whose bidding? I have not seen you here before. You speak a strange English, and it is hard to understand what you have said to me."

Malina leaned forward with menace in her dark eyes. "You hear what I say, that is all that matters. Wash the young woman and find some clothes for her to wear before Named-Lakota comes to his lodge."

With that, Malina lifted the flap and went outside. She did not care for any of them and she was determined to give all newcomers as much trouble as she could. Now, Named-Lakota was a different story. Half-Indian, half-white, handsome and brave, she had her sights already set for him and her daughter, Pepita. Malina only wished that Pepita was not such a shy girl, shivering in her moccasins every time a brave came near her. Malina was going to make sure she gave the yellow-hair much trouble from sunrise until sunset. Named-Lakota will never look upon such a skinny one! But Kachina—that young woman was going to be a hard one to get rid of.

When Akando mounted his horse to ride back to the reservation, Malina had been watching from beside her tepee where she had been making a new dress out of doeskin for her daughter. It was time for her to return to Named-Lakota's tepee, enough time had passed for Kachina to have finished her task.

Lakota stood laughing with a group of braves and others who had been welcomed into Black Fox's camp. The "others" ranged from Kiowas to Comanches, half-breeds to white trappers. There were even some Mexican-Indians Black Fox had welcomed. Black Fox himself was away with his wife just then, visiting another Kiowa camp several hundred miles away to the north.

"Ah, there he is," Lakota exclaimed when he saw Little Coyote peeking out from behind the tepee he and the young men had been admiring. Lakota had been laughing at a primitive painting Black Fox's nephew had been allowed to paint on his uncle's tepee. The painting depicted Little Elk capturing a white woman, dragging her by long hair into a caricature of his own tepee. "Where have you been hiding yourself, Little Coyote?" Lakota asked as the former came sheepishly out into the open.

The crowd of chuckling young men dispersed just then, leaving Lakota and Little Coyote alone. Before Lakota could question him further, Almanzo came riding into camp, having gone hunting with some of his friends the week before. Lakota greeted his longtime friend by making the sign for "Kiowa" in the sign language of the plains tribes, holding his right hand close to his right cheek, the back of his hand down, fingers touching and slightly cupped while his hand moved in a rotary motion from the wrist.

"Dark Horse." Lakota greeted Almanzo by his Indian name, leaving off the last word, "Son." He found some of the Indian names too much of a mouthful—and Almanzo agreed by shaking his head, saying, "I like this shortened version of my name much better. I shall be known as Dark Horse only, from now on," he said, laughing as he tossed his right leg over and slid from his black horse.

Little Elk came running up just then, begging to care for Dark Horse's beautiful horse. "I will rub Tachón down and walk him for you," the youngster said, laughing as the black horse nuzzled him sharply.

Lakota laughed, telling the boy, "Just don't paint any pictures of the black one on your uncle's tepee. I don't think Black Fox would appreciate too many more of your pretty pictures, Little Elk."

The lad shrugged, having a hard time understanding the mixed Kiowa and English. Little Elk grinned happily when Dark Horse handed Tachón over into his care. Dark Horse turned to Lakota then, speaking low. "I shall have to teach you the language of the plains better than that, my friend."

"Hey! Come back here!" Lakota shouted as Little Coyote went running off to join a group of Indian girls walking over to admire the freshly captured mustangs in the corral. But Little Coyote kept walking, losing himself in the crowd of giggling maidens.

"What is that all about?" Dark Horse wanted to

know, gesturing to his companions to take their kill to the women for cleaning.

"Let's walk a while," Lakota said. "There is so much I have to tell you, much you won't be able to believe."

Kachina and the "white-eyes" were laughing and joking when Malina tossed back the flap and entered unannounced. Her dark eyes went round. She could not believe the sight that greeted her. The white woman who, she had learned by the grapevine, had been given the name Aiyana, was dressed like a yellow-haired Indian doll!

Willow's hand went automatically to the turquoise headband that circled her forehead, down to the soft doeskin dress with the beaded V bodice, and then her hands pressed nervously against her thighs where the skirt clung gracefully to her youthful curves. Her young breasts were proud and prominent. Her cornsilk hair had been washed free of the dust, until it shone like a fine bolt of spilling silk. The doeskin matched her beautiful eyes—and it was then that Malina went at her with claws bared.

"You white harlot!" Malina screeched, flying at the white girl who stumbled back and came hard against Kachina. "Where did you get that dress? It is Pepita's own. How dare you!"

Before Malina could land a blow on Willow's head, Kachina stepped in front of the girl and brought up her arm to deflect the blow meant for her new friend. They had become friends instantly, liking each other from the start of their stumbling conversation. In fact, they had found themselves to be in much the same predicament. Only Kachina held much shame and humiliation inside, horrors she could tell no one ever.

"Stand back, woman!" Kachina warned. "Leave my new friend be. She is not to blame. It is your own daughter Pepita who gave me the clothes just the day before. Pepita does not like the colors of the beads you have chosen to sew into the bodice. Look how pretty she is in the yellow and brown beads your daughter so detests." Kachina saw that she had hit a sore spot; she decided to drive further into the wound. "Pepita says she would much rather have red and green."

Malina wailed, her eyes wet with tears. "That is my daughter's headband the white-eyes wears." She pointed with a wavering finger.

"Pepita prefers the bittersweet color of beads."

Tearing at her hair, Malina flew from the tepee. Her screams of outrage could be heard all the way to her own place. Lakota and Dark Horse turned from their conversation to watch the woman run in a crazy zigzag pattern to her tepee, her hand clamped over her head as if expecting a thundercloud to descend on her any time soon.

Lakota and Dark Horse exchanged glances and then stared in the direction the terribly upset woman had come from. Their path changed course, and instead of going to the spring they headed for Lakota's tepee.

Now Willow's eyes flashed with anger as she heard two Indians speaking broken English outside the tepee. "Who is this Lakota?" she asked Kachina. "I heard those Indians saying that I am meant to be Lakota's woman."

Kachina only smiled sadly, knowing that this young woman had much to learn in the way of being a captive. How well she herself knew!

"It does no good to fight, Willow," Kachina said, reaching out to console her, but Willow drew back, even more angered.

"He won't! He won't!"

Just then the flap of the tepee was flung aside and Lakota stepped into the now dimly lit tepee. At once, Willow sprang at him like a cornered mountain lion, striking out and smacking Lakota across the face. Startled, Lakota found himself stumbling backwards through the flap, surprise written on his face. Reaching up and feeling the blood trickle down his cheek from the wound, Lakota moved again toward the tepee.

Willow now turned to Kachina, hissing, "See, I told you no one would take me!"

At that moment, two large arms encircled her like the sturdy limbs of a tree, rough and tan. They yanked her clear off the ground, and her feet dangled in the air. It was done with such force that it knocked the wind from her and she could only gasp for air. Now, as if almost in a dream, Willow seemed to be floating through the open flap. She could hear women laughing and men jeering as she struggled valiantly to get free, but she was held as though in a vise in those strong arms.

Willow could feel the sheer strength and power in his body as he moved through the camp toward the song of a spring in the near distance.

When they came to the edge of the water, Willow was tossed like a bag of grain unceremoniously, head first, and submerged in the water. As her head came up, her eyes were blurred and it was hard to see anything, save for the voice that came to her. It sounded somehow familiar to her.

"That should cool you off!" said Lakota with a snort following. He spun on his heels and walked away from the water, passing Malina who had followed him down to the spring. "Take her to your lodge and clean her up again."

While he walked away, Willow pounded the water with clenched fists, screaming, "How dare you!" She raised a foam in the water as furious as a tumbling waterfall. "Oh . . . you *ohhh!*" she sputtered.

Lakota only laughed softly to himself, recalling the vision of loveliness she had made in the Indian clothes before he had dunked her in the water. He had changed, and Willow Hayes had much to learn about this new man he had become.

Willow climbed up onto the bank, not knowing that Malina watched her with malicious eyes. Her hands were trembling as she tried to wring the water from her hair. She was soaked, the lovely Indian dress ruined. But worst of all, her pride was hurt. She had never been so humiliated in all her life!

With a nasty ring to her laugh, Malina approached Willow and stood with her hands on her large hips. "You are not so pretty now, white-eyes."

Willow merely stared at the thick green grass that surrounded the spring. The water burst from beneath a cliff, a thick, rushing volume of pure blue that made delightful music as it tumbled down the slope. White daisies poked their slim heads out of the grass and then Willow saw the three-petaled blossom blooming near her—the very same white flower with violet heart that a mysterious, painted Indian had once presented to her.

Named-Lakota entered the tepee and stared around blankly. He was thankful that Kachina was not present, for he wanted to be alone just now to think. Walking around, he relived the feel of Willow in his arms and knew again the passionate desire she had awakened in him. He wanted her, badly, he confessed to himself. She was the only woman who had made him experience such confusing emotions. He had thought he had gotten away from it all, feeling himself renewed by nature and his blood brothers in the camp. But when Willow arrived so unexpectedly she had thrown his emotions into turmoil once again. He had lost his heart to one woman once, and he was determined not to lose it again!

Chapter Eleven

Gazing into the low fire, Willow sat with her legs tucked under her. The pretty doeskin dress had not been ruined in the water, after all. Kachina said all this did was make the dress "fit" her shape better, and then she had laughed.

Now, while Kachina slept peacefully on a buffalo robe in the back of the tepee, Willow remained awake, unable to forget the humiliation she had undergone that afternoon. This Named-Lakota was a beast, and she thanked God that he had not returned to the tepee!

The moon was a half yellow circle in the night sky, and Willow found herself drifting outside to admire it. She walked a little, listening to the low sounds of night creatures and the tall grass swishing beyond the tepees.

Looking over the tepees in the camp, she again noticed that Named-Lakota's tepee was the only plain one here. The others had realistic pictures painted on them, pictures that Kachina had told her recorded significant events in the owner's life. These were the usual warlike exploits, or perhaps a visionary experience. Kachina remarked that the Kiowa also kept calendric hides on which were depicted the outstanding events of successive years.

Kachina did not say which tribe she belonged to, and Willow did not ask. The Indian girl seemed to keep some things inside she didn't want anyone else to know about. Willow respected this.

Willow had never been this thoroughly confused, and her bewilderment had solely to do with Lakota. He bore a striking resemblance to Talon Clay. He even walked like him. Sounded like him. But there was only one thing out of place—Lakota had dark hair.

The song of the spring beckoned her. As Willow walked across the moonlit valley floor, she wished she had Istas to ride. With his long strides and manly strength, Lakota had made it to the water's edge in no time at all.

Willow could see that it wasn't far now to the spring. In fact, she had only gone a little way. Looking back over her shoulder, she saw that the shelter of the camp on the small rise was very near to the spring.

Approaching the darker glade surrounding the cool, singing waters, Willow slowed her stride. She should not have come to this spot—it only reminded her painfully of the demeaning scene of the handsome Indian tossing her so unceremoniously into the water. Couldn't he tell that she would become no man's kept woman? He must have been aware of this fact when she flew at him and scratched his face. She hadn't meant to become so vicious, but maybe this would teach him to stay away from her and go to find himself another mistress!

Deciding it best to return to the tepee soon, Willow,

in last-minute peacefulness, breathed in the sweet, redolent fragrance of spruce and cedar wafting about on the night air. It was like a savage paradise here!

The never-ending waters burst from a leaning wall of cliff and made delightful music down the slope. At the bottom, the pure waters meandered between tree-bordered banks far as the eye could see. Where did it go from there, Willow wondered curiously. The song of the stream must go on forever and ever.

Gazing up to a higher slope, Willow promised herself she would climb there one day. Suddenly, most amazingly, she found she did not want to return home. Nor did she want to go to Harlyn Sawyer's rancho to become his wife.

Her only desire was to stay here for a while. She had found a great friend in Kachina. She loved the savage beauty of this place. She was happy . . . what about Named-Lakota? What was she going to do about him? She could find so much peace and happiness if he were to go away.

Just how was she going to deal with all these conflicting emotions raging through her like a wild, tumultuous storm? Everyone has a twin somewhere in the world, Tanya had once told her upon returning from New York. There, in the school, Tanya had met a girl who could pass for Willow's twin. Well, she had met Talon Clay's in the flesh! And what . . . handsome flesh—

Only thing, how was she to fight these familiar feelings he awoke in her? He was Talon's twin enough when it came to making her feel all tingly and hot inside just looking at her!

"Aiyana . . ."

Spinning about after hearing a deep voice call to her in her Indian name, Willow's eyes searched the surrounding area. But all she could make out was dark shadows. Was one of those shadows a human being? It must be, she told herself, for she had heard distinctly a man call to her. Her nerves leapt then as the voice called yet again to her.

"Who . . . who's there?"

"Lakota. Come here. I am lying in the grass waiting for you."

"Like a snake," Willow said under her breath.

"Come here, and lie down beside me."

"Like hell I will," she hissed low.

"I heard that!" Suddenly he leapt before her very eyes, golden chest bared, a necklace of eagle talons and bear teeth dangling between his pectorals. They ceased to rattle and Lakota grinned handsomely. "A kiss is all I ask of you . . . Aiyana," he said, and fell into a fit of giggling.

Willow's nose twitched with the sneaking suspicion she was smelling strong alcohol, spirits the Indians called firewater. That was it, and by the smell of this man he had been imbibing quite a lot. She began to back away from him, looking this way and that trying to decide the best avenue of escape if he should become violent. But he didn't seem to be in any such mood, for he was grinning stupidly from ear to ear.

"Aiyana—my but you're lovely." He reached out but she jumped aside. "What? No kiss for Named-Lakota?"

"I'd much rather kiss a—a fish!"

"You asked for it." He lunged forward to scoop her up into his arms and she looked at him in disbelief for all his drunken agility. "You want to kiss a fish. You will kiss one, Aiyana."

Willow eyed the water he was carrying her to and it hit her all of a sudden just what he intended to do. Oh no, not again!

"Let me down!" She kicked the air, her legs scissoring, but she could not reach his body for the hem of the dress Malina had given her had no width for freedom of movement.

Just as Lakota was about to hoist her into the air in readiness for the toss, Willow found a new target winding his long hair about her fingers and giving a hank a twist with all her might. Her other hand snaked up his neck and she found she had two handfuls now!

Lakota felt as if a small mountain cat had attacked him. She had scratched him and left a thin, bloody line down his cheek earlier. Now she was tearing his hair out by the very roots. This was enough to take all in one day from one small woman—

Hoisting her into the air in a swift motion, Lakota whirled her around and positioned her so that her slight frame came up hard against him. She stood on her own two feet now, her eyes spitting golden fire up at him. He had waited long enough—the game was up! His lips crashed down on hers and took them savagely, burying her mouth between his own, testing, delving, and then devouring her flesh whole.

Willow felt her knees shiver and then begin to give way. Was this the way Indians kissed? He was setting her afire. Her bones were turning to jellies. As the kiss deepened, she found herself sinking to her knees. Her eyes had closed somewhere during the kiss, and now as she opened them she found herself lying on the grass, Lakota stretched out along her side. Why was he staring at her?

"D-Did I faint?" she tremulously asked him, trying not to gaze into his wondrous eyes.

"You always do, Pussywillow," he grinned.

"I—" she stuttered. "*You!* Talon Clay Brandon, you really did go away to become a savage!"

"I am a savage," he said with a low laugh.

"Let me up," she snapped. "You have no right treating me in such a—a bad fashion. Why, you aren't even a true Indian."

He lowered his face and kissed her softly. Then his head lifted and he murmured, "Oh, but I am a savage, sweet Pussywillow. Now, give me your lips once again and let me have your tongue this time."

"You're drunker than a skunk!"

He flopped onto his back and before she could snap at him again, she heard him snoring loudly. Eyeing a water skin one of the maidens had forgotten and left hanging from a branch, Willow smiled mischievously as she went to take it down. It was heavy, full of spring water. Good. It was just what she needed. Now all she wanted was a—knife.

Finding the needed weapon hanging at his ankle, she leaned over him cautiously to slip the knife from its sheath. Positioning both the water skin and the knife over his head, she punctured the skin and sliced along the bottom to allow a sudden gush of water to splash over his face.

"Wha . . . ?"

Sputtering and coughing, Lakota rolled onto his elbow. The walnut-and-bark dye began to run in dark rivulets down his cheeks, and when the stuff dripped onto his chest, he looked down and knew what had happened. Then, snapping his head up, he saw her running from the spring, laughing as she went.

Her taunting voice tinkled back to him on the night wind, and he shrugged, curling up into a virile ball of heavenly man, his snores melting into the nocturnal symphony that the creatures started up again after the light steps had disappeared into the night.

Willow was awakened rudely when a strong hand clamped over her mouth where she lay on the buffalo blankets and soft hides of other animals. The moon filtered down through the smoke hole and time stood still while Willow was being held by viselike arms. They felt familiar, but she couldn't be sure—

Scant seconds before her knee lifted to thrust painfully against his most vulnerable spot, Lakota had been searching out the secrets of her soul, through her dark-shadowed eyes. Through the very pores of his flesh he searched for the truth of her love for the man she had run away with to marry.

"Where is your man?" he hissed against her face.

"Talon Clay?" she asked as he lowered his fingers to rest on her chin. "Is that you?"

"Named-Lakota."

"No. You are not . . . I saw the dark stuff run down your face with which you had your hair dyed."

"A woman dyed it."

"There. You are Talon."

"But here I am known only as Lakota and you must call me by this name. Now tell me where is your man? Why wasn't he abducted along with you?"

"Why? What do you want to do with him?" She

began to push him away, for he was much too close for any whit of comfort.

He only pulled her closer. "Do as I say, woman. This is my lodge and you won't push me away."

"You—have changed, Ta—Lakota."

He smiled then. "Lakota cannot change; he is new."

"B-but you told me to call you Lakota. You are confusing me."

"And so you should be." He squeezed her arm. "You are confusing *me* all to hell."

Afraid of what he was saying and thrilled at it at the same time, she said, "What do you—mean?"

"I mean—I have it in mind to make love to you, Willow, Aiyana. I am going to make love to you—now!" he hissed into her ear.

"No—you cannot b-be serious!" She looked up at him and shivered violently. *I am a virgin. It is not right!*

"Come with me," he said and standing, he pulled her up against him.

"No—please no."

"Nothing can change my intention."

"You are mad. You have become a crazy Indian." He tugged on her wrist and she warned, "I will scream."

"No one will save you from it. You are mine for this one night."

"Talon, please don't talk this way, please." Her eyes begged and beseeched him. "One night!" It suddenly struck her what he had said. "I'll never let you have me—for one night!"

"Well then—many nights."

"No!"

"Come along now, love."

"Stay away from me—I don't k-know who you are—anymore!"

"Take off your clothes—I don't want to hurt you or have to use force."

Willow was desperate. "I—I am married!" she blurted, biting her tongue afterwards for the lie.

"You are *what?*"

"Married," she said quickly, before she changed her mind. "To Harlyn Sawyer."

"When?" He peered at her suspiciously.

"On our way—" she shrugged— "to wherever he was taking me."

He reached out to take her by the shoulders and give her a sound shake. "On you way to *where?* Where was Harlyn Sawyer taking you?"

"I—I don't know." If she and Harlyn had to get away from this crazy savage, she wanted to make darn sure he, Lakota, or whatever his name was, didn't find out where she was headed!

All of a sudden Willow realized that Harlyn Sawyer was on his way here—and of course, so was Kijika. She looked at Lakota again, her eyes searching his. Where had she seen those eyes before . . . ? Kijika? Oh dear God! No, it could not be! It better not be!

Feeling faint, Willow leaned against the lodge pole, murmuring, "Get me a cool cloth—please."

"Oh no. If you are going to faint again—do it on your own this time!" And then he was gone.

Lakota walked in the hushed night air. His head ached; he had drunk too much of the firewater that

Trapper John Summers had brought into the village that night. He and Little Coyote and a few of the other Indians had shared the firewater.

The village still slept. The shadows surrounding him were peaceful and he found a soft place to sit beside the spring where the sweet vegetation grew. He thought back, his deep green eyes in serious reflection.

He recalled to his mind's eye the day he had returned to Sundance, meaning to become reformed of his crooked ways as an outlaw. It was his second meeting with Willow Hayes.

When she had seen him, her cheeks had become tinted a breathless petal pink, and a lock of gleaming hair that fell across one cheek had looked like a skein of yellow silk on cherry velvet. He remembered telling her she was like no woman he had ever met. He had been about to enlarge on that, but he was at a loss for words for the first time in his life before a woman. There had been, from their first meeting, something so pure and golden about Willow Hayes, and he had wondered back then if she was just putting on airs. But he had soon learned, over the year, that there was nothing two-faced and deceitful about her. So far as he knew. And he'd learned to read most women like a book.

Lakota only knew that there was something excitingly different about Willow Hayes. Back then he had thought that there would never be a future for him and Willow. There had been times when he had been hard and ruthless, robbing folk while they eyed him with suspicion and dread. Too, there had been countless numbers of women who had known him for the debauched outlaw he was.

Lakota sighed raggedly, feeling loneliness again wash over him as it had back then. He had been afraid to stain the lovely slip of a girl whose heart showed in her eyes. She had been in love with him, he knew, her first love, he guessed now, as he had then. She had gazed at him with those soft, big, brown eyes, not knowing how lovely and vulnerably innocent she appeared to him. He had loved the shine in her long hair as it caught the light and had wanted to confess this to her and so much more, but he had held himself in check.

But now, now Lakota realized that he loved Willow Hayes with all his heart and soul. What was he going to do about it? His body ached for her. There was no other woman on earth who could bring him to ease his torment.

Again, as he had been then, he was aware of his fast-beating heart, of his thrumming pulses. He still could not forget that first wild kiss. How her innocence shook him! She had been like a shy wind of flame. He had gotten himself so tangled up in those velvet-brown pussywillow eyes. She was like a fawn, shy and wild; but she was more of a woman now.

Lakota shifted his weight and leaned to one side in the thick grass. Life had failed him in his youth; he had felt cheated. He had fallen head over heels for an older woman. But she had cruelly mocked him, even as she had brought him his manhood at a tender age. He had wondered back then if he had ever driven the shame of being cast aside by Garnet from his mind. She had pushed him from his beloved Sundance and he had gone to live with the Tuckers. Carl Tucker, a rowdy sort even at a young age, had taught him everything about malicious mischief and seducing women. Already taught by Garnet, that had come easy, pursuing women. They trailed after him like annoying flies; even now in the village dark-eyed maidens and older women pursued him. All women turned him cold—all but Willow Hayes.

The spring murmured softly and the insects sang their melancholy notes as he continued to reflect back in time. Back then he had revolted and become lawless, and his blood had surged like that of a savage. He had embraced the world of blood and violence, of fevered lust for money and women, women and yet more women. Lusty women. He remembered having bedded three or four of them in the same night. He had wandered into a valley of crime, of downhill evil. And Tucker had been right behind him. That manner of love had not been love at all.

At Rankin's fandango, he had felt his jaded heart turn over. Willow's hair, like fine gold dust, had been swept back, and her pretty pink dress was adorned with lovely eyelet lace. He had the idea he could have taken Willow anytime, whenever he wanted to. Poor willow-eyed creature, he had thought, she was his for the taking. He had seen it in her eyes. She would never have told him no if he had had it in mind to make love to her; and he had thought about it all the time. Respect for Willow Hayes had won out, however, and he had turned his lusty mind-wanderings aside. Somehow, seeing her as she had been then, so vulnerable and innocent, he had decided that the time was not right, and maybe it never would be for them. He could not have her, could not have the kisses she so sweetly offered him. He could not touch her cameo flesh.

But now he felt his loneliness more than ever. It was a physical pain. He was in love with Willow Hayes, and he decided he would make her his; he had to—before the sun rose over the horizon.

PART THREE

Savage Bride

. . . these wild ecstasies.

—Wordsworth

Chapter Twelve

Named-Lakota never reached the tepee where Willow and Kachina slept again. Nightwalker, Kijika, was just returning, as the first colors of dawn were tinting the eastern backdrop of sky.

He had only paused long enough to stroke Cloud's neck when he looked up and sighted Nightwalker and the other Indians strung out behind him. Was that some sort of wagon or rig, too, that he could just faintly make out? How had the conveyance made it down here from above? It must have been some going for whoever had ridden inside. And was that the minister from the reservation with them, Jim Nibaw, the man he had met not too long ago when he visited the valley with Trapper John Summers? Lakota frowned. What was the minister doing here, at this ungodly hour of the morning?

Nightwalker detached himself from the others and kneed his dark horse over to the tall figure standing at the corral. "So, my son. You have caught the white horse. I have hunted this great one for years. Why did I not see this one before when you were here? He is yours, I can tell. He shies away from others. Why did you hide him from me? When you came here, you were riding another horse."

Lakota shook his head at so many questions. "I am not surprised to see you enter the camp like a silent spirit, Nightwalker." He still had not gotten used to calling him Father; only occasionally did he find himself automatically saying it. "I know now why they named you Nightwalker." Lakota smiled up at the man astride the magnificent stallion. "Cloud followed me here." He shrugged. "He follows me everywhere, even if I ride another horse. I think he's jealous."

Nightwalker's tired eyes widened. "You let such a magnificent specimen of horseflesh run loose? I would never think of doing such a thing."

Lakota chuckled warmly. "He doesn't have wings and he will not run away. I tamed him too well for that."

Nightwalker snorted, saying, "He is only tame for you, my son." The faint rosy glow in the east had been gradually deepening and the gray blanket slowly lifting from the land. "Where were you going just now when you should be sleeping soundly on your mats?"

Lakota almost laughed out loud as he said, "What mats? I don't seem to have any to call my own for the past week."

A darkening of the brow went unseen by his son. "Who would dare throw you out of the lodge that I, Nightwalker, had especially erected for my son?" he said with thunder in his deep voice.

Lakota smiled and responded sarcastically, "One woman . . . now two." He paused to see the incredulous look cross Nightwalker's face before he went on. "Of course, I could always sleep with them, one on either side of my mat. . . ." Suddenly he had a very good idea that Nightwalker knew what was going on, at least partly. "An old friend of mine from Sundance dropped by, and since she didn't want me in my own tepee, I saw no other way to keep her happy than to move out myself. As for the other woman, I am getting to that. Her name is Kachina. She's my captive." He dropped it there and waited.

"Captive? An Indian woman?"

"You heard it. She's Apache. At least she was with Apaches when we overtook them and raided their camp and stole all of the mustangs. She was naked."

"She had no clothes on?" Nightwalker's shoulders stiffened as he asked the question.

"Not a stitch. Beautiful and naked."

"Did you take her to your mat?"

Nightwalker waited in suspense for his son to asnwer.

"No."

"Why not?" Nightwalker made to slide from Mah Toh's back and then paused, waiting for an answer. "If you do not lie with women, then do you prefer your pleasure elsewhere?"

Lakota coughed. "That depends on what you mean by that word. Elsewhere could be anywhere. I do prefer the gentler sex, if that's what you mean."

"Did you take a prisoner?" Lakota asked quietly, not looking at his father. "I saw the wagon, if that's what it was."

"Buggy." Nightwalker kept looking ahead across the valley, from range to rampart.

Lakota murmured in thought, then said, "Harlyn Sawyer's buggy?"

Now Nightwalker swung around to face Named-Lakota. "You are very observant for thinking it was only a wagon you sighted in the time right before dawn. You know everything, then?" He looked into the deep green eyes, so like his own. If only they could both have the dark hair, but this was not so. Martha had had the yellow hair, just like her handsome son.

Lakota nodded. "You took her captive. Why?"

Avoiding the question, Nightwalker's voice was gruff when he spoke. "Never lie to me; this I will not tolerate. You shall be sent from me at once if you speak to me of untruths."

Lakota sighed, quite sure of what was coming. "What do you want to know?"

"One thing: Do you love the little white woman with the yellow hair?"

As he clenched his hands at his sides, Lakota's next words were wrenched from his lips. "Yes," he said, "yes I do."

"Like a man, then, you must do something about this at once. I have brought Jim Nibaw from the reservation. Do you agree with what I am about to set into motion?"

"Nightwalker . . . Father, I can't marry Willow Hayes!" He whirled to come face to face with his father.

"What!" Nightwalker said in gruff interruption. "You can do anything if your love for a woman is great. Is your love great, my son? Does it eat away at your vitals when you cannot hold her and kiss her—and make wild love to her on the mats? Does your heart gallop like your swift mount thunders across the plains when she is near you?" He watched as Lakota nodded after each one of his questions. Then, "Do you want to throw her down on the mat and tear her clothes from her lovely body and ravish her until she screams for you to cease?"

"Oh—" Lakota groaned painfully—"God, yes!"

"Then come with me."

In a soft doeskin dress with beaded white bodice, Willow stood in the middle of the tepee, off to one side of the cookfire, and glared at Malina. Willow tore at her freshly braided hair and stomped her moccasined foot.

"I will not marry him!"

"You have had him waiting half the day, white-eyes."

"Talon Clay knows when Willow Hayes makes up her mind about something that it sticks!"

"Who is this Talon Clay, that you keep saying his name?" Malina viciously asked, hating the white girl all the more for having been chosen by Nightwalker to become his son's wife. Named-Lakota, with the green eyes and golden skin, was like a shining, virile Indian god to the young maidens here. Who would *not* want to wed him?

Malina continued to press the pacing blond. "Who is he?"

Willow stopped and whirled to face Malina. "He is this Named-Lakota, who else. Bah!" Willow jerked her chin up defiantly. "So you say he is. But to me he is Talon Clay Brandon, and my sister is married to his brother, Talon's brother who used to be a Texas Ranger!"

Kachina stepped closer to her friend. "Is this so? Ah, I have been feeling this, that you have known Lakota before. It was in your lovely eyes the first thing this morning when you discovered your young man had had his hair dyed by one of the women of the camp. I did not even know he had hair other than the color of dark berries. He fooled me well. Still, he is very handsome, Willow Hayes, Aiyana." Kachina smiled at the pretty Indian name. "You should be proud to become such a one's wife."

Her eyes flying wide, Willow faced Kachina. "He has Indian blood, Kachina. I could never marry him now. Once, not too long ago, I loved Talon Clay, but now—now I find he has the blood of the savage in his veins." Her soft brown eyes clouded with unshed tears. "I couldn't love him now; no, he frightens me half to death."

"Malina." The younger Indian woman turned to the other. "Would you leave us now?" She nodded, her eyes telling Malina that she might be able to get the white girl to come around and not be so stubborn in this matter.

Malina nodded back. She was in no position to argue, for she had been ordered to get the white girl ready for the wedding. But Malina had not succeeded; maybe Kachina would where she had failed.

"Willow, Aiyana . . . can I call you Aiyana?" Kachina went to sit by her friend on the pile of buffalo hides.

"Call me Willow, nothing but Willow. I am not an Indian squaw, and I shall never be one, either." She looked at Kachina out of the corner of her eye, saying, "Never!"

"Willow," Kachina began again. "Nightwalker says you must join with Named-Lakota. We have been through this for a long time this day. Lakota is waiting for you, but he does not want it to be force he has to use. I think, Willow, that he will use force soon."

"How?" Willow snapped, looking at Kachina more seriously now. "Do you think he will come in here and drag me out by the hair?"

"I was outside a short time ago," Kachina went on, avoiding Willow's question but watching as she listened intently to what Kachina had to say. "There is a man here by the name of Sawyer, and I cannot recall the first name of the white-eyes—"

"Harlyn Sawyer. Of course! He would be here, because he came in with Nightwalker. Oh, and I know what Nightwalker's Indian name is . . . it's Kijika. That green-eyed Indian fooled me! He's Talon's, I mean Lakota's father. What a coward he is, he would not even bring me in to face his own son. Nightwalker knew what he wanted all the while. He wanted me to become the savage bride for his half-breed son!"

Kachina's eyes flew wide at the hateful word she had been called by the people in the white man's forts. "Do you . . . not like half-breeds, Willow Hayes? Does this bother you—to be a friend to one or to join with one in marriage?" she asked slowly, measuring each word carefully.

"It would be degrading to be the bride of a savage, or a half-breed!" Willow said with a toss of her bright head.

Kachina at once moved away from Willow Hayes. With her back turned, she said, "And it would be bad to be a friend of one such as this?"

Willow stared at Kachina's beautiful black hair, sleek and straight as an arrow down her proud, straight back. "You are Indian; you are my friend."

"I see." Kachina said softly. "And what if I should be half-breed? Does this bother you even more than if I was full-blood?"

"I—" Willow thought for a moment. Then she said, "No, I would still like you, Kachina. You are my very best friend."

"Well, then." She whirled about. "Why are you so afraid to marry Lakota, the one you know as Talon Clay?"

Willow moaned as if she were in pain. "I will have to go home one day, Kachina, and will have to face my sister and her husband."

"Yes?" Kachina blinked, trying to understand.

"Well, you see, my sister's husband does not like savages either—" Willow clamped a hand over her mouth at what she was about to say. "Kachina—my sister's husband is Talon Clay's brother. He will run him off Sundance property when he finds out his brother is a—a half-breed. Ashe Brandon is going to go crazy when he finds out that his mother ran off with a savage!"

Kachina shrugged. "He should not be too crazy when he realizes that this was what his mother wanted."

"But—did she?" Willow searched Kachina's face.

"She must have. Why else would Nightwalker want you to join with his son so badly? He must have loved the white woman very much."

"Yes," Willow breathed, "as much as Talon loved Garnet." Then Willow looked up at Kachina. "I cannot marry Lakota, Kachina. His heart still belongs to another."

"You are still afraid of him. You think he has become a savage. Why do you not forget what he is on the outside and see him for what he is on the inside?" Kachina's face hardened then, at what she had to say next. "They are going to torture your friend, this Harlyn Sawyer. I heard it being said."

"What?" Willow spun about and as she was heading toward the flap, she heard the first piercing screams. She stopped, looking at Kachina who had come up beside her. "They can't do that. What will make them stop, Kachina?"

"For you to be joined with Lakota, that will stop them."

"Who said this?"

Kachina looked toward the flap as another scream pierced the air. "Lakota himself said if you do not come to him soon, he will continue to torture this Sawyer until he dies."

"No!"

The Indians were in good humor, laughing and joking among themselves. Some of the things the English-speaking Indians and Texicans were saying made Willow blush where she hid behind a large tepee. They had no idea that a female was present, and Willow had never felt her cars burn so hotly!

Then, as she crept closer, staying in the shadow of the tepee, what she heard next caused her heart to thud and her hands to grow clammy. Some of the men were boasting of their own wedding nights, comparing them, and laying bets as the outcome of Named-Lakota's wedding night!

Closing her ears to what they were saying, Willow's thoughts returned to the real reason why she was here spying on them. Something about the way the man's screams sounded had caught her attention a short while ago when Kachina had gone out to join the others and try to find out what was happening at this time.

A sharp scowl crossed her face and distorted Willow's delicate features when the high male scream came again. She was peeking around the tepee and saw where all the noise was coming from. It was not Harlyn Sawyer who was doing all the screaming, but Little Coyote—he was in on this deception too!

Keeping close to the tepee, Willow spun about to return to her own tepee. So, they were putting on a little act for her benefit, trying to trick her into yielding under pressure and marrying Lakota. Oh, the deceit of young men!

Willow finally realized what she was doing when she hid behind a tepee staring at the dark patch in the distance. The corral—if only she could reach it without being seen.

This would be no easy thing to do!

She had to get away from Talon; he frightened her as this savage Lakota! It would be no Christian marriage—a heathen wedding, no less. When he took her to his mats it would certainly be living in sin, and that she was not going to allow to happen!

A short time later, Willow saw that she had not prepared herself for this part of her desperate plan. When she came upon the mass of beautiful wild mustangs she wondered how she was ever going to find

Istas among them. Then Willow imagined herself lying naked next to Lakota, the savage stranger Talon Clay had become. Nothing now could have deterred her from her flight.

A sound from behind her sent a little quiver of apprehension over her. She could not know that Lakota had left Jim Nibaw's side when he first detected a movement behind his tepee. He decided he had only imagined something was there, but then while he was speaking to Jim Nibaw he saw the same flash of white and gold ripple again in the corner of his vision. With his eyes ever-widening, he watched the flash of dainty white legs and streaking hair go from behind first one tepee and then another. . . .

Now, his large powerful hand shot out and jerked Willow to a halt when she had set off in a run again. His hand twined and twisted in the golden tresses while the pangs of a consuming and increasing love played havoc with his temper.

"Where do you think you are going?" he ground out, pulling the little face closer.

White-faced, Willow could only gape at the handsome savage in tight buff buckskins, colorful feathers and turquoise beads shining in his hair flowing to his waist!

Willow's escape attempt had failed, and she had given up all hope of remaining untouched by the handsome savage Lakota.

"Nightwalker said to 'join with you.'"

Inside her tepee where Lakota had taken Willow to be alone with her, she stood stalling for time, but she saw his patience was thinning rapidly. She had refused to look at him as she said the words.

"What do you think that means?" Lakota asked.

Willow's ears were attuned to the plaintive singing on the night wind. "I—do you mean—for us to *really* become man and wife—truly?"

"What else?" Lakota said impassively.

He searched into her big brown eyes and had the strangest feeling she was pulling his heart right through his soul like a big knot.

For a breathtaking moment Willow stared at him. This was not the Talon Clay she had known so well over the past year and more. A deep and quivering trepidation seized her. The laughing, gentle outlaw-reformed-mustanger who had told her wild, funny stories, discussed horses with her, and made her feel happy and carefree with him was changed beyond recognition. She watched his mouth tighten as he waited for her to say something.

Who was this savage-looking male? Could this be the same young outlaw she had fallen instantly in love with? Her heart pounded. Her limbs trembled. Before her stood a ruthless, savage warrior, and she decided he was utterly incapable of compassion or mercy. He would show neither when he forced her to become his bride.

"Talon Clay?" she said tentatively, thinking that if only she could reach him, plead with him to quit this nonsense and return her safe and sound to Sundance, things would be like they used to be.

"I am Lakota," he said. "My Indian name you know by now, there is no need to instruct you on it over and over again."

Still stalling for time, she said, "How do I have proof you have let Harlyn Sawyer go?"

He smiled one of the rare smiles she had seen since she had arrived in Black Fox's camp. "Come outside with me," he coaxed, "and you will see him being released when I give the signal to the braves across the way."

When they stepped outside, Willow came up unexpectedly close to Lakota. Looking up into his handsome face, she saw his skin was made even bronzer from the many campfires that had been lit in the last quarter-hour. Sharp lines defined and were cut into Lakota's face, and his remarkable eyes made him look even fiercer with the passion that flared brightly within their depths. He returned her gaze in full measure, softening his look, and Willow trembled.

"There," he said, giving the motion. While she watched Harlyn Sawyer being released, his heated eyes moved leisurely over the gentle outline of her breasts beneath the soft white beaded buckskin bodice.

Lakota was imagining how Willow's petal-soft peaks would bloom within his mouth, how it would feel to suckle them. Now his loins were beginning a deep burn and his manhood had never before felt so heavy and hard. He would have to go easy on her and not hurry his possession of her. Willow was no saloon girl to be roughly tumbled and later shoved aside. This woman he was going to love savoring for as long as possible.

Peculiarly, Willow was happy to see Harlyn Sawyer ride off into the night. She felt Lakota's rapt gaze on her and lifted her chin a notch to look up. His eyes locked with hers. Willow felt as if her breath was being knocked out of her.

Before she could guess his intention, Lakota reached out and touched her lower throat where her pulse was beating a wild, tuneless rhythm. His head bent, and lips, warm and thrilling, brushed Willow's. Lakota took his time kissing her lightly, merely brushing his lips back and forth. The muscular tension in his body was like a tightly coiled spring ready to be set loose at the slightest touch from her. Tremors of desire quaked through Willow.

When he finally lifted his head, her passion-dark eyes staring helplessly into his, Willow felt as if all the breath had been knocked from her.

Lakota wanted to tell her how much he desired to be with her, to go into her body and fill her deep inside. To taste the sweet honey of Willow at last. In the past he had restrained himself from having her, afraid he would hurt her because she was so small. He had relieved his fears on this matter, speaking to Nightwalker and another woman of the camp who had borne several children. If he was gentle, he could not hurt her, no matter how small she was inside, for her woman's body would learn soon to accommodate him, no matter how large he was.

His emerald eyes narrowed hotly as they traveled slowly down Willow's body and then back up.

"I have wondered about you for a long time."

His words startled her, and she had to tear her eyes from his. Without looking up again, she said, "Harlyn wondered about me . . . too."

His mood changed swiftly and he ground out harshly, "What does this Harlyn mean to you? Not your husband really?"

Willow was not thinking much about Harlyn Sawyer at the time. Lakota was speaking with his body to every fiber of her being. "The man I—I was going to marry. The man you sent away. . . ."

He stiffened. "You lied and said you married him on your way here—or to wherever he was talking you. But you're still—a virgin—"

The light from the campfires flitted over his high, taut cheekbones. Why hadn't she realized before that Talon Clay had Indian blood in him? And what about his brother, Ashe, who had fought with the Indians—why had it escaped his notice Talon was a half-brother, that they had not been sired by the same father?

"Answer me, Willow. I don't much care what Harlyn Sawyer thought or wanted from you. You are mine now and you will be answering only to me—from now on!"

"No," she quickly came back. "I won't answer to any man. You are in my past, Talon, and I don't want you anymore!" She stared up at him, searching his taut face while realizing that she hadn't really wanted Harlyn Sawyer at all. She had been fooling herself. "Come to think of it," she said after a moment's thought, "I don't think I even—know what love is."

With menace in his deep, slow voice, he said, "I don't remember mentioning anything about love, Willow." He stared deeply into her startled eyes. "I never did trust any woman." He was getting angrier by the second and his eyes were raw and pained. "Not one damn bit!" he finally ground out.

Willow breathed in sharply and felt her eyes burn with hot tears. "Then leave me go, Talon Clay. You only want me for your savage pleasure—your squaw!"

Whirling from him, she ducked inside the tepee. Lakota stared down at the ground, then up again. Jim Nibaw and the others were waiting. It was as well that Willow could not see the dangerous glint that had come into Lakota's eyes, and his tall, lean body going absolutely rigid.

Chapter Thirteen

Indians began to drift out from their tepees as they heard the marriage ceremony was about to begin. The man named Harlyn Sawyer had been brought back by Named-Lakota himself, and this time the torture was real. Lakota was doing something the Indians had never seen done before—pulling out the man's hairs one by one.

When Willow could stand the screams no longer, knowing for certain it was Harlyn Sawyer they tortured this time, she ran from her tepee and caught Lakota by the arm. He turned about at the soft touch of her hand on his arm.

"You wanted me?" he said. His hair shone like dark flames in the light of the campfires surrounding the area where Harlyn Sawyer had been tied to a stake.

Willow stared. She did not recognize this man at all. Maybe she had come upon the wrong man. Above the fringed buckskins emphasizing the long muscles of his thighs, his chest was bare, and there was blood on it. Across his strong, proud chest a medallion of pounded gold winked back at her, the face of the sun proclaiming his birthright as a warrior's son. Looking closer, she could make out the moon, earth, fire, rain, and even what looked like it might be a portrayal of wind. Willow stepped back.

"You were searching for me, Aiyana?" Lakota said softly as he studied her reaction to the scene. He had not pulled all that many hairs from the man's head—but Sawyer could sure scream loud from a little hair pulling and a few drops of blood. It looked worse than it actually was.

"Please," she began, watching Harlyn Sawyer finally pass out after he had glared at her, as if his pain was entirely her fault. She cringed as another hair was yanked out and Harlyn came to for a moment to yelp. Then his head lolled against his shoulder once again. "Please . . . Lakota . . . I will do anything you say." Tremors of great fear shot through her. "I—I will even consent to become your—wife." She watched him nod slowly and step away from the slumped body.

When at last he stood before her, she said, "Is there no—other way?"

His head moved a little back and forth, his lips softening with a tender smile. "No other way for what, Aiyana?"

Willow swallowed hard, fighting against the desire to run. "Never mind," she said, and walked beside him as he took her arm.

Jim Nibaw had been one of the reservation Indians awarded a bachelor's degree; he had gone to a private school, a seminary, which was supported by the more highly developed society in the older states. The literacy of the region could not have been supported without the steady flow of young teachers, professors, clergymen, lawyers, and academicians arriving daily by the handfuls in the West. Jim had only been out of school for two years and had already married fifty-nine couples; today would make it sixty.

Surprised that it was to be a Christian wedding, Willow stood beside Lakota, even more surprised to learn that she was being joined in holy matrimony to *Talon Clay Brandon*. Jim Nibaw even knew her full name. He was coming it to now, for Lakota had just said another "I do."

"And do you also, Willow Margaret Hayes, take this man to be your lawful wedded husband to have and to hold from this day forward till death do you part?"

"I—I do."

"With the power invested in me . . ." he went on slowly, "I now pronounce you man and and wife!" Jim Nibaw grinned, closing his huge black Bible. "You may embrace now."

The murmur of contented chatter in Indian and in English surrounded Willow while Lakota bent to kiss her tenderly on the lips. Then he drew her closer, up tight against his lean, hard frame, his fingers digging into her upper arms. He laid his cheek against hers, pulling her fiercely to him.

Afterward there were games and dancing, whoops from the Indians and wild hollers from the trappers who had come with John Summers, just in time for the celebration. There had been a hunt just that day and meat hung from a tripod at the edge of the fire, delicious aromas of crackling buffalo meat filling the night air.

When the fires died down and people began to return to their homes, the married couple were allowed to go their own way. Dark Horse had been steadily gazing at Kachina the whole evening, asking her afterwards to walk with him. Willow overheard Kachina saying "No," as she went to stay with Wolf-Eyes-Woman for the night to afford the newly wedded couple some privacy in the tepee.

Highly nervous alone in the presence of her new husband, Willow said, "What should I call you now that we are man and—wife," she asked, with some trouble over the words.

"The same. Lakota. When we leave this village someday you may again call me Talon. But not now; I want to be Lakota for as long as I possibly can."

"You want to hide from reality, that's what."

"No."

"You want to hide from your brother, Ashe, then."

"Don't speak of him now."

She looked back at the dying campfires, not even thinking or caring where they were walking to. "What do you want to talk about?" she said, playing for time. If only she could get to Istas, and then to Harlyn Sawyer.

He turned to her, taking the cold hand in his own. "The time for talking is over, Aiyana."

"D-Don't call me that—please."

All her senses were being absorbed by the man walking with her. She trembled as a strong, sure arm slipped about her waist to draw her closer to his side.

A clean, musky male scent from Lakota's skin

pierced her senses. Ripples of delight at this male aroma coursed through Willow. She could not know that Lakota's need was becoming urgent and he was beginning to perspire a little.

"Come," he said, taking her elbow, "let's go out by the water. It is cool there."

"I—I'm not warm."

He smiled to himself. "You will be, Aiyana. I am told that all wedding nights get warm sooner or later."

It was no use telling him; he continued to call her by the Indian name anyway. Her eyes widened then as she watched him take an Indian blanket down from a tree branch and spread it over the moist earth. The song of the spring danced along Willow's nerve ends. The water sparkled as the new orange moon arose. Behind them were the low campfires, the popping of wood from a distance, sparks going into the night like yellow diamonds rising to join the millions of silver ones in the vast bowl of sky. A comet streaked above. A dog barked.

Hypnotically, she walked with Lakota to the water's edge. She had felt a strong sense of danger earlier standing next to him, becoming his wife. She knew he had been waiting for her to say the words that would make her his. Now all she felt was extreme nervousness at being alone with him.

"Come and sit with me now," Lakota said, coaxing her with the gentle tone of his voice.

He led her to the blanket and they stood over it, then Lakota tugged at her hands and together they knelt on the square. His long, square-tipped fingers cupped her face as Lakota gazed at her for a long time. His eyes cherished every gentle angle, every soft curve. While his eyes made sweet love to her his other hand swept down over her, memorizing every detail of her lovely body. Everywhere he touched there a trail of flame was left behind.

"Aiyana, pretty little flower." He bent his head to brush her lips tenderly and taste the corners of her mouth.

Now his hands slipped around to the back of her, cupping the firm contours of her buttocks and bringing her near the proof of his hard desire. The sky and stars above spun. Willow felt dizzy from the wave of intense desire that swooped over her and soared in her blood. She was suddenly so hot she feared she was going to faint.

"Lakota, please, don't—kiss me anymore. I'm afraid you won't like it if I—faint."

"You can faint, little one." He nibbled at her throat. "I will bring you around after a while." Now, unceremoniously he lifted her off the blanket. "Let's cool off in the water."

Alarm raced through her. "No—I don't want to go in the water. Please—Lakota."

He brought his face close to hers and smiled. "It's not in my mind to toss you in again—are you afraid that's what I will do?" He waited for the negative shake of her head. "I only want to taste your wet skin—love."

"M-My wet s-skin?"

Setting her down at the water's edge, Willow pressed her fingertips to her mouth as he began to pull off his clothes in front of her. Even in the frail moonglow he could see the rosy blush spread upon her face as he stripped down to his nakedness. He put his profile to her, and Willow choked down a gasp at the sight of his exposed maleness. Sheer terror washed over her at the thought of being ravished by the huge, pulsating manhood. He could only hurt her terribly with that! She arose now.

Starting to back away from him, Willow said with a gulp, "I—I think I-I am going to sit down—" she waved a hand behind her—"on the b-blanket."

He was on her in an instant, swooping her up into his arms and carrying her to the water's edge. This time he laid her down, her feet dangling in the water. Willow's wide, soft brown eyes fringed by heavy lashes could only stare helplessly up at Lakota as he began to remove her clothes.

In the moonglow Willow's sweet body looked tawny in color. Beneath a long, graceful throat her naked shoulders were delicate. Lifting her naked from the earth, Lakota's eyes dipped over the silken fall of golden hair that fell softly over high, firm breasts. When his fingers slipped up her rib cage to cup the underside of a breast, Willow caught at his wrist. She could feel the muscles leap at her touch.

"I will not savage you, sweet Aiyana. What do you fear from me?"

"I once wanted you as Talon Clay Brandon, but now I don't know you any longer and—and you frighten me," she said in a whispery soft voice.

He came against her then, pressing his mouth close to her damp cheek. He lifted his fingers and touched the fresh moisture clinging to her lashes, below her eyes. "You are crying—why? I am not going to hurt you. I am going to love you with much care, and be inside of you before you know it." He swallowed hard, praying that he could make a swift entrance and be done with her maidenhood once and for all.

"I would like to go into the water now, please."

As if her word was his command, Lakota lifted her again and waded out into the bubbling middle of the spring. She was delighted to find that it was nice and warm in the center. Shivers of fear had begun moments ago, but now she felt relaxed in his arms as he carefully stretched her out on top of the water.

Lakota wondered if she could hear him sizzle as his body entered the water; he couldn't seem to hear much of anything for all the deep noises like a thousand bees buzzing in his head. His desire for Willow was overwhelming. He wanted to be pressed so close to Willow that not a breath of air could pass between them.

"You are very beautiful," he murmured, sliding his hands over her as he stood her up.

The silver-blue water rose to the peaks of her breasts, and as Lakota stared, he felt himself throb almost painfully. When he drew her into the circle of his arms, she felt his hugeness press into her. Then her breath caught as he lifted her off the bottom, carried her high, lowered her some, and brought her belly to press against his chest.

"Talon . . . I mean Lakota, put me down."

"Not this time," he said firmly.

Settling her against his waist, he wound her legs about him, carrying her like that to the water's edge. He groaned with the hurtful urgency of his passion. Lowering her only enough to make his entry swift and sure, he bucked forward to drive into her. He was met with the hard wall of her maidenhood.

Seeing the shocked expression cross her face, Lakota

backed away and lowered her all the way to the damp grass. He wanted to say he was sorry for being so selfish and in such a hurry. A virgin was a new experience for him, one he was not going to enjoy very much at first. He had been afraid of hurting Willow—he still was.

"Don't hurt me, Lakota," she implored him. "I can't stand pain very much."

"I promise you, sweet, when I have you at last you will be ready all the way for me. Just relax . . . feel the water."

For several minutes Lakota did nothing more alarming than kiss and caress her with tenderness. He had been hasty before and meant to make up for it. Searching with his mouth, he went on to explore her cheeks, her eyes, the dainty line of her jaw. Swiftly he found the sensitive places below her ears, along her throat. He savored each moan that told him she felt pleasure at what he was doing. Finally his lips found hers, his tongue probing as he tasted her.

Stretching out full length just over one side of her hip, Lakota continued to kiss her. Pure longing shot through Willow as the lean strength of his fingers stroked and caressed her bare breast. It was the first time he had ever really touched her breasts fully. Her throbbing nipples thrust against his golden touch. She gasped and he thought he had frightened her again.

"Let me show you," he said thickly, "Willow, Aiyana, let me show you how good it can be."

Lakota began to prepare her for him. Though he was not experienced with virgins, he knew he must make her thoroughly moist before entry. His body was so swollen he feared ripping her apart. Not even his fully erect manhood could make him rush this.

Now Willow was moaning brokenly. She was beginning to arch against him, and he was meeting every inch of her with feverish delight. I will make you burn with pleasure, Aiyana, he was thinking.

"I—I never felt this way before." She moaned her words, and arched her hips when he took her nipple into his mouth. "Oh God!" Her head rolled from side to side.

His fingers found the velvet of her inner thighs and began to stroke upward. She could feel the hardness of his manhood straining against her thighs, and a warm wetness began in the core of her. He was probing inward now, his every movement setting off waves of grinding pulsations inside her. With his mouth he suckled and tugged at a peak of her breast, and Willow could feel the long, swollen shaft lying hot and hard against her.

Tentatively she lowered her hand, shaping her fingers to the sinewy contours of his manhood. Lakota gasped as the small hand closed about him. A deep agonized sound tore from him. He moved away from the small hand that had begun to move up to his swollen head.

"Don't do that," he rasped. "If you arouse me just a little more I'll have no choice but to take you at once."

He lowered his head to kiss her again, taking her lips with wild passion this time. While he continued to kiss her, he slid her buttocks down to the edge of the water, her feet dangling in it and her legs parted.

Willow began to shudder uncontrollably when the water lapped between her thighs. His finger slipped inside and found the very core of her. But when he would have pressed home he again found the maidenhead giving him resistance.

Lakota shifted his weight and Willow reached out, afraid that he was leaving her. When she opened her passion-drugged eyes, she could see his head hovering over her belly. She gasped in surprise when he slithered into the water, the movement bringing his face between her spread legs. He moved closer, while her eyes widened in bewilderment.

"Oh, no . . ." Surprised darkened her eyes to deep brown. "No, please don't . . . !" But he had already moved to taste her intimately. Willow groaned and her head was flung backward.

Inexorably Lakota forced her legs wide apart, his mouth enveloping her most sensitive point. As he had with her breasts, he suckled her. Moans and mewls were tearing from her throat, and she twisted frantically between the lapping of the water and the almost painful possession of his lips and tongue.

When she cried out and bucked against him, Lakota moved up over her. She was covered with a fine sheen of perspiration, her hands clenched spasmodically at her sides.

"Willow," he breathed against her cheek, "Aiyana . . . sweet, sweet love."

"Lakota!" she cried out. Then again, "Please . . . !"

"It is coming, darling . . . now."

A tiny spasm of fear went through her then as he grasped her hips, and, bringing her to the water again, he stood hip-deep and began to enter that first bit of her. Her passage was small and tight, he discovered, but he found her gratifyingly moist with honey. His massive length entered her body a little more, and then she gave a little gasping cry as she tore.

"Oh please . . . stop . . . that hurts. No . . . more!"

Breathing heavily, Lakota tipped her hips upward and used his hand to rub his shaft against the sensitive palpitating bud of her womanhood. When he knew she was on fire for him, Lakota's abdomen clenched and he leaned forward with a powerful surge. He tore through the barrier, but did not go deeply into her yet.

Cries of pure ecstasy poured from Willow. The fleeting pain was nothing compared to the joy that followed swiftly. Now there was only the pressure of fullness, and a small ache in the walls of her as he began to thrust and wrench. When he began to press deeper, he filled her completely, with some left to spare.

The grinding force of his thrusts drove her deep into the grass when he climbed from the water, still inside her as he clutched her hips, covering her body with his full length but not crushing her.

Willow's head began to toss wildly. Her hips arched to meet every surging thrust. She grasped handfuls of grass and began to sob at the tension that was building so intensely as to be almost painful. The pressure had built until Lakota could stand it no longer. Surging pleasure ripped through him; he knew she was climbing with him. Waves of rapture carried them higher and higher, the pressure building. Lakota drove home, putting all his thrusting power into the last surge that brought them to the pinnacle of ecstasy together, the shattering climax wrapping them in a cocoon of rapturous splendor.

Tenderly he drew her close when it was all over. Tipping her head back, Willow stared into green eyes shining with the wonder of what they had just shared. The moment they had reached the crest together had been pure bliss. It was in her mind to ask him if he had ever shared this perfect moment with another before. But she couldn't bring herself to voice her fears that if it had been this good with others, then she would not be the last woman he would find such sweet ecstasy with. But he seemed to read her mind, and she thrilled to his words.

Caressing her sweetly curved hip, looming over her, Lakota lowered his lips and brushed hers. With his eyes gazing raptly into her face, he said ever so tenderly, "I love you, Aiyana . . . I love you." His hand moved from her hip to his chest, near his heart. "You are in here now and I will never release you. No one has ever captured my heart and soul as you have this night." Tracing her jawline with sensitive fingers, he said, "I know you are the most beautiful woman I have ever known. I must tell you this—there has not been another woman since the day we met."

Now Willow looked away from him. Disappointment in him flared in her. How could he lie to her this way? Her eyes had not deceived her when she saw Talon Clay going into the woods with Hester—and then there was the day not too long ago when Hester, her bodice gaping wide, had followed him from the line of thick trees. When Hester had spotted her in the buggy with Harlyn, she had looked so smug and sneering.

"What is it?" Lakota asked, cupping her chin and forcing her to look back up at him. "Something is troubling you now."

"I—I can't tell you," she said, feeling shy all of a sudden. She would be mortified should he learn of her jealousy. "It is really—nothing."

"Oh yes, there is. It is bad, I can read this in your face. Tell me."

"No." Tears were starting, and she soon would be unable to hold them back. "Please don't ask me, Talon, Lakota."

"Do you love me?" he said fiercely, pressing against her hip bones and cupping her chin roughly.

Tearing her chin from his grasp, Willow began to roll away from him. She didn't get far. Dragging her beneath him, while he breathed heat into her face, he loomed over her on all fours. Willow looked up. He was like a savage cat trapping her under his huge paws.

"Something bothers you badly about me. Does it have to do with other women?"

Intense shivers of pleasure and fear tingled over her flesh. She could smell his angry heat and manliness. She could sense his displeasure over her silence. And she could feel rather than see his eyes boring into her steadily, for the high moon was directly behind his head.

"I am waiting impatiently, Aiyana."

"You can wait all night then. I won't tell you." Willow rolled her head to avert her eyes from his beautiful male body hovering so close to her thrilling flesh.

With a savage movement, he lowered his face and brought it close to hers. She turned her face aside even more, unconsciously bringing her ear close to his lips. Nibbling her earlobe, he repeated his statement of impatience.

His breath was hotter now and it was all she could do not to swing her face around and offer him her throbbing lips. She gasped next when his tongue circled her ear and then thrust itself inside.

Silently Lakota vowed to hear her fears, no matter what he must do to get her to talk. Gazing down at the delicate line of her chin gilded by moonlight, his eyes darkened with deep-seated worry. This worry was becoming profound. Then he thought he had found the answer.

"Willow, Aiyana," he called softly into her ear. "Hear me; I have something to say to you."

"Come down here and stop looming over me. I am not going anywhere, you don't have to imprison me like I'm some—trapped animal."

The combined effects of fear and desire were proving to be overwhelming to Willow. She feared him one minute and wanted him to make love to her the next. But this time her passion was driving her mad; she wanted him so badly that her insides were wrenching and pulling in a grinding heat she could barely stand anymore.

"What do you want to tell me?" she said, almost losing control of her voice.

"It was about a year ago that I told you about all the other women I have bedded and warned you to steer clear of me. Am I right?"

"Yes," she said in a small voice. Breathlessly she waited or more.

"It is true that I have not had another woman since I met you. Now what is it that troubles you so much? Those women were sluts, darling, and meant nothing at all to me. They were loose-moraled women and always got just what they were looking for. One of them got into my blood," he said, not telling her that it was Garnet Brandon, "but that's over with now. Her memory has been replaced with a love so pure and shining that nothing can ever erase it. Never," he said fiercely, his eyes blazing. "Do you hear me?"

Willow felt him shaking her by the shoulders, and she turned her face aside, whimpering with the bittersweet pain his merest touch was making her feel. Her head flung backwards, and her eyes rolled. "Lakota . . . love me . . . I want you," she panted. "Please, take me . . . now."

With a deep-throated sob, Lakota gathered her hips and drove himself deep inside her moist core. He molded his hands to the firm contours of her shapely buttocks and lifted her until her back left the ground.

When her head was rolling frantically from side to side and soft cries were urging him to go faster, Lakota slowed and then pulled himself all the way out.

Crying out loud, Willow jerked forward to reach for him. "No . . . please . . . don't leave me now . . .please . . . please . . . !"

Leaving her open to his ardent gaze, Lakota pressed his palm over the place his huge, throbbing manhood had just quit. He rotated his palm, knowing his actions were driving her mindless with passion.

"Tell me now," he rasped over her.

"H-Hester . . ." was all she could get out, mewling in her throat while he punished her by staying away.

"Jesus," he groaned. "You are blind if you believe that I had anything going with her."

"I don't care—just fill me again, Lakota, please. I want you in me again."

"I care," he hissed fiercely, drawing her up against his chest and shaking her. "I haven't had Hester for three years. Believe me, my pure sweet darling, she's the biggest slut around twenty counties and she comes pretty damn close to Gar . . ."

Willow froze. He had almost said her mother's name. He hated her bitterly. Suddenly she realized the staggering import of his never finding out she was Garnet's daughter. He must never ever learn this!

"I believe you," Willow murmured, pulling him close and wrapping her slender legs about his waist. "Now, love me, Talon Lakota—love me and never stop!"

Chapter Fourteen

Cloud galloped across the wild prairie while Willow clung to Lakota from behind. Riding bareback, with only a rawhide rope for a rein held loosely in Lakota's grip, he laughed for the sheer joy of living, and Willow joined in, pressing her happily flushed cheek against his back.

As it was cooler in the north near the river, they both wore soft buckskin shirts, leggings—Willow wore a deerskin skirt—and knee-high moccasins. Lakota's outfit was fringed and beaded here and there, while Willow's bodice was hung with shells and brightly colored feathers.

Willow Aiyana and Named-Lakota seemed to those who watched them ride out of camp to be like an Indian god and a goddess, both fair and beautiful, vivacious and virile. And very much in love.

"Look!" Lakota shouted, lifting one hand to the sky.

Tossing back her head, Willow caught sight of a single hawk wheeling in the air, soaring so gracefully until it spotted its prey and then, swooping down with talons outstretched, it made its landing in the tall prairie grasses. The hawk issued a loud victorious cry, and settling its huge wings, the bird disappeared from view.

Hugging Lakota, Willow watched the sagebrush and prickly-pear cactus being left behind with the Spanish dagger. Ahead were the rolling high plains, the river with its cottonwood and willow clumps. They were going to the same spot where they had made love the day before. Willow now shivered in anticipation, her pulse racing wildly with her heartbeat.

The land here was hilly, and from the banks of the river it was hard to see if anyone was coming. Cloud was slowing to make the descent down the last short hill. The cottonwood trees that grew along the river bottom seemed like giants, their whitish-gray furrowed trunks larger than a man could reach around. Willow stared up in awe as she had the day before, when she had stared up passion-dazed as Lakota made wild, sweet love to her. Some trees towered four times as high as a tepee. The cottonwood leaves rustled continually, gently, whispering of shade and—privacy.

Before Lakota could dismount, Willow reached around, and pressing her warm hands below his waist, embraced him fiercely. Letting go of the ropes, allowing Cloud to roam where he would, Lakota's fingers sought Willow's. He weaved his hands with hers, guiding her down to press her palms against his hardening shaft.

A soft, quick breath was released from Willow. Was he always like this when he was around her? But then, even when he was in the company of others, she noticed he looked unusually large even at rest. No matter what he wore, as Talon or Lakota, he always seemed conspicuous. Even while she anticipated the inevitable joining, she wondered how her small body had ever been able to accommodate him.

As she pressed against him now, Willow's breath shortened and her heart was pounding like a horse in a fast gallop. The tips of her breasts were rapidly becoming hard.

Lakota pressed her hands harder, saying in a low, amused voice over his shoulder, "Am I enough for you, Aiyana?"

Willow tried pulling her hands free, but he held them close and cupped her fingers to his contours. "Am I?" he asked again and was pleased with her mute nod against his shoulder. He said tenderly, "And you will always be enough for me, my sweet Aiyana, more than I could ever have hoped for."

Giving the command for Cloud to stand still, Lakota slid off his horse and reached up for Willow. Their eyes met for just a moment and then he was helping her down, slowly, his hands lingering at her tiny waist. Her body suffused with heat while he continued to gaze into her eyes, Willow knew that his capacity for passion was great, but no greater than her own where he was concerned.

His arm wrapped about her waist, her head resting against his shoulder, Willow and Lakota walked silently to the grove of cottonwoods. Some of the largest trees had trunks that divided near the ground, and their giant limbs sloped enough so that they could be climbed if someone had it in mind.

The midday sun found them, putting a mellow spotlight in the place where they stood together wrapped in each other's presence. Leaning back, Willow reclined along the slope of an almost flat trunk while Lakota's ardent gaze followed her until she was looking up into the leafy bowers.

"It's warm here," she said lazily, stretching her arms high above her head.

"Warmer than usual," Lakota remarked, stepping to put one leg on either side of the giant limb. He leaned forward, placing his hands beside Willow's arms, one on each side of her head.

Forming an impish smile, Willow whispered, "Are you going to make love to me right here, my handsome savage?" Her body trembled erotically at the thought.

Lakota nodded mutely.

"Oh no, you won't—"

When she would have lifted herself all the way with a shove from her elbows, Lakota met her halfway, his sudden, fierce kiss driving her back to her reclining position.

Thinking this was merely a game he was playing, Willow tried to wrench herself free. When he lifted her blouse and bared her breasts to his warm perusal, she knew he was dead serious about making love to her here.

"No—" she laughed, not able to contain her mirth. "We'll fall off!"

"Not if I am holding you fast to me," he said, his meaning becoming quite clear in her eyes.

He gave her little time to consider the possibility further. Pressing closer, his lips lowered to claim hers in a kiss that was both savage and sweet. "I think that we'll have little time for rest this afternoon," he whispered against her ear. He would not tell her now that he had to return soon for the buffalo hunt and spoil the golden September day. He wanted to be with her for as long as he possibly could.

"Why do you need rest?" she murmured, taking little nibbles at his lower lip. She giggled softly, saying, "Why do I need rest?"

He nuzzled her throat. "To keep up our energy supply?" He chuckled and answered his own question. "Just in case we are raided by some warring Indian tribe. If I was away from the village, you would have to help gather the old people and children to safety."

She lifted her head to kiss the underside of his chin. "Are you going away, Lakota?"

He shivered at her delicate touch and groaned when she moved her lips to the hollow of his throat. His hair glistened in the pale sun as he slightly turned his head. "For a while," he confessed. He pressed between her thighs with his palm. "Just for a while."

Sunlight filtered through the leafy branches and fell across Willow's naked breasts. A rosy peak glistened moistly as his lips left it and went on to the next. Willow swallowed hard. "Oh . . . Lakota," she groaned. "Lakota . . ."

Alternately his fingers gently massaged her breasts with his hot, moist mouth. Now he cupped a round firm globe while his tongue flicked and his teeth nibbled gently. Between her thighs he rubbed himself rhythmically, his loins causing a heat to spread right up into Willow's secret core. He trailed fiery kisses from her breasts back up to her lips, which were open and inviting the wet thrusts of his tongue.

With one hand he parted her thighs, using his middle finger to massage her. Arching her hips, Willow brought him inside her, and he stroked until she was tossing with hot desire. She was so weak with longing that while he was removing his clothes, she could only look up at him. Tossing his clothes aside, he returned to help her with her own.

Searing bolts of pleasure tore through her when his naked flesh came against hers. He entered her satiny folds swiftly, cupping her hips and tipping her upward. Willow cried out loud, then again. There was no pain, but the pressure of his fullness had surprised her. He was so heavy and hard inside of her that she felt like she was a part of him.

"Willow," he gasped roughly, "Jesus . . . you're so warm and sweet. Like warmed honey. Your passage is still small and tight," he breathed into her ear, "can you feel me carry you—when I would draw out?"

Following the question, he lifted his head and was looking right into her eyes. Willow felt her cheeks burn with heat, but she was not embarrassed as he continued to gaze into her eyes while making love to her.

The powerful, surging body above her drove Willow into new realms of ecstasy. Then he changed and moved in deep, slow strokes. He teased her by withdrawing and then plunging, sinking his full shaft into her, over and over, until she was gasping and panting hotly.

"When Lakota . . . when," she was begging now, her nails digging into his shoulders.

Ever-increasing sounds of ecstasy mingled as their bodies separated and then came together again. They were so wrapped up in their loving that neither noticed when Willow began to slip from the trunk. Willow's eyes had closed while her neck arched. Lakota's head was flung way back, his feet wedged in the division of the trunk.

When she finally began to really slip away from him, Lakota jerked upright and reached out. In the process, Lakota's one foot remained lodged in the trunk while his other came free. His eyes widened as he saw Willow being flipped face forward to the ground. Her arms flew out to brace her fall, and by the time Lakota had freed himself, Willow was rolling onto her back and laughing so hard that she sat down and began to cry, too.

When Willow looked up and saw that Lakota, standing there stark-naked, was beginning to chuckle, she began to laugh all the harder, until she was laughing and crying so energetically that Lakota couldn't tell one from the other.

"Oh!" Willow pointed, feeling like a little girl all over again. "Look at you!"

Looking down at that part of him that had so recently been deep within her, Lakota saw that his passionate desire was swiftly coming to rest. But when he looked at her again his brow darkened. He was being tossed back in time again. Garnet . . . why was he so painfully reminded of that horrible woman again? This was Willow, his wife, his beloved. He looked at Willow again. She was looking up at him in mock-reproach, her baby finger resting between her pearly-white teeth. He looked at her hard. For now she seemed so like another, with her cornsilk hair mussed over one eye, her delicate features set in provocative play. This was a newer, riper Willow that he had never known before. There was a new radiance to her translucent skin and there was a new sheen in her hair he had never seen. In fact, she was far lovelier than that slut had ever been!

"Come," he said gruffly, holding out his hand. "We should go back to the village now. It will be getting dark soon."

With his back turned to her while he gathered up their clothes, Willow looked at his magnificent nude body and felt fear wash over her all of a sudden. What was wrong? Why didn't he want her anymore? There was unfinished business here . . . *what was wrong?*

"Lakota . . . ?"

"Don't stand around, Willow, get dressed." He avoided looking her way while he stepped into his breeches and laced up the fly.

He had called her Willow. Somehow this disappointed her. While they had been loving he had always called her Aiyana. She walked silently beside him while they went to find Cloud. He was not far off, standing at the line of trees where they found him. The big white was acting oddly, as if he had been peering into the adjacent trees right before they came up on him.

"Whoa," Lakota said, gently smoothing the nervous stallion. "What is wrong, boy? Did you see something?" He peered ahead into the trees and frowned down at the ground thoughtfully.

"Is something wrong?" Willow came up to where he was holding Cloud's rope halter.

"I'm not sure, but I have this strong impression that someone, or more than one, has been standing here. See the faint prints?" He looked up as she nodded. "These are not ours."

A soft gasp fell between her lips. "They were watching us then. . . ." Her eyes dilated at the thought of being spied on—while they made love!

Lakota did not look at her as he leaped onto Cloud's back and then reached down for her. When she looked up at him tartly and stepped back, he said impatiently, "Come on, we have to get back to the camp and report this." He kept his arm out while Cloud began to prance away from the recalcitrant human on the ground.

"No. I am not going anywhere with you."

"What?" he said, his face altering from alert watchfulness to disbelief. He leaned on one knee and looked down at her hard. "Did I hurt you, Aiyana? I am sorry if I did, but I didn't know you were going to fall off the trunk."

All of a sudden Willow beamed, inside and out. He was calling her Aiyana again. He had not been disappointed in her, after all. His haste to dress and be away must have come from a sense that danger was lurking near. Wasting no time, she came into the circle of his reaching arms and felt herself being lifted up behind him.

All the way back to the camp, Willow snuggled close to her husband and pressed her cheek into his buckskin shirt. She sighed in contentment, knowing everything was going to be just fine.

Dreadful Fox and One-Eye remained hidden in the bushes. They were young pirates of the plains who raided other tribes and whomever they came across for horses, food, and women; now they were acting as spies for a man by the name of Tucker—alias Randy Dalton. But they called him Tucker, as he preferred.

The two Indians had been watching the strange, beautiful couple make love in the trunk of the cottonwood for many hours now.

"When do you think they will finish?" One-Eye, aptly named for his missing eye, asked.

"Who can say?" Dreadful Fox answered, breathing hard. "These two enjoy each other very much, my cousin."

One-Eye stroked the Apache club he carried; it had a wooden handle and a stone head, both of which had been covered with buckskin sewn together with sinew.

One-Eye was having difficulty breathing himself, since he had never seen two more magnificent human beings joined together in the act of mating. All One-Eye had ever connected with the act of coupling was a series of grunts and groans and a quick animal release. But this was something out of the ordinary, and as One-Eye watched the small-built woman giving as much as she was receiving, he began to understand why the white-eyes Tucker wanted this sun-haired beauty. He would not mind adding her to his own collection of squaws. Perhaps when Tucker was finished with her . . .

"We will go now," One-Eye said to Dreadful Fox. "We have seen enough! Now we must wait for the White Indian to leave the hidden valley of Chief Black Fox."

"We will take the chief, too?" Dreadful Fox blinked in confusion.

"No. Jim Bluecoat has said that Chief Black Fox is away to the north with his family. We only want the yellow-hair who Bluecoat says the Kiowas have named Aiyana."

Dreadful Fox shot one more look over his shoulder at the lusty scene, then reluctantly followed his cousin, asking, "What does this mean—Aiyana?"

"Jim Bluecoat says Nightwalker calls her Little Moon Flower; this is Aiyana. She is the captive bride for this half-breed Named-Lakota who makes love to her now in the cottonwood."

"She lets him take her like that without a fight?"

One-Eye's one good eye narrowed. "He has captured more than her lovely body, it seems."

Flinging back his long stringy black hair, Dreadful Fox held the back of his mount before leaping onto it. "Do they hold others captive at the camp of Black Fox?" Dreadful Fox wanted to know, thinking of obtaining a captive woman for himself.

"The Horse Indians have many captives, mostly Mexican. But these two white-eyes are new; and they have the Shoshoni woman Kachina they took from us when they killed half of our men. This white man goes by the name Harlyn Saw-yer. He has failed to bring the yellow-hair Aiyana to Tucker."

His one eye burned fiercely. They would have their revenge for the stolen mustangs and the beautiful Kachina. There were now only thirty and five of his men left. "We will not fail. Be still. They are coming. We must make haste before the White Indian spies us!"

Willow watched Lakota pull himself up onto Cloud's back in one fluid motion. With bow and arrow, lance and club, and deerskin leggings, he became a fiercely handsome Indian buffalo hunter astride his white warrior horse.

Nightwalker was in the lead, Little Coyote, Named-Lakota, Dark Horse and all the other braves strung out behind him. That left only the women and old men and a few children in the camp, besides Harlyn Sawyer, who had been left in the custody of Jim Bluecoat. The warriors' wives were going along, too.

Many Feathers came to stand beside Willow, his wrinkled face looking like yellow parchment beneath the warm September sun. "You should not be sad to see your husband go on his first buffalo hunt," he scolded Aiyana.

Willow hadn't realized the old medicine man had come to stand by her until she heard his slow, guttural voice. She looked down at Many Feathers, for he was several inches shorter than herself. She smiled at the old man, but said nothing.

"There is nothing to fear," he said and walked slowly back to his tepee.

Watching Willow from four tepees away was Jim Bluecoat. Beside him on the ground was Harlyn Sawyer, unshaven and dirty in the same set of clothes he had been wearing on his arrival in the camp. He had flatly refused to wear the "stinkin' Injuns'" clothing offered to him by Wolf-Eyes-Woman, Jim Bluecoat's wife. She snorted his way now as she entered the tepee and secured the flap against the wafting of his strong body odors.

Jim Bluecoat continued to stare after the line of proud hunters, all of them tall and handsome. He was a half-breed too, but the others had not welcomed him into the camp as easily as they had Named-Lakota. He had been there longer than the tall "boy" with the dark green eyes, but then Jim Bluecoat was not Nightwalker's son, either. Chief Black Fox seemed to favor Nightwalker for some reason . . . he had heard they were related in some way.

None of this mattered to Jim Bluecoat now. All he wanted was to get his hands on the white horse belonging to Named-Lakota. The wonderful white stallion fired his blood and made his heart sing when he gazed upon its magnificence.

The Great One made a perfect buffalo horse, and he would be the same in the hunt as he was in battle. Jim Bluecoat had seen the horse when he was allowed to go along once before. The white one owned great speed and was fearless. He would enter the fringe of the nervous, fleeing herd without guidance by reins. He had enough swiftness to avoid the charge of a wounded bull buffalo. He had the deep wind to stay with a racing herd for miles.

With hot jealousy Jim Bluecoat watched the white horse from afar. Even from here he could see the horse toss his proud head and prance high above the ground, as if his hoofs had wings. He would have this great one someday.

Jim Bluecoat spat on the white man who had failed Bimisi, "slippery" Tucker. He and his Apache friends would not fail.

Chapter Fifteen

Kachina's long hair blew softly in long black spirals about her creamy tan cheeks. There was a new excited flush about her face and her step had grown lighter. Her years numbered about twenty but she felt as if she was a small, happy girl again. All this, despite the tragedies she had undergone the past three years.

At the moment, Kachina and Willow were returning from just north of the camp where they had gone to gather wild plants for herbs and berries to make pemmican. Not only was pemmican nutritious, but it could also be stored away in rawhide cases called parfleches. In the parfleches the pemmican would keep for months.

The men had been gone for two days now. The day before, Kachina had taught Willow how to make the pemmican. With a stone maul, they had taken the preserved buffalo meat after it had been left to dry and pulverized it; then the powdered meat was mixed with ground and dried berries and fat. The result was the high-protein food pemmican.

Many-Feathers waved to the young women as they entered the camp and then continued on his daily walk to the farthest corral and back again. He was on his way now; but it would be a while before he returned.

"Hello Harlyn," Willow said as she and Kachina paused to visit with the only prisoner not allowed free roam of the village. Willow had a strong impression Harlyn's incarceration had sprung from her husband's bidding.

When Sawyer would not speak, Kachina, feeling sorry for the man, tried a few words with him. "It is a nice day, Saw-yer, do you not think?" She looked at Willow and then back at the white man.

The once handsome Sawyer glared up at the beautiful Indian girl, snorting, "What's nice about it?" He leered openly at the scooped bodice of her doeskin dress, his bleary eyes taking in the creamy tan perfection of her flesh.

"How long do they plan to keep you prisoner?" Willow asked, lowering her voice so that Jim Bluecoat could not hear from inside his tepee.

He peered up at her and then away, sneering. "Why don't you ask your Injun lover? He knows everythin' about everyone and watches every move everyone makes—'specially you. Damn half-breed, he practically runs the show around here. Ask him!" He waved his hand, dismissing them abruptly.

When Willow had not moved away from the smelly Sawyer, Kachina touched her arm. "Come, Aiyana, we will go make something to eat now. There is nothing you can do for him. They will let him go when the time is right."

"Yes—I suppose so."

Kachina tied the ends of a piece of hide to four poles, then filled it with water and meat and vegetables. To make the water boil she then dropped hot, fist-sized stones into the pouch. Soon the delicious odor of meat, wild peas, and prairie turnips filled the air inside the tepee. But when it was time to sit down to eat, Kachina only stared into her bowl in a state of dreamy reflection.

Though the meat was stringy, it was delicious, and Willow chewed hungrily until she noticed Kachina had not taken one bite yet. "I thought you were so hungry, Kachina. Are you feeling well?"

Kachina's face became animated then as she pulled out of the romantic trance she had been in. Her huge doe eyes sparkled. "Oh yes, I am hungry." She attacked her food, using her fingers to eat while Willow used the copper spoon Almanzo, Dark Horse, had given her one day not too long ago.

When Kachina thought of Dark Horse she tingled from head to foot. Ever since he had come to the tepee with Lakota just five days before, Kachina had walked around in a hazy cloud. He had continued to stare at Kachina when Lakota picked Willow up and bore her to the spring. She had turned to find him watching her and the laughing comment she had been about to make had died on her lips. Dark Horse had been studying her in such an unusual way as to make Kachina's blood turn to fire. How she had desired to be with him, to talk with him. Yet she had denied him a walk with her in the moonlight the very night Willow and Lakota had married.

Very carefully now so she would not arouse any suspicion, Kachina brought up the subject of her heart's recent palpitations. "How well do you know Dark Horse?" she asked softly.

The question had emerged like a tender caress, and Willow's head shot up. She stared straight ahead, thinking she now knew the reason why Kachina had been so distracted the past few days. Willow smiled to herself, knowing exactly how Kachina felt, for she had often found herself stumbling over her own feet when she had first met Talon Clay, the man who was now her husband. Even lately she often found herself gazing off into nowhere.

"I've known Almanzo for quite some time, Kachina." She smiled. "At one time—" Willow bit off, looking down to see Kachina's hand suddenly resting on her arm. Questioningly, she looked into Kachina's blue-black eyes.

"Almanzo?" was all Kachina said.

"Yes, Almanzo Rankin. Rankin is the name of his mother's distant relatives. At least, this is the way Nightwalker explained it. The Rankins adopted Hungry Wolf's Son Dark Horse when Hungry Wolf passed on to the spirit world." She exchanged a smile here with Kachina. "At one time everyone thought Almanzo was Nightwalker, and he allowed everyone to continue thinking this. He was like a mystical Indian god or—" She waved her arm—"whatever you would call such a being. The line of Nightwalkers has weakened, Named-Lakota tells me. *He* was actually next in line to receive the title Nightwalker, but his father decided to call him Named-Lakota; don't ask me why."

"I know what this Lakota means," Kachina began. "It is a name in the Plains Indian language which means all-togetherness. Lakota is the name of the Teton division of the Sioux Nations. Those Siouan tribes moved this way and mingled in marriage with the Comanches and Kiowas and white captive women—but not the Kiowa-Apaches."

"What . . . ?" Willow sought the word. "What tribe are you from, Kachina?"

Proudly, Kachina said, "I am far from home. I am Shoshoni."

Without looking at Kachina now, Willow asked something that had been on her mind ever since meeting Kachina. "Do you have white blood . . . Kachina?" Willow swung her head around to look directly into the midnight-blue eyes then.

"Yes. It is true I have white blood."

Willow nodded, spooning a slice of prairie turnip into her mouth and wondering when her beloved would return. Her heart was heavy, she was missing him so terribly.

Sneaking off while the camp slept and Sawyer sawed logs beside his tepee, Jim Bluecoat went to meet Tucker in Apache Territory. He would ride most of the night and not return until late in the morning. But then, and he smiled cruelly, he would not be coming back to Black Fox's camp unaccompanied.

Four hours later he came upon the camp where Tucker and the Indians had settled for the night before reaching Apache Territory. He had crept up to make sure these were not Kiowas or any of the Horse Indians, for they would demand the reason for his leaving the prisoner unattended to go sneaking off into the night by himself.

Jim Bluecoat faced Tucker now. "Nightwalker has finally gone hunting with his men and left the camp with only old men and women to watch over it." A greedy gleam came into Jim Bluecoat's eyes as he envisioned himself taking the Great One for his own. Then he shivered when he looked at Tucker's face, wondering what had happened to the man's eye. Where before there had been a gray-blue eye there was now only a white film covering the eyeball. Not only that—Tucker walked with a limping gait.

"Heh, heh," Carl Tucker chuckled nastily, rubbing his big hands together before the hot, licking flames. "Is the girl there?"

"There are two young women in Black Fox's camp. One is fair, the other the beautiful Shoshoni, Kachina."

"I knowed that!" Tucker snarled. "I want to know about Willow Hayes—no one else. She's the one I'm after."

"She is Willow Hayes no longer."

Jim Bluecoat jerked backward as Tucker lunged at him, snarling, "What the blazes you talkin' about!" His hair fell about his forehead in greasy strands. "Is she dead, you tellin' me that, man?"

"She is Willow Margaret Brandon n-now," Jim Bluecoat got out finally, only repeating what Jim Nibaw had said during the ceremony.

"Brandon!" Tucker roared. "I hate that name Brandon." He snatched up Jim by his blue coat lapels. "You better be tellin' me the truth, half-breed . . . else I'm goin' to string you up by yer family jewels . . . heh, heh, heh. You hear me, half-breed?"

"I hear you—white man."

"Heyy!" Tucker roared, sending Jim Bluecoat flying with a solid right punch to the jaw. "Now," he said, shoving his way through the line of laughing Apaches milling around the fire. "Let's go kill us some old folks and take up some captive women—yeah!"

Willow froze in place near the spring, then whirled about. A strong feeling had come over her when she picked up the filled water bags and started back to camp. She lifted her head higher now . . . was that the pounding of horses' hooves she heard?

Straining her eyes, she could see nothing up there but the first pale streaks of pink dawn. That could not be thunder she had heard; the rent in the sky was summer blue—then what was that noise she could hear growing steadily louder?

Now she could hear shouts in the distance, and when she turned with fast-beating heart in the direction of the voices, she dropped her water bags and set off into a run.

"Kachina!" she shouted at the top of her lungs. "Kachina!"

Feeling her heart pound, Willow ran until she thought her lungs would burst. She knew these riders could not be Ashe Brandon coming with the drovers and mustangers; Tanya and Ashe still thought she had gone away with a nice, handsome stranger to get herself married. Even if they thought she should have returned by now for a visit, Willow knew they would never come looking for her, not unless they had news she was in trouble. She had no time to wonder what everyone at Sundance thought of both her and Talon Clay's disappearing almost at the same time.

Stumbling over a pile of wood at the edge of the village, Willow clutched her side and gasped for breath. She looked up from her bent position, out across the village. Where was everyone? Had they already found a hiding place? Then she spotted Kachina, passing from one tepee to another, carrying a bowl of something steaming toward Harlyn Sawyer. Almost simultaneously, Kachina and Harlyn looked up as the ear-splitting yells began.

Kachina screamed and dropped to the ground close to Harlyn. Exploding rifles sounded all around, almost deafening Willow where she crouched shivering behind the stack of wood. She squinted her eyes, trying to see through the swirling clouds of dust and smoke. Then she saw them. Old people and small children running frantically from their tepees in all directions.

Willow's nerves began to tingle in fear. There was no chance for her to join the others. Then she almost stood as an image with parchmentlike flesh and kindly eyes came to her mind. Many Feathers—where was he? She could not see him. Her head swiveled in the direction of the corral. Lord no! Would the attacking band go there to steal the horses too? She had to get to Many Feathers somehow and help him to a safe hiding place!

Willow turned to look back over her shoulder. What was she going to do? her heart cried. She could hear Kachina screaming, and Willow knew the lovely Indian girl was being yanked up onto a horse by a warrior with a fearsome painted face.

There was no help for Kachina, Willow thought sadly. She must get to Many Feathers, if she could. Half-crouching, she started to make her way toward the corral where the wild, beautiful mustangs were kept. Just before Lakota had left for the buffalo hunt, she had watched him break a spotted devil of a horse. His whole body was muscled bands of magnificent steel, and her own cried out for that strength she was so badly in need of now. For a moment she thought how cruel life would be to her if she never saw Lakota again. They had only just begun to love!

The chilling, heart-rending cries of terrified old women and children followed Willow as she ran, tripping and falling, getting up again, dodging obstacles that seemed to leap up in front of her as she ran, on and on. She had to get to Many Feathers before the attacking Indians did.

Before Willow ever reached the farthest corral, an Indian with terrible war paint on his face was bearing down on her. Her doeskin skirt rode high on her legs as she ran, her hair streaking wildly behind her. One of her arms flew out as if she was reaching for something in the air, something, someone to help her. She had never seen such fierce-looking savages!

"No, not now, not now," her mind kept repeating with the violent beats of her heart. But the savage was swooping toward her—closer, closer!

Dreadful Fox could feel his heart keeping time with the thundering of his horse's hoofs. Here, almost in his clutches, was the pretty white flower Aiyana he had watched making love with the White Indian. He could make her his, take care of her after Tucker was done with her. She was a prize he would treasure, Dreadful Fox thought, and he would not be rough with her as he knew Tucker would be.

Flashing hoofs reached Willow's line of vision right

before she was swooped up into strong arms as the horse kept right on going. Gasping and sobbing, she felt herself being stroked gently while the galloping horse slowed to a jogging trot. Before she even saw the burning smudge in the sky she smelled the acrid smoke. Finally she looked up, seeing several tepees going up in flames, hearing the screams of those burning to death, those being the eldest and unable to run. When she heard the gurgling scream of a child, she leaned over the strong coppery arm and vomited.

Wiping her mouth with the back of her hand, Willow looked right into the blackest eyes ever, hissing, "Murdering savages!" She pounded at the hard, fleshy chest. "I hate you . . . !" Pushing away from the young Indian, Willow looked up just in time to see her worst nightmare, in the flesh, riding toward her. . . .

It was . . . it had to be . . . Tanya had said she was the cause of Tucker's having shot himself in the leg, and Tanya had been the one to injure his eye—an eye that was totally white and horrible to behold—

Carl Tucker—a nightmare come to life!

Many Feathers rose heavily from his hiding place, tears coursing down his deeply lined face. He had once been a proud Kiowa warrior, but the passing of time had made him an old man. Once he had thundered with a proud chest across the plains on a great steed. Now that same chest was sunken. Now he saw his helplessness in his old age. He had not been able to save those old friends he held most dear. He even had grown fond of Named-Lakota and his sweet bride Aiyana.

Now Aiyana was gone. The hated Apaches with their

bimisi white leader had taken her away. He had seen this band of Apaches; they were the worst kind of Indian. They were a motley group that had been banished for their evil deeds and now preyed on others, even stooping so low as to take a white man to be their leader. He was afraid Named-Lakota would never see his bride again . . . if only they would return before the renegade Apaches got too far away with their prize.

Trudging slowly back to the camp, Many Feathers steeled his old heart for the utter destruction he was about to see . . . he could already smell the acrid smoke, see it being scattered in the wind and carried away. . . .

The hunters returning to the village were full of joy. After the last buffalo had been killed, the young wives camped nearby had come in to help the victorious hunters. Each brave's wife identified her animals by the specific markings painted on her warrior's arrows. There were only four men who did not have their wives with them; and two of them, Little Coyote and Dark Horse, had no women they could call their own yet. And Nightwalker's wife was no more.

Nightwalker laughed softly while Tall Deer's seven wives did his skinning and butchering for him. "The better hunter a man is, the more people he can afford to support in his lodge."

Named-Lakota leaned an arm on his lifted knee, saying in a voice of amusement, "Who will skin and butcher our meat, Nightwalker?" He recalled the confused and terrified buffalo swirling in circles, the Indians riding about them and firing arrows while some charged with lances, dust rising high into the air above the battleground.

"Why have you not brought your wife, my son?"

"She would never make it as a squaw," Lakota chuckled, watching some of the Indian women already packing buffalo hides and meat on pack horses to be taken back to the village.

When they turned to join the others to make the trip back, Lakota noticed they had left the buffalo hearts littered on the ground. With a questioning eyebrow, Lakota turned to Nightwalker, asking, "What is wrong with the heart of the buffalo? It appears they are leaving it purposely behind."

"It is true, Lakota. We believe that the mystical power of these hearts will help to regenerate the depleted herd of buffalo. Everything else is put to use. Even the horns, bones, and hides become useful as household items." Nightwalker laughed low, adding, "Even the dung of the buffalo is saved to use as fuel."

Lakota joined his father in laughing, joking, "I hope the women wait until it is dry before picking it up."

"Do you not feel proud that you have killed your first buffalo this day? Look, one of Tall Deer's wives has cleaned both yours and mine. Tadewi is proud of you; think how proud her grandfather Many Feathers will be. He has grown very fond of you and Aiyana, my son."

Now Lakota grew serious. "Nightwalker . . . Father, when will you return to the reservation?"

Nightwalker sighed, saying, "Only once in a while. There was a woman there that I had been staying with . . . but she has passed on now. I will continue to bring the mustangs to the reservation, that is all."

Lakota would not bring up the subject of his mother, Martha, for he had seen the pain in his father's eyes just now. Dark Horse had told him that Nightwalker had been very much in love with his mother. He himself could handle this now . . . but how was Ashe going to take this news? Surely he did not relish the thought of being the one to tell his brother, but who else was there to do the telling? One day he and Willow would have to return to Sundance and face the music—and Ashe.

"What is your age now?" Nightwalker asked his son quietly.

"I am not sure—somewhere around twenty-six, twenty-seven, maybe a little older."

Nightwalker chuckled. "You do not even know."

"But you do, you're telling me?"

"I have been doing some figuring. You will soon be twenty and eight!"

Lakota whistled. "Jesus . . . that is old. I'd better make up for lost time," he said with a wistful twist to his mouth, melting inside when he thought of a pair of fawn-colored eyes and hair the color of liquid sunshine mixed with wild honey. He should not have left unfinished business behind—that had been a mistake. But he was prepared to make up for lost time now and mend any mistakes he had made. He thought of her meeting him with open arms, and he smiled.

There were no shouts of joy at the success of the hunt, no children coming running to greet them. All that greeted the hunters and the women who had gone along to do the butchering was silence . . . silence and devastation.

Lakota's eyes burned brightly with tears, and it was not from smoke. The smoke had long ago dissipated. He was battling emotions he had never felt before, feeling as if his heart was being ripped apart. Even the horse he rode hung his usually proud white head dejectedly and trudged through the burnt-out rubble and debris. Here was an old woman with her brains bashed out. There was an old man lying facedown on the ground like a broken puppet whose strings had been cruelly severed . . . Cloud automatically halted before the pile of black rubble that had once been Lakota's tepee.

A white-hot stab of pain attacked Lakota in the chest. He was shattered to the very depths of his soul. His eyes searched reluctantly for a lock of honey-light hair, a flash of brightly colored beads, any clue that would declare the evidence of her death.

No! This cannot be! She is not dead! his heart cried. He lifted his face to the gray sky and a deep, rumbling sob rose from his throat. *No!*

"Why do you weep, my son?"

The softly spoken words dragged Lakota back to the living, for he had felt his soul had died there a moment ago in the blackened rubble with his love. He turned to see the caring face of Nightwalker, and there, beside him, was Many Feathers!

When Lakota finally spoke he sounded as if he had contracted a cold, and the usual ring of clear white surrounding his green eyes was red and bloodshot.

"She's gone." He turned his face to the sky as it began raining, and laughing ironically he repeated, "She's gone . . . we had only started to know each other—" he groaned— "Oh God! what will I do without her." He turned to Nightwalker with tears hovering on his dark lashes. "She is my heart!"

"Who is it you weep for, Named-Lakota?"

His father was speaking to him again, but Lakota hardly heard the words, he was in such pain and grief.

"She is not dead to you," Nightwalker said slowly, thinking she might as well be—she was in the hands of the most dreaded band of Apaches ever to roam the plains.

Lakota went stock still. He stared at his father, narrowing his reddened eyes. "What are you saying?" he said slowly. His eyes left Nightwalker and swept back and forth across the village, but he saw no one, nothing but the carnage of death and utter destruction. He leaped forward, shouting, "Where is she, then? Don't play with me, Nightwalker!"

"I am not toying with your emotions, Lakota. I only wait for you to calm yourself before I speak of what we must do to get the woman back from the—" his voice dipped to a hiss— "Apaches."

Lakota was almost afraid to ask which band of Apaches had taken the women captive. "Is it the— Ipa'Nde?"

Nightwalker only nodded, yes he was afraid this was so. Staring-eyed, Lakota could only look past Nightwalker and Many Feathers to the rainswept skies above the high plains, feeling a terrible anger tearing and pulling at his heart.

Tall Deer and Little Coyote crept up on the camp of the Ipa'Nde, the Devil's Band of Apaches. There were two men in the camp with bad eyes, one was Indian with his entire eye missing, the other was a man called Tucker, for Tall Deer and Little Coyote could hear Jim Bluecoat saying his name.

Tucker's voice carried to them now: "Shut up, man, if you say my name once more I'll slit your throat from ear to ear! Might be some Injuns snoopin' around what can hear you. I don't want my name bandied about, hear?—That's good."

"You killed my woman," Jim Bluecoat spat at Tucker's back when he spun away from him. Tucker turned back to face Jim Bluecoat. "She is not here—you murdered her!"

"Awww, she's all right, Bluecoat, we just couldn't bring 'em all with us."

"What if they come looking for the women, what will you do then, Tucker?" Jim Bluecoat asked, narrowing his eyes.

"I'll be waitin', that's what. All I really want right now is the Brandon man. I aim to get rid of all Brandons." The vision of a gorgeous redhead came to his mind and he thought, Well, maybe not all Brandons—for Tanya was a Brandon now, by way of marriage to Ashe Brandon. He still felt a hankering for her . . . but now that Willow was here and she had filled out so nicely, maybe he wouldn't be needing Tanya Brandon anymore. Mentally he rubbed his hands together. Maybe he could have both Brandon women when the time came—Willow was a Brandon now, too. Man! Two gorgeous women, and Saw Grass joined with Sundance. He would live like a Texas king!

Up in the tall grass on a small hill, Little Coyote and Tall Deer took in the conversation that wafted their way. Tall Deer shook his head, unable to understand all that they had been saying—this Tucker talked so strangely.

"Come, Tall Deer, we will go back to tell the others what we have found and what we have heard."

That night, the Horse Indians surrounded the camp of the Ipa'Nde and crouched low. Lakota almost went crazy with the need to kill when he spotted his most hated enemy—Carl Tucker!

A thrill of premonition raced over Willow's flesh when Tucker called her to come out of the crudely erected tepee. It smelled badly inside and she was glad to be able to get out for a breath of fresh air. But when she stepped out she went absolutely still. Her eyes lifted ever so slightly, to the small incline rising from the hastily erected camp. There . . . she felt something, what was it? She lowered her eyes at once when Carl Tucker got up and began walking toward her.

Lifting her chin, Willow looked unafraid into Tucker's face. Kachina had whispered to her inside the tepee, referring to Tucker as a Devil Man. Willow had agreed. Kachina did not even know just how bad Tucker really was. This was the man who had tried to rape her twice, had kidnapped her sister Tanya and tried to kill Ashe Brandon, had successfully murdered many of his own friends—and God only knew what else he had in mind.

Willow's eyes shifted a little to the right. Glancing over Tucker's shoulder, she focused her eyes on the wavy ridge. For only a fleeting moment she thought she had seen the silhouette of a tall man casting a menacing moonshadow on the Apaches below. She had felt a familiar flash of something . . . but it was gone as quickly as it had pierced her senses.

Reaching out with a big hand, Tucker lifted the beaded fringe decorating Willow's bodice and let it slip through his fingers, ever so slowly, menacing her with his one good eye. The other socket, where there had been some color before, was now a milky film too horrible to look at.

"There are too many of them," Nightwalker was whispering to Lakota. "They outnumber us. Look how many guards they have around the tepee where the women are being held."

"We will have to attack when they sleep," Dark Horse said in sign language.

"We will kill only the guards," Lakota said, pointing to each one of them. There were four around the tepee.

"We must be careful," Dark Horse said. "If we slip up, the women might be killed." He was thinking of Willow, true, but ever since he had learned that Kachina had been captured by the Apaches again he had felt something wrench his heart. He knew it was not just pity, or compassion—it was more. He wanted to get to know Kachina better; there was something special about her, and he had a burning desire to learn just what it was that attracted him to her.

"Damn," Lakota swore and clenched his fists when he saw Tucker's fingers becoming more familiar with Willow, brushing the front of the doeskin dress with the back of his hand.

Lakota was so happy to see his beloved alive, he wanted to run down there, slay all of the Apaches single-handed, and sweep Willow into his arms. A fierce surge of protectiveness rushed over him, and it was all he could do to keep himself from leaping down there and doing as he wanted. But there were captive children in the camp too; he must also think of them, as Nightwalker had warned earlier.

"Put her back in the tepee," Tucker was ordering one of the half-breed renegades. It was then that Jim Bluecoat walked into the circle of firelight, his eyes narrowing shiftily upward.

"Traitor!" Dark Horse hissed, clutching his bow and reaching for an arrow.

"Stay your hand!" Nightwalker ordered, clamping an iron hold upon Dark Horse's wrist. "You shall have the occasion to put him away soon enough."

Dark Horse's fingers clenched and unclenched rhythmically. "We will attack like our Comanche brothers—when the moon is high and full!"

The moon was finally high in the sky, full and lemon-yellow. Nightwalker sent eight of his men off in a running crouch down the hill. They were the most silent, expert warriors he knew of. They could slit an Apache's throat without a breath of notice. All were fast asleep, all but the guards. These were watchful men, but they did not have eyes in the back of their heads, Dark Horse thought as he crept up and slashed a throat with the speed and efficiency of an attacking tiger. At once his hand covered up the mouth and throat that was gargling on its own blood, silencing the Apache forever.

Lakota could not contain himself any longer, and set off down the hill as Nightwalker's hand reached out and snatched nothing but a handful of air. Lakota was heading for the tepee that held his wife and Kachina. Once Aiyana was safe, Lakota would go after this Tucker—Nightwalker was sure of it!

Several tepees away, Carl Tucker came awake with a

start. His shifty eye darted this way and that, and his flesh prickled telling him something was wrong. Peering out the flap, keeping it open with his head, he hitched up his pants and swiftly reached for his guns. Amazingly, he saw very clearly with his one good eye—and what he saw now caused him to bolt from the tepee and head directly for his horse. Injuns! Kiowas! There could be a whole tribe of them out there . . . he had to get away!

Inside the tepee where Kachina and Willow sat huddled together there was nothing but the cold ground beneath them. They had been given no blankets for warmth, no fire was going, and the night was growing chillier by the minute. By morning they knew they would be blue from cold.

"I hear s-something," Kachina said, her teeth chattering.

"It's only the guards, Kachina." Willow took up her friend's hand and began rubbing it between her own.

Willow looked at Kachina. More than cold was making Kachina shiver, there was something else, a nightmarish brand of fear that made Kachina's usually lovely face a terrified mask of apprehension.

"Do not let them get me, Aiyana," she stammered. "It is terrible what they do to a woman." She began to shiver uncontrollably. "They hurt me over and over . . . please do not let them do that again."

With wide-eyed comprehension, Willow stared down at Kachina's bent head, long strands of gleaming black hair covering her face. She looked suddenly like a frightened little girl, rocking back and forth and crying in silent, hearbreaking sobs.

"Kachina," Willow took hold of her friend's shoulders, putting her head next to Kachina's. "Kachina, please don't cry. Listen, we'll get out of here. I promise I'll think of something. They won't hurt you," she said with fierce determination in her voice, "I promise I won't let them do—that to you again."

Kachina's head jerked upward. "Do you hear that? They are coming for us now . . . hide, hide, we must hide, hurry, Aiyana."

"Kachina! Stop it!" Willow shook the Indian girl. "There is nowhere to hide." Her eyes widened in shock then as the tip of a blade poked through the side of the tepee wall and slashed downward in one neat, fierce stroke. "Oh . . ." Willow felt as if she would faint.

Just then a long, buckskin-fringed leg poked through and the body followed, slipping inside in one fluid motion. Fierce elation swept Willow, and pulling Kachina up with her, she swept them both into Lakota's waiting arms.

PART FOUR

Savage Love, Sweet Love

. . . aching joys . . . dizzy raptures.

—Wordsworth

And summer pools could hardly cool
The fever on my brow!

—Thomas Hood

Chapter Sixteen

Pulling Willow into the protective circle of his arms, Lakota kneed Cloud away from the Apache camp. He could barely give credence to the fact that his woman was alive and well—and she appeared unharmed.

Lakota touched Willow's head and brushed a tender kiss across her cheek as he pulled her tangled hair back behind her ear. Gently then he rested the side of his face against her head, his chest and arms curving about her like a spoon.

"I love you, Aiyana Willow," he murmured fiercely.

"Oh, Lakota—I thought you would never get to us in time! I don't know what that devil Carl Tucker would have done with us!"

"I never thought to find you and the others in one piece." His lips brushed her forehead, as he gently asked, "Did he touch you in any other way?"

"Lakota! Look!"

Willow screamed as the Apaches gathered on the moonlit rise began to descend. Lakota had only a moment in which to check to see if Dark Horse,

Nightwalker, and the others were with them. There were only fifteen of their own Horse Indians. The rest had remained to help the women rebuild the camp and to guard the valley in case the Apaches returned for the mustangs.

A swift estimate told the Horse Indians they were outnumbered, fifteen to their thirty-five or forty.

"We cannot fight!" Dark Horse shouted. "Not with the women with us. We will have to make a run for the plains. Once we're there, the Apache ponies will not be able to keep up with our mustangs."

"I would not be too sure about that," Lakota said. "But I am willing to try!" He gave Willow a swift look of love before setting Cloud into a long, stretching run. "Hiyaa!" he shouted over his shoulder, sweeping up his lance and shaking it in the air. "Try and get us now, you evil bastards!"

From a hill not far away, Carl Tucker watched his prey vanishing like thin smoke. Foiled again, damnit! The dark side of his face that the moon did not find was cast in eerie shadow, while the other side with the milky socket looked even worse. He could go down and join the Apaches in the chase. Or he could stay right here and see if they returned with prisoners. He decided to hang back and let the Apaches do all the dirty work. All he wanted was the one they called White Indian—that was Talon Clay Brandon. So, the kid had become a savage—a very frightening one at that, one Carl would not like to meet alone on the trail. He had always thought Talon had some wild blood in him. Let him run with the savages, he thought. He wouldn't be running for much longer. He planned to see that all Brandon men were wiped from the face of the earth. All he had to do was get one prisoner; then he could send word to the other brother—and then he would have them both. The girl was not working out as well as he had thought at first. Damn Brandon men—they always saved their women in the nick of time! Well, next time there won't be any saving them—the whole lot of them are going to die!

Quitting the edge of the slope, Tucker carefully returned to the camp and found a good place to conceal himself and his horse, to await the Apaches and see if they brought any prisoners back.

Kachina's captor still held her tightly, one arm about her waist. There was no radiant animation on her face now. Her almond-shaped eyes were not dancing. There was none of the stoical Indian courage that should have shown her heritage. She didn't know where the Apache was taking her prisoner this time; she only knew they were racing over the earth at a tremendous rate of speed.

Dark Horse stifled a yell of exultation. Their party had left the Apaches behind! He could see up ahead that Lakota had glanced back to see the line of Apaches stretched across the dawn-lit horizon, and now Lakota raised a fist in the air in an expression of exultation—they had made it! The horses up ahead began to slow their furious pace, and Dark Horse did the same. A smile with some jealousy curved his lips when he saw that Lakota was bending his face close to his wife's. But his smile ended when he felt Kachina begin to shiver against his chest again.

"You are safe now, Kachina," he said softly against her hair. "You have nothing to fear any longer—they are gone."

Fear coiled in Kachina's belly at the sound of the deep male voice murmuring in her ear. She didn't want to surface from this nightmare, not again, not this time. If she held herself inside, then she would not be hurt, would not feel when they violated her body this time, would not hear their harsh, guttural sounds above her.

Dark Horse stared down at the shiny dark head in concern. "Are you all right, Kachina? Why will you not speak?"

"No . . . do not . . . please do not hurt me . . . again."

Startled by the fear in Kachina's voice, Dark Horse stared at the disheveled figure hunching over the horse's neck. It seemed to him she was trying to get as far from him as possible. When he reached out a hand to touch her head, Kachina's body tensed. He had barely touched her and she was pulling inside of herself. A pitiful sound reached his ears, and he frowned darkly.

Now Dark Horse understood what was wrong with Kachina. When he had shown interest in her welfare, Lakota had told him he had found her naked when they had attacked the Apaches and taken the mustangs. Lakota had had to save face and treat her as his captive, for he had not the stomach to take the Apache scalps. Lakota had taken Kachina to his tepee, but not to his mats. He had sensed the dark fear of man in her.

Dark Horse was angry with himself for having been so rough with her when she had struggled as he was ordered by Nightwalker to carry her to his horse; and this anger increased when he thought of the terror Kachina must have known at the hands of the Apaches. If he had been given the chance, he would have killed every last one of the Ipa'Nde Apaches!

Looking down at Kachina's slumped figure, he eased her carefully back into the band of his arms. She was sleeping restlessly now. He stroked her black silk hair with a tenderness he had not felt since he had carried Tanya Brandon into her house following the frightful, ugly scene during which Carl Tucker had taken her hostage.

Kachina stirred and began to whimper, though she did not awaken. Dark Horse leaned forward to encompass her fully in his secure embrace. The sound she had made had been the whimper of a frightened child. "There is nothing for you to fear," he crooned softly. "I am here and shall protect you forever, Kachina."

Suddenly Dark Horse realized what he had said. If Kachina had been awake he would have committed himself to something he was not prepared for. Still, he had said the words. But why? He went back in time, to almost two years ago. His wedding day. What should have been his wedding day, but had turned out to be a drastic mistake. He had been in love with the sweet, virginal Ellita Tomas—so he thought she had been untouched by man. Right before the wedding vows were to be spoken, a friend of his had walked up and revealed the less than virtuous character of the woman he was about to marry. She had been used by another man, and God only knew how many before him. The wedding had never taken place. Right before all their guests, he had shamed Ellita Tomas by calling her a whore, thrown her to the ground and walked away.

Kachina whimpered in her sleep again, trying to pull away from the steel bands that held her. Dark Horse stroked her again, being careful not to brush her breasts accidently. He knew she would react violently, or pull even further into herself, if the smallest touch of intimacy was made.

Dark Horse was fighting his own battle. He had never felt such a sense of protectiveness toward a woman, not even Ellita Tomas. For only the second time in his life, Dark Horse felt a full awareness of what Kachina was suffering strike him. Tanya Brandon had been the first one, and he had felt her pain as if it had been his own. He might have fallen in love with her, but Tanya's heart had already been pledged forever to her husband. Now he and Tanya were the best of friends, and he would return to Sundance soon for the "drive" to Abiline with the rest of the drovers and mustangers. For a brief moment he wondered if Lakota would be going back with him—and Aiyana Willow.

With Kachina's body so close to his, Dark Horse began to feel something he knew would be better left dormant. Her softness was beginning to excite him. Her womanly odor was dizzying his senses. She was vulnerable, and if he wanted he could renew her trust in man. Unable to stop himself, Dark Horse leaned over Kachina, and brushing the long spirals of hair aside, he kissed her tenderly at the corner of her lips. She stirred but did not awaken. Then Dark Horse smiled to himself when she snuggled closer and purred in contentment.

Up ahead of all the others, Lakota reached downward and laced his fingers with Willow's. "Are you sleeping?" he said, nudging her softly with his chin.

Shifting a little in her seat on Cloud's back, Willow pressed back against Lakota. "No," she said, "but I ache in every bone of my body."

"It has been too long since you have done any strenuous traveling, Aiyana." His lips were soft and cool against her ear.

"I still can't believe what happened. Everything took place so fast."

"Do you want to talk about it?"

She described the entire horrible scene, telling him of the senseless killing of old women and men, and of how she had tried to get to Many Feathers. "Is he . . . ?"

"He is unharmed." He gazed deeply into her eyes when she twisted to look up at him. A lazy, sensuous smile came over his face. "You should see yourself, Aiyana; you look just like a wild Indian yourself. But a much prettier one than the rest of us."

Then she remembered. "Kachina . . . how is she?"

"She is back there in the most reliable arms she could be in."

Glancing back to the last horse, Willow smiled when Dark Horse bent over Kachina and kissed her temple with a tenderness out of place with his usual behavior. Dark Horse—Almanzo as she had first known him—was never seen in the company of women for very long. She had had her suspicions about him, never thinking to see him care for another woman after Ellita Tomas had disappointed him. He was always hunting, never remaining in one place for very long.

"You are thinking very hard about something."

Lakota broke into Willow's ruminations. "Can I be a part of it?" he asked, stroking her thigh and causing tingles to run from her belly to her breasts.

"If you keep that up, bright savage, I won't be able to think at all!"

"You sound as if you have recovered swiftly, Aiyana. Now tell me, what were you thinking so hard about after looking back to see your friend safe and sound in Dark Horse's arms?"

"About Dark Horse. I remember him as Almanzo Rankin and how he almost came to marry Ellita Tomas."

Lakota chuckled. "He is still Almanzo Rankin—when he is not in Black Fox's camp or with the Horse Indians. Same as me; I will be Talon Clay when I return to the civilized world."

For now Willow did not want to think about what that would entail—Talon Clay returning to face the wrath of Ashe Brandon. And most certainly "resourceful Ashe" was to find out soon that his brother was only his half-brother—and then all hell was going to break loose!

"I mean," Willow began again, "the manner in which Dark Horse—Almanzo treated his bride-to-be. He almost killed her for keeping secrets from him."

His voice becoming gruff, Lakota said, "I would have wanted to do the same if a woman had lied to me over something so important. She would never see the end of my anger!"

Willow trembled inwardly, hoping never to have cause to lie to Lakota. It would be a dark, terrible thing to face him in the morning. But she had no worry here; she kept nothing from him, nor would she ever. She did not dare!

The campfires in the valley cast their friendly glow on the trees and the moving people. Cottonwoods, pines, and mesquite trees were cast in burnt-orange and goldenrod hues, for the sun was just spotlighting the way as the weary riders came in, and touching the tips of trees, painting them lavender. Teary children slid down off the mounts of the Horse Indians, some running to find their parents, some standing looking lost after all that had happened to them. One such bewildered child began to weep, and Lakota, seeing this, kneed his mount over to where she stood waiting for someone to come get her.

Lakota dismounted and scooped her up into his arms. "Are you looking for your mother, Chay-NOH-ah?" he said her name, which meant White Dove in perfect Indian.

Tadewi and Tall Deer spied their daughter just then, and so did Grandpa Many Feathers. They all came forward to reach for the little Indian girl, all encompassing the suddenly happy child in their warm embraces. Tadewi looked into Lakota's eyes and her gratefulness shone in her own. At first when Lakota had come to the camp Tadewi had not liked him much. She had thought he was just another curious white-eyes, like so many other hunters and gold seekers, and she had thought him to be unfriendly. She had boldly told him there was no gold there, and he had surprised her by saying that Tadewi was the only precious "Sunshine" there, making her blush.

"Here you are, Sunshine," he said now, winking at Tadewi. "Here is *your* gold."

"I am forever indebted to you, Named-Lakota." She

smiled up at Aiyana then, still waiting patiently on the big white horse. "Your wife waits for you. Come to share our meal with us soon—" She glanced around at the tepees just being erected by the women and at the younger men busy cleaning up. "Come when our home is in order. You will be welcome, you and your wife." Tadewi then smiled at White Dove and hugged her as she walked over to where they would erect their new tepee. All of Tall Deer's other wives came rushing to Tadewi, taking turns in hugging the child, and then they all joined Tall Deer's older children.

Heaving a deep sigh, Lakota walked over to lift Willow down from Cloud. Eyeing her husband with much speculation, she pulled his eyes back to her when she touched him on the arm. "You are staring at Tall Deer's harem. Are you wishing you had more than one wife? Am I not enough for you, my savage lover?"

"Enough!" Lakota roared, lifting her off her feet and twirling her around. He came to a stop and chuckled deeply. "Enough?" he repeated, a question this time.

The gold flecks in her eyes sparkled. "What are you trying to say to me, Lakota? Am I enough or not?"

"You, my pretty little Willow flower, are too much." He bent to kiss her lips, while the busy people in the camp pretended not to notice and kept right on working with smiles on their faces. "I can't seem to get enough of you—you!" Then, softly, into her ear he whispered, "Wait until later, when we have our new tepee erected. I'll show you just how much you are, Aiyana."

"We'll see then." Willow walked away from him, leaving Lakota to stare hungrily after her as she went to the spring to wash up. Halfway there, she turned back, her eyes searching for Kachina. She had totally forgotten about Kachina and she wanted to see how her friend was doing.

Kachina was not very well; she was still in a frightened daze. Dark Horse had set her down against a thick bole of a cottonwood. Bewildered, she looked up at Dark Horse again, unable to recognize the kindness in his eyes, that he was a friend, not an enemy. Dark Horse looked down at her, aching to take her in his arms. He wanted very much to soothe away all her fears with tender caresses, to keep her calm and at ease with him.

"Kachina," Dark Horse said with all the pain in his heart he was feeling for the beautiful Shoshoni woman.

She only huddled deeper into herself, thinking she heard this man call to her in unfriendly tones.

"Kachina." Dark Horse knelt down at her side and took her hand. "Trust me and I shall help you all that I can."

From the back of the burned-out tepees Willow watched Dark Horse try to reach Kachina. The Indian girl had suffered much at the hands of the Apaches, and the fine thread that had held Kachina's subconscious nightmares in check had finally snapped. Willow did not know whether she should try to reach Kachina or allow Dark Horse to try and reach her. Then a thought occurred to her and she walked softly to the couple beneath the trees.

"Dark Horse." Willow came to stand beside the man she had once been in awe of. "Let me try. I think Kachina is afraid of all men at this time."

Innate good sense told Dark Horse that the woman knew what she was doing. And he trusted Willow.

Reluctantly, he gave up his vigil and stood back while Willow knelt beside Kachina and took the Indian girl's hand in her smaller one. Several softly spoken words fell on deaf ears at first, and then, slowly, slowly, Kachina began to respond. Her eyes flickered first, then her head came up. She blinked.

"Aiyana . . ." Kachina cried, throwing herself into Willow's arms. "You did not let them get me . . . you are truly my friend!"

Turning away, Dark Horse began to walk slowly back into the camp. It was plain for anyone to see that Kachina was afraid of men—had come to not trust any of them. He would never forget her as she was this day. He had never seen a woman look more beautiful and utterly terrified. He had once cornered a young doe in a tangled thicket and had been unable to bring down the death-stab to end the creature's life. Now Kachina painfully reminded Dark Horse of the doe awaiting the killing stroke of the hunter.

"Dark Horse," Lakota called, seeing his friend just coming out from under the big cottonwoods ringing the immediate camp. He walked up to Dark Horse. "Have you seen my wife? I've been down to the spring where I thought she was going to bathe, but she was not there."

"She is with Kachina."

Lakota started to move away from Dark Horse, saying, "Well, I will just go and talk to her, then. I want to tell her that the tepee . . . what is it?" he asked Dark Horse who had placed a restraining hand on his arm. "Yes?" he said, looking down then up again. He grinned. "Did you have something else to tell me?"

Starting out slowly, Dark Horse finally said, "Kachina is not—" he searched for words—"she is not well."

"Was she hurt, then?" Lakota's eyes wrinkled in concern.

"Time alone will ease the problem that plagues Kachina . . . I think I want her, Lakota. But for now I must tell her that she has nothing to fear from me and I will not touch her unless she herself desires this. I must go slowly and do everything I can to win her trust."

Lakota drew his lips together and blew softly. "This is serious. I think we should go and talk. Would you like that, my friend?"

Nodding, Dark Horse said, "I would very much like that."

Later that evening, while Kachina slept peacefully in the new tepee, Willow went off by herself to the spring to bathe. Submerging herself entirely, she felt the mineral-rich warmth soothe her tired, aching muscles . . . and soon she was engulfed in a sensual daze.

Unaware of anything but the dreamy delight of the midnight-blue water gently massaging her slim body, Willow's eyes closed in pure ecstasy. There was only one thing that was better than this, she thought with a deep purr in her throat. It was not long before Willow realized she was being watched, and she could almost feel the heat of Lakota's gaze searing her wet flesh.

Lakota stood at the water's edge surrounded by the moonlight beaming down. He hunkered down then, to get a better view. Gazing down at Willow, his silvered green eyes darkened with desire. He let his fingers trail in the water as he said, "You have been avoiding me all afternoon."

In a husky-sweet voice Willow answered him. "You have not been around for me to avoid you." She leaned back and arched her throat, soft and velvety like swan's down. Her eyes were dusky and mysterious as they swept over him in a provocative scour.

"I have been around. You just didn't see me for all your occupation with Kachina." He held up a hand when she shot him a look. "Do not get me wrong, though, I think it's wonderful that you take her under your wing—such a beautiful wing, at that."

All of a sudden she was watching him tear off his smoke-stained buckskins and fling them aside impatiently. She watched his bronze face, his sleepy smile as he slipped gracefully and fluidly into the water.

With a low growl of pleasure, he said, "I'm going to get you—Aiyana Willow."

"I am waiting, my savage love." Her laugh emerged huskily. "Come and get me."

Standing before her now, glistening like a bronze god, Lakota cupped her face in his large, lean hands and drew her to him. His lips were crisp and cool; hers were soft and warm. Yet, when they came together it was like a volcanic heat rush fusing them. Arching her body into his, Willow could feel he was already swollen in passion. Again she wondered briefly how he could fit into her with such ease. The only time he had hurt her was when they had first joined, and then when the pressure had built and he had been close to release. She hoped that she would come to fit him like a glove so that every moment could be spent in glorious ecstasy.

Lakota's deep kiss went flaming through her body,

her bare breasts becoming hard and taut, her pelvic area grinding hotly, coiling and uncoiling, unleashing all the passion she had stored away for days since that last unconsumed joining. Just when she thought she would faint from wanting, he lifted her, cupping her buttocks, and, with the thrusting power of his manhood, he entered her swiftly and easily.

"Just ride me now, love," he gently urged, beginning to move her up and down with deliberate slowness, initiating her into the movements.

Willow sank irrevocably into him while his prodigious shaft invaded the secret recesses of her womanhood. He filled her with a pressure that was almost unbearable, stretching her tightness to the utmost. Her nails dug into his shoulders; her head was flung back in the savage moment of rapture.

A low growl of pain came from Lakota. "So impatient, my love? You are going to leave your—mark on me."

A wanton, wild desire had been driving her, and when she realized through the daze of ecstasy that she was scratching him with her nails, she bent forward and kissed the tiny wounds better. Still inside her, Lakota carried her like that to the water's edge. His narrow hips kept up their thrusting while he tumbled her into the grass. They rolled upon the mist-dampened earth, thrusting, arching, straining, loving again and again. Willow felt as if she were lost in a vortex of savagely throbbing lustful pleasures. Every inch of her skin was on fire!

Fluids of love flowed between them, wrapping the lovers in passion's flames. He repeated the rhythmic strokes and a sweet rapture began to torture and claim

Willow, her undulating body crying out for release from love's torment. Then, when she thought she could stand the torment no longer, Lakota drove himself with a deep thrust that snatched her breath away. Ecstasy lifted like rising mist that hovered before the flaming sun, only to be consumed. The climactic end burst into radiance for the briefest time, taking them to dizzying heights of rapture and beyond. His climax was so powerful that Willow cried out at the hard, hot spurts that spurred her on to even greater pleasure, until she shivered in bittersweet delight.

Still hot and hard, Lakota took her with him as he rolled onto his back. Sighing in the greatest contentment a man could know, he gazed up at the millions of twinkling stars, stroking Willow's head while murmuring all the words of love that had sought release from his frenzied mind as he had searched for the Apache camp where Tucker and the Indians had taken her. He had promised himself he would let her know all that was in his heart if and when he found her. This night, he had found the perfect time to pour out his heart.

"Lakota, Lakota, I love you too, with all my heart and soul." She pressed her cheek lovingly against his chest, listening to the powerful thuds of his heart.

"Don't ever leave me," he beseeched her, "stay with me always and forever. If you ever chose to leave me something would die inside and never come to life again. I never thought I would be able to love again. . . ." He slid across the last word, and realizing his mistake, he went deathly pale. There was no taking back what he had said. He waited in breathless anticipation.

"I know you loved another woman before me,

Lakota. We have been through this before, and though you had denied her claim on your heart, I knew beforehand of your attraction to an older woman. Her name was Garnet Haywood Brandon," she said, hating herself for the lie. For Garnet's last name had been Hayes. Her mother. But he must never learn this, she thought, fear of that happening making her feel dizzy and faint. He hated women who kept secrets from him, and she would never tell him that she had one, even though she realized he craved a trusting relationship.

"She used to keep secrets from me, just like my mother Martha kept them." He continued to stroke her back, tangling his long fingers in her hair while his hand went up and down along her spine.

Willow blanched. Now she knew why he craved the trust so badly. The two women he had loved most had lived in a world of their own, never giving, only taking. Garnet had used him cruelly for her own lustful appetites, taking the boy to her bed when he was still wet behind the ears. But Willow could not hate her own mother; she only hated what she had been. She hated to admit that her mother had been a loose-moraled woman, but there was no other word for it.

Far in the back of his mind danced the wanton wisp of a woman. But she seemed to be drifting further away, and each time Lakota made love to his wife, Garnet's image seemed to grow fainter. She was not in his heart; never that. The love he had felt for Garnet had been made of nothing but already disintegrating particles of lust. He had already despised the woman while he still craved her body. There had been little conversation between them; only their bodies had spoken to each other day after day while she taught him all there was to know of becoming an expert lover.

Stroking Lakota's chest, Willow sighed pensively.

"What was that all about?"

"Oh . . . I was just wondering if we will return to Sundance soon. I miss Tanya and baby Sarah. The babe is growing, and I hate to be away so long from her. They are so cute when they are passing from the crawling stage to the walking one. I used to play with her and hold her when Tanya was busy. Now I wonder who is watching her and playing with her in my place."

Lakota smiled down at her head. "Miss Pekoe, maybe . . . say, you should have thought about all this while you were running away with Harlyn Sawyer." His voice dipped lower. "Did you really want to marry that whey-faced dude? Tell me now—did you?"

Rolling over her, Lakota stared down into brown eyes alive with sparkling moondust. Willow laughed nervously, wondering what to tell him. She thought of the first thing that came to her mind—the truth.

"I ran away from Sundance because I had it in mind to get away from you. I—" she began tearfully— "I hated the idea that you—you were in love with a ghost. You almost raped me thinking I was her—Garnet." She took his face in both hands, cupping his taut cheeks. "Never let her come between us, Lakota, promise me this."

The chill of a late-September wind made Lakota shiver for a moment, but he thought afterwards it was more than the night breeze that caused the rampant shivers in his tall frame. Thinking it was a shiver of passion, Willow let the moment pass. He was kissing her again, moving hot and magically inside her again.

Yanking his head down with a handful of hair,

Willow hissed, "Promise me. . . ."

"I promise."

Then the savage mist of ecstasy engulfed them, taking Willow and Lakota up and away.

When Willow awoke, joyously, she saw back over her shoulder the people already beginning to move about the camp. Another tepee was being erected, and she wondered who this one was for. The tepee was actually very easy to assemble, and two women could erect one within an hour. Feeling warm and pleasant beneath the buffalo robe, Willow watched with chin in hands while the Kiowa women bound their three main tepee poles with rawhide toward the tips and raised the tripod, adding extra poles to the circular framework. They tied the poles again at the tips, hoisted the heavy fitted cover of buffalo hide with a final pole, and unfolded it around the framework to a beautiful cone. Willow noticed that this tepee was very large, decorated with religious symbols and pictures commemorating a warrior's deeds. The central figure in the hide was painted black and resembled a fox. All the other hide-covered tepees were the plain tan color of the buffalo from which they were fashioned, blackened at the top from smoke.

"Fox," Willow said to herself. Lakota stirred and she said, loud this time, "Black Fox!"

"Wha . . . ?" Lakota blinked, looking down at the warm robe and wondering when Willow had gone off to fetch it during the night. When he had fallen asleep, she had been there wrapped in his arms. "Did you say Black Fox? Why did you say Black Fox?" He blinked up at her sleepily. "Chief Black Fox?" He sat up now. "He is here?"

The buffalo robe slipped down over Lakota's lean, gorgeous form, and two maidens passing on their way to the spring giggled behind their hands nervously. When Dark Horse appeared with a sheepish look on his darkly handsome face, Willow and Lakota exchanged looks.

"Did you cover us up?" Lakota asked Willow.

"No. I thought you covered us up." Hastily she looked to Dark Horse and then back to her husband. "You didn't cover us up?"

"No." Lakota reached for his buckskin shirt and pants. "But I think I know who did."

Grinning hugely, Dark Horse chuckled. "You two are nature lovers, I presume?"

"Oh no!" Willow dived beneath the buffalo robe, taking her clothes with her. Muffled sounds of embarrassment filtered through the hide while Willow tried to clothe herself under it. When she emerged, looking like a small wildcat, Lakota and Dark Horse began to laugh. "What is it?" She looked down at herself.

Willow was rattled. Both her blouse and her skirt were inside out. Then her eyes narrowed mischievously as she studied Lakota. "I would not laugh if I were you, Named-Lakota." Her voice was a happy singsong as she stood and brushed grass off her clothes, then cocked her hands on her hips. "Stand up, smart aleck!"

Shrugging as he stood, unable to see what all her persnicketiness was about, Lakota looked down. He still failed to see what was so amusing. Now Dark Horse was laughing, not at Willow but with her.

"Will you two cut that out," Lakota demanded, "and tell me what is wrong with the way I look?"

Sidling up to Lakota, Willow went around in back and pinched Lakota in the derriere, playfully stating, "You better do up your fly, bright savage." Then she sashayed to the woodpile where Kachina was outside watching them, a faint smile on her lips.

After checking himself out fully, Lakota stood with hands on hips, staring at the sky and shaking his head. "Bright savage." He laughed at the facetious endearment. "I'll know better next time than to laugh at my wife."

"She took the buffalo robe," Dark Horse reminded him. "What will you do now? Walk through the village like that?"

"Why not? She did it."

"So she did." Dark Horse grinned again, showing a mouthful of straight, white teeth. He walked over to where Lakota stood, and stepping behind him he said, "Should I do up your fly for you?"

"No. I'll just stand here and catch a cold. That is where my head is, anyway." He shook his head and began laughing very loud. "Willow, Willow, when will she ever stop her harassment of my splendid male form. Damn—" he slipped his pants down, and, right before all the giggling maidens, he reversed them and stepped in the proper side— "but I love that woman!"

Chapter Seventeen

Finally they could hear Chief Black Fox and his party nearing the village, with a trembling wave of hoofbeats on the earth. The Indian scout who had gone out to meet them returned to say they were bringing in two hundred horses he and his warriors had caught in the mountains.

Women began to go out and scour the area for driftwood. A rich smell of food cooking began to permeate the valley. Cooking pots steamed; broiling meat dripped buffalo fat onto dung-coals. The drummers were bringing out their painted drums and setting them up while some brought out rattles made of gourds or stiffened hides, and even dried buffalo scrotums would swish to the measure of the drums. This night there would be much feasting and dancing, ceremony and giftgiving.

White Dove had just stopped by to show Willow her new doll, made of stuffed deerskin. She chattered away in a mixture of Indian and English, then went skipping on her merry way to join the children running squealing among the tepees. Willow paused a little longer outside the tepee, watching the happy youngsters chasing each other while the older boys pretended they were hunting, attacking grasshoppers and dragonflies with pint-sized spears.

It was quite a spectacle when Chief Black Fox rode into the village with his family. He sat his spotted horse straight and proud. His face was finely chiseled, with high cheekbones, a long, straight pointed nose with flaring nostrils, small, close-set eyes, and a very sensuous mouth. His blue-black hair was parted in the middle and atop his head sat a fox's tail, dyed black all over, and from beneath the tail a long braid hung down his back. Colorful beads and dyed thongs of leather were tied about the headpiece and left to trail along his head. Another fox fur hung about his neck, this one silver and black. His skin was the darkest bronze Willow had ever seen, and she had to admit he was a quite attractive and powerful figure.

"This is Chief Black Fox?" Kachina stepped from the tepee she shared with Willow—for the time being.

"I believe he is the reason for all the excitement the past few days." Willow smiled. "He must be the chief. I have never before seen such a strong, handsome face."

"I have." Kachina smiled back at Willow. "My mother."

Willow gasped. "Your . . . mother?"

"It is so. She was half-breed. When she was only twelve she was given to a man in marriage. My father was a subchief of the Shoshoni. They were all killed, even my brothers and sisters, when the Apaches attacked our village. The bad Apaches I speak of had wandered far from their own territory to pillage and kill."

"I hope they do not return." Willow realized that

Kachina was finding it easier to talk about her fears the last few days. "Nightwalker says now that Chief Black Fox has returned there will be a council to decide what to do about the attack they made here and to prepare for another if one should come. Nightwalker has said that he hopes Black Fox will want to eliminate the Ipa'Nde altogether."

"I am all for this." Kachina giggled, feeling her old self again now that Dark Horse, Lakota, and Willow had been so helpful in drawing her from her pit of fears. "Listen to me, I am sounding more like you every day, and you are beginning to sound like a real squaw."

"I really do feel like a savage bride at times!" Willow laughed. She put her arm about Kachina, squeezed her waist, then went to find her husband.

As evening came on, the younger maidens replenished the wood on their fires to make light for eating and dancing. The sounds of merriment carried on the night air, drawing everyone out of their tepees to join in the celebration. The chief, seated in the midst of all, began the feast by picking up a plate of buffalo meat his wife, Morning Dove, had set before him. After selecting the choicest pieces he handed the plate to the next in line, Nightwalker, and then Black Fox's son, Little Fox.

Seated beside her husband, Willow licked her fingers clean of the buffalo grease. Her lips were shiny and slick, and seated where they were at the back of the circle, in dark flickering firelight, Lakota leaned close to her and kissed her mouth, licking at the pink bud of her upper lip. Like the newlyweds that they were, they fed each other from the one platter balanced upon Lakota's knees.

"Happy?" Lakota asked, gazing into the brown eyes flecked with gold.

"You have made me very happy, bright savage."

He chuckled, asking, "Why do you call me bright savage? Do I shine or something?"

"Well . . ." she said, studying a choice piece of meat, "you are more fair than the others . . . your body is not as bronze, and you are very smart to have picked me for your squaw."

"Oh?" He wiped the corner of her mouth clean with the tip of his finger. "Why is it that I am smart?"

She leaned against him and splayed her fingers across his bare chest. "You chose a woman who loves you very much. Would you want anything less in a woman?"

Looking deeply into her eyes, he said low, "She must love me with all her heart and soul. She must be willing to die for me. For I would die for her if I had to."

"You have made no secret of your feelings." The expression in his eyes snatched her breath away . . . it was so . . . loving. "But would you really die for me if you had to?"

"You are the only woman who holds my heart, and I will cherish you forever. Does that sound like a man who would do anything for his love?"

As she could not bring herself to speak in this exquisite moment, Willow only nodded mutely. Gazing down at his beautiful bride, Lakota knew a moment of worry. He was painfully aware that she was in danger now that Carl Tucker was once again in their life. He had vowed last year to kill the man if he wasn't dead already, but hide nor hair of him had not been reported by any of Sundance's men; it was as if Tucker had vanished from the earth's face. Now he was back, and he was up to his old tricks. Why, he wondered, did Tucker want Tanya or her sister so badly? What was on Tucker's mind? He would have to do some hunting with Dark Horse again, only this time they would be hunting for Tucker.

Seated on the ground with Pepita on one side and Kachina on the other, Dark Horse was thinking his own thoughts about Carl Tucker. He not only worried over Willow but now Kachina. The beautiful Shoshoni had gotten into his blood, but all of a sudden she was shying away from any contact with men, especially those seeking to court her. How easy it would be to take advantage of her helplessness, he thought. She was here as a captive, but Lakota did not hold her as such. He himself could press his case, but he felt she was not ready for courtship yet. All it would take from her would be a look, a gesture, a spoken word, and he would sweep Kachina into his arms and comfort her in the manner she needed to be comforted. He would show her the sweetness of love, of giving without fear. He was eager, and excitement surged through him.

"You are not eating," Kachina said, breaking the long silence between them. The only one near enough to be heard by them was Pepita, keeping up a string of lively chatter in broken English. Malina sat next to Kachina, saying nothing. She had not been the same ever since her daughter had been taken captive and returned deflowered by the Apaches.

"Maybe he is not hungry," Pepita said, speaking for Dark Horse. Pepita had come out of her trauma unscarred and no memory of the degrading shame remained to haunt her as it had Kachina. In fact, she had boasted to her mother of the handsome warriors that had taken her to their mats and she said she enjoyed every moment because she had not struggled.

Malina was seriously thinking of setting up her daughter in her own tepee in the village; and everyone knew what that meant. The braves would be free to come and go as they wished in Pepita's tepee.

Now Pepita leaned heavily upon Dark Horse's arm, and her words were soft, for his ears only. She told him what her mother was planning to do, and she asked him: "Would you come to Pepita's tepee? It would be a pleasure to service you, Dark Horse."

Disgust for Pepita's kind leaped into Dark Horse's onyx eyes, and he was painfully reminded of another woman just then. Ellita Tomas came to mind, the woman who had almost become his bride. Ellita had allowed herself to be bedded before their wedding day, and he, Almanzo, had gone into a rage. He had trusted her, believed her to be pure and untouched by man. She had been deceiving him all along, crawling into bed with another while his heart beat for her and his loins burned to be joined with the beautiful woman who was to become his bride.

"What is wrong?" Pepita put on a pout.

Kachina chose that moment to look down just when Pepita's hand came to rest on Dark Horse's thigh. Acutely aware of distress in the area of her throat and chest, Kachina tore her eyes from that spot and looked elsewhere. She watched the impressive chief and his lovely wife for a time, but found her gaze being drawn back to that part of Dark Horse's person. Only minutes had passed since Dark Horse had plucked Pepita's questing fingers from his thigh, but he did not miss where Kachina's curious gaze came to rest now. When she looked up into his face, her eyes were melting.

This was the signal Dark Horse had been longing for and waiting for. He lowered his head to say something in Kachina's ear.

"The maidens are just beginning their dance. It is proper to leave the circle now." He saw as he spoke that Kachina's pupils were very large, the deep blue in them standing out like a moonlit pond. "Will you walk with me?"

Shivering inside, Kachina nodded. Dark Horse helped her to her feet and Kachina rose with a pounding heart. Looking at him now as she was, Dark Horse was sorely reminded of that cornered doe. Lifting a hand to cup her cheek, he lowered his head and spoke softly, reassuringly.

"Hear me, Kachina, and understand well, I will not do anything you do not want me to."

In a voice so low and soft, she returned, "I know you will not, Dark Horse, for I trust you with all my heart. You and Lakota and Willow have become good friends to me. I do not believe you would hurt me after you have been good medicine for my soul. You would be what the whites call an Indian giver, and you are not this, I know."

"Your words are kind and I take them to my heart, Kachina. Come, we will walk now while the moon is climbing in the sky. I have a desire to see you laugh with the moon on your face and the stars in your hair."

Kachina stepped into the grass beyond the edge of the camp and ducked under the low-swooping branch of a cottonwood. She was walking before him and her laughter tinkled back to him. "You are a poet, Dark

Horse, with your pretty words. Are they meant to flatter, perhaps?"

Signal number two. Dark Horse watched her step over a fallen branch with agile grace and felt his heart pick up speed.

Pausing beneath the umbrella of heavily sagging branches, Kachina waited breathlessly for Dark Horse to come to her. Her heart was in such a turmoil she could hardly breathe normally. She seemed to be holding her breath then as she felt him approach, each soft step he took seeming to reach up inside of her and yank at something.

For several minutes, Dark Horse stood looking down at her, trying to see her face in the moonlight to read her mood. She had given him shy, indirect signals—but signals, nonetheless. He was vividly aware of her as a woman and of his own tumultuous desire. He knew that to win Kachina's trust he would have to proceed with caution and care.

"I can see you now," he said with a smile in his deep voice. "The moon is on your face—move a little more to the left. There, stay right there."

Her laugh was gentle. "I believe Dark Horse likes the moon."

"Only when a certain maiden is beneath it." He realized his mistake and hoped she had not heard his soft intake of breath.

"It would be nice if that word still applied to Kachina," she said with painful regret in her voice. "You have made a mistake in your words, Dark Horse, but I do not wither because of it. I have already forgotten. I liked your words, and I wish they truly were meant for me."

Tilting her chin up, Dark Horse gazed into the moon-glazed eyes. "Kachina," he caressed her name with his tongue, "you are a maiden to me still, and I tell you I will never have the intention of hurting you." His throat clenched before he went on. "You must trust in this."

Softly as a child, Kachina said, "I believe you. I—I only wish I was good enough for you, Dark Horse, b-because I think you like me." She swallowed hard. "You do . . . like me a little?"

His eyes darkened with anger. "Good enough!" He took her by the shoulders and shook her gently. "It is I who should be saying this to you!"

Her eyes became alarmingly round. "You?" She shook her head. "But I do not understand."

Letting her go, Dark Horse spun away and went to lean against the massive bole of the cottonwood. His voice was muffled as he spoke over his shoulder. "Kachina, Kachina, your heart is good and pure as gold. Mine is black and soiled. You do not know what I have done in my lifetime."

Kachina stepped closer. "You are not bad, Dark Horse. You are kind and gentle and . . . you brought me back to life."

Still he did not face her. "Aiyana Willow did that."

With gentle and soothing hands, she slowly massaged his shoulder. "It was you who rescued me."

"You are wrong. It was Lakota."

"But you were there right outside to take me in your arms and carry me to your warrior horse."

He looked along her arm. "How did you know that?"

"Willow has told me. She watched how you carried me in your arms with such care, as if you had taken up a child. The other warriors were gathering the children while you had eyes only for me."

He snorted. "That is selfish."

She laughed. "But you were thinking of me." Her hand splayed over his back muscles. "Why do you think of me so much, Dark Horse?"

Now Dark Horse spun about and drew Kachina to him, and Kachina came up against him so hard that she felt that heated, by now familiar shape of impassioned man. She reacted violently, pushing at him with balled fists.

"Hush, Kachina," he crooned. "Be still, my heart. I only want to hold you."

"B-But not so close."

He pulled back and Kachina at once felt the cold emptiness that he left her in. Dark Horse felt it too, and he stared down at Kachina, his heart in his eyes.

"It is lonely without you in my arms," he said with profound feeling.

"I know. It is lonely without you . . . too, Dark Horse."

He stared down at a triangle of moonlight lying across her chest. "I would make love to you, Kachina, if only you were not so afraid, and if only you would be my—wife."

Tears threatened to choke out her voice as she whispered, "You would want Kachina to be your wife after . . . after she has been dirtied by so . . . many hands and m-men's bodies?"

He reached out and grabbed her, his fingers biting into her shoulders. "I do not care how many have had you," he hissed deeply. "After you become mine, no one shall ever dare touch Kachina again!"

"You do mean this." She stood there aghast at his declaration. Staring into nothingness, she placed her back to Dark Horse. "I cannot do this thing to you, Dark Horse. You will forever be sorry that you took to wife a soiled woman."

He gripped her from behind, grinding out between his lips, "I told you, Kachina, it is I who am not worthy in your eyes. I have discovered much about myself this past year. I would have married once . . . she decieved me and bedded with another before we were to be married. Word came to me by a friend . . . not from her own lips. But I did not give her a chance to speak her heart, I cast her aside on the ground in front of everyone gathered there to see us wed. She was shamed and degraded before all her friends. It was bad of me to treat her so unkindly. Do you not see, Kachina?" He pulled her around to face him.

Every word had pierced her to her very soul and she stared at him in disbelief. "If you would not have this woman because of one indiscretion, how can you say you want Kachina who has been taken by so many that she should not be alive this day?"

Dark Horse cursed her and reached out to slap her cheek, but it was only the kind of slap that stung rather than hurt with a painful throbbing. Coming to her senses and realizing that Dark Horse meant every word he said, Kachina reached out and took that same hand that had slapped her, and laying it on her face, she caressed it with her cheek.

Stepping closer, Dark Horse laid his cheek on the other side of her face, so near her lips. A slight turn brought Kachina's lips into the hard curve of his own. His lips softened and slowly, slowly, closed over hers in the gentlest kiss imaginable. Pulling her against his chest, Dark Horse kissed Kachina with a soft pressure that sent shock waves coursing through her body. She had never known the gentle kiss of a lover, for Kachina had never been kissed before. The only kind of kiss she had ever experienced had been a cruel slanting of wet lips, hard bites, and tongues thrusting until she thought she would choke from the saliva dripping into her mouth.

Kachina had never known desire before, either. It swept through her now like tidal waves. Her heart pounded like a fast drum against an even stronger drum. Her knees went weak. There were stars not only in the sky but behind her eyes. She broke away before embarrassing herself by swooning in his arms.

"Dark Horse!" Kachina gasped. "You leave me no breath." Shyly she looked down at the ground. "I feel a little weak."

"I feel *very* weak," Dark Horse confessed. He lifted her chin, murmuring, "I want you so badly that I hurt, Kachina. I have never known such desire for a woman. Will you be mine?"

"D-Do you love me?"

He pulled her into the warm, secure circle of his arms. "Do you feel my heart pound?" he asked her.

"Yes."

"Do you feel . . ."

She looked up at him. "Dark Horse? What?"

"I would not ask you the next question in my mind, Kachina."

"Let there be no secrets between us, please?"

"Do you feel my . . . desire?"

Shyly Kachina slid her hand down his side and

flattened her palm against him, saying, "Yes, I feel it."

"Kachina," he rasped, pushing against her fingers spreading over him. "Kachina . . . I want you. Do not be afraid, my love, I will not hurt you. Please, Kachina." With his hands on her shoulders he urged her to the earth with him. "Let me love you."

Her head came to rest against his shoulder. "The others will see us here," she said.

"No one comes this way, Kachina, not this night." He smiled into her hair, adding, "I saw Lakota and Aiyana Willow quickly making their way to their tepee . . . I think they would like to be alone for a time."

"I have been a bother to Aiyana and Named-Lakota when they should have been alone together as man and wife."

"Soon, my heart, you will share a tepee with me." He tipped her chin up. "I will wait to love you until that time if that is how you wish it to be. Just say the word and your word is my command."

"I truly want what is happening between us this night, Dark Horse. Come," she said, standing and reaching for his hand. "Come with me to the tall grass beyond."

This was all Dark Horse needed to hear from Kachina's lips. As he followed her lead he felt jubilant, and a surge of tenderness went through him. He trembled at the force of his emotion. He caught up and spun her about to face him. With his hand in hers, he spoke carefully.

"Kachina, if we had met at another time and another place I would have courted you properly and brought the bride gift to your father." When she would have protested, he shushed her with a finger. "You did not listen, Kachina, I said another time. You would have been a maiden and I would have courted you properly and with the approval of your family. With full observance of the customs and what is proper in your village, we would have become man and wife. You and I, Kachina—" he stroked her velvety cheek— "we know that it is not within the realm of possibility for us now."

"I know, Dark Horse," she said in a near-whisper. "I know you understand what is going through my mind. You are a very wise warrior and very kind. I know that you believe a good woman is meant to be pure and—and—" She did not know what she was trying to say to him.

He pulled her close to him. "You are a good woman and your heart is as gold, Kachina. Never believe otherwise, never believe that those savages stole from you your heart and soul. They might have taken your body, but I believe they never touched any other part of you."

Heavily she leaned against him, murmuring, "Oh, why did we not meet long ago, my love? It saddens me to know that others have come before you."

He stroked her hair that was blacker than midnight, and silkier than the finest silk itself. "But look, Kachina, look at the good that has come from the bad. If the Apaches had not taken you captive, you and I might never have met. I know this is a terrible thing to say, but sometimes we must suffer the pain of night before the final joy that comes in the morning."

"Press your lips to mine again?" Kachina wound slim, coppery arms about Dark Horse's neck, her fingers sinking into the fattest part of the black braid that hung down his back like a thick arrow.

With infinite tenderness, Dark Horse kissed her full, moist mouth long and breathlessly. When she began to shiver in her inadequacy he murmured against her cheek, telling her what he would have her do. Stepping back, Kachina reached down and lifted the hem of her doeskin tunic, drawing it up over her head. When she stood naked before him, taking her own braid in her hands to unplait it then shaking the wild black cloud free around her, only then did Dark Horse remove his own clothes. He knew that her body would have been lovely to look upon, but he had never dreamed she would be this exquisite.

Before melting with her to the grass, Dark Horse put his fist to his chest, near his heart, then with hand extended he opened his palm to her. Taking the extended hand, Kachina pressed it over her own heart. In love's oldest primitive ritual, they sank to the grass with Kachina stretched out on her back, Dark Horse above her. His onyx eyes delved into the midnight-blue of hers, while his hand gently smoothed her hip as he nestled himself slowly against her thighs. He told her gently that what was to happen between them would be natural and a thing of beauty. There would be no pain, only pleasure.

"You must believe this, Kachina."

"You have my trust. . . ."

"Completely? You will not question anything that I might do?"

"Nothing."

"And withhold nothing from me, Kachina. I would have you as if you had become my wife in every way.

Without the spoken words, very soon our love shall make us like man and wife, but if anything displeases you or makes you frightened I would know this at once." He touched her gently between the thighs. "I would . . . kiss you here . . . I want this to be perfect fulfillment for you."

Mildly shocked yet tingling with anticipation, Kachina nodded mutely. He kissed her thoroughly on the lips, her throat, then moved to the straining peaks of nipples. The warm wetness of his tongue bathing her nipples, first one then the other, made Kachina arch as a gasp of primitive delight escaped her. She had meant to lie still and allow her mind to stand back while he pleasured her. But she found that to hold back the smallest whimper would be unfair; now she wanted to scream for the sweet ache that was spreading through her like wildfire.

"Make all the noise you want, Kachina," Dark Horse said, feeling triumphant, "no one will hear."

While he said this his hand was smoothing the prominent section of her belly, his fingers questing into the silken black hair that grew over her mound. Discovering her tiny pearl, he moved with rhythmic strokes, then sank further into the velvety folds of her. He gazed tenderly into her eyes, delighted at the blue sparks of fire emanating from their depths. His own desire grew, and he became so hot and hard he feared his throbbing length might hurt her. He determined to go easy on her.

Dark Horse slid lower in the grass, while his hands spread her legs wide apart. For a moment Kachina felt embarrassed and tried to close her legs against him. But when he laid his cheek so tenderly against her thigh and flicked her lightly with the tip of his tongue, her thighs automatically opened for him again. Swift, wet strokes drove her mindless as he found her most sensitive point. He arched her hips upward, and when she was trembling with her first release, Dark Horse moved up over her and entered her with ease while she was yet in the tumblings and grindings of pure ecstasy. At the height of her greatest pleasure, Dark Horse penetrated with his whole shaft and filled her while she opened and closed about him like satiny folds of a petal caressing him. When she swooned, Dark Horse slowed his strokes until her consciousness returned. Now her hands reached out to clutch his back, urging him to move faster. When it began to happen to her again, Dark Horse joined her, and together they experienced the explosion of ecstasy's joy. They climbed rapture's peak and took off soaring, gazing at the glory of love's heaven before falling side by side into the cottony clouds of golden afterglow.

Pepita moved on silent feet through the grass toward the grove of cottonwoods. She had seen all that she wanted to see. Dark Horse had chosen the beautiful Kachina over Pepita. First Named-Lakota and now Dark Horse. Pepita had once been timid and shy; but no longer. She would win one of these magnificent warriors for her own. A mischievous smile touched her full mouth, lifting her wide cheeks, settling her dark brown eyes into a malicious sparkle. Pepita just might have both of them, one dark, one fair. One for each night—and maybe altogether. First she would have to do some planning. Where was Jim Bluecoat? He would help Pepita. He did not like Lakota, and he seemed to have an eye for Lakota's woman, Aiyana. When Jim Bluecoat returned she was going to summon his aid, for she was going to need all the help she could get.

After several hours of wonderful ecstasy in Lakota's arms, Willow turned to her husband with a worried look. A faint smile touched Lakota's fully satiated lips.

"Worried about Kachina?" He moved over her, looming above her huge and dark in ember-glow. She was so soft and delicate snuggled against him, pliant in the aftermath of their lovemaking. They had soared to rapturous heights, once, twice, three times.

"Yes. She left the circle of firelight just as the dancing began."

Now Willow smiled as she remembered Kachina and Dark Horse going off together. "They have been gone an awfully long time. Do you think she's all right?"

Lakota hummed for a second, then said, "I think she is enjoying herself."

"I hope Dark Horse does not frighten Kachina. She has become very skittish around men, and Dark Horse is especially imposing. He is so much a—man."

"What does that make me, then?" Lakota swept her naked body with an ardent eye, then kissed one rosy peak.

"You and Dark Horse are much alike. You are both such . . . such—masculine creatures."

Rising off the soft furs and hides, Willow pushed at Lakota's shoulders. Then she reached down, causing Lakota's huge body to quake with immeasurable joy at her touch. Willow was amazed at finding him still so hard . . . and long . . . and thick.

"Oh . . . you are so—"

As she began to remove her hand Lakota caught her wrist and held it. "The time for modesty has passed, my love." He tutored her movements, showing her best how to please him.

When she was just beginning to enjoy the power she had over him, able to stir him to such prodigious size, he pulled out of her hand. She stared down at the angry, throbbing length, amazed that her small hand could bring about such pleasing results.

"Why did you pull away?" she asked Lakota. "I was just beginning to enjoy pleasuring you. I didn't want to stop."

His smile was disarming, stealing every last vestige of power from her limbs. "I don't think you would have liked the surprise that comes with this form of pleasuring your husband—not yet anyway. We are too recently wed."

Thinking for a moment with bent head, Willow finally caught on and brightly said, "Oh . . . well then, if you don't think I am a big enough girl."

Gripping her shoulders, he whispered as if someone stood just outside the tepee flap eavesdropping, "You are a lady now, my wife, and good ladies don't always go in for such play, at least not to the end results." His eyes darkened suddenly. "Whores get paid for that, Willow. They even use their mouths. Married ladies want their husbands to be inside them at such a time."

"Huh!" she sniffed. "You said yourself 'We are too recently wed.' What do you mean then, bright savage?"

He had said the wrong thing; he knew it now.

"Oh . . . so you'd rather have a whore pleasure you." Springing up from the mats, she glared down at him.

He sighed. "I never said . . . that."

"Did you ever pay a whore?"

"Willow, let's not get into this . . . you know what my past has been. If you want a surprise, I will give you one." He smiled. "But I would much rather be inside you when the fireworks go off."

Pulling her soft tunic over her head, Willow jerked the thing down and stepped into her moccasins. Leaning on one elbow while surveying her brusque motions amusedly, Lakota asked where she thought she was going.

"To the spring—to wash."

"Oh no, you don't." He was up on his feet in an instant. "You might just encounter some lust-crazed Apaches, or you might step on Dark Horse and Kachina . . . I don't think they would appreciate your coming upon them and surprising the hell out of them."

Unconscious of her actions, only knowing how angry and jealous she was, Willow cocked her hip and tossed the long yellow wave over the right side of her eye. His green eyes narrowed dangerously at the same moment the image of Garnet came to Lakota's mind.

"You look just like a slut when you pose like that, you know," he ground out, wanting to hurt her for some reason he could not understand himself. Just that she sorely reminded him of another woman just now.

"A . . . what?"

Spitfire angry, Willow slipped off one moccasin and threw it smack into his face. When she bent down to remove the other moccasin, intending to use it as the second missile, Lakota gathered up his clothes and quit the tepee before Willow knew what was happening. The silken fire of his hair was the last thing she saw in flight out the tepee flap.

Willow faced the embers glowing in the meager pile of wood. She could put some more wood on. She could go to bed . . . now that she was alone. She and Lakota had exchanged the fiery darts of their first argument. Alone now, she sank onto the soft, fluffy bed of animal hides and furs. Her tears glistened in the dark, glossy fur. She lay her head down. Tears turned to soft sniffles. She closed her eyes. She slept.

Chapter Eighteen

Beneath a dark moon Lakota leapt onto a pinto stallion, and for the first time spurred the horse brutally. He quit the camp like an arrow shot from a taut-strung bow.

Harshly the wind slapped his enraged face, and his vision blurred. He eased up on his mount and headed east after climbing from the valley, putting the spirited pinto to a long, easy lope. The Indian mustang moved smoothly across the league-wide basin. Now Lakota was traveling fast over the weird moonlit country, and the miles were put swiftly behind him.

Halting his thunder-breathing mustang, Lakota looked back the way he had come. Behind him all was dark; he could only make out the high spots that the moon bathed eerily in silver glitter. His strong hands gripped the mustang's coarse black mane; the horse was restless and wanted action. His bare feet spurred the horse, and together they flew, making short work of the miles that spread before them.

Lakota was trying hard to erase Willow and her hurt

expression from his mind. An ache was deep inside him, one he could not name. In the past he could have put the ache down to lust for a woman—any woman. When Willow had come along he had not wanted other women, and he had finally realized he desired Willow as he had never wanted any woman before in his life. All his dreams and wonderings about her had been vague though, some sweet, but mostly questioning. Voices had clamored from the past, as they did now, clamoring for a hold in the unknown depths of his soul. So, what the hell . . . how could he blame Willow for that loose-moraled woman's behavior just because Willow happened to be the woman's spitting image at times? Why did he suddenly feel he must be merciless to the girl who had roused this tumult in his heart? Why did he want to avenge himself upon the innocent one because of his frustration?

Here Lakota frowned—or was Willow all that innocent? Was there something she was hiding from him? Why did he get the feeling at times that she was keeping a secret?

Willow had watched him often back at Sundance with those big staring eyes. Pretty eyes. Nice, soft figure. She had caused him to become so hot and frustrated, sometimes he had felt like dragging her into the stable and having his way with her.

A sudden, hot anger at himself, at Willow, at Garnet, possessed Lakota. Wheeling the spotted mustang with a bound, Lakota plunged into the shadows and moonlight, a beautiful wild sight in the savagery of the land. The mustang's black mane whipped back, and Lakota's own hair was silhouetted like a conquering banner across the Comanche moon.

The long fringe of Willow's doeskin skirt made a gentle *whoosh* as she walked to the spring. After donning the skirt and blouse, she had brushed her unbound hair, then braided it into one long plait down her back. Her hair was so long now that it brushed below her buttocks, well over four feet long. A white leather headband, narrow with trailing ends, completed her outfit.

Morning breezes had been ruffling the flap of her tepee when she awoke to find herself alone on her soft bed. Sitting up, she had wondered how long it would be before Lakota came. When he still had not shown up by the time she was dressed for the day, Willow had really begun to worry. She had to fight against a new fear, the distressing thought that she might have really angered him this time. But what had she done that was so bad? He had said she looked like a slut. Willow knew there had never been another soul who had thought, much less said, such things about her.

The sounds of the camp were behind her now. When she halted before the inviting blue pool, Willow felt a dart of longing pierce her soul. They had made love for the first time here. Remembering the strength and hardness of his long, lean body, gleaming bronze in the moon's rays, she began to shiver and a low moan broke from her.

Lakota, Lakota, what horrible thing stands between us?

From the chamois pouch she always wore concealed

on her person, Willow lifted out the portrait locket. Opening its tiny catch, she found Garnet Hayes Brandon staring provocatively out at her from the heart-shaped prison of gold. Staring so intently at the ghost who was her rival for her husband's love, Willow did not hear the soft whoosh of deerskin as Malina crept up on her and hid behind the brush.

"Are you the cause of all my heartache, Mother?" Willow said, holding the locket up and away from her. "When will you release your evil hold on Talon Clay Brandon, my husband Lakota?"

Her breath catching softly in her throat, Malina stared covetously at the lovely bit of gold fashioned in a heart shape. Her eyes sparkled with greed. There was a painting in this precious trinket . . . and Malina could hear the strange speech the yellow-hair made to it, calling the picture Mother. Malina must have this little treasure. She could entreat Pepita to be a good girl with such a gift as this.

While Malina continued to watch the girl studying the pretty locket, she began to devise plans of how she could snatch the thing from Aiyana. It must be done carefully, for she would not want to incur Lakota's wrath. He had become a well-liked figure in Black Fox's village. Strange, when she could not sleep last night for worrying about Pepita's future, she had stepped outside her tepee and seen Lakota pulling on his shirt and heading toward the nearest corral, where the most troublesome horses were kept.

Malina watched Aiyana with the locket until her envious desire devoured her. How was she going to get her hands on that pretty piece? Even if she did, how could Pepita wear it without drawing attention to the stunning heart? The chain on which it hung was so fine that at first Malina thought there was some magical force that suspended the locket well below Aiyana's lifted hand. Then she had seen the delicate chain that held the heart as the sun found the valley and gave the thing glittering substance.

Gold! Malina thought. The precious metal that made men go loco and kill each other to obtain it. She knew where there was such a cave that grew this precious gold. It was far from here. Badman's Cave. She had seen it once when she was a little girl traveling with her Mexican family, long before the Kiowas had captured her. Her husband had been slain months before by Apaches, but her precious Pepita had lived. Her Indian husband, Deer Path, had died only weeks before Named-Lakota and all the new ones had come to stay. She had never known the lasting love of a man, not even Deer Path's. The old Indian had only used Malina and her daughter for work. His first wife, Wolf-Eyes-Woman, was Malina's enemy even now.

When Malina could not see what Lakota's bride was doing with the precious locket anymore, she crept to the next group of bushes nearest Aiyana.

What happened next caused Malina's dark eyes to go round, her mouth to sag open wide. The beautiful locket was sailing in the air, catching the sun, shining dully, up, up, suspended against the lavender-gold morning sky for a fraction of a breath before falling, falling, the heart first, then the chain, as Malina watched its diving descent into the blue pool. Mesmerized, Malina stared at the water's tiny ripples moving out from the exact spot where the locket had gone in.

As she watched Willow turn and walk away, Malina marked the spot well in her mind. In a very few minutes she knew she would retrieve the shiny object and have it for her daughter. When Malina knew she was alone, she waded out into the water, looking somewhat like a buffalo cooling itself off. Now she slid down, breaking the surface of the water, disappearing from sight.

Within a few moments she rose with her arms stretched ever upward, the locket dangling from her fingers. Her hair was plastered wetly to her skull. Her deerskin tunic clung heavily to her thick frame. On her face was a triumphant smile as she began to leave the water and head for her tepee, the locket clutched tightly in her large hand.

All that next week during her estrangement from her husband, Willow worked alongside Kachina and the women of the camp to keep her mind off her problems. They gathered fruits and nuts and wild vegetables, they prepared the pemmican constantly, sewed hides, and dug fall roots with sharpened sticks. The women of the camp who fashioned the most intricate designs on clothing or prepared the greatest number of hides gained the same prestige among her peers as a warrior who performed bravely in battle.

One beautiful night when the moon was a huge yellow chunk above the valley, Willow could not stand her restless frustration any longer and quit the tepee's confinement. No one was there to ask where she was going. Kachina was off with Dark Horse somewhere, visiting with the younger Indians in one of the lodges set up for games and entertainment that night.

On her way to the rope-corral where Istas was kept, Willow considered her free access to the valley. She could escape, if she had it in mind, and return to Sundance. But Sundance was a long way from Black Fox's camp, several hundred miles or more. Harlyn Sawyer had recovered from wounds suffered the day of the Apache attack. Willow had been shamed to discover upon returning that Sawyer had pretended death until the Apaches had departed with their captives. He was recovering fast, and ate just about everything she prepared and brought to him where he had been moved to—outside Little Coyote's tepee. Jim Bluecoat was not welcome in Black Fox's camp. He was a traitor, and the Indians would kill him on sight.

Willow had learned to ride without a saddle, only an Indian blanket between her and the horse's back. She bent low now over Istas's back and urged the fine mare into a run; soon they were flying across the valley floor. This day she had chosen to leave her hair hang loose, and it flew wildly now about her shoulders in yellow spirals.

How exhilarating! she thought. The wind whipped at her cheeks and lifted her unbound tresses in willful abandon. The moon was bright and the valley's wild beauty was mysteriously phosphorescent. The night was captivating, and she felt a catch in her breath.

Rounding a rock wall, Willow pulled Istas up short. Below she could see an orange fire blazing, blue smoke curling up into the night sky. A lone figure sat before the fire, his shoulders hunched forward while he whittled a stick, pieces of it flying into the flames. The voice lifted up to Willow and she started.

"I know someone's up there. Come down and show

yourself," Lakota said, unable to see who had come upon him. The white horse nickered in the shadow of the rock wall, and Lakota said, "Easy boy, we don't want to frighten our company away. Come down and show yourself before I am forced to come up and get you." He sat with every muscle tensed and alert in the event of trouble. But he didn't expect much in that area, for no Indian would come upon another so noisily in the night—especially not in Black Fox's winter camp.

Willow's heart thudded. She had two choices: Go down and face Lakota, taking the chance he might think she had followed him. Or turn Istas around and flee like the wind, for Lakota would be sure to chase her just to find out who had been spying on him. She chose to run, only because it was a beautiful night and a shame to spoil its enchantment for either one of them.

Whirling Istas with the braided reins, she put the spurs to the horse, her moccasins a soft continual thudding against Istas's ribs. She was soon flying across the valley floor.

"Come back here!"

Behind her Willow could hear the angry shout, and the sound of a horse pounding after her. The wind caught at her, tangling her yellow-gold hair. Willow felt a strange rush of fear and excitement both. Her heart pounded. Her throat burned.

Thundering after the intruder on Cloud, Lakota could make out the free flying hair. It flew in silver flashes about the woman's head, woman yes, for it could not be a man. He knew suddenly who it was he pursued. She was going to kill herself if she didn't slow down. He cursed and leaned low over Cloud's undulating back, feeling victory as he pulled closer to the spotted mare.

"Pull up!" he shouted as he drew close to Istas's wildly streaming tail and flying hooves. But his words were snatched up and away by the wind of Cloud's passage. "Damn you!"

Willow could hear Lakota shouting at her, but she could not make out what he was saying. A glance over her shoulder told her he was rapidly closing the distance between them. Willow felt reckless and defiant as she pushed Istas to her limit, knowing triumph as she increased the distance once again.

But Cloud was a lion of wild horses. With a little more pressure applied from Lakota's knee-high moccasins, Cloud seemed to leap into the air like a Pegasus, until finally he was even with Istas. Willow's eyes widened as Lakota reached over and pulled up on Istas's braided reins, slowing the horses down until they both halted, side by side.

When at last Willow could catch her breath and look at Lakota, what she saw in his face caused her to blanch. His mouth was a thin, grim line. Her own mouth began to tremble as his fingers clamped on her wrist and tightened. He spoke then, looking at her with menace in his flamelike eyes.

"Are you trying to kill that horse?"

"No." She tilted her chin defiantly. "No, I am not."

"What then?" He jerked her wrist, pulling her closer.

Jerking the reins hard, Willow backed Istas up and moved out of his reach. She jerked again and the horse reared up, curvetting while flashing her sharp hooves dangerously.

"Come back here," Lakota ordered. "I am not

finished with you!"

Sending her wild tresses back over her shoulder with a flip of her wrist, Willow glared at him. "But I am finished with you, savage, and I don't have anything more to say to you. I don't have to explain my every move to you."

Cloud's eyes looked like fire as Lakota kneed the stallion closer to them. "You are my wife and I keep track of everything you do, day and night."

A soft snort huffed from her nose. "Well then, if you know my every move, bright savage, what am I doing out here in the dark all by myself . . . tell me that?"

An ominous narrowing of his green eyes told Willow she had overstepped her bounds. Still, a defiant spark remained. Hastily she asked, "What are *you* doing out here?"

"What I do is my business."

"And what *I* do is yours too, huh?"

"I have already said that."

He moved swiftly then. Receiving no warning, Willow felt strong fingers clamp over her wrist, and this time she was hauled from her horse and positioned before Lakota none too gently. As soon as she was against him, Lakota felt his pulses leap and his aching loins respond to her softness.

"You feel good, woman," he rasped into her ear. "I don't know how I've lived without you being next to me these past seven days." He nuzzled her throat and cupped a breast that fit perfectly into the palm of his hand.

"Lakota," Willow groaned, "Lakota, I need you so much. I am yours, beloved, all yours. Please, Lakota, take me somewhere."

"I have a blanket," was all he said.

Istas followed the white stallion, slowly at first, and then faster, trotting and then galloping. They returned to Lakota's campfire where he lifted her gently down from Cloud's high back and took her fully into his arms. She came up hard against his strong frame, lips to lips, her breasts flattened against his chest. Lakota was trembling in his great need. Her small hands kneaded his shoulders as tremors of desire quaked through her body.

"Lakota, I love you . . . oh I love you so much!"

The breathless sound of her panting voice in his ear drove Lakota a little crazy. He swept her to the blanket and pressed her down there. While she emitted little cries of impatience, he shoved her skirt up, and positioning himself over her he plunged deep within her. Her head jerked and she stared up at him in bewilderment.

"Wait . . . Lakota . . . please wait." Willow bit her lip and tasted blood. She heard him groan above her.

Thrashing her head on the blanket, Willow waited until it was all over and his end had come. She couldn't understand why he did not fit her this time. It was her own fault. She had begged him to take her somewhere at once.

Ready for more, Lakota began to move hard inside her again.

"Lakota . . . give me time to catch my breath!"

Moving like lightning, Lakota grabbed Willow's arm when she rolled to her side to escape him. He turned her to face him again, drawing her against the solid rock hardness of his thighs. He molded their bodies snugly together and Willow cried out at the bold member pressing so insistently inside her tender flesh.

"Lakota—you must wait," she cried.

She buried her head against the hard groove of his collarbone. "Please, there is so much—pressure."

Surprise flashed in his eyes and he held himself away from her, incredulity in his voice, "What—? Aiyana? Look at me." Lakota lifted her chin tenderly. "You are yet so tight, my love . . . there was pressure only for a moment and then it was gone. Wasn't it?" He shook her gently, then stared down at the lines in her forehead. Had anger and lust consumed him so greatly that he had been too forceful for his love? "Aiyana—I promise never to do that to you again."

"You mean," she swallowed, you mean you will never make l-love to me again?" She watched a new frown form on his brows.

He gripped her shoulders hard. "How long did you have this discomfort? God, I can tell by the shadows in your eyes just now that it was constant." His head went up while his eyes rolled back. "Damn, I knew you were too small for me." How about the last times they had made love, had he been too hasty then?

Lakota's pained expression returned to her small face. Miserably, he groaned. "How, I wonder, am I going to hold myself from you now, Aiyana." A thought struck him between the eyes then. "Were you . . . ready for me?"

Staring at him, she said, "R-Ready? What does that mean, Lakota?"

With happy tears shining in his eyes, he lifted her and hugged her to him fiercely. "Oh, my lovely bride, I thought so. I was too hasty in my actions. Next time I will know better than to take you so forcefully. You anger me at times—Aiyana Willow. It's just that . . . you are so different from other women."

There, he had said it. She was different from them, even different from Garnet. But he would not mention her now, not at a time like this when the moment was hanging by a thread. He had a great desire to love her this night, to love her tenderly, to display all of the gentle love that was inside him for her.

"I wanted you," she said with a new shyness, "then why was there discomfort when you—you took me so quickly?"

"Because, sweet love, you *thought* you were primed for me. You see, God created you differently, while I can be ready at the drop of a pin—I mean, just looking at you when you stand a certain way or smile at me with your pussywillow-brown eyes."

Willow looked down and then up into his eyes again. "Will it always be like this? I mean, do we always have to take time to prepare me for you?" She was compelled to look down again, feeling embarrassed in this conversation.

His eyes hungered for her to look at him. He tilted her chin up so that she was forced to see into his eyes that were lit by the campfire, displaying all the emotions he wanted so desperately for her to understand. "Darling," he began, using his old endearment for her, "until my body has stretched you sufficiently, we will have to continue with this love-play." He grinned down at her. "I know one thing—"

"What is that?" she asked, feeling lovely ripples moving from her groin into her belly.

"You become excited just talking about it." He smiled, then stated the obvious. "I'm still inside you.

Feeling better all the time—much better." Thrusting forward and back, his shaft stroked her gently while two fingers began a rhythmic massage at the sensitive pearl of her, bringing on necessary fluids for comfort.

Bending over her, Lakota suckled at one nipple until it stood to attention, then bathed the other with his tongue. He swirled the moisture all around, while she began to purr.

Now she was clinging to his powerful muscled back as he moved to possess her fully. His loving became slightly rougher, but the pleasure she was receiving this time made her forget there had ever been any pain. He was a big man for her to be able to receive all of him, but she knew in time they would come to fit each other with ease.

Ecstasy burst over them now, sending them both far from earth. Lakota cried her name into the wild mane of her hair, then took her with him to the starlit heavens of rapture. At that precise moment they looked at each other only with their senses.

The days passed for Willow in a happy blur. Kachina and Dark Horse had been joined as man and wife in a quiet ceremony two days before, and they now shared their own tepee just as Willow and Lakota did. The warriors rode out every day to scout the area and check for Apache "sign," and then when Lakota returned Willow managed to keep him well distracted for the remainder of the day. Many were the hours of laughter, and lazy, loving smiles, and tender afternoons spent in walking or joining Kachina and Dark Horse in a ride across the valley. Then there were the starlit nights, dark fires, and rapture beneath the moon or the conical shape of their sanctuary. She was happier than she had ever dreamed was possible.

Oversleeping one morning, Willow awoke to find she was alone. With a lazy yawn, she rolled over and hugged herself, remembering the joys of the night before when she had received Lakota in her blankets. Barely had they returned from the heights of passion when they climbed again to the earth-shattering pinnacle of wondrous delights.

Sighing and stretching like a contented kitten, Willow rolled onto her stomach and leaned on her elbows. As she stared, the flap to the tepee stirred, as in a restless wind, or with the passage of someone walking by. Shivering, with a sudden sense of foreboding, Willow sat up with a terrible sensation of loss sweeping over her. Shaking her head and denying the strong feeling of presentiment, she stood and donned the chamois robe, taking her clothes with her as she headed to the spring.

The figure of a young woman lingered behind the tepee Willow had just stepped from. A haughty smile played on Pepita's mouth as she fingered the locket she had pulled from beneath her bodice. Watching the yellow-hair walk to the spring, Pepita toyed with the locket, peered at the lovely woman inside, then, dangling it for a moment by the chain around her neck, she slipped it back where it rested in the cleft of her rounded bosom. Her dark eyes watched the yellow-hair until she was out of sight, then Pepita walked back to her own tepee.

* * *

"I would like to take Kachina to meet my godparents," Dark Horse was saying. "It has been many months since I have been home."

Lakota and Dark Horse had been out for a day of hunting, just the two of them, and now they returned to Black Fox's camp just as the sun had set and the campfires were smoking. Lakota wiped the dust from his face, his eyes straying to his tepee where his love awaited him.

"She can wait a few more minutes," Dark Horse said, though he anticipated entering his tepee to find Kachina busy in her sewing or her cooking. The role of wife became her; she was more beautiful than ever. "Well? Are you staying, or are you homesick too?"

Lakota snorted through his long, straight nose. "Homesick maybe, a little. But I don't relish the thought of facing my brother and Tanya. Can you imagine the responses we will get?"

"Are you going to tell him?" Dark Horse said.

"Tell him that his only brother is part savage? Not likely. Not right away, anyway."

Dark Horse handed the reins over to the boy who came running up to care for Tachón. Lakota removed the braided reins from Cloud, then the saddle blanket, and, giving the stallion's rear a slap, sent Cloud galloping off to his freedom. Lakota loved Cloud, and all wild mustangs, and thought they should all run free—once they learned who was master. All he had to do was give a loud whistle and Cloud came flying out of the blue at him. But each horse owner to his own, was his motto.

Shaking his head, Dark Horse said, "It is not fair for you to hold back this knowledge from your brother.

You and Ashe have become very close—" he laughed—"even though you chose to dress in Indian style around Sundance."

"I believe Ashe hates all Indians," Lakota told Dark Horse.

After thinking this over for a moment, Dark Horse went on. "Ashe did not hate me." He grinned. "He did not love me, but we got along after he came to know me better." Dark Horse's voice lowered so it would not carry. "I think your brother had a worry that I might have been enchanted by his woman. This was true, but that was before I discovered that Tanya's heart was truly with her husband. I felt her pain; that was all."

Now they were walking in the direction of the tepees, their long legs in knee-high moccasins covering the distance swiftly. They agreed to speak more on the subject of making the journey home as a group when the women sat around the fire with them later, when the last of the supper chores were completed. Dark Horse waved as he slipped into his tepee, and Lakota made his way to his own. He was eager to feel his love come into his waiting arms.

"Lakota," a voice purred. Lakota saw the figure of a woman on the periphery of his vision. He turned and saw it was Pepita and almost groaned at the delay he knew was coming.

His regard swept the black-plum eyes, the black hair swept intricately in a topknot of braids, then went down to the assorted red beads adorning her bodice, her sleeves, and the hem of her short doeskin dress. "*Hola* Pepita. You are—ah—looking very—uhmm—colorful today. Is there something about a special occasion I happened to miss hearing about?" His whole body was yearning toward his own tepee and the adorable woman waiting there.

As Lakota was speaking as politely as he could to Pepita, Willow happened to step outside to toss a bowl of water off to the side. She froze. Her eyes dilated. At the moment Pepita's arms were encircling Lakota's neck, bringing the roundness of her breasts to press against him, while one of her knees pushed between his legs. Willow went alternatively hot and cold all over. She felt faint and sick to her stomach. Unable to watch the lusty scene any longer, she stared at the ground in a daze, and keeping that pose, she backed into the tepee and let the flap down quickly before Lakota saw her.

Disentangling Pepita's arms from about his neck, Lakota took her wrists in a firm, crushing grip, his face lowering close to hers. He spoke to her in English. "The last woman that did that to me earned the name slut where I come from, Pepita, so if you don't want me giving you a bad reputation you better steer clear of me." He shoved her back forcefully. "Do you understand? I'm sure you do, I have heard you speak English."

Tossing her head, Pepita brought the locket from between her breasts and waved it before his eyes, taunting him. "Pepita has something that mamá gave to her . . . it was the yellow-hair's, but she did not want it. She threw it into the water. Now it is Pepita's." Taunting him further, while he stared at the dangling object that was a familiar thing from out of the past, Pepita tucked the heart between her bosom once again. "If you want it, *muchacho,* you must come to get it."

Fuming inside the tepee, going from anger to bitter hurt, Willow paced its confines. When she could take it no longer, telling herself that Pepita was only playing up to Lakota, she lifted the flap to peer outside to see what was taking him so long.

"Come to get it." Pepita tossed back her head then as Lakota did just that, slipping his hand inside her bodice. But once he got hold of the locket, Pepita pressed herself closer, gripping his hips while making a grinding rhythm with her own. "You will like Pepita, I show you how to really make love." Before he knew what was happening, she reached up to cup his chin and glue her lips hotly to his.

Having seen quite enough, Willow ran to the fluffy bed and threw herself down. Sobs began to wrack her slight frame, and her tears ran freely down her flushed cheeks. No, no, *no!* Her mind screamed. Not Lakota, not her love. Oh God, please let me wake up from his nightmare!

Outside, Lakota now shoved Pepita back so hard she fell with a thud to the ground. His fingers came away with the locket still in his grip, and he flicked the catch, already knowing the face that would look out at him once he opened it. Devilishly, Garnet smiled at him from her heart-shaped prison, taunting him in her death even as she had while alive. Looking at the woman who had caused him all his misery while he was growing from boy to man, he wondered why he had even taken it from Pepita. It was apparent she had stolen it from Willow, and it was a lie that it had been tossed into the spring by its owner. He was about to toss it back into Pepita's lap when her singsong voice lifted to him, causing his blood to run cold.

"Hah! Your woman is loco. She stands by the water before throwing the thing in while she calls the woman in there her *mother.*" She watched happily as Lakota stared at her as if she had sprouted horns. "I am not the loco one; do not look at me like that. It is your woman who is this. She speaks to her *mother,* and then throws her picture away." Now she sniffed. "Will you give it back to Pepita?"

The only answer Pepita received was a cold one, as Lakota spun on his heel and headed back in the direction he had just come from. Pepita watched him stuff the locket into a slot in his breeches. Then she covered her ears while he whistled shrilly for his horse. When she stood and dusted herself off, Lakota had vanished.

PART FIVE

Savage Tears

Tears, idle tears, I know not what they mean;
Tears from the depth of some divine despair
Rise in the heart, and gather to the eyes.

—Alfred, Lord Tennyson

Why linger, why turn back, why shrink,
My Heart?

—Percy Bysshe Shelley

Chapter Nineteen

As dawn crept over the sleepy Indian village, Willow slowly awakened to the sound of someone moving about in the tepee. She grimaced. Whoever it was was not being very quiet.

Willow suddenly realized that Lakota had not come to sleep in his bed all night! Then the anger of seeing him in Pepita's arms the evening before returned, and she stared at his back while he rummaged through the parfleches in search of something.

Her eyes narrowing over Lakota's strong, lean back, she began to wonder what kind of man he was that he could so casually slip from her arms into another's. Then she thought she knew. During the week they had been apart, she had fought against the aching fear that a passionate man like Lakota would not go long without a woman. But even as she thought that perhaps during their separation he had turned to Pepita, a thread of doubt remained. Still, had she disappointed him in some way? Last night she had seen him ride off into the foothills again . . . why?

Willow closed her eyes for a moment, then forced the words to her lips. "Where have you been? I—I have been waiting for you all night. Lakota? Why won't you say something? Anything."

"All right," he hissed over his shoulder. "Shut up!"

Going white in the face, Willow sat up in the soft bed while her eyes frowned over his tall back held so rigidly from her. Willow's heart beat painfully as she came to her knees, his words penetrating the haze of her recent awakening. Her soft, hurt, brown eyes swept over his tall, lean frame and she yearned to go to him and ask what it was she had done to cause this indifference to sprout in his heart. She decided to remain silent, however, though her heart was beating like a wild ceremonial drum.

Dark clouds rose over the valley just then, darkening the door just as the approaching storm rolled in with a growl of thunder. Gloominess settled inside the tepee, and neither stirred, not Willow, not Lakota.

Then Lakota broke the silence as he growled over to her. "Fetch some wood for the fire. It's going to get chilly in here."

Standing, Willow shook out her long, tangled mane of yellow hair. "Chillier than it already is?" she snapped, unable to contain her growing anger. "I don't think a fire will help much in *here.*"

As she fetched her clothes and began to dress, a feeling of unease seeped into her flesh. Waiting a few minutes had not brought a ready retort back to her. He was so cold and indifferent he would not even take the time to argue with her. Had Lakota actually gone and fallen for Pepita's kind? Unlikely! she thought. Besides, Pepita reminded her too much of Hester.

Paling in the face, Willow froze at the entrance. Was that it? Could Lakota's soul be so tainted from all the loose-moraled women of Hester's kind? There had been all those saloon girls. And then Hester. Garnet . . . she hated to think about it further.

"Be sure to collect some more wood from the woodpile," Lakota ordered as Willow was stepping outside. "We are almost out."

Her eyes were hurt as she became visible at the entrance again. "But . . . it is raining."

"Are you afraid of a little water?"

His back was still turned and Willow smiled at it. She couldn't help herself, even if he turned about and saw the ray of hope crossing her face. At least he was talking to her now, and that was a fair sign he had trouble avoiding her completely. Deciding to press the moment, she stepped back inside with the armful of wood, and setting it down, she began to build a fire. When that was done, she sat back to wait.

After several more minutes, Lakota whirled to face Willow. "You haven't gone to fetch more wood." His eyes narrowed to mere green slits. "Why not?"

Looking up at her savage love, Willow knew that there was no human, no woman alive on earth who could take this man from her. Just let her try!

"I'm warming myself," she said in a little voice.

"Well, warm yourself after you return with the wood."

Her tawny eyebrow shot up as Willow said, "You could make the warming come a little quicker if you helped a little bit. . . ."

Walking over to her ever so slowly, while Willow stared at his coming, her nerves thrilling to every step, he stopped before her and hunkered down. Her eyes made love to every harsh plane and angle that seemed to have appeared overnight on his face. He looked somewhat older, and she became alarmed momentarily, before the sweet, languid fire filled her bloodstream. His hard, warm hands cupped her cheeks on either side, his palms almost covering her whole face, while his fingers formed a bridge over her eyebrows. When his voice emerged it was soft and dangerously cool.

"I wouldn't warm you if you were the last female on earth."

With that he stood and vanished from the tepee. Willow's entire body became one mass of hurt, growing progressively more painful to bear. Before her sightless eyes wavered only one vision—the terrible gleam that had been in Lakota's eyes.

With slim grace, Willow lifted herself and found her bed. Rain drummed on the tepee and splashed softly through the village, repeating the words over and over . . . *last female on earth . . . last female on earth. . . .*

"Aiyana . . . Aiyana . . . may I enter?" Kachina continued to call softly from outside the tepee. The sun had come out, and she waved to Black Fox as he rode by in a proud, grand fashion on his jaunt through the village, checking this and that, greeting his people with his warm, friendly smile.

Turning over in her fluffy bed, Willow heard a voice invading her mind and she emerged from the cloud of a deep, healing sleep. Her friend was calling . . . but from where . . . ?

"Kachina?"

"May I enter?" The lovely Indian woman had been standing outside for a full two minutes or more now. "I will go if you are trying to sleep, my friend. I am sorry to have disturbed you." She turned to go back to her tepee, but she really had no desire to return just yet. Something was troubling her friend's marriage—Kachina had read this in Lakota as he and her husband went out to check the corraled mustangs.

Before Kachina could walk away, Willow appeared at the opening and held the flap aside. "Kachina?" She waited until her friend turned back to her tepee. "Did you want to see me?"

Kachina took one look at Aiyana Willow and rushed to her side, picking up her listless white hand. "What is it? Can you tell Kachina what is ailing you? Ohh, you are not . . . not in the family way, are you? Is that why you and Lakota have quarreled?"

"I am not in the family way, Kachina."

"I have been worried about his manner this day and thought something amiss." She let it hang.

"Kachina." Willow became alert for the first time in several hours. "What are you saying? Has Lakota told you something—" she frowned— "something I myself don't even know about?"

"May I come in?"

"Oh . . . yes." Willow stepped to the inside to allow her friend to enter. "I'm sorry—I was just surprised, that's all."

Seated beside Kachina on a couch of buffalo robes and other softer hides, Willow told her friend the whole story, including the part about when she had looked outside her tepee to find Lakota and Pepita locked in a lusty embrace.

"I can't understand him, Kachina. Why would he seek another when we had been so close the . . . night before." Willow wasn't even aware that tears had come to her eyes, but she felt a painful constriction in her throat and chest.

"My friend, sometimes those who love each other hurt each other, sometimes meaning to and sometimes not."

"I don't understand that," Willow said, sniffling and shaking her mussed blond head.

"You might have hurt Lakota somehow to cause him to display this anger to you." Kachina's laugh tinkled brightly for a moment. "I have learned so much about love since meeting Dark Horse." She became serious once again. "What have you and Lakota quarreled over?"

"That's just it." She sighed. "Nothing."

"There is nothing other than the wood he wanted you to carry this morning? Nothing at all?"

Willow shook her head. "I don't think so." She couldn't very well speak to Kachina about the personal matters they had hotly discussed, but maybe there was a clue in that after all. Thoughtfully Willow said, "Whenever I look at Lakota in a certain way, tilt my head, or make eyes at him teasingly, he seems to go stone cold hard on me. He ignores me as if I . . . have a disease!"

"You say he rode out after this—uhmm—embrace with Pepita and did not return all night?"

"That's right." Willow sighed, swallowing the choking lump that had been in her throat ever since they had started this conversation. "It almost seems they had a—a lover's quarrel!" She laughed despairingly over the last word. "I—I just don't get this at all, Kachina, and I feel like I'm going crazy because of it."

"No." Kachina crooned, placing her arm across Willow's shoulders. Her smooth, coppery hand lifted to smooth back the wave that always fell over one of Willow's eyes. "You will not go crazy, because Kachina is here and together we will solve this strange mystery between you and Lakota. He loves you with all his heart, you know."

Tears were flowing freely down Willow's cheeks now. With a lot of noise, she sniffled. "How do you know that?"

"He tells my husband how he worships the ground your moccasins walk on and even the air above your lovely head. Lakota has told Dark Horse that you are a very special woman, and if anything should ever happen to you he would wither away from sadness and pain."

"But everything has changed since then, Kachina. Something bad has happened overnight to make him feel this way." Suddenly a thought came to her. "Kachina, Lakota has said that if a woman, namely me, ever held something important from him, like a secret, he would be angry enough to want to strangle her."

"And, Aiyana, what deep secrets do you hold from him?" Kachina, wisely observant, asked her.

"I—" Willow swallowed hard. Then she whirled to face Kachina squarely. "I don't see how . . . how it could have anything to do with us now. He couldn't know, you see. There is no chance of his finding out that . . . that the woman he was once in love with was my—my mother." When Kachina shook her head in confusion, Willow went on. "My mother, Garnet Hayes Brandon, is dead and buried now. Talon Clay—Lakota—was just a boy when my m-mother seduced him." Kachina's eyes had grown huge, but Willow kept on. "Garnet had lived at Sundance before I ever arrived there with my father. . . ."

"How is this, Aiyana?"

"She—" Willow hung her head in shame— "She ran away from us when we were all small children, deserted us, three children and our father. When my Pa finally caught up with the place where she had gone to live, Garnet was already dead. That's how I figured it anyway, that my Pa had been searching for Garnet and—and he just got to her too late."

"He stayed on at this place called Sundance then and raised his children there?"

"Yes." Willow nodded. "He died there, too; not much more than two years have passed since his death."

"I am sorry to hear this." Kachina placed a comforting hand on Willow's arm. "My parents died a very tragic death, but now that I have come to know love I feel close to them, closer than I have ever felt. Their spirits are with me every day now, and they are very pleased that Kachina has found her happiness in life."

"Yes," Willow murmured. "I thought I had found mine, too."

"You still have this happiness," Kachina said softly. "It is just being held back for some reason, for a time, and then it will return, my friend. Plenty of happiness for you and Lakota. I know this. You and Lakota have sweet love for each other. It is the kind of love Dark Horse and I share, the kind that will never pass away." She patted Willow's hand. "You come to our home now and have something to eat."

"I am not very hungry, Kachina."

"Even so, you come anyhow and keep Kachina company while she eats." She giggled as a thought struck her. "Maybe we let Lakota and Dark Horse eat first, like good squaws, then eat afterward, while they watch?"

"I don't think Lakota would look at me, Kachina." Willow sighed. "Not even for a moment, the way he's acting toward me."

"Come, and we will see."

Later, while Kachina was serving the meat-and-vegetable stew she'd prepared, Willow placed the platter of Indian bread and berries on the wood dining slab set up between the two men. Lakota avoided Willow all the while, and he ate very little. Dark Horse and Kachina exchanged glances now and then, while Willow just hung in the background feeling totally out of place and dejected.

Kachina herself began to feel that the couple's future looked bleak indeed, and then she caught Lakota stealing a glance at Willow. She read much in his eyes in that brief space of time. Love. Frustration. Bitterness. And hate. Also Kachina had seen misery and regret and a certain brand of sadness swirling in the deep green of Lakota's stunning eyes. But it was the hate that Kachina could not understand. This troubled her very much.

All of a sudden Willow could not stand Lakota's silent unconcern and detachment. He was purposely avoiding her! She couldn't take it a moment longer.

When the scream rent the silence in the tepee, resounding against the conical walls, Kachina placed one hand over her mouth and the other upon her breast. Dark Horse sat looking up at his wife silently. But it was Lakota who reacted most strongly to Willow's ear-piercing scream. Slowly he rose from his cross-legged seat on the floor, walked over to Willow's ramrod-stiff body and slapped her in the face unceremoniously.

She slapped him right back.

Dark Horse and Kachina held their breaths.

"Come with me," Lakota said, grasping her by the wrist.

"No." She pushed down on his hand, trying to shrug out of his hold. "I am not going anywhere with you!"

Having no other choice but to watch the couple argue, Dark Horse went to stand beside his wife, taking her hand while he smiled reassuringly into her midnight-blue eyes. He was telling her not to have a care, that Lakota and Willow would iron out their own problems. But Kachina continued to watch, fearful that they would come to more blows than they already had.

Lakota tugged at her wrist, saying, "Now, you will come with me."

Willow tried slapping his hand away, but her slaps fell ineffectually on his wrist. "No. No. Go back to your new love, Lakota—take her with you wherever you want to go!"

Lakota peered closely at her, sputtering, "What?"

"Yes—" she finally answered, looking very petite with him towering over her to the full height of his anger, "and you know very well who I am talking about. I won't say her name."

"Yes . . . I think you better tell me. That, and much more explaining."

Before she blinked another eyelash, Lakota very unceremoniously swept her out the door. He had bent over before her wide, shocked eyes and hoisted her like nothing but a sack of potatoes over his shoulder. Dark Horse kept back a grin while he watched Willow pound Lakota's back with angry tight little fists. Kachina placed a hand over Dark Horse's wrist, and he covered hers with his own, patting her with the same reassurance his eyes had earlier held. Then he turned and reached behind her, scooping her bottom into large hands while pulling her close for the wild kiss he pressed to her lips. Shortly Kachina's arms were winding about Dark Horse's neck, while her softly swelling hips met his lean, hard ones. Then they forgot everything else as love's kindling became a roaring flame of passion.

Amid shrieks of outrage and kicks that came close to his groin, Lakota bore Willow to the edge of the village and stood there whistling for Cloud. He had only to wait for several minutes listening to her shrieks turn into muffled sobs and tears of utter frustration and weariness, before the sound of hoofbeats were coming toward them. The deep red haze that was the afternoon sun loomed behind the magnificent white, giving Cloud a startling, ghostly appearance. And to Willow, who was looking at the thundering horse upside-down, he seemed to be coming right for them—too fast!

"That half-wild stallion is going to ride right over us!" Willow yelled as best she could in her ungainly position. "Hurry, Lakota, put me down!"

Now she could feel the thunder of the horse right through Lakota's body, sensing through her own excited nerve endings the tremendous powerhouse that was bearing down on them. Any time now they were going to be crushed. Willow threw her arms up over her eyes, tensing for the horrible impact that was to come.

The thunder had ceased. And . . . someone was laughing!

When Willow opened her eyes she received a second shock. The mighty white stood there blowing, his graceful neck curving while his head came toward her and she felt his hot air puffing against her face. Velvety lips nuzzled her cheek as the long white face nodded—as if he was letting it be known that there was nothing for her to fear, after all.

Then Willow glared at the big horse. "Well, so you're laughing at me too, are you?" She could still feel Lakota's shoulders going up and down in silent laughter. "You can both stop now. The humor is gone, though I never saw what was so funny in the first place!"

Next she was standing on her own two feet, swaying dizzily in momentary vertigo. When Lakota and Cloud ceased to whirl in her vision, she found herself staring into the darkest, most unreadable green eyes. It was as if she had been suddenly plunged into a frighteningly mysterious forest with no way out. She had no conception of what he was thinking, or feeling. Looking at this stranger, Willow began to weaken and fail in courage.

It was the time of sharing tables, and not a soul stirred outdoors in the peaceful Indian village behind the two people and the beautiful white horse cast in bronze by the fiery banners of the setting sun.

"Aiyana . . . why?"

Like a dagger of sun, the gilded arm of the man reached out to stroke the golden face of the young woman standing still as the statue of a dainty Venus. Her eyes were tipped upward. The sun painted her yellow as a British guinea. She is like a shy, yellow fawn, Lakota was thinking. But in his demure bride lurked the heart of a temptress. A spotted fawn. One that hid its true colors. He would sooner carve out her heart than learn she had deceived him well and good.

With the sunset, changing from shades of goldenrod to burnt-orange to red-violet-purple, came the encroaching raw sienna and blue-gray in the foothills where the shadows had just begun to deepen. Just as one last dagger of sun struck the earth, Lakota lifted the despised treasure up in the air and the sun struck it, too.

"Oh." Willow gasped when her eyes slipped from his to see what it was he held against the sunset. She stared, mesmerized, every bone in her body melting and freezing over. Soon her whole body was one chunk of shivering ice. "Oh . . . my God," soft as a breath of air, her voice escaped through stinging cold lips. "How—where did you get that?"

"Recognize it, do you?"

"Y-Yes, of course. It—"

"Was your mother's?"

Her eyes went wild as she gasped, "H-How d-do you know th-that?"

"A little bird by the name of Josephine." His eyes narrowed, then flared wider as he closely regarded her face.

Willow knew the Spanish pet name for Josephine. "Pepita?" She shook her head. "But . . . how did she . . . ?"

"Malina told Pepita and Pepita told Lakota. Simple," he said with a low snort.

Willow frowned, tiring of his nasty little game wherein she had become the defenseless victim.

"Not simple," she snapped. She pointed at the locket. "How did Malina . . . ? Oh." Malina had been tracking her steps to the spring; she had seen her out of the corner of her eye . . . was it only several days ago?

"I can see in your eyes the game is up, Willow Hayes."

"Willow . . . *Hayes?*"

"That's right." He stared down at the small breasts rising and falling rapidly over the erratic thumping in her chest. "I just divorced you."

A frown line appeared between her fine, tawny eyebrows. "You can't do . . . that. Not that easily."

"I can do anything I want, Willow Hayes." He taunted her like a stallion trapping a filly in a small corral. "Anything, I want." Slipping a rough hand over her throat, he traveled lower and cupped and fondled a breast until it hardened beneath his touch, a touch that had no more intimacy in it than a man handling a dead fish.

Shamed that her body could so easily respond at a time like this, Willow reverted to anger and slapped his hand away just when his fingertips had been tweaking a nipple into erection. Like a frightened, hissing kitten,

Willow stood her ground.

"D-Don't fondle me l-like I'm one of your saloon girls, Talon Clay. I'm not one of them . . . I'm not a whore . . . and I'm not *your* plaything either!"

"No. You're a deceiving little slut just like your mother was." He snatched her to him, his hot breath raining sparks over her alarmed face. "Would you like to know how Garnet seduced little Talon Clay?" He shook her, snapping, "Would you? No? I'll tell you anyway. Picture this if you can . . . gorgeous Gar-net," he drawled her name while making a salacious gesture with his hand, "always after unsuspecting little boy, until one morning she slips her lily-white hand . . . oh yes, pure white, because *Mistress* Garnet never soiled them . . . she slips it under the table while poor, dumb son sits across from Papa with red face and a hardness in his groin that reaches the underside of the table." He made another salacious gesture with his hand and Willow reached out to slap it aside.

While Willow slapped her hands over her ears—still able to hear some of his words—Lakota taunted her cruelly by going on and on and on. What he went on to describe made Willow's hatred for her own flesh and blood grow, while her heart twisted in agony for the tall boy who had been unsuspecting of their ill-fated love affair from the start, always believing in a fantasy world where a golden-haired siren would sweep him away like a knight would a princess on a white charger. From a world of care. Of need. Of wants. From a world where adults paid him no more mind than they would a stray pup with mange.

"What does this have to do with me?" Willow cried, looking at him now and afraid of the moisture that had appeared in his eyes.

"You?" Lakota cried back, his voice pitched several octaves higher than his usual tone. "You? . . . you ask me? I'll tell you. She's the witch you were spawned from." He sneered as his eyes roved over her lovely, detestable face. "So like your own mother." His fingers lifted to sift through the golden hair that had come loose about her small, dirt-streaked face. "The same hair—" his lips went to her ear with a hiss— "that I used to run my fingers through when we made hot, passionate love. Ah yes, aren't you a fortunate woman to have a husband who has been taught everything there is to know about making love from your own mother?" Breathing mockingly into her ear, his fingers slid down her body and stayed there.

"Stop!" Willow shoved away from Lakota with all her might. "Stop . . . damn you . . . *stop!"* Clamping her hands over her ears, she shook her head in a pitiful motion and sobbed as she slipped to the ground. "Don't . . . tell me . . . any . . . more—" Now she sat on the ground. "Just leave me alone—"

With a heart-rending moan that could even have startled the big white and sent him sidestepping dangerously close to Willow, Lakota threw himself on top of the horse and went flying to the hills. Looking up with a streaked face, Willow watched her love ride forever out of her life. It was over . . . all over. . . .

Chapter Twenty

Wolf-Eyes-Woman employed sign language in order for Willow to understand her. For ten whole days now Willow had been in the charge of Wolf-Eyes-Woman, and she was becoming sick and tired of slaving and sweating beneath the woman's iron rule. And if Willow did not do as the woman dictated? Usually she went like a naughty child to bed without her dinner. That was not so bad. But it was the striking on her limbs and the poking in her soft places with the sharp sticks that Willow could not tolerate, that stung almost as badly as Lakota's paying no attention to her. Almost, but not quite.

Carrying an armful of wood, while Wolf-Eyes-Woman trailed behind like the stealthy creature she was named after, Willow trudged to the woman's tepee. Wolf-Eyes-Woman was a widow with nine children, children who also carried sharp sticks just like their mother. Willow could count more than fifty Comanche breeds that had come to the camp with Black Fox this time around. His people were allied with the

People, as this particular band of Comanches called themselves. Of course, the whole tribe wasn't with them, just those that were allied with the Horse Indians—one of whom happened to be the vicious Wolf-Eyes-Woman, half-Kiowa, half-Comanche, and God only knew what other blood flowed in the tyrannical woman's veins. Lakota could not have placed her in the charge of a more unsympathetic human being—if Wolf-Eyes-Woman even was that.

As the woman pointed imperiously to where she wanted Aiyana to put the wood down, Willow's brown eyes followed the sharp stick warily. Just as she was bending over to relieve her arm of her burden, Willow felt several sharp jabs in her already tender buttocks. Whirling about, she caught the culprits this time, grabbing three sticks out of three pairs of grubby brown hands.

"One. Two. Three," she counted as she snatched each stick away.

"Hu!"

Yelping, Willow spun about. Automatically she dropped the three sharp sticks and rubbed her aching backside while facing the terrible wrath of Wolf-Eyes-Woman. Dejectedly she looked around the oversized girth of Wolf-Eyes-Woman, unable to find anybody who could really aid her in this. Dark Horse had taken Kachina to meet his godparents, taking Little Coyote and a few others to travel with him. The latter was planning to hunt the hills surrounding the Brazos and the Colorado while Dark Horse and Kachina visited. Willow had not been informed they were gone until two days following their departure. Harlyn Sawyer had become Malina's slave, and she was never allowed to visit with him. Nightwalker had traveled with a band of Horse Indians to Clear Fork Reservation, but should be returning any day now. Lakota was practically a nonexistent figure in the camp, only returning from a hunt now and then to make certain Wolf-Eyes-Woman was doing her job. That left Willow all alone to fend for herself. She was surrounded by hate. Black Fox could not even help, and besides he was always busy in this Pipe Council or that.

Soon, she thought, there was going to come along the ways and means for her to escape. Tears came into her eyes when she thought of Sundance—oh God, to go back home and get away from this horrible place!

"Aiee!" Wolf-Eyes-Woman poked Aiyana in the arm until she drew blood. She stared down in horrible fascination at the white woman's blood. Wolf-Eyes-Woman had never done this before. She backed away. Now she was afraid of what the breed Named-Lakota would do to her for drawing this blood on his woman.

Malina saw her chance to taunt her enemy and came flying from her tepee, wielding a hide-comb like a dangerous weapon over her head. "Now you will have much trouble, Wolf-Eyes-Woman," Malina said in her broken Comanche. "I am happy to see I will finally have my revenge on your black soul. Named-Lakota cherishes this woman and will kill whoever harms a hair on her head."

Willow rubbed her sore arm while her eyes went back and forth. Her Indian vocabulary was limited to understanding only a few simple words from each tribe.

"Idahu!" Wolf-Eyes-Woman called Malina a "snake," spitting out the word as if she herself hissed.

Feeling insignificant and alone in this Indian world, Willow crawled into herself while the women argued back and forth and the children glared their hostility at her. She looked around at her surroundings. This had once been a happy place for her and Lakota. And now, no thanks to her mother, she had become miserable beyond belief!

How could Talon Clay do this to her! They did not belong here, either of them. Well . . . maybe Lakota did. But she belonged to the world of the civilized, where the homefires burned brightly, the "little house," Tanya and baby Sarah, Ashe, Samson, and Clem, even the mustangers and drovers.

Lakota was a savage. He had truly become Lakota of the Northern Kiowa-Sioux and forgotten he was a young man by the name of Talon Clay Brandon!

This man had become a mere stranger to her. She had allowed a savage stranger to caress her flesh, murmur love words into her ear, to enmesh her in what should have been a glorious union between man and woman, husband and wife, two souls beating as one.

Lakota did not even *sound* the same, the pulse and accent of his voice having been modified to the point where she did not realize he was the same person, at times. Particularly of late.

He wore a gold eagle feather in his headband. Even though the nights had turned considerably cooler, he sported the breechcloth and went bare-breasted.

Watching the blood drip from her arm, Willow wondered: What am I going to do? Named-Lakota had made her his captive, his slave, the one person he dumped all his bitter hatred upon. And all because she was Garnet Hayes Brandon's daughter . . . he had discovered this. No, it had been the Mexican women who had told him.

She would go to find him, this very minute, and demand release . . . she wanted to go home, home to Sundance!

While the quarrelsome women continued to hurl a combination of Mexican, Kiowa, and Comanche words at each other, Willow held her arm up against her chest and walked, while grumbling aloud, "I will not put up with this! He has made me his captive . . . I am not a slave! I am a free woman! We are not even truly married, not in the eyes of God!"

"Who says that you are not truly married with my son?"

Willow glanced down at the arms that suddenly held her by the shoulders, then up at the fringed chest she had carelessly charged into, and almost swooned with happiness. "Nightwalker! Oh thank God . . . when did you return?" She grimaced as he continued to hold her from him at arm's length.

"Answer me first: Who says you are not my son's wife?"

"I—I do."

"You and my son received the blessings of the Almighty God in accordance with the solemn observance of any house of Christian worship. Who has told you that Jim Nibaw did not truly join you and my son together? I see. This is only in your thinking, little Aiyana?"

"Yes, I did not really believe that the reservation Indian was a minister, in the true sense of the term."

"You can believe that you and my son are truly wedded and blessed in this union. I myself insisted upon the ceremony. Come, we will go to your dwelling and see about that cut you have on your arm. How did you receive this?" He peered down, studying the bloody hole in the soft flesh.

"I—" Willow looked Wolf-Eyes-Woman's way and said, "I did it while fetching wood for . . . Wolf-Eyes-Woman."

"Who has said you must fetch for the woman?" He propelled her towards her own tepee, where she had not slept in nine nights, but instead had had to find her rest besidc Wolf-Eyes-Woman on the dirt floor with nothing for a headrest but her own hands. "Who has said you must be her slave? Tell me . . . ahh . . ." A light shone in his eyes then. "I know who has done this. Has he finally discovered the identity of your mother?"

"H-How did you know?" Willow turned back to him as they entered the tepee and she blinked in the gloom of the place.

"Sit," he ordered, pushing her down upon the buffalo robes gently.

But Willow leapt to her feet at once, not wanting any contact with the place where she and Lakota had made such sweet, aching love together. In fact, her only desire now was to get away from Lakota, as far as possible!

Finding another place to sit while Nightwalker rummaged in the parfleches and then tended her wound, Willow listened quietly as he told her of the true, honest, pure love his son had been seeking. True, he had not discovered this in Garnet. But he had been searching for his own heart's love even at a tender age. When he had not attained true love with Garnet, he had been violently disappointed.

"You can see who he truly searched for, can you not?" he asked Willow.

Willow shook her head. "I don't understand that kind of 'searching,' I guess."

"How could Lakota truly find his heart when she was not yet there at Sundance?" Nightwalker asked her. When she said nothing to that, he went on. "She was yet to come to Sundance."

"I don't believe in this destiny thing, or kismet, but only do I believe in God's will." Shaking her head, she said to herself, "To think that I loved that savage at one time . . . I must have been loco!"

"Calm down, little one. You still love my son. It indeed was predestined that you and my son meet and fall in love. You get yourself all worked up over nothing. Come, we will walk outside."

Nothing was making any sense to Willow. Destiny . . . bah!

So many questions without answers filled Willow's head that she was made dizzy by them. And then, she thought of it again: There was always escape . . . if she could get to Harlyn and they could only manage it with so many red savages about. Comanches. The place was crawling with new ones every day. How could Lakota leave her in such a dangerous place!

As soon as Willow came out of the tepee, Wolf-Eyes-Woman was leaping at her, ordering Aiyana to be at her tasks. Rapidly, in Comanche, Nightwalker ordered her to be gone and never bother his *son's* woman again. Eyeing the "white-eyes" with hostility, Wolf-Eyes-Woman sneered and then skulked away like a dog slapped on the butt with a switch.

Lakota did not see his wife and his father walking in

the afternoon sunshine together as he hastened toward the corral with a wild Spanish pony strung out and trotting behind him and Cloud. If he had caught a glimpse of them he would have been highly agitated and displeased that her punishment as a slave had been ended by the hand of his father. He would not have approached Nightwalker, but later he would have punished Willow for not listening and staying put with Wolf-Eyes-Woman.

As it was, however, incredibly, Willow was enjoying her walk that afternoon with Nightwalker. They conversed not of personal problems or conflicts of the heart, but of the Indians, the new Comanches in the camp, and Willow began to find herself interested in the Comanches, with whom the Kiowa were allied. On the southern plains, no more warlike tribe existed than the Comanches.

"I believe that!" Willow laughed. "Wolf-Eyes-Woman carries a mean stick."

"One I mean to break very soon," Nightwalker commented. "No daughter of mine will be treated in such a manner! I must speak with Lakota and see that this punishment goes no further."

As Willow looked around her, she noticed that every one of the Comanches seemed industriously busy with one chore or another. Willow had earlier ignored their busy presence about her. Now there was more to see, now that she had somebody to share part of the day with her. Those days on Sundance property were long gone when she and Talon shared a happy camaraderie, when the sexual tension between them had been laughed and joked away in the light of day, and their friendship had begun to bloom like a glorious flower opening its velvet folds to the sun.

Willow sighed, wishing those sunshiny days back now. Just so she could *be with him.* If only she had never tried that gown on with the intent of seducing him . . . there had been a curse on that captivating gown of Garnet's!

A disturbing memory came to her mind then. Had Lakota meant to hurt her that night under the stars? Purposely hurt her? He had never been so hasty. And what other tortures would she have to endure if she was to remain his captive bride? When he took her in his anger it was frightening. Anyway, she did not want to make love anymore. She could still remember the burning pressure of his anger, the hugeness filling her when she was wary and unprepared. He had started out by being angry with her—he could never tell her otherwise!

All the other times their loving had started out with wonderful feelings. Delicious waves of pleasure had washed over her, even though she had rejected the frightening sensations at first. How could she have wanted Talon Clay to make love to her that day, so long ago it seemed to her now, when she had almost begged him to take her then and there beneath the cottonwoods. And he had become angered. Was it jealousy at the idea that she knew just what she was doing and might have been with other men before him? Willow wondered now how it all would have turned out if he had laid her on the ground as she had desired and made love to her? Would they be happily wedded at Sundance now with a babe on its way? Heaven forbid that she should become pregnant now!

When Willow shivered, Nightwalker inquired if she

was feeling all right. "Your face is a dark berry, Aiyana. You are sure?" he asked again as he turned away from staring at her reddened face. "You are not overly warm in those heavy buckskins you are wearing?"

"No. I am fine." She was tired, but she would not say so. She could not wait for the black canopy studded with stars to close over the camp so she could find her sorely needed rest this night on a soft bed instead of on the hard ground she had been forced to sleep upon. Fear that Lakota would come and find her there . . . well, she would just have to deal with that when and if the time came. Besides, she was furious at Lakota for his treatment of her, and this cooled some of her impending trepidation over what would happen later on.

Nightwalker knew who occupied the greater portion of Aiyana's thoughts this day.

Standing at the cleft in the high wall, Willow gazed out over the uneven ripples of buffalo grass in the distance and the shrublike mesquite trees blowing gray-green beneath the October sun. To the west, cacti sprouted in sporadic numbers out of the sandy earth, their dangerously hard thorns and growths pointing in every direction like so many road signs gone crazy.

Nightwalker told Willow about a certain type of plant, a cactus, that would cause a person to hallucinate if he was fed a part of it. He told her what part that was—he laughed—just in case she should find need of it one day.

Over the next several hours, Willow learned many things about the Comanches and Kiowas as she and Nightwalker strolled the camp and surrounding areas.

The Kiowa, who numbered altogether about sixteen hundred, embraced ten to twenty bands in all. Each one consisted of the occupants of twelve to fifty tepees. A new band came into being when a leader, like Black Fox, separated from the parent group and took with him a following of brothers and sisters, with their own spouses and offspring. The Comanches were their allies, and Willow laughed when Nightwalker told her that some of the Comanche names were Making-Bags-While-Moving; Those-Who-Move-Often—and Burnt Meat.

"What about someone like Lakota? How is it that he is," Willow paused to think for a moment, "can he actually become one of . . . them?"

"One of them?" Nightwalker asked with a low chuckle.

"A savage. He is half-white. If he would cut his hair, and put on normal clothes, he would *not* look much the savage." Willow looked up all of a sudden and drew in her breath softly, for Nightwalker was gazing into her eyes, unconsciously directing her attention to his own stunning eyes. "How do *you* come by the green eyes?" she was compelled to ask.

"Somewhere, way back, I am told, one of my great-great-grandmothers was a white woman. She was fair-haired like yourself. She, they say, had eyes as green as grass. Helsi was her name. She had sailed from the Old World. She was captured by a Siouan Chief." Nightwalker's eyes narrowed in thought. "We come from mixed breeds, my brothers and sisters, cousins, uncles, and aunts. Is this not also true of your people? We are not all what is called—uh—blue-blooded."

"So true. My family, too—I should say—*our* family. I have a sister and brother whom I love very much. We are a mixture of the Scandinavian countries, and—some other nationality I can't even remember now." Willow shrugged a dainty shoulder. "Blue-bloods are uppity anyhow, and I'm glad we're not one of those. I would really dislike having to be totally English, you know, from England? My sister Tanya, who has been to school in the East, says they talk through the nose and peer down that same nose at you if you talk like you haven't attended some fancy school or another. Reckon they'd really have a laugh if one tried to hold a conversation with the likes of me!"

Nightwalker laughed, a happy sound that rolled up from his deep-welled chest. "You are very intelligent, Aiyana, and you have much charm. I wish I could say you will go far in life, but that is not my fervent wish for you—"

"No," she broke in, "your wish is for me to stay here forever with your son who is a half-breed, one who will never fit in anywhere The whites will never truly accept him. Neither will the Indians. Not really. He is a part of two worlds. I can't share those worlds with him. But he is Talon Clay Brandon to me. He was born in a big white house with grand furnishings surrounding him. When he opened his eyes and first became aware of himself as a tiny human being, he looked into a white face, the face of his mother, Martha Brandon." Willow did not see Nightwalker's eyes flare up passionately at the mention of his love; she went on. "He grew up at Sundance . . . and he—"

"He learned the ways of a man with a woman, at a very early age. She was a bad woman, your mother."

Willow gazed to the far-off plateaus where a hazy lilac mist wound its way like a long snake down the sides. "You knew what she was even then?" she almost whispered.

"I have known this for a long time. I would have spared my son the hurt, but this was not for me to do."

"Why didn't you take him away with you?" Willow continued staring off in the distance.

"And steal him from his mother?"

"No. Why didn't you take him away from *her.*" A low, tearful sound was forming in her throat. "Didn't you know that she was tearing his heart to shreds? Why did you let her *kill* his soul that way?"

Nightwalker looked down at the golden head and felt as if a knife twisted in his heart. "Did she hurt you, too, Aiyana? I think she left you without a mother's love at a very tender age."

"You didn't answer my question, Nightwalker. You could have taken Talon Clay from her—why didn't you?"

Suddenly Nightwalker appeared older than he really was. "I cannot tell you, Aiyana. Sometimes we do the wrong thing. After all, we are all only human and have sinned one against the other." He studied her as she looked out upon the distant herds of wild game: elk, buffalo, antelope, and many other animals that she had never seen before she had come to Comanchería. "These roads that are *away ahead* will stay with me through life and after. . . ."

"What was that, Nightwalker? The words are beautiful."

"Part of a prayer, Aiyana. Come, we must return before Lakota."

Willow's pulse was far from being normal when she slipped between the flaps of the tepee, feeling a premonition.

"Oh."

Lakota stood not five feet from her, a tall dark figure, his expression indistinguishable against the background of mauve shadow. "I told you to stay with Wolf-Eyes-Woman," he ground out harshly.

His green eyes were hard, without any warmth in them at all, and they bore into Willow with relentlessly grinding force. "I—I am not just any old slavering squaw, you know." Her lower lip trembled as anger succeeded fear. "I am a *white* woman, as you well know. And . . . look at you, Talon Clay Brandon." As she said this, though, she was powerfully tempted to reach out her hand to touch his silken braid. "Why . . . you're nothing but a white-faced savage." As she went one further, she noticed how really bronze his flesh had become, all over, and his flesh contrasted with the bright-gold eagle feather he wore stuck in his headband.

Willow waited with bated breath, not daring to say more.

"You are my captive now. My slave."

And you were once a passion of mine, she kept to herself. Now . . . now she didn't know what he was to her.

"You mean I am Wolf-Eyes-Woman's slave." She wanted to call him Talon again, but he would only glare at her as he had moments ago. "When will you let me go? Why don't you just allow Harlyn Sawyer to take me away from here? That way I will never become a nuisance to you again." She looked up at him soulfully. "Please?"

As if he hadn't heard her words, he said, "You should be punished for disobeying my orders."

Willow stomped her foot. "Go ahead, then—punish me!"

He scowled darkly across to her. "I mean to do just that."

When he made no move toward her, Willow hung her head dejectedly. "I want to go back to Sundance," she said brokenly, "I don't want to be married anymore, not to you, not to anyone."

"I have already told you we are divorced."

"How?" She looked up at him.

"By my word."

"Your word is law, then?"

"Where you and I are concerned . . . yes."

When his eyes raked her from head to foot, Willow could read lust in them. "I hate what you are really thinking, Lakota, I hate what you really want from me. You think just because I resemble Garnet you can gain your pleasure and use me, and be rid of her ghost."

He stared rigidly at her. But how close had she actually come to the truth? He wanted to exorcise Garnet's evil spirit and the power it still held over him. He wanted to get back at Garnet through her daughter. He wanted revenge. Garnet had ravaged his heart with her wild, wanton ways and torn his soul to shreds. He needed . . . he did not know what he really wanted. . . .

"That is not my kind of game, Willow," he said coldly, hating himself for the lies he must tell her. "I desired her, true. But I do not need substitutes, either." He began to track her, and Willow stepped backward until her back met the lodge-pole. "You are here now. That's all that really counts."

No words of love. Willow looked from his eyes to his hard mouth. She wanted him to kiss her—she must be crazy!

He leaned forward and kissed her teasingly, spreading her legs apart with a knee thrust between her thighs. Heat leaped into her veins when his tongue went into her mouth. Her lips trembled under his. Her knees shook against his legs.

"Why," he began softly at her lips, "didn't you tell me she was your mother? Why?"

"I—I didn't know she was my mother. . . ."

When at last he straightened to look down on her, Willow found herself shaking. She was staring into raw green eyes, eyes that had deep sadness in them. His hand settled on her arm, then ran its length to entwine his fingers with hers. "How could you not know your own mother?" he ground out with low-pitched fierceness, pulling her to him again with a hard jerk.

Her head fell back as she felt his fingers knotted in her hair and yanking. "She left us. She went away when we were children. I never saw her . . . again."

"Do you expect me to believe you really didn't know your own mother even when you came to Sundance?"

"She was dead by then!"

Lakota felt as if he had been stabbed cruelly in the chest. All of the air seemed to go out of his tall frame then. Willow's face blurred before him as he pulled her to him again and indulged them in a deep, soul-reaching kiss that lingered and titillated with erotic caresses and thrusts in her mouth. Riptide tremors caused a violent disturbance at the apex of Willow's legs. Lakota trembled with uncontrollable heat against her soft frame, his hot hardness at testing to his great need.

When he pushed her back against the lodge-pole and shoved up her skirt, Willow caught his wrist. "No. Not this way," she demanded, breathless and shaken to the core of her very being. "You will not have me again, Lakota, not with this ghost between us. Never again. I mean it, Lakota; she must be gone forever from our lives."

Her eyes remained unemotional and withholding while his fingers caressed her softness, and, when he became bolder, she tightened her legs against his encroaching touch. He could see that she meant every word. With a lean, brown finger he brushed her bottom lip and then quit the tepee.

The long, beautiful string of undulating mustangs stretched out, with several of the Horse Indians and Kat'U bringing up the rear with Lakota. They were ascending the slope to the crack in the rock wall that would lead them to the hidden valley.

Standing beside Nightwalker outside the valley, Willow shaded her eyes from the fires of the setting sun. Then Talon's Cloud appeared, running against the broken mass of lavender clouds that floated in the west, golden-edged, in a sea of dark blue sky.

As the mustangs came on, the rose and amber lights grew stronger, brighter, and the shadows below grew deeper, the buffalo grass in the distance a blurred and grayish purple. The mustangs reached the dunderhead, which rang with a clatter under the hoofs of one hundred horses. From out of the gentle shadows they galloped to the sunset-flushed hill where below the camp was situated.

Now Willow could make out Lakota. Like a sun god he was, mounted on a black mustang, his own Cloud leading the horses out front into their captivity.

Willow's breath caught as she watched Talon's Cloud surmount the dunderhead at the heights. Willow stood enchanted. The stallion stood proud, unchallenged, shining silver and gold himself when the sun hovered on the rim of earth and sky.

Her heart mounted with the mustangs when Lakota looked her way. She gazed at him, then at the white horse again, recognizing in Talon's Cloud something within Lakota himself. Both were savage, not meant to be reined in.

With Cloud's long mane and tail flowing in the wind, his long profile against the backdrop of gold, he almost appeared ethereal as he stood and waited for the only master he would ever know on this earth to come up to him.

Her breath held, Willow watched man and beast; they melded into one, the sun dropping below the dunderhead. Time seemed suspended. A trick of the sunset's afterglow, Willow thought, nothing more. But the transfer of Lakota from the black horse onto Cloud took place during a moment during which the changing sunset blinded her.

Man and beast moved against the deep Indian red sky, and then they were off, a moving picture of extraordinary beauty and wildness. Willow felt a sadness moving within her. Everything was ready. She and Harlyn had made their daring plans. In two weeks' time she would be back at Sundance—if all went well.

Chapter Twenty-One

A lavender-blue dawn gave way as the sun rose higher above the grassy plains. Head nodding, Sawyer rode alongside Willow on the stolen Spanish pony. Patting Istas's silken neck, Willow looked over at Harlyn Sawyer. A lot of help he has been, she thought, snorting softly.

One hand splayed on Istas's rump, Willow again stared back over her shoulder, the way they had come. With a calm eye, she scanned the hazy blue ridge where the sky met the earth. At the start of their getaway she had been jumpy and jittery, expecting a band of Horse Indians led by Lakota to come swooping down on them at any moment to return them to the camp. But they had been on the trail now for ten days, and thankfully there had been no sign of a soul, not a white man, not an Indian, no one. There had been nothing but the great sighing of the buffalo grass, and now they were leaving that behind. Along the way, off in the distance, always to their left side, there were now some scattered trees to be seen, but away from the tiny streams of water there was no woodland whatsoever, only the endless elevated prairie. And still, the scenery was changing, ever changing.

Thankful though she was that their escape had been made good, amazingly, with the combined help of Malina and Pepita, the situation was becoming unbearable. She was tired, hungry all the time, aching all over in every bone of her body, parched in her throat during the day with their low water supply, and frozen every night under the one Indian blanket Malina had managed to throw to her at the last minute. Pepita had made sure Sawyer got one too; these women only wanted to see the last of Aiyana.

Most of all, Willow was tired of Harlyn Sawyer.

The man beside Willow came awake on his pony with a loud snort. "Wh-Where am I? Damn and tarnation—" He blinked. "Willow?" Sighing, then yawning, he said, "Where're we now? I sure am hungry." Scratching himself in the ribs and stretching wide, he yawned again.

"What else is new?" Bored, Willow watched the hawk that had been soaring above them the day before once again circle against the blue sky. The hawk's shadows traveled swiftly across the earth, and Willow craned her neck to watch it climb high in the sky. It was while she was watching the gliding flight of the hawk that her eyes shifted, lowered, then did a double-take as they widened considerably at the sight of the terrain just back off to their right.

Sawyer's stomach growled, and he frowned at Willow. "Why do you have to carry all the food and dole it out as you see fit? Just gimme another piece of jerky and I'll shut up until lunchtime."

In a low voice, Willow said, "There's not going to be any *lunchtime.*"

"What?" Sawyer glared at the little woman beside him, unable to understand the change that had come over her in the few short months he'd known her. It was unbelievable, but she had been transformed from a soft, timid little girl into a passionate, high-spirited woman. Still, he was a man, he thought, and he wanted his own way this time. He was going to get it too!

Reaching over, Sawyer grabbed at the parfleche tied to Willow's Indian saddle. "I mean to have me somethin' to eat, and you won't be stopping me this time, little wom*aaaaan!* Hey what'd you go and pinch me for? You plumb loco?"

Rubbing his arm where Willow had pinched him, Sawyer frowned darkly at her, wishing he had never let her talk him into breaking free from the Indians. At least there he had had plenty to eat, and someone was always passing the firewater jug his way. Especially Pepita, Sawyer thought, licking his lips. He always did have a hankering for them Mex women. He frowned at Willow again. A "pale-face," even though the sun had tanned her a soft golden shade. This here woman was more than he could take, though, and first chance he could he was going to find a way to get her to Dalton. He knew who Dalton was now. Tucker. That's who he was. Him and them grinning Apaches had raided Black Fox's camp. He'd heard one of the Indians call him "Tucker" right before Tucker himself got a shot off into his shoulder. Just for that, this here man planned to get revenge on Tucker's hide. He would bring him the girl first chance, then, when Tucker paid him in full, he would take care of Tucker himself. Ahh yes, he could almost smell victory already, and feel the rancho in his clutches.

"Sawyer!" Willow said harshly. "I told you to ride faster."

"What? And wear out my pony?" An ugly grimace crossed his thin face. "Are you loco, woman?"

"Don't you ever watch behind us?"

Willow waited until Sawyer had taken a good look, then turned about frozen as a statue. "Yes, we're being followed. I've been watching while you have been dreaming about food and God only knows what else!" Shaking her head in disgust, Willow wondered what she had ever seen in Harlyn Sawyer. But then, she had been an entirely different woman a few months back. Thank God she had never married this poor excuse for a man!

Halting his mount beside a few scraggly trees, Nightwalker gazed across the open country at the two riders. For many moons now he had been following in their wake, always watchful for any sign of danger. His eyes had a clean sweep of the land now, but soon the tall trees and hills, rocks and plants, would hide the riders from him, and then Aiyana would be on her own. May the Great Warrior go with her at that time, he thought.

Nightwalker had been saddened to see Aiyana go, but if she thought this was the best way, then it was what she must do. He had a strong feeling she knew what she was doing, for she was intelligent and strong enough for the plan of action she had undertaken.

Smiling, Nightwalker thought of how he had aided

her in her escape. Lakota had not read her plans in her moods and actions, but Nightwalker had been acutely aware of what it was she had begun to plan in her mind as much as two weeks ago. The first time he had noticed the change in her had been the day Lakota had walked from her tepee, and his look had been troubled indeed. That night, around the campfire, Nightwalker had turned around to see a new determination in her eyes. Aiyana Willow had become her own person; her will was strong now. She was going to succeed in her sought-after dreams. Though she did not know this yet. How much more pain would she have to endure before she triumphed, he wondered. And his son—perhaps his pain was the greatest at this time. He had kept this from him, that his woman had gone, but upon his return he would have to tell Lakota that she had unfurled her tiny wings and taken flight. She was homeward bound. Where did Lakota's heart truly belong now? Aiyana had chosen her path. Would Lakota follow and claim his bride? He could foresee many thorns yet left along the way for the lovers.

For several more days Nightwalker escorted his daughter-in-law from afar, knowing she had caught sight of him, and then he halted one day. It was time for her to go on her own. She had become strong. The little flower has blossomed and become a warrior woman. Pleased with this new revelation, Nightwalker turned Mah Toh's head north, back home to see what awaited him.

The first thought that came into Willow's head when the uppermost roof balustrade of Sundance house came into view was "home," and it was so good to be here. A warm sensation grew in her chest. This was home to her. Freedom from harm. Freedom from danger. This was where she had laughed and played, cried and sung, made wishes and prayed, grown from little girl to young woman. And this was where she had fallen in love.

As Willow was turning Istas into the long drive to the house, autumn winds swept before her as if clearing the way to make a welcoming path for her. A small dust-devil swirled across the lane before her in a state of excitement. Everything was so familiar and dear to Willow, and she felt choked up somehow.

Flanking Willow on the Spanish pony was Harlyn Sawyer . . . but she didn't want to think about him just now . . . just enjoy, she told herself, enjoy being *home.*

Though it was mid-November, there was still enough color in nature for it to look like late summer. Only here and there was the grass burned out in spots where the gardener had scythed it too short. Excitement grew in her as she drew ever closer to the house, and a choked feeling clogged her throat when she heard a baby's delightful, high screech. Giving the heels to Istas now, Willow hurried faster. Baby Sarah . . . she could hear her playing in the backyard.

Rounding the back of the house, Willow began to slow Istas. "Whoa, girl . . ." Then she was sliding from the horse. "Tanya . . . *Tanya!*" Now she was running.

The lovely redhead had stopped playing with the toddling babe to turn and see what Sarah was shaking her pudgy hands at. Straightening from her bent position, Tanya Brandon slowly looked the girl over—no, the woman who had just slid from the Indian pony . . . and she was calling her name now, running in her direction. In a few short moments before the blanket-draped woman came charging toward Tanya, the blanket slipping from around her shoulders, then being flung aside, Tanya's dumfounded stare took in the amazing sight. She saw what looked like an Indian girl, in well-seasoned buckskins, laced-high moccasins, fat braid . . . that braid specifically commanded notice. It was a *blond* braid.

Right before the gloriously tanned woman hurtled herself into the redhead's arms, Tanya's face lit up in recognition and her arms opened wide to welcome her sister. She had only been gone for three months, but to Tanya and Willow, who had always been so close, it felt like three years.

"Let me look at you," Tanya said, holding Willow at arm's length. Her eyes shifted to the bedraggled rider who had dismounted and was helping himself at the water pump, slurping the water down like a famished hog with its snout turned up. Sawyer had not even bothered to make use of the tin cup that hung from a string at the post. "Who is that?" Tanya asked, dearly hoping that this was not the same person Willow had gone off and gotten married to. "Is he . . . ? Are you . . . ?" was all she could mutter.

"Harlyn Sawyer," Willow answered. "And no, we are not wedded."

"Well . . ." Tanya began, hundreds of questions clamoring for attention in her head. "Did you get attacked by Indians, then?" She looked Willow over really well then, noticing the stunning difference in her sister. "You weren't . . . ah . . . they didn't—" She shrugged— "did they?"

Tossing back her head, Willow laughed with total abandon. When she stopped, her sister was looking at her a little worriedly. *Oh Tanya,* Willow was thinking, *if you only knew!*

"I'll tell you everything later," Willow said. "Right now I am in need of a bath, let me tell you." She laughed. "I think I have fleas."

"F-Fleas?" Tanya scooped Sarah up just then, as the baby had been whining and tugging at her skirt. "We will have to get you scrubbed down right away!" Looking over to the scrubby character slumped against the water pump, Tanya said, "What do you want to do with him? Certainly he is not coming into the house?"

"I'll take care of this," Willow said, leading Istas over to Harlyn Sawyer. She nudged him in the leg with a toe. "Sawyer! Get up. You might as well start earning your keep if you're going to stay on here for a while before you start back to wherever you came from." Cocking a hand on her hip, Willow looked down at the miserable lump of humanity, wondering how he had even gotten this far in life. "Sawyer, if you're not sick, you better wake up and get going."

With one jaundiced eye, Sawyer peered up at Willow. "Always naggin', aren't you? Sure am fortu—nate I never got hitched up with you, ma'am."

"Same goes here. Now get up and get these horses taken care of. The stables are over there." She pointed, and his eyes lazily followed the finger's direction. "Sawyer, if you want to *eat* and get something *powerful* good to *drink,* I suggest you get your rear moving . . . NOW!"

Tanya's eyes widened as Willow's last words did the trick to get the wily sluggard off his feet. Never had she seen a man in such a wearied condition move so fast. It was as if Willow had put a Fourth of July cracker under him. Tanya laughed; even baby Sarah chuckled.

"Sho' is noisy out here," Miss Pekoe drawled, popping her turbaned head out the door. When she saw the braided-and-buckskined woman, she let out a yell. "Why, if'n it ain't Miz Willow!" She grinned at the surprised Tanya then. "If this doan beat all git out! Miz Willow's done come home! There's gonna be some good ol' times at sweet ol' Sundance ta-night . . . Yessuh—" She did a little jig with her skinny feet—"Ah-hunnhh!"

The young woman playing on the hearth rug with baby Sarah wore a fresh deep-yellow gown of victoria lawn with a starched crisp finish. Baby Sarah had on a sweet little puffed dress of British nainsook, dyed a pretty pink pastel, soft finished, with a slight luster. Sarah's red curls were pulled back from her face in the same delightful fashion as Willow's.

"Weow?" baby Sarah said, pushing Willow's nose as though she were pressing on a button. She giggled and shrieked then when her aunty tickled her gently in the ribs with her thumbs while holding the baby's torso with both hands.

"Wil-low." The young woman repeated her name slowly for the chuckling baby.

From her squooshy upholstered armchair, Tanya laughed down at her sister and her child. "I think it will be a while before Sarah has her vocabulary straightened out. She says Mum, and she calls Ashe Poppy—"

"What's this? Did I hear someone call me?"

Just then Ashe Brandon entered the living room, his dusty breeches wrapped around long, lean limbs attesting to the fact that he had been out riding the range. There was no mistaking that this was Talon Clay's brother, and no one thought this more than Willow did at the moment. Looking up at him, Willow felt a pang of loneliness sweep her, her heart divided with the desire to stay and the desire to fly back to Lakota's arms. She knew she couldn't be two places in one time. If only—

"Well, I'll be damned," Ashe said, closely studying the lovely young woman playing on the carpet with his daughter. He smiled across to Tanya. "Thought we might have company when I saw the strange horses out there. Are you just company, or are you home to stay?" He thought he knew then when Willow exchanged a look with Tanya. "Didn't work out, right?"

"Ashe," Tanya said with a laugh. "Why don't you let Willow answer some of those questions you're firing at her?"

Ashe's presence had brought home so many questions Willow had failed to ask herself, until now, looking at baby Sarah, seeing Ashe and Tanya together. What if she was with child herself? She could right now be carrying Lakota's seed within her. What would he do if he knew this? Was he searching for her, even now? Did he care for her at all? Of course he didn't; otherwise he would not have treated her so badly!

"Hmmm." Ashe, looking down at this new Willow, decided he was not needed here at this time. "I think I'll go wash up for dinner, Tanya. Pleasure seeing you, Willow. I hope you're back to stay, and the little house is always yours, you know. Sammy's back." He smiled as her eyes lifted and lit up. "He's out riding with the mustangers right now, but they'll be coming in any hour. So, you stay around for a while, missy," he ended, using his old pet name for her. He walked over and dropped a kiss on his wife's forehead, "Ummmm, you smell good, love." He bent to give Willow and baby Sarah each a hug and then whistled on his way out the door.

Willow shook her head, saying, "I swear he falls more in love with you all the time, Tanya—" She smiled, adding, as she used to: "Sis."

"Yes." Tanya sighed, gazing dreamily in the direction he had gone. "I love Ashe more all the time, too. You recall it wasn't always a bed of roses, either."

Leaning on her elbow as she was, Willow's long golden fall of hair reached the floor and folded there like a bolt of spilt silk. Her hair was streaked here and there by the sun, her ends almost white, the others about her face pale honey. Tanya was amazed at the peachy-gold shade of Willow's complexion, and was somewhat curious about the firm, shapely muscles she had seen while Willow was in her bath.

"Willow, tell me, how did you acquire such a nice, firm shape? You used to be soft-looking as a kitten. You only told me you were at an Indian camp and they treated you—" Tanya shrugged, as Willow had— "so-so. What does that mean? You are so different . . . I can't get over what a change has come over you in such a short time."

"I married a savage, Tanya." Willow's eyes took on a waiting look.

"You married . . . a . . . savage." Tanya made it

sound like a statement of fact rather than a question. Finally Tanya collected herself, asking, "Well, what was his name? Was he handsome? Was he good to you?" Tanya swallowed hard, looking at Willow in a new light. "Aren't you going to tell me anything about your life in an . . . Indian village? Your . . . husband?"

"He is Named-Lakota."

"Lakota . . . that's nice."

"Named-Lakota." Willow laughed. "That is his name."

"Oh, I see . . . Named-Lakota." Her face split in a humorous grin. "Did you call him, uhmm, Named-Lakota? Or did you call him Savage Love?"

Stretching along the carpet, Willow chucked Sarah under the chin. "Both," Willow said. "He was both to me."

Toying with a strand of her hair, Tanya leaned forward. "Did you really love him, Willow? I mean, he didn't force you, did he?"

Willow fell to her back on the carpet, laughing. "What do you mean? Did he force me to love him, or to *make* love with him?"

"Ummm . . . both," Tanya said, her eyes big and blue.

"He forced me to marry him. Then I fell in love with him." Willow rolled over onto her stomach. "No. That isn't true at all. I have always loved Lakota, all my life I guess."

"Hmmm." Tanya looked down at the lovely ring on her third finger, left hand. "I guess you could say that I've always loved Ashe Brandon, too. But I knew Ashe when I was a little girl, you've only just met this Named-Lakota."

Her eyes sliding up to meet Tanya's, Willow gave her sister the most mysterious smile Tanya had ever witnessed plastered on Willow's face. It was almost as if Willow was keeping a deep, dark secret from her. And of course, she was, and only Willow could guess how it was going to affect Ashe and Talon Clay.

Chapter Twenty-Two

Gigantic cottonwoods swayed lazily in the afternoon breeze. It was a day like Indian summer, with a cloud-laden blue sky above and sunshine so mellow and warm it made one want to meander in pensive thought the whole day long, walking in and out of spindrifts of shade, and sharing the day with someone special. That was what Willow had been doing, walking and talking with her brother, who was younger than she by several years, and ruffling his carrot-colored hair while they played silly games on their walk together.

Samson peeked from behind a huge bole of tree, then, when his sister came closer and spied him, he jumped out at her like a bogey man, his voice going deep and fierce. "Scared ya that time, didn't I?" He skipped over to join her, taking the golden-tan hand in his. "How'd you get such a purty color, sis? You must've been out in the sun a lot when you were gone, huh?"

"You know what?" Willow smiled and waited for Samson to echo her last word. "You're still an inquisitive little nipper, aren't you?"

"Inquis-itive?" Samson said, cocking his bright head.

"Curious," Willow replied.

Samson's eyes remained fixed on his second-oldest sister as he walked. "Oh," he said. After a moment of quiet meditation Samson took up the conversation once again. "How come you're so different, sis?" He grinned impishly then, saying, "Did you grow up or something while you were away?" He peered down his lanky length, then up again into his sister's face, thinking she was completely grown up now. "I didn't get any bigger while I was gone."

Willow laughed, remembering the tales he had told her of his trip to New Orleans and his wild escapades. "That's not the way I see it, Sammy. If I remember right, and I should, you told me just this morning over breakfast that the pretty little daughter of the French maid trailed you everywhere you went."

"Naw, she was just a little girl." Samson blushed, denying that he had ever spent many thrilling days full of play rollicking in the narrow streets of the French Quarter with the Rankins' cousins. Especially darling Gabrielle, Rosa Rankin's cousin's mistress's daughter.

Clem waved just then from the line of bunkhouses, and Samson, already becoming a man's man, looked over toward the stables somewhat wistfully. Noticing this, Willow decided she had taken up enough of Sammy's time, even though he thoroughly enjoyed the time he spent with his sisters. But Sammy had grown up with them, two young women always hovering over him like overly protective angels seeing that he came to no harm.

"Go ahead, Sammy, join the men."

"Really sis? You won't be lonesome?" He looked with longing across the greensward as Ashe came outside with several of the mustangers from out of the stables, meaning to go out and check the fences that might need fixing. Again, as they had discussed the subject the day before, Samson asked Willow what she thought had become of Talon Clay. "I'm worried, sis; no one's seen him for a long time now. You heard Ashe, he's worried, too. What's wrong, sis? You look kind of funny, just like you did last night at dinnertime when we were talking about Talon Clay and what might've become of him. You seen him, haven't you? I always know somethin's up when you start chewing on your fingernails. See, you had your baby finger in your mouth." He watched as she let her hand drop to her side once again, this time a bit wearily. Reaching up, he planted a surprisingly strong hand on her shoulder, asking her, "Sis . . . what's wrong?"

"I—" Willow found she didn't know where to begin. "Maybe we'll talk about it someday, Sammy, soon . . . I promise." She smiled. "Think you can wait until I'm ready?"

The lad hooked his thumbs into his belt, aping the way Ashe stood when he was making up his mind about a matter that needed serious consideration. "Guess so." He squinted his sherry-brown eyes in the sun. "Yeah, but don't you be wandering too far away from home. Hear?"

"Hear, yessir!" She tipped her wide-brimmed cowboy hat and nodded strongly. "Don't you worry none about Willow Hayes. . . ." *My name's not Hayes anymore, Sammy,* she wanted to say, *I'm a Brandon now, just like Ashe made Tanya one. Wait until you hear that Talon Clay is my husband . . . my savage love.* "See you later, Sammy. Don't get into too much mischief."

"Naw," Samson called back to her over his shoulder as he went trotting toward Ashe and the others, "I don't do much of that anymore, sis."

Willow ducked under some low-swooping branches and then resumed her walk, this time alone.

Sunlight and shadow played over Willow's winsome countenance as she walked through the woods where solitude held the earth in its embrace. She wore a cornflower-blue frontier dress that brushed the lower branches with a soft whooshing sound as she stepped here and there. Dreamy reflections stirred in her, and from out of the past she recalled moments of sweet joy she and Talon Clay had shared together. . . .

In the beginning, at Sundance, they had been awed by each other's presence; oh, she knew Talon Clay, the outlaw, had been smitten with her . . . at first. Then a transformation had occurred, after Talon returned from running around with his outlaw sidekicks. There had been an aloof carelessness about him. He had avoided her and hadn't tried to touch her physically as he had when first they became acquainted. That evening, as the sun was just being immersed in the fiery copse of wood, when she had chased after Talon to warn him that Rangers were near, she had truly and deeply fallen in love with the handsome outlaw. His beautiful forest-green eyes had engulfed her heart and soul, roamed over her flushed face and touched her shivering form here and there. Half afraid, desperately wanting him to kiss her and hold her, she had taken the initiative. When they embraced, it was explosive, his arousal plainly evident in the tight buckskins that brushed roughly against her. Passion's first kiss had drowned her in a sea of shimmering sensation. Her breath had shortened, and her body had become flushed with suffused heat.

As Willow emerged from the wood into a sunlit clearing she felt the mild caress of the autumn breeze that lent sweetness to the earth. Brightly feathered creatures winged busily around their nests caring for their youngsters. Giant trees swooped heavily over Strawberry Creek, which coruscated under the sun, its lazy blue waters showing intermittently through the trees. Before Willow stood the sadly neglected house, Le Petit Sundance, half finished, with swallows flying in and out of open squares meant for windows.

As she drew near it, Willow conjured up an image of a crowded sun parlor, with the Brandon men and their families gathered in it. She stood directly below the unfinished gallery now, looking up, a haunting feeling coming over her, and it was almost as if Talon Clay's tangibly felt presence there beside her was truly a reality. This was Talon's house, but would he ever return to complete its construction?

It was a one-story structure, surrounded by a gallery, surmounted by a hipped roof, but its most curious feature was its framing. The walls consisted of posts sunk in the ground and set closely together, laid vertically instead of horizontally; it was what the French called *poteaux-en-terre,* meaning "posts on earth."

Climbing the stairs, Willow crossed the front gallery, seeing already that the unfinished house was badly in need of paint to keep its fresh wood from turning dark with ugly stains. When she stepped inside and walked the center hall dividing the house, her high-laced shoes rang hollowly against the wood floors running to the barren walls. In the rear gallery the stairs that rose upward went nowhere, and she went to stand at the top looking out over the breathtaking grounds of Le Petit Sundance. Her heart twisted as she thought of what might have been. Talon had become Lakota, her savage love. Would they ever be together again as they had been in the Indian village?

A choked feeling rose in her throat and Willow could no longer halt the deluge of tears that flooded from her burning eyes at the possibility of being divorced from the man she loved with all her heart and soul. Loneliness was a cruel thing, and now she knew it in its most terrible form.

Rushing down the steps heedlessly now, Willow forgot to lift her skirts high and tripped on a loose stair. She found herself reaching for nothing but empty air, and then when she knew she was falling she braced herself for the pain to come, but when she was tumbling over and over there was nothing but release from the real hurt she had been feeling moments before.

Striking the boards below, Willow felt all breath go out of her for several moments as her lungs struggled to adjust to the shock of the fall. She lay there for what seemed a long time, unable to move for fear that something was broken. Soon she discovered hot tears were rolling along her cheeks and into her hairline. From where she lay Willow could sight along the floor to the line of trees where the woods began. Her eyes widened. She had just seen movement there!

Forgetting she might be hurt, Willow sat up too quickly. She felt bruised and badly shaken, but that was about all. As far as she could tell she wasn't hurt, yet later might be a different story and she might find herself really one massive ache all over.

Whoever had just emergd from the woods hadn't seen her yet, or else he was pretending she wasn't there, Willow thought. Still seated on the gallery floor with her legs tucked underneath, Willow searched the man's countenance until she could make out his identity.

"Harlyn Sawyer," she said under her breath. What was the man doing here? Was he spying on her? Had he followed her from the line of bunkhouses out back of Sundance? Ridiculous, she told herself. And even if he had been out walking, so what? He was free to come and go as he pleased, Ashe had given him a few jobs to do around the place. Still, now that he had recovered from his exhaustion and his minor wound, why hadn't he moved on so that he could return to his rancho? Surely he was not going to stick around in hopes of pursuing her hand still? She might as well set the man straight on the matter. She was still married to Lakota as far as she was concerned.

"Sawyer," Willow called, drying her tearstained cheeks with the back of her hand. "Wait up!"

Sawyer paused in midstride and turned to watch Willow limp over to him. He damned the situation. Sawyer had known all along that Willow would come here, for he had often seen her gazing from the hill in this direction. He had come himself to see what it was that could be such an interest to her. He had asked a few questions about seeing the half-finished house for himself, and had discovered Talon Clay Brandon—that cursed half-breed—had begun work on this place called Le Petit Sundance, and had left it undone to go chasing off somewhere. He had overheard Ashe Brandon cussing his brother out real good, and then the next minute Ashe was staring off to the hills with a worried frown creasing his brow.

Now, today, Sawyer had followed Willow from a distance, knowing she was headed for the unfinished house, no doubt going there to moon over that half-breed husband of hers she left behind at the Indian village. Knowing Willow and her adventuresome spirit, he had loosened that stair days before in hopes that she would take a bad tumble. But, curses, she had only sprained her ankle. He was grateful to whatever God looked over her that she hadn't broken her damn fool neck! He wanted her hurt a little more than merely a sprained ankle so he would be able to take her away. A busted arm or leg would do. But no such luck; she was much stronger than he had believed her to be. Next time he might just kill her. Of course, he could always tell Tucker that it had been accidental, that he hadn't meant to go to such lengths. Then again, he would not get paid if he brought Tucker a pretty corpse. Tucker wanted her alive and well to use as bait for the Brandon men.

"Pretty day, ain't it?" he said as Willow Brandon neared. "Say, what happened? You look as if your horse threw you." He lifted his head as if to search for the mentioned horse.

Narrowing her gold-flecked eyes over Sawyer with suspicion, Willow pushed the straying yellow wave away from her eyes and brushed her skirts off with a hand that still trembled. She looked up at Sawyer when she was finished and was straightening her back. There was a strange look in his mysterious brown eyes just then—she had caught it, and she held the image in her mind so that later she could reflect on its meaning with more accuracy than the moment afforded her now.

"I'm all right," Willow said, limping beside him as they walked through the tall grasses and dried summer wildflowers. "I asked you what you were doing here?"

"You did? Well, Mrs. Brandon, if you did I sure didn't hear you, now did I?" He looked at her with a frown of concern. "Are you sure you're all right? What happened, anyway?"

Her nose wrinkled, smelling a rat. "Let me ask you you how come you're so talkative all of a sudden? You sure weren't much company in my presence all the other times, save for that first day we met."

"Ah yes, now that was some fine day, when I first looked upon your purty face." He looked down at her as if to study her keenly this time. "You sure have changed, become mighty purty, if I do say so myself. You was nothing but all meat and no potatoes before, Miss Willow."

"*Mrs.* Brandon, to you."

As they neared the big house, Sawyer said slyly, with a lift in volume, "Mrs. Brandon—"

Whirling about to come squarely in front of Sawyer, Willow hissed, "Keep your voice down!"

"What? Why, Mrs. Brandon, don't tell you you ain't told your folks you done gone and got yourself hitched with Talon Clay Brandon, second heir to Sundance property. You haven't?" His brown eyes narrowed with deviltry. "Why not, Mrs. Brandon, don't you think they should know about the happy event that took place in . . . an Indian village?" He whispered the last words in a low hiss.

Willow halted her steps beside him. "What is it you want, Sawyer?" She knew he was after something.

"I just want you to go away with me. Help me get some gear together; stealing a wagon won't be nothin'."

"*Again?* Go away with you again?" she squeaked. Willow shook her head in utter disbelief. "You must be crazy!"

Suddenly he was staring straight ahead, as if he was seeing something he couldn't really believe. Following his steady gaze, Willow saw Hester Tucker sashaying toward them, her blond hair done up on her head in frizzy curls, her lips painted a garish shade of red. His eyes nearly popping, Sawyer followed the sensuous rolling of her hips, and no one knew when his baggy, borrowed pants began to feel snug in the front. Sawyer had been celibate for too long now, his last woman having been Pepita. He saw Hester only as an end to his mild discomfort, and had no heart as to what she would think or feel afterward toward him.

But Willow was not looking at Hester so much as she was at the woman the silly blonde had brought along. She was very slender, with a pretty white face that looked curiously as if it had been lavishly patted with powder. Bright splotches dotted her high cheeks, also a curious shade, this one pink. As she walked closer to Willow, Willow could see her strange yellow-green eyes; and she had black hair, black as ink.

"Willow Hayes," Hester greeted her with an affected air. "Won't you meet Fleurette Baudier." Hester sniffed haughtily. "She's French."

"Obviously," Willow said, like a grande dame herself. Ooooh, how she would love telling Hester that her name was not Hayes any longer but *Brandon.* Wouldn't that set Hester back on her heels and curl her hair! "Hello Fleurette," Willow greeted without pretense, sticking her hand out.

The pretty girl eyed the outstretched hand for a moment and then took it with a smile on her rosy lips. Willow bet herself those were artificially colored, too.

"Halloo," Fleurette said in a heavily accented voice, removing her lily-white hand from the graceful blonde's. "You are very, ahh, petite, Mademoiselle Hayes. Ah, but so pretty."

You're not so bad looking yourself—a little on the skinny side, Willow almost said but thought better of it. Instead she softly said, "I've never met a real French girl, I mean Frenchwoman. Did your folks come from France?" Willow blanched, feeling like a blundering idiot.

Tinkling laughter filled the air. "No, no, mademoiselle, we are born, all of us, in New Orleans in our family. The coming from France was accomplished by my ancestors, ah, but do not ask me how long ago that was!" She laughed again and exchanged a look with Hester.

"Well, who's going to introduce me to these fine ladies?" Sawyer said as he drawled the words in his best southern accent. "I been standing here awonderin' and awaitin'."

Taking a deep breath as if it pained her to speak, Willow said, "Hester Tucker meet Harlyn Sawyer, and Fleurette Baudier meet Harlyn Sawyer. Harlyn Sawyer meet the ladies." She couldn't help herself then, she turned aside and muffled a low giggle with her hand. *If Hester Tucker was a lady, she was willing to eat anybody's hat!* Lady-of-the-night was nearer the truth.

Hester gasped then as Willow straightened after she had made a pretense of coughing in her hand. "Willow Hayes! If you don't look dark as an Indian squaw. And your hair—tell me, have you been using white vinegar on it to make it so light?"

"Ahh," Fleurette came to Willow's rescue, *"petite mademoiselle* looks simply *ravissante!"* She leaned closer to the blonde, tapping the dainty wrist as if she held a fan. "Tell me, how did you obtain such a ravishing color . . . ? Have you been . . . sunning yourself . . . in the, ah," her voice went below a whisper, mock-scandalized, "the nude?"

"Ohhh," Willow purred, "but of course." Straightening from her slightly tipped position to better hear Fleurette's whispers, she said, loud enough for them all to hear, "I did it while riding on a white stallion!"

Hester's eyes widened in shock, and some curiosity. "Did *what* while riding a white stallion?"

Lifting her shoulder provocatively, Willow purred, "Why Hester, surely *you* know. . . ."

With that Willow left them all standing staring after her, struck with wonder. Fleurette thought the girl possessed fire and spirit. As for Hester, she was the most dumbfounded, for she did not recognize this Willow Hayes at all!

Leaf-patterned shadows created ever-shifting, ever-flickering, gray scenes across the quilted bedspread, a swath of the same glancing over the wood floor of the little house. The place was neat and orderly, the blankets folded tidily at the foots of beds, every bare spot of wood polished to a high sheen and smelling of rosewater and beeswax; the bedcovers had been freshly laundered and hung out on the line to dry afterward so that they smelled fresh as springtime, and every dish and pot and pan was in its rightful place in the corner cupboard. Even the puncheon floors had been sprinkled with rosemary and peppermint, then swept clean of the herbs with a broom, leaving a pleasant scent behind in the rooms.

"How *quaint."* Fleurette chirruped as she stepped into the house without bothering to knock or call out. "I have sent the drover back to Rankins to pack all my bags and bring them here." She walked around, delighted with what she saw. "Charming," she said, stooping to touch a pink and blue braided rug. "Did you make this yourself?" She stood, directing a white finger toward a wall hanging. "And this?"

"Yes, to both," Willow returned. "Fleurette, I know you want to stay here . . . but you see, I may be going back to teach school soon."

"I do not mind, *cherie*. I will love being alone here." Returning to the door, Fleurette leaned against the door frame, her arm high above her head. "Charming," she repeated, "I Love it here. Oh please." She whirled to face the lovely blonde. "Say you will allow me to stay. It is really much too hectic at the Rankins' . . . they have company," she added, with a pout.

"Oh?" Willow was curious. "What kind of company?"

"Their son is there, Almanzo Rankin." Fleurette spun to face Willow then. "And he has his wife with him—she is an Indian! La! She is the stuck-up one. I have never seen such a haughty face. I do have to admit she is quite lovely . . . for an Indian squaw. You know, he could have done better if he would have married my cousin; she is a cousin by what you say, ah, tail of the shirt, I think it is. It is strange how Ellita did not come along when the Rankins visited New Orleans to see *maman* and myself. My *maman* is an old friend of the Rankins'. La! but your younger brother is a mischievous one! That one was forever chasing that sweet youngster Gabrielle. And countless other pretty mademoiselles, I might add." Stopping to catch a breath, Fleurette blinked at the suddenly quiet blonde. "Something is wrong, Mademoiselle Hayes?"

"No, nothing is wrong." Willow turned her back on the chatty young woman. She was not much younger than herself, Willow could tell. Fleurette Baudier had much to learn about peaceable Indians . . . and won't she be surprised to learn that this supposed haughty Indian woman, Kachina, was her very own friend. Very soon, Willow knew, Kachina would be over to visit her, for no doubt she had heard via the grapevine that Willow *Hayes* had come home to Sundance.

Turning back to face Fleurette, Willow said, "Fleurette, why don't you teach me how to speak a little French." Willow smiled. *"Oui?"*

"C'la vie. Say no more. I will teach Willow Hayes how to speak *all* French!" Fleurette pealed away in a string of longwinded giggles.

The converted barn now stood ready, complete with belfry and bell, to call all the children to school. There was an old water pump outside, and of course the essential red outhouse out back.

Willow experienced a wave of nostalgia as she tied her horse outside, almost expecting the wide doors to burst open and spill out a yelling, shoving group of children, the children of all ages she had taught here.

Surrounded by giant cottonwoods and live oaks, the red painted schoolhouse silently bid Willow welcome home, and suddenly she wished the schoolhouse could really talk. All of the folks in the two counties were proud of their school, which had in the past served as a church and a barn. Now the frame building was lighted by six large windows, and Willow knew that the new school furniture inside consisted of a tall bookcase, a long teacher's desk, and various size chairs and "desk boards" to accommodate twenty-five pupils.

Stepping inside, Willow was disappointed to see that no new teacher had taught school here . . . where did that leave the children? she wondered sadly. *No school?*

It was indeed sad, for the school had of late been equipped with all the necessary apparatus: a huge globe; a set of colorful maps; a thick dictionary and stand; a set of spelling-and penmanship charts. Willow felt suddenly choked up as she spied Pa's tobacco tin, which she had carried her lunch in. She usually ate outside with the youngsters when the weather permitted; it usually did. While she ate on the one stair, she watched the girls sitting in a circle on the ground playing a game of pat-a-cake. She remembered one boy by the name of Shawn, who'd walked five miles to school, though when it was raining hard Pastor Cuthbert would take time off to pick Shawn up in his wagon. What had been Shawn's last name? she tried to recall. School had never been dull with that lad around, he'd had a good aim with the spitballs!

"Hallelujah!" Pastor Cuthbert exclaimed from the door, which stood open to allow a bright ray of sun to wash the floor up to where Willow was just in the process of turning about. "If you don't look like an angel straight from heaven." He rushed forward to greet his favorite schoolteacher; he'd had a time of it trying to replace her, but no one had been able to fill the bill as far as Cuthbert was concerned. "Are you back to stay? I certainly do pray you are. You would be amazed, child, at how many youngsters are wanting to come to school." He shrugged. "There was no one." His eyes moistened and he blinked. He was really happy to see Willow Hayes. "If our children and their parents continue to show their good will and interest in the future, this school will always be on a level with the best schools in Texas . . . my dear, are you ready to teach? Four days a week?"

Looking across the room to the large blackboard she'd used to write letters upon, now still bearing the lopsided, half-erased scrawl of a child, she noticed it had come loose and been repositioned at a crooked angle on the wallboards. Willow softly gave him her answer: *"Yes."*

Breathing deeply, Fleurette stepped outside the little house. She flung her heavy black hair over her shoulder, stopped and sank into the thick grass outside the house. For the first time in what seemed ages, she was allowed some time alone to meditate by herself. Always at home she'd been surrounded by so many uncles, aunts, and gossipy, partying cousins. They all lived side-by-side in New Orleans, residing in noisy *soigne* townhouses, in which she thought she'd surely go crazy.

Ah, Fleurette thought, it is nice to be away from it all. She was a nature lover at heart, and she was afraid she'd never get used to the hordes of suitors vying for her company at the Mardi Gras or at so many soirées . . . nothing was a novelty to Fleurette any longer.

Sundown had blazed across the earth, but now the violets and grays of twilight bathed the grounds that surrounded the girl lounging in the tall grass. She closed her eyes then, and before Fleurette knew it the twilight was deepening, her eyes opening to the sweet, dark shadows she was immersed in. As a tall figure moved forward stealthily, Fleurette's lids closed again over her yellow-green eyes.

Fleurette received no warning of the man's coming.

In the rapidly darkening area, Talon Lakota could not see who it was lurking in the grass outside Willow's house. Whoever it was though, he'd make sure they moved on and did their sneaking elsewhere. He was here to see Willow, and he wanted no stranger distracting him from his mission.

Simultaneously Talon covered the mouth and lifted the person against him, exerting little pressure on the frail arms he'd suddenly encountered. And Fleurette could only imagine she'd been attacked by a lean, muscled cougar; there flashed in her mind for only a second's time the tale Samson Hayes had related of the large golden cats that roamed the hills of Texas. She struggled to be free, but the arms that held her immobile were like bands of raw iron. Suddenly Fleurette had a hard time believing this was truly a human being, a man, who held her. She soon grew weak and leaned against the man, smelling the disturbing male scents he gave forth, and feeling with repulsion his strong male body pressed against her to hold her still.

"*Mon Dieu,* unhand me!"

Hearing strange words spilling from a woman's mouth, Talon stepped back and looked down at the frail thing he'd been holding. Her odd-colored eyes were wide, and he knew he'd frightened her out of her wits. Hair as black as a raven's wing framed a milk-white face, and Talon had a moment of unease when he stared into the ghostly countenance of the wild-eyed woman, thinking he'd come across a disembodied spirit. He'd never believed in such things, and besides he'd grabbed hold of her and felt her warm flesh, smelled the delicate scent of the expensive perfume an unquestionable lady who ran a boardinghouse down in San Antonio often had worn.

Her odd-colored eyes dilated with shock as they brought into focus the golden "mountain cat" who had attacked her. Slightly uptilted eyes, green she thought, stared curiously down at her. Surrounding the long-lashed eyes was a lean rugged face, all sharp angles and flat-planed, high cheekbones, with a mouth that looked as if it had been carved out of bronze. In fact, he appeared to be that color all over . . . Fleurette flushed at where her curiosity was taking her. She stared boldly upward again, her awestruck eyes coming to rest on the light hair, chopped shoulder-length, silken hair that swayed when he moved the slightest bit. Around his forehead, tied in a knot in back with trailing ends, he wore a turquoise headband. He could be an Indian, she thought, but concluded after remembering the buckskin attire she'd seen often here that he was a normal human being after all.

"Who are you?" Talon inquired, standing with his arms cocked at his hips.

"My name is Fleurette Baudier!" she said in a flurry of perturbation. "I happen to be staying here with Mademoiselle Willow Hayes for a time." She missed the momentary flaring of green eyes. Shakily Fleurette cleared her throat. "She will return shortly, she has only gone to visit the school briefly," she warned; just in case he had any ideas of lingering. "And you, who are you, sir, and what are you doing here?"

Chuckling low, Talon announced, "Ma'am, I happen to live here." He nodded then, and tipping his head to her, said, "Good evening." He strode off the way he had come, this time in an upright stance.

Not long after the startling intrusion on her privacy, Fleurette had returned to the little house. She'd tried her best to make herself a cup of herbed tea, but her most valiant efforts proved utterly futile. Not only did Fleurette spill the tea leaves all over, but she burned her lily-white hands with the scalding water she'd somehow managed to heat over the hearth. That had been another chore in itself, the building of a fire.

"I don't know if I shall be able to take this much longer," she told herself. "I do believe I prefer to be waited on much better . . . but I do long to be off by myself meandering and daydreaming." She looked around, wondering what she could prepare for herself that would be easier and safer. "If only that rogue had not come along to spoil everything this evening." Hearing a sound at the door, Fleurette looked up and saw Mademoiselle Hayes standing there.

"What rogue were you talking to yourself about, Fleurette?" Willow asked as she came into the room, inquisitively studying the nervous girl.

"You don't know how happy I am to see you, mademoiselle!" Fleurette came around the table in a rustle of emerald-green silk. She'd changed her dresses several times that day, and each time had been disappointed with her countenance. "I've had quite a time, let me tell you! First I was attacked by a most rude male person, he . . ."

Willow stepped closer, perusing Fleurette's highly flushed face. "What male . . . person do you mean? There is not one soul here who would dare attack you, Fleurette. Ashe chooses his hired hands well."

"I would not know about that, but this young man certainly did come on strong. Why," she said excitedly, "he came very close to ravishing me, he did." She strolled around the table, patting her hair. "He took liberties that would shock you, mademoiselle!"

Automatically Willow murmured, "Carl Tucker."

"Who? Did you say Tucker? You did, of course. Well, tell me, what does this Tucker look like? Is he heavy, or thin?"

"Why don't you just tell me what this man who attacked you looked like, and save us some trouble, Fleurette?" Willow didn't know why, but suddenly she'd begun to feel an inner trembling.

"I did notice one thing," Fleurette said with a

desultory smile. "He was like a lean, golden mountain cat, the ones your brother Samson spoke to me about. I couldn't help gazing into his incredible eyes, hmm, dark green I believe. Around his head he wore a headband."

Willow's heart had begun to pick up its beat, and her head felt as though it was reaching the stars in the sky. "What color was his hair, Fleurette, can you tell me?" If it was her love, then Fleurette's answer would be: Like golden wheat.

Recalling the fluidness of the young man's silken hair, Fleurette swiftly answered, "I was so frightened, I do not recall."

Disillusioned and close to tears, Willow sat down on the puncheon bench, a painful "oh" falling from her lips.

Chapter Twenty-Three

"Why didn't you tell me that last night?" Willow stormed at Fleurette, her arms flailing in the air.

"But mademoiselle, you did not ask me if he *resided* here at Sundance." Slyly, Fleurette contemplated her next question before asking it, "Ah . . . so who is this man who holds such interest for you, mademoiselle?"

"Damnit Fleurette, stop calling me *mademoiselle!* I am Willow . . . Willow, oh, never mind the last name!" she snapped irritably, mixing the buckwheat batter for pancakes with a frustrated beat.

"Hayes, that is it, Willow Hayes."

"Yes, yes," Willow said, spooning applesauce into a bowl to go along with the buckwheat pancakes, "if you say so."

"What has you in such a dither, mad . . . ah, Willow Hayes?"

"Just Willow, if you don't mind." Halting the preparations for breakfast, she stared out the window in a dreamy state of reflection, wondering how it would be to have Talon holding her in his warm embrace.

"My savage love," Willow murmured, not conscious that Fleurette was studying her closely, much too closely, with a mischievous light in her odd-colored eyes.

Indeed, Fleurette's mind began to churn with mischievous schemes; perhaps Fleurette was going to find something else here besides relaxation.

One morning when Indian summer spread its soft, warm blanket over the earth, Willow rode Dust Devil across the pasture before sunrise. Oak and mesquite woodlands, fantastic formations of rock and cactuses, blue gurgling streams, and grass-rich meadows alternated across the land.

Halting above the wide, meandering Emerald Creek, she gazed down the hill and felt more alive than she had in a long time. Wild grasses spread beneath her feet, and Willow inhaled the damp, sweet odor of wild hay. She walked down the boulder-strewn slope leading to the lazy ribbon of the creek.

Holding her breath, Willow spied two deer, a buck and a young doe, silhouetted against the sky blooming dawn rose and red in the east. The doe stepped daintily along the trail, and not far behind trotted the intent buck with his magnificent rack of antlers. Looking neither right nor left, the buck pursued the coy doe, which kept herself just out of reach. It was mating season, Willow realized, when the bucks lost some of their fear of man, the reason why he had not become alarmed at sensing her there.

Willow walked uncertainly through dawn's hazy rose light, watching the deer break their silent interlude to trot away toward the oak thickets along the creek's edge. She paused for a moment to watch the sun burst gloriously above the trees at the east bank of the creek. Sweeping over the land, the first rays shot across crags, prairie, woods, and water. Trees turned to cinnamon, orange, and russet, and wind rippled over the water, shattering shafts of sunlight into a million red-gold flecks. The trilling of birds opened the morning's symphony, and then from the woods a variety of wintering songbirds supplied sweeter melodies.

Willow then looked up, struck by the sudden silence in the air. Everything had come to a standstill, even the busy twittering of birds. Staring around, Willow could find no movement in the trees. She looked around, startled by the sudden winging of a bird from one tree branch to another. Catching a strange scent on the wind, Dust Devil raised her head and nickered a warning, nudging her master with her huge, velvety nose.

"We better return, huh, girl?" Willow said, feeling gooseflesh rising on her arm and along her spine. Mounting up, she put the soft spurs to Dust Devil and the strong mustang took the hill in powerful leaps and pulls. Soon they were disappearing over the top, Dust Devil's long charcoal-gray tail the last thing the cursing man saw.

Returning to where he had hidden his mount, a good ways off, Carl Tucker kicked tufts of earth into the air, scuffing the toes of his already scarred boots.

Talon Clay Brandon's face was symmetry itself. He'd forgotten what it felt like to get a haircut, and he cursed now every time Clem's scissors nipped at his nape.

"Hold still, whippersnapper, it was you what had the idea to cut yer hair shorter . . . dagblasted shears, don't know what's gotten into them." He chuckled. "Most likely needs some sharpening after being in hair the likes of your'n. What're you tryin' to do, fella, pretty yourself up for little Willow Hayes? Always thought you had a hankerin' for that one. Now you come back from wherever in blazes you went off to this time, expectin' the lass to be waiting fer ya." He peered into Talon's strikingly handsome face then, whistling. "Sure been a long time since I been seein' a prettier face than what you got, boy. Say now, sure don't think I should be callin' you lad anymore, not nowadays anyway. You shore did do some fine growin' up, Talon Clay. Yessir, Willow's sure gonna take a good look at'cha this time!"

When Talon stepped into the adobe kitchen after sniffing out the berry tarts Miss Pekoe had whipped up, he found himself getting a good scolding as the black woman brandished her spoon above his head, then stared slowly while a plump cherry ran slowly down the man's chin. Looking up again, she smiled a huge, toothy grin.

"Why if'n it ain't you, Master Brandon. Jes' look at you, if you doan look like the fine gent'mum, yassuh! Where you been, boy? I mean, *man,* 'cause you sho is a man . . . all man." Giggling in a low, throaty voice, Miss Pekoe dared to ask, "What happened to that long, shining cornsilk hair you used to have all over your head?" She giggled again. "I always wanted to put a pretty bow in your hair. If you aks me, I like youse much better this way."

"Well, Miss Pekoe," he said, hugging the skinny

maid around the waist. "I'm afraid I must say I'd like you a whole lot more if you had meat on your bones. But you sure do have pretty eyes, Miss Pekoe."

"Ah, go on with you." She brandished her huge wooden spoon again. "Youse jest wantin' to get another one of those berry tarts, Master Brandon." She chuckled, waving her spoon. "Go ahead, stuff youself, I kin always make more. Ashe's always comin' in here stuffin hisself, too. You Brandon men sure do like the berries, and I sure am glad Mister Brandon come to fetch me here, 'cause I sure do like making all these goodies."

"You should eat some yourself, Miss Pekoe," Talon instructed, popping another syrupy cherry into his mouth. "Uhmm, damn but I sure have missed your cooking, woman."

"That'll teach you never to leave your home again." Suddenly she leaned closer, her black eyes curious and big. "You done seen li'l Missy Hayes yet, Master Brandon?"

"No." Talon glanced away and then back to the woman. "Why, should I have?"

"Ah, go on with you, I knows you was sweet on that gal. She been walkin' around here all pie-faced since she come back from almost marrying that poor excuse for a man, Sorry Sawyer, and I sure do think she been mooning about you, Master Brandon."

"Why is that?"

"Doan know, jest got a feeling, that's all. And you was always staring at her like a sick calf, you was. Miss Pekoe doan miss nothing when it comes to ro-mance."

Talon chuckled. "So, who is your latest flame, then?"

This time Miss Pekoe gave Talon Clay Brandon a

little tap on his head with the bowl of her spoon, chuckling low as she snorted, "Ah, you be moseying along now, Master Brandon, Miss Pekoe's got work to do." Before the young man made it all the way out the door, Miss Pekoe halted him, saying, "Mister Ashe knows you done come home, and he been lookin' for you. Don't you think it's time you quit playin' hide'n seek with him?"

Talon, poking his head back in, whispered loudly, *"Mind your own business, Pekoe."* Then he winked and vanished from the doorway.

When he'd gone, Miss Pekoe shook her turbaned head, murmuring, "Uhmm, uhmm, that sho is one fine-lookin' buck!"

"Well, well, just look what the horse dragged in," Ashe Brandon exclaimed when Talon Clay entered the stable and halted at the stall where his brother was pitchfork-deep in manure and hay.

Talon chuckled. "You still shoveling the sh—" he placed a finger over his lips— *"shh—shhh"* he finished, for Tanya Brandon had just walked up behind him.

"What is all the secrecy about?" Tanya came around and faced the young man in buckskins, smelling clean as lye soap, with a fresh haircut and shave. Her eyes widened in surprise, a very pleasant surprise at that. "Talon Clay Brandon, is this really you? Lord, you almost gave me heart failure looking like that!"

"Like what, ma'am? I didn't look at you rudely, did I?" He grinned impishly.

"Why, you—you're all grown up." She smiled affectionately at her husband. "Just like your older brother. And you knew what I meant, too, so don't play games with me. When I became a Brandon woman, I also got some more smarts. You can't pull the wool over my eyes."

"Tanya—" Talon pulled the gorgeous redhead into his arms and gave her a big hug— "you grow beautifuller every time I see you. Ooops," he said, glancing down at her belly. "Sorry if I hugged you too hard, I had no idea you were in the family way." He grinned. "Again."

Astonished, Tanya said, "How did you know? Ashe and I have told no one . . . ah, darling," she said to her husband, "when did you tell your brother? I thought we agreed to announce it this evening at dinner?"

Ashe looked dumbfounded and shrugged. "Never said a word to him, love, honest to God." He looked at this new man who was his brother, inquiring, "How did you know, Talon?"

"Oh, come on now," Tanya put in, "I heard Talon 'shh-ing' you when I walked in."

Sheepishly, Talon declared, "That was something else, ma'am, you see Ashe here was shoveling, ah, *manure,* like he always does, thinking he's a hired hand instead of the boss of Sundance."

All three of them laughed collectively then. "I do hope you're staying long enough for dinner, Talon, before you go riding off into the sunset again?"

"Oh . . . I think that I'll be staying a while before I head out again."

"Where to this time?" Ashe wanted to know, thinking his brother might sail away to China or some other faroff place like India and become a wealthy merchant.

Gazing thoughtfully down to the floor, Talon damned the boots that were beginning to pinch the toes that had become used to moccasins over such a long period of time. Now he seriously wondered if he would ever get used to the harder leather again. Talon looked up, right into his brother's cat-hazel eyes. "Ashe," he began, then tried to go on, "I—I don't know how to tell you that—" he shrugged— "that I really have no idea what I will do or where I'll go next."

Tanya and Ashe exchanged puzzled glances. Clearing his throat, Ashe leaned the pitchfork against the stall, and with one arm about his wife's waist and the other about Talon's shoulders, he said, "What say let's go and wash up for dinner." He looked down into his wife's wondering eyes. "Tanya, see that a place is set for Talon and our female company . . . Fluerine or whatever her name is." He sent her from his embrace, giving her backside a pat. "Maybe you can get your sister to help you." Feeling his brother's involuntary shiver go through his arm, he asked Talon if he was cold, and Talon said: "No, not at all."

Mustering every ounce of confidence she possessed, Willow braced herself for the moment Talon Clay would enter the room with Ashe Brandon. While she helped with the placing of the dishes on the long linen-draped table, Fleurette kept up a lively string of inane chatter that was driving Willow to the breaking point. Because she couldn't make out what Tanya was saying about Talon's new appearance and wanted desperately to hear, Willow was prepared to stuff a gag into Fleurette's mouth!

"Willow?" Tanya was talking to her. "Do you, or don't you?"

"I'm sorry, Tanya." She turned her back on Fleurette and said with a glance, "I really couldn't hear what you were saying."

"I was merely asking you if you wanted to fetch the white wine."

"No," Willow answered, "I really don't care for any, thank you."

"Well . . ." Tanya cocked her slim arms on her hips. "You might not want any, sister dear, but there are others who might." Tanya laughed then. "Go and fetch it? Thank you," she said as Willow turned to leave the dining room. "Fleurette," Tanya said, facing the slim French girl, "are you nervous or something? No? I'm sorry, I thought you seemed to be. Are you missing your family then?"

"Oh . . . yes, I suppose I am missing them a little, madame."

"Oh please, you may call me Tanya, Fleurette."

Staring around the lovely room, Fleurette said, "Why do you do so much of the work yourself . . . Tanya? Do you not own a houseful of maids?"

"Just a few," Tanya said wistfully. "I love to keep busy, for you know they say that idle hands are the tools of the devil." She laughed softly. "Besides, I wouldn't want to grow fat just sitting around with the baby all day."

"She is very pretty," Fleurette complimented. "What is her name?"

Setting down a silver spoon, Tanya frowned but did not turn about. "We said her name many times while we were playing with her this afternoon, don't you remember, Fleurette?" Something was occupying the girl's mind, and Tanya tried to think of what it could be. She did not really seem to be missing her home, she'd said as much. Then what could it be?

"Oh, but of course . . . Sarah. It is a very pretty name—it means princess, does it not?"

"Yes, I do believe you are correct. Sarah from the Bible; she was first named Sarai, but it was changed to Sarah, which means princess, or 'one who laughs.' There." Tanya straightened. "How does it look?"

"What is that, madame?" Fleurette stared vacantly into the sapphire-blue eyes.

Tanya shook her head. "The table!" She laughed aloud. "How does it look?"

"Perfection itself, madame." Looking around the room, Fleurette nodded, not seeing anything out of the ordinary, just shining dishes and silverware, fresh-cut winter flowers, and a linen tablecloth with yellow roses embroidered in the edges.

Exiting the room, Tanya shrugged and slowly shook her head. This Fleurette was certainly a strange one, to put it mildly. She bumped into Willow who was carrying two bottles of wine, one red, one white. Tanya looked dubiously at the bottles.

"Two? You'll have us all inebriated before the meal is over." Tanya laughed in a throaty chuckle.

"Miss Pekoe, she said 'One is for the gent'mums, and de other is for de womenfolk'." Willow wrinkled her nose in distaste. "And none is for Willow . . . Willow—"

Tanya raised an auburn eyebrow, asking, "Willow . . . have you forgotten your last name?" Tanya sighed, biting her lower lip meditatively. "You and Fleurette both act as if you're in a daze and can't think straight . . . or else both of you are in love."

Hastily Willow announced, "I'll get these to the table right away." Over her shoulder she asked, "Is the corkscrew still in the same drawer of the buffet?"

"Naturally." Lifting her shoulders, Tanya heaved a deep sigh, then went on her way to call the men to dinner and let Miss Pekoe know they were ready to sit down.

Willow's eyes were large and luminous when Ashe and Talon Clay stepped into the room . . . and then her jaw dropped as Talon stepped from behind Ashe, his shocking green eyes at once finding her where she sat at the table. Having a hard time breathing normally, Willow snapped her mouth shut and looked anywhere but at Talon Clay. Deciding she looked too obvious ignoring his presence, she let her gaze roam the top of his head every once in a while. Her heart was beating so rapidly she thought she was surely going to faint any moment!

"Willow . . . ? Willow . . . ?"

"Hmmm?" Willow turned to find Fleurette nudging her with her elbow, and she stared at the black-haired girl as if she was looking straight through her. "Did you say something?"

"That's *him!*" Fleurette hissed, her eyes growing larger and more interested by the moment. What a gorgeous hunk of man, she was thinking. Never had she felt such a strong pull between herself and a man; always she'd found this flaw or that to eventually cross the man off her list as suitor. "*Mon Dieu,* this one is simply gorgeous!"

Now Willow saw red, and she felt her claws sharpening beneath the table. "Men are not *gorgeous,* Fleurette, how can you be so, so—" she used a word she'd heard the girl use before— "such a naïveté?"

"La! But this one is!"

"I thought *this* one almost raped you?" Willow could feel the hot breath charging in and out of her flaring nostrils.

"Oh, but of course, he can do so anytime he chooses." When Fleurette looked at her dinner companion she flinched at the hostile look she was receiving. "La, but I suppose mademoiselle has made designs on this one—"

"I'm going to make designs on you," Willow whispered hotly, "horse pies right on your powdered white face!"

"La, you are only jealous, that is all. So, he is not yours; how can you act in this rude manner to your house guest? I shall not stay in your home a minute longer if you persist in treating me so poorly."

"If you stay in—" Willow bit off, for she'd glanced across the table and found Talon sitting straight across from her, his eyes boring right into hers, his mood toward her icy politeness when he spoke her name in greeting her. "Hello, Talon," she found herself answering. When, unwaveringly, he continued to stare at her, Willow found herself squirming in her chair.

"Does mademoiselle have ants in her drawers?" Fleurette leaned over to say in a mock-sweet voice. Just then Fleurette's face lit up considerably, and she exclaimed over someone who stood in the doorway, "Hester! Do come in and join us, please!"

Blinking and frowning at the same time, Tanya looked up to see her overdressed neighbor standing there. "Yes," Tanya said, exchanging a look with her husband, "please join us, Hester, there is plenty for everyone here." She leaned over to whisper in Ashe's ear, "Do you mind if we do not announce our surprise tonight? I think I just might retire soon; it's been a hectic day, and Sarah has been cranky. What? Yes, darling, my maid is taking good care of her."

"Welcome, Hester." Ashe stood to his feet then. "Have a seat." He waved an arm. "Anywhere you like." When he saw that she had done just that and had seated herself beside her old lover, Talon Clay, Ashe looked down at his wife and took her hand in his as he sat back down and patted it. "Who," he said only for her ears, "do you think will light the fireworks first?"

"Talon Clay . . ." Hester drawled, her long lashes batting swiftly. "Is this really you? Lordy—" she placed her hands over her breast— "you sure do steal a girl's breath away." She slanted a coy look in Willow's direction before going on, dragging her eyes slowly back to Talon, "Where've you been keeping yourself? Who'd ever know when you've become such a man of mystery."

Girl, you don't know the half of it! Willow kept to herself, her own smug expression being batted back and forth between Hester and herself. She had one artful cat sitting beside her and the other wily one across from her, both sharpening their claws against her. Willow coolly regarded them both, leaning forward a little to spoon into her mouth some of the steaming vegetable beef soup Miss Pekoe had served in a large tureen.

Gazing directly into Willow's lazy-lidded eyes, Talon set forth to answer Hester Tucker. "Would you believe it if I told you that I've been living in an Indian village, where there's nothing but Comanches, Kiowas, and a motley band of half-breeds who'd sooner slit your throat than look at you, that is if you don't belong there. The women are beautiful . . . there was one especially . . . with hair like—"

"Butter. Please pass the butter." Willow quickly slashed through Talon's sentence, speaking the request loud enough for puzzled eyes to turn her way. Tanya especially was looking at Willow with serious consideration—and then her blue eyes slipped over and studied Talon Clay with quiet deliberation.

Curious as a cat, Hester leaned eagerly toward Talon Clay, purring, "With hair like jewels sparkled in it?" Patting her hair, she stared right into the deep green eyes.

Talon nodded, saying, "Like diamonds and topazes were in the locks."

"I have heard that Indians take scalps." Fleurette broke into the conversation. *"Mon Dieu,* have you ever taken one yourself?"

Talon chuckled. "Indian or white?" His eyes narrowed over the skinny girl frighteningly.

"La! You are a savage, *monsieur!"*

"Oh poo!" Hester scoffed. Setting down her refilled wine glass, she again leaned closer to Talon, rubbing her breast up against his arm. "Can you say that he *looks* the savage now?" She put the question to Fleurette.

"He did so more the day before today. La! But he did frighten me so, coming up upon me where I was resting in the grass near the little house and watching the lovely sunset. But now, I see he has done away with some of his hair, and he looks, ah, more gentlemanly today." Fleurette tilted her face downward and looked up demurely from beneath her spiky black lashes.

Finally Ashe entered the conversation, having cleared his throat first to announce he was doing so. His brother had been projecting a vision to him, and in his mind's eye he'd seen him fitting in very well in this Indian camp he'd spoken of. "I'll bet Almanzo had something to do with your going to live in this Indian camp, am I right?" Ashe asked Talon.

"Correct," Talon returned. "It was Almanzo who took me there and introduced me to a man by the name of Nightwalker. Kijika—that's his Indian name."

"Oh yes, I see," Tanya exclaimed, feeling her husband's eyes suddenly on her with curiosity. She blushed prettily before she went on, "And what was your Indian name, Talon Clay? Rather," she said, looking at Willow momentarily, "I should ask, did you have an Indian name?"

For a moment Talon stared across the table at Willow. He could see that her lips were trembling slightly, as if she were about to speak but couldn't quite get the words out. How greatly he had missed her when she'd gone from the camp. The intimacy they'd shared was still alive, burning in his flesh. With moist eyes, Willow gazed back at Talon. He had hurt her, but she'd not let him see that hurt. No, never. But in her heart and soul she could never forget the love they'd shared. Both were thinking their own thoughts . . . was this the end of their love? Or was it only the beginning of a new life?

"My name was—" he was staring right into Willow's eyes— "the same as it is now."

Willow released her breath, not conscious she'd been holding it until she let it go. Now, while everyone was talking at once, asking Talon excited questions, Willow exchanged a look with her sister. And Tanya knew . . . oh yes, she knew everything. Now the only question remained . . . would she tell her husband? Or would Tanya leave things alone?

Gray turned to blue as the sky lightened, lambent morning rays aswirl with dove-white clouds that moved toward the sun that was just rimming the horizon. Moving through the trees swiftly, Willow spurred Istas while Dust Devil followed not far behind and nipped her rival for her master's attention on the rear now and then. Whenever Willow chose to ride Istas, Dust Devil would clear the fence and go flying after the pair. But when it was the other way around, Istas chose to stand contentedly cropping pasture grass, her huge, liquid eyes gazing into a world apart from man.

Splashing across Strawberry Creek, already seeing Le Petit Sundance basking in morning's first glorious rays, Willow urged Istas up the short hill at a faster pace. She laughed happily then as Dust Devil shot mischievously past them, the gray mustang's long, sturdy limbs stretching and pulling in a stunning play of muscles. Willow's hair came loose from its tidy roll at her nape and flew all about her flushed face in wild disarray.

Le Petit had become her favorite haunt lately.

Willow halted the spotted mare and stroked the black mane. "Isn't this just the most beautiful spot in the world?" she said, bending Istas's ear back and scratching it. "Oh, you!" Willow exclaimed, patting Dust Devil's long velvet face coming up with determined force against her hand. "Here," she said, digging into the deep pocket of her divided skirt and bringing out a lump of sugar, "this is for you, sweetheart, and one for you, too." Istas curved her long neck back to find Willow's hand and nibbled the sugar from her.

"Do I get one, too?"

"OH!" Willow whirled about to face the owner of the dangerously deep soft voice.

"Morning."

Green eyes smiled up at her and Willow's heart picked up a crazy, exaggerated beat. It was Lakota's voice but Talon Clay who gazed up at her, one hand splayed on Istas' rump. Actually he was both, yet this man who stood here now with such a changed countenance was a complete stranger to her. Gone were the long braid, the fringed garments, the knee-high moccasins, and the beaded headband. If she had to describe his appearance now she'd have to say he was a clean-shaven, ruggedly handsome individual, with hair so healthy and thick that it stood away from his well-shaped head, combed slickly back away from his tanned forehead and the sides of his face. With most of the sun streaks out of his hair the strands appeared darker, with only a glint of gold here and there.

Willow found she was swallowing hard, and her hands were nervously warm and sweating. Was this the same man who'd given her exquisite joy while she lay so close to his heart? Why had he returned to Sundance so swiftly on the heels of her escape? Did he still hate her for being Garnet's daughter? What is going to become of us? her heart was begging for him to let her know.

"Do you come here often?" Talon inquired, taking a bite from a big, juicy red apple. He smiled as the mares began to smell his tempting treat.

Her mind was spinning back in time to the sunny day they'd first met. "I live here," she answered automatically, as if they were beginning all over again.

He slowly grinned. "Here? Nobody lives here, this house isn't finished . . . or haven't you noticed?"

She tossed her head, sending her golden mane flying; and when she was still again, the huge wave half covered her right eye. "I've noticed many times; I have been this way . . . often."

"Is that so?" He stopped grinning. "Why?"

"I've made no secret of it. It's beautiful here, and I like to come here alone, to walk, and sometimes I don't think about anything at all."

Now he was leaning his elbow against Ista's hip. "When you do think, what comes to your mind, *Miss* Hayes?"

Willow shook the thick waves that hung to her waist and tightened her fingers on Istas's reins. "Not you, if that's what you're thinking, Talon Clay." Before she realized she'd been so cruel, though not sorry for it either, she found he'd reached up for her to halt the motion that would send Istas flying.

"Hush. Do not fear," he murmured, pulling her down to stand close to him.

Balling her hands into fists, Willow shoved at his chest and bent her knees to keep him from drawing her closer to his virile frame. "I'm not afraid of you, Talon Clay, I just don't like you much anymore." She ceased her struggles when he suddenly went motionless and stared down into her face—as if he was seeing a stranger instead of the woman who'd been his loving wife.

Taking her by one arm, Talon swung her behind him, and then his body followed as he pressed her against the bole of a huge tree. His eyes were boring into hers when his lips began to lower, his thighs holding her prisoner. Seeing his intent, Willow jerked her face aside and squeezed her eyes shut tight. With his lips close to her ear, Talon breathed deeply of her lavender scent before he spoke.

"Have I turned so ugly that you must turn your face aside? Don't you think my kisses will excite you as they did before? What is it, Willow?"

"Yes, you are ugly, Talon Clay." She opened her eyes without looking at him. "And you are right, your kisses will not thrill me anymore. I hate you," she said, believing she actually did at times, especially after his cruel treatment of her. "Don't you remember what you did to me? How can you forget so easily? I'm not some ignorant squaw you can throw upon your mat and have your way with anytime the mood strikes."

Angrily he pressed closer, pressing the taut muscles of one leg between her knee. "I'll have you whenever I want." His lips nibbled at the chin turned toward him. "And I'll have you now."

"No," she snapped, finally turning to stare him down. "You won't have me now, and you won't have me ever." Remembering the pain he'd inflicted upon her, she drove the blade deeper. "I never did love you, not Lakota, not you, Talon Clay." She blanched when his eyes darkened till there was no green in them, no color whatsoever. "Yes, you see women can amuse themselves too for a time, and then we can move on to other . . . loves." She skipped over the last word.

"Is that so?" His eyes blazed, sending dark fires everywhere. "We'll see about that, won't we."

Before Willow could think to react, his lips were glued to hers, while his large hands cupped her cheeks on either side. His huge body shivered with ecstasy at the feel of her soft lips beneath his. The more she fought him the angrier he became. When she would not kiss him back, he tore his mouth away, and she could see as he looked down at her that his eyes were glistening with frustration and lust.

"Fight me all you want, Willow, but the more you struggle the more quickly you'll satisfy me."

When he came back at her for more of the same, Willow bit down just as his tongue was thrusting into her mouth. He tore his lips from hers, and taking her by the shoulders, he lifted her several inches off her feet. She looked down, wanting so badly to kiss him back and hold him, to draw him within her shivering warmth. She wanted desperately to believe there could be a future for them, but there would be nothing, not until he rid himself of Garnet's terrible memory and came to her with a freshly opened heart.

Talon stood away from her, letting her feet touch the ground. With his back turned, he ground out, "What do you want, Willow? Do you want me to say I love you?"

"You love me, Talon, with your body." She looked aside, unable to look at his long, lean back without the desire to run to him and clutch him close. "When you love me with your heart, then you will know that there is nothing left for me to want."

Walking over to where Istas and Dust Devil stood at right angles to each other happily munching grass, Willow mounted up and rode out of the clearing. A pair of troubled green eyes watched her go.

Chapter Twenty-Four

The ring of hammer and nail echoed across the land while Le Petit Sundance neared completion. Sammy and Clem were busy wielding the paintbrush, painting the gallery posts that supported the hipped roof white. Talon and Ashe were just hanging the heavy, paneled front door. Almanzo and a few of the drovers, those that were handy at carpentry, under Clem's supervision, naturally, were placing the windows, which were set at the outer edges of the walls, providing window seats inside the house. Outside, the wooden drapery and lively railings typified the exuberant carving that characterized the carpentry of the early nineteenth century. Up on the roof still more men precariously clad the bare wood with shakes. Inside, architectural details included pine floorboards, paneled doors shipped from New Orleans, and brick fireplaces. All in all, the house was a meld of the old and the new.

"It is going to be a very happy place to dwell," Kachina said to no one in particular, but her dark blue eyes remained riveted on Willow.

Sarah played on the blanket amid the women, while Willow twiddled with a rattle that Clem had fashioned out of hand-rubbed Louisiana cypress wood for the babe. She held it up now, invitingly. "Here, Sarah, come and get it." When the child toddled over to her aunty, Willow reached out and hugged Sarah around the waist. Her eyes lifted often, roaming over Talon's bare torso, which gleamed impressively when he happened to step out into the sun and leaned against the railing while he drank from the spring-cooled water jug. Desire burned in her eyes, but when he glanced her way she was always looking elsewhere, or reaching for the child.

While Talon drank the water, he gazed over the rim of the fruit glass and watched Willow with intense green eyes. He had caught her looking his way often out of the corner of his eyes, and when he turned to look directly at her she sent her eyes chasing off anywhere but in his direction. Until the moment he'd come through the door at Sundance, he'd thought never to see her looking at him that way again. He'd made no secret of his longing for her the past week, but all she ever did was evade him at every single turn. He had deluded himself by thinking she would come to him on her own. Grimacing now, he thought that if it was going to be up to him to do the chasing, it was going to be a cold day in hell when he caught up with her!

About to go inside and see where help was needed, Talon's side vision caught the flash of horses and wagon bumping along the new road that was being cut into the grass and earth by much traversing of late.

"Damn," he swore, seeing that it was only Hester, "not her again." Whenever Hester showed her face around Sundance, which was again often, Talon was reminded of her brother, Carl, and his vow to murder the bastard one day. Carl Tucker had escaped his clutches twice now, and if there should ever come a third occasion Carl was going to find himself cornered like a mustang in a box canyon.

That in mind, Talon saw no need to greet the sleazy blond, so he disappeared inside, feeling three pairs of female eyes driving into his bare back. Two he cared nothing about, the third, well, he was going to have to see where the future took them. In the meantime, he was going to keep damn busy and take a dip in the freezing creek each and every midnight!

Willow's eyes followed Talon until she could see the bronze of his flesh no longer. He had been letting his hair grow again, and it was almost shoulder length, growing so fast that one could almost watch it lengthen before one's eyes. Willow preferred it shorter, for the darker hairs at the nape of his neck curled in tempting locks there.

Seated on the edge of the blanket, dressed in an India lawn dress that perfectly matched her eyes, Fleurette had carefully watched Willow and Talon as they covertly tried to study each other while the other wasn't looking. There was a battle going on between the two of them, and Fleurette wondered if she would be endangered by stepping into their line of fire. La! But what could it hurt? Surely not herself.

"So, here you are," Hester laughed, going over to plop herself down on the blanket beside Fleurette. "Your cousin has come to fetch you home, and is he furious. He has been trying to hunt you down all morning."

"André?" Alarmed, Fleurette's gaze flew down the path. "La, what is he doing coming to fetch me? I can make it home on my own." She shot a look at Willow as she played, as usual, with the little one. Not bothering to hide a smirk as her eyes passed over the Indian woman, she went on in a high voice. "Monsieur Rankin was going to see me home . . . ah, that André, he is forever panting at my heels. I have told him over and over to leave me be. I do not wish his simpering company."

Graciously waiting until Fleurette had completed her tirade against her cousin, Tanya now spoke up, unable to contain her curiosity. "He is your cousin, Fleurette—then why does he pursue you so? Plainly, he knows he cannot ask your hand in marriage."

"Oh la! but he can, madame. In New Orleans it is the fashion for cousins to marry with cousins, and my parents even encourage André in his suit. He is a skinny weasel, forever sniffing maddeningly into his handkerchief."

Keeping her head down, Willow smiled to herself secretively. Finally, Fleurette was on her way home, and not a second too soon, she thought happily. The French girl had shown her true colors several days after she had moved into the little house with Willow, and that included the bit of nasty mischief Fleurette had created in devising the outrageous tale that Talon had been unable to hold himself from ravishing her at first meeting on the spot.

Hester Tucker was seeing herself mirrored in Fleurette's actions, seeing that devious plans constantly ticked in her brain, and Hester did not like what she'd been perceiving. For days now she'd been watching Willow and Talon Clay, and the sweetest love she'd ever imagined possible was taking place before her very eyes. But the two were blind . . . didn't they realize what a perfect love was theirs for the taking? Having watched them, Hester at first had been jealous, but that emotion had been weeded out when she decided this was what she had always been hunting for, a love so stunningly captivating it would knock her off her feet. And she would have it, if it took her years to find!

Steeling herself for the verbal blows that always fell when Fleurette and Hester combined forces to attack her, Willow lifted Sarah into her lap and busied herself by playing with the child so she wouldn't be forced to acknowledge either one of them. Lately she was especially bothered by Hester's presence, for she could never forget that it was Carl Tucker who had tried to kill the Brandon men and had almost succeeded in raping her. And after the attack on Black Fox's camp, when Carl and his filthy Apache friends had taken her and Kachina captive, she had come to realize there was nothing the man wouldn't do. She was certain he was out to get the Brandons—and she, too, was a Brandon now.

"Willow," Tanya addressed her sister, feeling the need to be away from Hester, for only bad memories came to her whenever Carl's sister was visiting their property, "Give Sarah to me now. I'd like to go inside and see if the men would like something to eat from that picnic basket we packed."

Clutching Sarah tighter, Willow said, "I'll stay with

her, Tanya; you go inside and maybe you can find some time alone with Ashe for a few minutes."

"Oh . . . all right." Tanya rose from the blanket, smiling when Kachina came to her moccasined feet and brought the huge picnic hamper with her as she stood. "Thank you, Kachina." She leaned to whisper something in the Indian woman's ear, and Kachina nodded and reached out to gently pat Tanya's still flat stomach.

When Tanya and Kachina had disappeared inside the house, Willow set forth to give her full attention to the child, who was toddling about the corner of the blanket and then falling down with high-pitched shrieks at her cute antics. The child reached at once for Willow when Hester moved closer and chucked Sarah beneath her chubby chin. Hugging close to Willow's bosom, Sarah peered at Hester Tucker with big, round eyes and pulled at one of her bright red curls with cherub fingers.

"Weow!" Sarah announced haughtily, staring at her aunty while she patted familiarly the diminutive blonde's face. "My *Weow!*" she shouted, defying either of the young women to challenge the fact.

"Is she afraid of me?" Hester asked, taking the first step in becoming friends with Willow. In the past they'd always been rivals for Talon Clay's love, and Hester had, from the first day they had come face-to-face, hated Willow with a passion.

Willow blinked, hardly believing Hester was speaking to her in a civil tone instead of with her usual vicious tongue. "Sarah's not afraid," she said, "hardly that. She's just not used to . . . strangers."

Leaving all her affected airs behind, Hester said in a hurt tone, "I can hardly be called a stranger." She laughed then. "I've practically lived here at Sundance the last two years."

Willow said nothing to that. Suddenly she was leery, for Hester had never been up to any good when she visited Sundance. The only word Willow could think of in describing Hester was wicked. The whole family was that, rotten to the core. Even Janice Ranae, their mother, was not to be trusted. Long ago Tanya had discovered Janice Ranae was no friend. And Carl—he was the worst one of the whole lot!

Just then Talon came over to join them, walking with a chicken leg in his teeth and a fruit jar swinging from one hand. Setting the fruit jar down on the blanket, he brought his other hand from behind his back and stuck a white wildflower in Willow's hair.

"Howdy ladies," he said, almost choking on the word when Hester turned about to face him. Hester was no lady; she was a whore.

Just as Talon was hunkering down beside Willow, grinning into her flushed face while he continued to munch the chicken leg, Fleurette chose the moment to leap to her feet and begin issuing dainty little shrieks. She sped around the blanket and rushed right into Talon's arms, almost knocking the man over while he was trying to finish his chicken. The half-eaten morsel went flying as Fleurette landed smack in the middle of Talon's lap, while Talon sat down hard, his legs sticking straight up in the air.

"Help me! *Mon Dieu,* save me."

With Fleurette's cheek pressed to his, her excited body almost flattening him to the ground, Talon found he could do nothing but take the woman by her tiny waist and try to lift her from him. But the action only brought Fleurette closer to the hard male body, until she was lying pressed familiarly between Talon's legs.

Talon grimaced, trying to lift the woman from him, but she continued to push him back until Talon began to grow weak from trying to hold back the laughter that split his insides. "For being so . . . skinny, woman, you sure do weigh like a passel of horses! Hey, come on, stop that . . . what's bothering you?" He couldn't help but laugh then, but halted abruptly when Willow glowered at him through her pussywillow-brown eyes, stuck her chin high, and rose to her feet with Sarah in her arms. From his grounded position, he called to her, "Willow, where are *you* going? Damn." He shoved Fleurette until she had come loose and was flying in the air. But Fleurette's hand clutched at Talon and as he was rising she grabbed hold of him and this time he landed smack on top of her.

"What is with you, woman?" Talon shouted, yanking Fleurette up with him as he finally succeeded in coming to his feet. Looking over her shoulder, Willow had seen everything. He'd never seen her so indifferent toward him, except maybe when he'd taken liberties near the creek with her. "This isn't my fault," he stormed, glaring into Fleurette's flushed face. "*You,* I see now what you were trying to do, and I don't like it one bit."

"But *monsieur,* I had a spider crawling up my leg!" she cried, pouting her red lips.

"Where is it now, *madem—oiselle?*" he asked mockingly.

"I—I do not know." She made a show of brushing at her yellow-green skirts then, lifting the hem far too high for propriety's sake and then dropping it with a shake.

Coming to her feet, Hester advised her, "Give it up, Fleurette, can't you see you're only making a fool of yourself? Mr. Brandon is not interested in you, and he never will be, either, his heart is with—" she sighed—"with Willow Hayes."

Leaning forward, seeming to bring both women into his confidence, Talon, smiling genuinely at Hester for the first time in ages, said, "Can you both keep a secret?" His answer came as a collective nod. "Good. Willow's last name is not Hayes, not any longer."

Smiling knowledgeably, Hester nodded, looking off into the direction Willow had gone with Sarah. But Fleurette had no idea what was going on, so she excitedly asked, "Who is Willow's husband? What is her last name?"

"Are you sure you'll keep it a secret? Cross your heart?"

"*Oui,* yes!" Fleurette executed the childish gesture; then waited impatiently to hear what Willow's last name could be.

With a sly grin, Talon asked, "What begins with B?"

"Ahh." Fleurette rolled her eyes. Then she gasped, blurting: *"Brandon?"*

With a lusty laugh, Talon leaned forward, his bare chest glistening bronze in the sun; as she stared mesmerized into the commanding green eyes, Talon opened her hand, and placing the chicken bone in her palm he squeezed her fingers shut, softly announcing, "You win the prize, *mademoiselle!"*

Remembering his determination to move slowly in

on her, Talon stepped into his house looking this way and that for Willow. He found Clem and Ashe working diligently over a pine floorboard, laying the planking side by side and filling the small holes in with wood putty. They were arguing over the best way to shim the plank for a perfectly tight fit and they gave Talon no mind, so he passed unnoticed into the hall and then into another room. Here the drovers were just putting the finishing touches to the window seat, ready to move on to the next room. Stopping to discuss with their boss a certain cut they'd like to make, none of the men noticed the slender beauty enter until she made a little sound in turning around to go back the way she'd come. Catching the flash of amber India lawn, Talon happened to look up just as Willow was in her turn.

"Willow," he called her back. "Don't go, I'm almost finished here."

"I—" She blushed when the other four men turned to see her standing framed just inside the freshly hung door trim. "I was looking for Kachina . . . have you seen her?"

Ducking his head in a mode of decorum, Vernon offered, "Saw the pretty squaw with Almanzo; they was goin' back in the wagon with Missus Brandon."

Somebody took a deep breath and Vernon looked about to see who'd made the sound, but he couldn't rightly tell. Handing Vernon a blueprint, Talon walked over to where Willow stood indecisively, dismissing the drovers with a flick of his hand. He smiled down into her eyes, and Willow mistook the fierce gleam of his gaze for lust. She had no idea she'd provoke that response just by walking in on him while he stood in discussion with the Brandon drovers. A low masculine chuckle reached her ears now.

"I love you in that dress," Talon said.

"I—" Willow couldn't think of anything to say back to him. Shaken by his words, she turned around and showed him her back. "I think I should be going back to Sundance now; it's getting late." Seeing the moon rising in the east, she gazed out the many-paned window to a sky that was yet showing its blue shroud.

His breath was hot in her ear. "Stay." He was standing very close.

"Talon . . . I can't." She made to move forward, but he caught her by the elbows, bringing his cheek to rest on the side of her head. With unshed tears in her eyes, she broke from his gentle hold. "I'm sorry. I have to go."

Rushing after her, Talon darted in front of her, breaking her flight. From the room across the hall, Ashe and Clem looked up from their labors for a moment, wondering what was going on, why Talon was keeping Willow prisoner. Putting a hand on Clem's shoulder, Ashe encouraged the older man to ignore the lovers and return to the task. When they were unobserved once again, Talon put his hands together in a prayerful gesture, bringing his long fingertips up to take her chin on either side.

With his arms so near her breasts, Willow had a hard time keeping her voice steady. "I can't stay here with you, Talon." She took his hands and placed them at his sides. Leading him over to the wall where the others couldn't see, Willow stopped and spoke in a low voice. "We are not man and wife any longer, so how can you even think to ask me to stay here with you?"

"No man has put our marriage asunder, Willow; tell

me if you think this is so?"

"You said it yourself, that you and I were divorced from each other. Don't you remember?"

"Yes, I do now that I think of it." He reached for her hand to lace her fingers with his. "But that is not true, Willow, we are still man and wife, and I ask you to tell me what man would say we are not?"

"Jim Nibaw?"

"The preacher?" Talon tilted his head. "The very same who married us? Willow, what nonsense is this?"

"I just wanted to make sure it wasn't a fake ceremony." Embarrassed by her trickery, she stared down at the dazzling pine boards they had laid just that day.

"Willow, Willow," Talon shook her gently. "I married you for better or worse, remember? Here." He took her hand and placed it over his chest on the left side. "Now I give you my heart . . . it's what you wanted, wasn't it?"

"Yes Talon." Then her eyes bored right into his. "Are there any ghosts left?"

His eyes flinched. Willow had caught him off guard. She studied him a moment longer before she sadly smiled into his eyes and walked along the hall to the door. What had hurt her more than anything, though, was the fact that Talon Clay had not been caring enough to say he was sorry for all the pain he'd caused her . . . and he'd not said he loved her. He had tried but failed miserably.

Tanya had tried persistently to get Willow to come to Talon's house with her and Ashe, since Fleurette and

Kachina were gone, having left for their homes before the cold weather set in, and there were no other women for Tanya to visit with. But Willow always came up with the ready excuse that she was tired from being at school with the children, or that she had some things that needed attention in the little house. As Samson was always staying overnight in one of the bunkhouses, Tanya took Willow's story that there was either wash to do or meals to cook as a poor excuse for not going to Talon's.

"Besides, I have to finish this dress," Willow was saying now, "otherwise it won't be ready in time for the . . . party."

Jasse, the black maid who was very talented with the needle, besides being Sarah's nursemaid, stood now with pins in her mouth putting the finishing touches on Willow's creamy off-white gown. The bodice scooped dangerously low, displaying far too much flesh and pushing it up until Willow was almost spilling out, and Tanya and Jasse had decided the best action here would be to add a valance of crisply starched standing lace to conceal the daring view. Tanya was fussing with the piece while Jasse waited patiently to pin it on.

"Oh no," Willow objected. "First I'll take the gown off, or else you'll make a human pincushion out of me, Jasse!"

"Jasse never stuck you," Tanya reminded her sister.

"We will get a better fit, Missy Hayes," Jasse said.

"If I don't breathe, you mean," Willow laughed, meaning to rise from the chair she'd been perched on for too long for comfort's sake.

"No, you don't," Tanya said. "Here, Jasse, give me those pins. I think Sarah's crying, anyway."

"Yes'm, Mistress Brandon." The black girl handed Tanya the pins, not afraid to touch the white woman with her fingers. There were no slaves here at Sundance, and Jasse had been fortunate to have been sold to Master Brandon on the auction blocks. When Ashe Brandon had given the shocked Jasse her freedom, Jasse had been given a choice as to whether she wanted to be left to her own devices or come to Sundance with him; Jasse had chosen to become a maid for the woman she'd had doubts about at first. But when Jasse was introduced to the missus she'd at once seen that the beautiful Tanya was a generous and kindly human being. Jasse, like Miss Pekoe, preferred to address the folks they worked for in a servile fashion, but it was done more as a grateful gesture than anything else.

"I will see to her at once, mistress," the black girl said in her delightful Creole French accent, her grammar cultured and precise. Jasse had belonged to a white woman, Carolinian by birth, who had come to live as a bride in New Orleans and had thought nothing of giving Jasse a sound beating once in a while, just for good measure, to keep the black girl in line.

"Thank you, Jasse. We will all have lunch together when we are finished here."

"Oh yes'm, Jasse would like that very much." Her plum-black eyes twinkled happily. "I will make sure that Miss Pekoe prepares a sweet for us, would missus like that?"

"That would be delightful, Jasse."

"I will see that it is done, then." With that, Jasse went to care for the whining child.

"She's a dear," Tanya said through a mouthful of

pins, prepared to begin the pinning of the valance at Willow's shoulder. "Oh look," she mumbled, "the thing's twisted again."

"Good," Willow said, coming to her feet. "I need a break anyway." Walking to the French doors, she stretched her arms this way and that to get the kinks out.

"Willow," Tanya began while she worked to untwist the stiff confection of creamy lace. "Why don't you return to the house? It is almost finished now; they are bringing furniture in already. It's very impressive, Willow, dark oak in the spanish style, with large, deep chairs, and lovely cream-white drapes. And the huge four-poster bed; why the wood is so heavy and dark—Talon Clay has been asking for you, and I've been giving him the excuse you've been working hard at school and need to rest. He asked how you occupy your time the three days you are not in school."

Staring out the window, feeling dangerously daring in the low-cut gown, Willow asked, "What did you tell him?" She cast her sister a sidelong glance before returning her gaze to the window.

"I told him you take care of the little house and—rest." Tanya shrugged, almost finished with the lace.

"Well, did he believe you?"

"I'm sure he didn't." Tanya stopped what she was doing to study her sister long and hard as she came to her feet, setting the lace down carefully on an end table. "Uhmm, Willow, I meant to ask you before . . . I haven't found the time to, I mean . . . I know Talon is your husband." She took a deep breath, then began again. "Maybe you don't want to talk about it . . . I won't pry, sis. But if there's something I can help you with, I wish you'd not be afraid to ask. What are sisters for if not to confide their troubles in, to know the other is there if she is needed?"

Whirling about to face Tanya, Willow rushed across the room, sobbing out the words, "Oh, Tanya, I love him so much, so much it hurts."

Stroking Willow's long yellow hair, Tanya murmured, "I know, Willow, I can tell. Ashe knows it, all the men know it. The only thing is, Talon doesn't know it."

"Oh." Willow stood back, drying her eyes with the back of her hand, sniffing loudly. "He has told me he loves me, Tanya, but I'm not sure he meant it."

"He is Lakota . . . Named-Lakota."

Nodding, Willow said, "Yes."

"He has . . . Indian blood?"

"Yes, his real father's name is Nightwalker."

"How—can that be? Almanzo is Nightwalker."

Willow shook her head, looking very beautiful and enchanting in the unfinished gown. "No, Almanzo is Dark Horse."

"Then . . . your story you told last year was about Talon Clay, I mean Lakota. He is truly the next in line to inherit the name Nightwalker."

"He is." Breathing deeply, Willow went on, "I don't know if he will; it is up to him if he wants to return to the Indian way."

"It seems he will not. Why would he be building The Little Sundance if not to live in it? I think he wants to have you with him, Willow. Don't you see, this is Talon's way of showing he wants to settle down and begin a family with you."

"A—a family?" Willow's eyes went round and liquid

brown with large flecks of amber-gold swimming in them.

"Of course, a family. He loves you, silly, can't you see that?"

"He has a strange way of showing his love, then." A frown marred her delicate brow. "He practically tries raping me every time we are alone together."

Tanya laughed, saying, "Silly, he only wants to make love to you. You're his wife, so why shouldn't you give him what he wants. It's so simple, Willow; you want him too, you and he should get together and make love like the world is going to end tomorrow!"

Looking down at her weaving fingers, Willow softly announced, "He has ghosts, Tanya, and you know what kind."

Now Tanya's blue eyes were wide with alarm. "Oh no, not the same ghost Ashe carried with him for so long, until I finally rid his memory of her."

"Tanya! How did you do it?" Willow was excited to think she'd rid Talon of Garnet's ghost once and for all.

"What works for one won't always for the other, Willow. I could tell you, but you'd not be doing what you think is best, something of your own devising. And Willow, remember Talon had a devastating relationship with our mother, unlike Ashe who never went to . . . bed with her. Talon most likely sees her in you, and the only way this ghost is going to be banished is through a love so great that Talon will finally see it is you, only you he wants and not only for—"

Willow looked Tanya squarely in the face, asking, "For what? Are you saying . . . lust?"

"Yes, not only for lust's sake. Love is giving of one's whole self. Has he done that yet?" she asked her mesmerized sister.

"No." Defiantly, Willow said, "And I don't want to see him, you can tell him that for me! You're right, all he sees in me is a piece of . . . of fluff, that's all!"

Willow and Tanya turned to the doorway leading into the hall just then, for they'd heard a sound there.

"Ashe!" Tanya exclaimed, her heart beginning to race. "How long have you been standing there?"

His eyes were dark, dangerously dark. "I've been here long enough."

"And how long is that?" Willow asked her brother-in-law as she stepped from the window. She stopped then, seeing his eyes growing increasingly wide as they were riveted to her bosom. Realizing what was making Ashe's eyes pop, she went to fetch her light green shawl from the back of the chair.

"That's some dress," Ashe told Tanya. He grinned mischievously then, asking, "Are you wearing one like that to Talon's housewarming, love?"

"I—" Tanya laughed then, the tension leaving her as she realized Ashe had not heard all of their conversation. Yet, sometime soon he was going to have to learn his brother was only his half-brother. "No, Ashe. And Willow's gown is not finished."

"Too bad," he remarked, grinning wolfishly at the diminutive blond. He sighed, adding, "But you're right, love, if she wore the dress as it is I'm afraid the hands would be swarming about her like bees in a blooming rosebush. And—" he began anew, thinking of his jealous brother where Willow was concerned— "we don't want any sort of trouble at the party."

Chewing on her lower lip, Tanya stared meaningfully at her sister, who sat daintily upon the chair, her fingers clutching the shawl together at the center of her chest. Willow caught Tanya's silent message at once, knowing her sister thought the best time to tell Ashe that he had a half-brother was right now, this moment. already they'd waited too long, for a secret kept in the mouth was like a wild bird in a cage. Taking a deep breath Willow nodded. The time had come.

"Ashe, I have something to—"

"Mr. Brandon!"

The three of them turned to the French doors at the same time, Ashe being the first to recognize the voice of distress. Eating the distance to the doors swiftly, Ashe yanked them open and went to lean over the gallery rail to see what Vernon was so excited over. The man was all red in the face and his horse was nervously pulling taut the reins that Vernon was jerking on to keep the horse from running away.

"Hurry boss, you better come right away . . . there's been an accident! It's your brother!"

Willow tried to rise from the chair, but a sudden paralysis along with a wave of nausea imprisoned her on the spot. Black ominous clouds roiled before her eyes and she stared into the darkness in horror. She was fainting, she knew it, but she clung tenaciously to the silver thread of consciousness, dragging herself up by her furious will to rise and go to her love. In moments she was standing tremblingly on her feet, the shawl slipping from her shoulders to the floor. She stepped upon the forgotten wrap then in her haste to follow Tanya and Ashe out the door.

PART SIX

Sweet Love

Make haste, my beloved,
and be thou like to a roe or
to a young hart upon the
mountains of spices. . . .

—Song of Solomon

O past! O happy life! O songs of joy!
In the air, in the woods, over fields,
Loved! loved! loved! loved! loved!

—Whitman

Love makes all things right, for it
Heals the sorrows of the Heart.

—Anonymous

Chapter Twenty-Five

The Spanish mustang came to a thundering, dust-raising halt before the freshly painted, petite mansion. Willow, the first to arrive in all due haste at Le Petit, was met at the front of the house by three of the drovers who had been there the last time she had; and several mustanger friends of Talon's were there, too. The handsome, dark-haired mustangers, knowing Willow's modest nature, suppressed grins at catching her by happenstance in a most charming state of near undress. Being in such a state of distressed agitation, she entirely missed their actions, which showed the time for being alarmed had passed. But it did flash in her mind for one quicksilver moment that the men's emotional states were not what they should be at a time like this. She could only put it down to the potent fumes that were wafting about in the air, and she couldn't know that they had only shared a little tot with their boss, he who'd had a bit more than they.

"Where is he?" Willow brushed past the covertly smiling men, who were beginning to understand the young beauty was not so indifferent to their boss as she pretended to be.

"Back here," said Zeke. "All the way to the back of the house." He winked at his fellow mustangers then as she swooped before them and led the way herself.

Before Willow reached the gallery she heard the sound of a lusty cowboy song. The ribald words burned her ears, but she pressed onward, realizing as she neared that it was her love singing the bawdy tune. Over her shoulder she said, "Oh, you had to get him drunk . . . it *must* be bad!" She kept moving until she stepped out onto the gallery, her eyes dropping at once to the man propped against the heavy rail there. Then her gaze was compelled to the stairway, the very same that she'd taken a tumble down, and she took in the hole where once there had been a stair.

Talon's song came to an abrupt halt as soon as he saw Willow standing there like a gorgeous angel. He took in the worried lines marring the perfection of her flawless face, and her eyes, which were measuring the extent of his hurt as they sped from his head to his feet. He followed her line of vision to the staircase, the one he'd been damning for the last hour. Before that, he'd been walking up the stairs, his hands deep in his breeches pockets, enjoying the wildly wooded beauty of his own backyard. He'd not been watching where he stepped next, dreaming of a lovely lady walking with him hand-in-hand, and he'd had a rude awakening when he had been daydreaming over a sweet kiss. He'd been stepping onto a stair where there suddenly was nothing but air, his arms flapping wildly about to regain his balance . . . he'd looked like a bird shot from its nest, Clem had related afterwards, for he'd stepped onto the gallery in time to watch—for that was all he could do—he'd watched Talon Clay do a last-minute turn in midair and come landing smack dab on his face, the sound of muscle and bone crashing into the deck.

Talon now grinned roguishly up at Willow. He'd been about to take another swig from the bottle he was clutching when his gaze dropped from her frowning face to her amply displayed bosom. He coughed then, once, twice, setting the bottle that he suddenly didn't need aside. As she rushed forward after seeing his wounded knee, the pants cut away to expose the badly bruised and bloodied leg the men had rushed to get to, she was unaware that Talon's gaze was riveted upon her bosom. Talon gulped repeatedly as the creamy perfection of her spilling mounds neared, and he thrust the bottle outward and up for Zeke to take.

"Here, I-I don't need this," Talon was saying, and then he frowned to the men, his meaning for them to get lost quite clear. He had no time to further study the delicious beauties set before him then, for Ashe and Tanya were just arriving on Willow's heels. Reluctantly he looked away from his wife and acknowledged Ashe and Tanya's presence with a sheepish grin.

"What in God's name did you tangle with?" Ashe wanted to know, moving closer to the wounded leg to survey the damage.

A board that looked suspiciously like a stair appeared in Talon's hand as he revealed, "This. It's the nineteenth or twentieth stair on the stairway to heaven." He looked purposefully down at Willow's bent head, and when his hand reached out to hover above the silken yellow veil that was her hair Ashe drew Tanya back into the house, telling her Talon was going to live and he didn't need them hanging around at the moment.

"But Ashe, we just can't leave, not now. How will he get to bed?"

Ashe grinned. "Willow will help him."

"But . . . Ashe." Tanya wondered then how much Ashe knew of Willow and Talon's relationship.

"Love," Ashe murmured, cupping his wife's lovely face in his big, warm hands, "Talon knows Willow a lot better than I knew you when we were first falling in love. I know my own brother, and I know they are not strangers to each other. I don't know when it happened, but it wasn't all that long ago. Don't worry, Lady Red, there's a bed, and there's food. What more could they need just now?"

"All right, we'll go back home and leave Clem here. Sammy's outside too; he's already seen Talon."

"Tanya dear . . . Sammy and Clem are going back with us too."

"But—"

"No buts. If there's going to be a wedding around here soon we're going to have to give the lovers plenty of time alone together."

"Ashe, I have to tell you something."

Tenderly he cupped her face in his big hands. "What is it, darling lady?"

"I—I love you, Ashe."

A deep chuckle sounded from Ashe's wide chest. "I know, love. I love you, too. Remember, we tell each other every night—several times before we fall asleep."

"Yes." She sighed then, feeling defeat wash over her as they stepped out into the gray shades of twilight. "I just wanted to tell you during the day." How was she ever going to tell Ashe about Talon Clay—about Named-Lakota? She just prayed for God to give her courage and the favorable occasion to disclose Willow's secret.

While Ashe and Tanya were stepping outside, Willow was just lifting the wide stair to look it over. "Talon, I have to tell you," she began, studying the stair so hard she missed seeing the darkening fires in his eyes. "I also took a tumble down those stairs, and I think there is more to this than meets the eye."

"You think someone has been planning a double murder?"

"Yes!" She pushed herself to her feet, carrying the evidence with her as she walked over to stand beneath the open staircase that wound up to the unfinished attic. "Someone is trying to kill one of us, Talon, or the both of us, like you said."

"Ridiculous!" Talon scoffed, feeling the effects of the liquor beginning to wear off already. He grimaced as he shifted on the floor and tried to prop himself up better against the railing. "How do you like this?" he snorted. "They've all gone and left me here to try and get to my bed all by myself! Helpful bunch, aren't they." Closely he watched Willow out of the corner of his eye. He groaned aloud when he noticed he'd gotten her attention. "This floor sure is getting hard, *ohhh damn,* how am I going to get into bed with this leg! It sure does hurt something terrible." He groaned again as he pretended terrible pain while he tried rising to his feet.

Rushing over to Talon, Willow hunkered down beside him. "Here, lean on me, and we'll get you to bed. That's right, put all your weight on my shoulders."

He said with a low moan, "If you say so. Lord, it

sure does hurt pretty bad. Ah, Clem thinks I might have broken it."

Willow gasped. "Your leg? You broke your leg?"

"Ah no, love, just the knee-cap." When he saw her knitting her brow from the corner of his eyes, he rushed on. "But I guess it is crushed pretty bad, and I don't even know if I'll be able to walk—" he looked down into her eyes as they rounded the corner leading into the bedroom— "without a . . . limp."

"A limp! Oh how terrible." She envisioned her virile love limping his way through life until he became an old man with an ever greater disability because of the wound.

She was so engrossed in helping her husband to the bed that Willow did not take the time to look around at the handsomely furnished room. When he was at last sitting on the edge of the bed, she looked up and noticed her surroundings. Gasping softly, she said, "It's a wonderful room, Talon!" She walked around, her fingertips trailing along the deeply carved wood of the Spanish four-poster. She smiled back at him, unconscious of the charming picture she created gliding about the master bedroom like an enchanted princess. "The colors are so warm. Oh!" She rushed over to the massive dresser with an oval mirror set into a recess, and examined a tortoiseshell comb, brush, and mirror set. "It's beautiful! I've never seen anything like it . . . so dainty," she ended softly.

"They belong to a very beautiful woman," he said in a whisper-soft voice.

Her eyes tilting up at him, she dropped the brush to the floor. Bending to retrieve it, she said, "Oh, I didn't realize you had a . . . you didn't tell me—" She clamped her mouth shut. "I'll just put it back," she said after a moment.

When she turned from the mirror and took in the painful grimace he wore as he tried to lie back on the bed, she rushed over to place her hands beneath his arms and help him slide to the headboard. She cocked her head sideways then. Her curious glance had returned to the perfectly carved heart that decorated the massive headboard; there were two names deeply engraved in the center of the heart. As she made to move closer to read it, she found her wrists caught in a strong grip, and then she was being pulled away from the headboard.

Willow glanced up into Talon's face hesitantly. "I'm sorry, Talon, I just wanted to see the heart closer." She stared across the room to the lovely tortoiseshell set, then back to the wonderfully carved headboard, linking the two together with Talon's revelation of minutes ago. "You can let me go now, Talon; I won't pry into your personal life again." When he released her, she rubbed at her wrists, declaring, "For a wounded man you sure haven't lost any of your strength, Talon Clay."

She flushed painfully as he returned, "My leg is wounded, love." Sighing deeply, he looked down the length of his body. "Everything else seems to be working."

Walking over to the dresser, Willow found a lamp there and lit it. "It is getting dark." She turned to face him. "I should be going back to Sundance now."

Green eyes narrowed. "This is Sundance, I've already told you that, Willow." He shifted his propped weight and gave a low moan. "Are you going to desert me, too? I might find that there's a need to go to the, ah, convenience during the night. What then?"

Her eyes large and round, Willow found herself staring at the wounded leg. Here, she had been worrying over the idea that Talon might make a repeat performance of trying to get her into bed with him. Worrying—when he might awake in the night and fall down the back stairs in going to the convenience and break his darn fool neck!

"I will stay." Flushing again, she asked, "Is there another bed in the next bedroom? And I'm hungry—where's the food?"

Chuckling, Talon said, "Relax, Willow, I'm not going to attack you; besides I'm hardly up to it. To answer your question, yes, there's a bed in the next bedroom, and there's plenty of food in the kitchen. Where do you think I've been living the past month?" When she had no ready answer, he said, "This is my home now, and it is here I will stay until I'm an old man."

Looking up from the thick green carpet, Willow encountered eyes the very same shade. His eyes had been studying her face, but now they dropped to the creamy expanse of breast and shoulder she unconsciously had been exposing all along to his heated gaze. What she didn't know when his face began to redden was that his body had begun to react in a very positive way to her presence, with a flush of virile passion. Again she rushed to the bedside, alarm in her voice.

"Talon, do you have a fever?" She leaned forward to feel his forehead, bringing into view the flawless creaminess of her flesh before his gaping eyes. Talon tossed his head far back and groaned loud:

"Oh Lord, I am in pain!" He peeped from one eye as she rushed to the foot of the bed, chewing on her knuckle. *"Ahhh,* I don't think that I can stand it. Willow, do something quick, please." Peeking down at her alarmed expression, Talon's eyes took in the hardened evidence of his desire, a desire that pained him more than any wound ever could. "Oh sh—" he began, ending with *"shoot!"* as he covered the bold evidence with arms crisscrossed over his body.

Willow blanched. That she would have to come into such close contact with his body while trying to help him in any way she could caused an erotic shiver to course along her limbs. Glancing up at the carved heart again, then over to the tortoiseshell set, Willow shivered with the thought of Talon in another woman's arms. It filled her with jealous fury. She must have been a woman he'd known before they had gotten married . . . but then why would he have her name carved with his inside the heart? She was certain she'd seen two names linked together there . . . but she could be wrong.

"Would it help," Willow began tentatively, "if I bandaged your leg?"

"Not much, but there's some salve in the drawer beside the bed if you would be so kind as to rub some on it. The stuff might help to draw some of the pain out." He groaned again for good measure.

Moving to the heavy, ornate table beside the bed, Willow tried hard not to glance over at the heart in order to read the names forever inscribed so beautifully in the wood. Besides, she really didn't want to know the woman's name. Looking away, she returned to the side of the bed, opening the tin of Harte's Salve, feeling

Talon's eyes watching her every move. Taking up a bit of the stuff, Willow's small hands began a slow massage near his kneecap, and when she was about to rub the salve into the wounded area he spoke softly to her.

"Higher, Willow."

There was a question in the eyes that turned to study his face, a silent question that asked if she'd heard him right. "But," she argued, "the wound is centered in your knee." Her gaze fell of its own accord then, roaming over the moistly glistening wide expanse of his deep golden chest. Her eyes slipped a little further, to his sucked-in waist, then on down to the huge phallic outline she could make out beneath his ragged breeches. Her gaze lifted and locked with his. When she saw the green flames ravishing her from head to breast, the flat tin of salve dropped from her nerveless fingers and rolled across the carpet, then rang in a little twirling song before it finally lay still on the wood bordering the carpet.

"Willow."

Before she knew what was happening, Talon was sitting up in bed and reaching for her arm. "I can read your feelings, Willow, you've made no secret of them." He caught her wrist. "I know you want me as badly as I want you, and I aim to show you just how much!"

When he dragged her across the bed and into his lap, she cried out. "Your leg! You'll hurt your leg, Talon."

He clenched his teeth and muttered through them, "Forget the damn leg!" His eyes glared into hers. "It is my body that is aching with desire!"

She struggled to gain her freedom, sobbing, "For whom, Talon? Who is your desire for, some saloon girl, or maybe it is Fleurette, am I right?" Determinedly, she would not look up at the headboard but clamped her eyes shut tight. "You had enough time to get to know Fleurette as a bed partner! Did you promise to visit her in New Orleans?"

His knee entirely forgotten, Talon hauled her up against his naked chest and hissed through his teeth, "Fleurette? I'd rather ride an old haybag than that young, skinny nag!"

She pushed away from his chest. "You would ride anything right now, that's how great your lust is!"

"Lust?" He sneered into her face, dragging her back up to him. His lean, brown fingers hooked into the scooped neckline of her new gown and the carefully stitched material separated under the downward stroke of his thoughtless hand, the sound of the tearing loud even in the huge bedroom. He did not stop there. Before she had a chance to cover her naked breasts, he plunged his fingers into the waistline of the creamy white gown, and while Willow gaped downward he rent the fine material the rest of the way, destroying totally what had once been a beautiful gown. With a savage glow in his eyes, he muttered hoarsely, "That's lust." Like a burning brand, one hand reached out and cupped the soft fullness of her breast in his palm. "So is this," he said, then reaching lower, said, "And this. Yes, I lust for you, Mrs. Brandon, and nothing is ever going to change that." His hand roamed the gentle swell of her hips. "I will always know a savage love for your body—always and forever!"

When he pulled her even closer, Willow tried breaking free and twisted against his greater strength. That strength ruled her now, holding her like silken chains. While she struggled to reach the side of the bed, her dress came away completely and she kicked it aside, for it was only keeping her imprisoned next to him. But she saw that she was wrong; his arms were the only thing holding her captive. Now her softly rounded hips accidentally brushed the hardest part of him and aroused him even more. But it was too late to think that if she'd not struggled so hard he would have cooled his ardor.

"You are mine, Aiyana! Mine forever. . . ."

Rolling Willow onto her face, he pinned her there with his good leg while he struggled out of his ragged breeches. He chuckled as she emitted muffled shrieks of outrage. When she was rolled back to face him once again, she saw his eyes rake her from head to bare feet. He grimaced once as he came to his knees and towered over her. The sight of his long, throbbing manhood came into view, and not for the first time she felt raw fear at the possibility of being torn apart by the hugeness of him.

"No!" she cried out in terror, for his desire was the greatest she'd ever known it to be. For one aching moment she wondered how he could manage this when he'd no doubt lain with Fleurette countless times while she'd stayed at Sundance!

"Yes!" he shouted right back at her.

With a violent lurch Willow tried escaping him the back way. It was a huge bed, and she had only gotten the top of her head to the edge when he caught her about the hips. He panted from the efforts of trying to chase her across the bed with his hurt knee, but he caught her easily enough. When he noticed how close his lips were to her thighs, he grinned devilishly. Reaching up, he grasped her wrists, pinioning her arms tautly against the bed. His lower half held her slender limbs captive. She tried to renew her struggles.

"If you let me do as I want, Willow, it will be over the sooner."

Seeing it was useless to struggle, which only seemed to excite him further, Willow lay still and waited for him to do what he would with her body, which was vulnerable to his slightest wish now. But she'd never felt so trapped, so unable to have her own way in the situation. Yet, if she had time to think about it, Talon seemed to come out the winner more often than not.

At the same moment Willow began to untense, Talon's touch became gentle, less demanding. He had never physically hurt a woman, least of all Willow. His hand slid along the silken curve of her hip, moving upward to cup the underside of a breast he could feel had become larger, fuller, more than the thimbleful he'd become used to. He smiled to himself, thinking the woman-child was at last ripening to full maturity. Dear God, how he'd missed this woman!

Talon hoisted himself up and over her, gently resting atop her while his good leg supported most his body off to one side a little. He took her shoulder into one palm, and as he bent to capture her lips she met him halfway with a cry of painful need, opening her mouth to the deepest thrusting kiss she instinctively knew he wanted to give. At will, her hands began to roam over him, discovering anew the rippling muscles of his back and shoulders. Sighing into his mouth, her fingers moved lower, to the slight indentation of his pelvis. He moaned deep in his throat as she became much bolder, finding the hard, slightly rounded curve of his buttocks, and pulled him closer to the concave area of her pelvis. She moved upward a little, bringing the softness of her thigh slowly closer to the straining member lying hot and hard against her.

"Lakota," she murmured passionately, "my savage love."

Her small hands moved between them suddenly, and Talon gave an agonized gasp. Exploring him, her fingers closed around the hard ridge, and he automatically bucked forward, bringing himself closer to her inner thighs. When she grew bolder yet, he grasped her wrist as his face appeared above hers.

"Love, sweet love, if you continue here my self-control will surely break. I want to savor this moment a while longer."

While she lay still as he'd demanded, she felt herself floating on a sensuous cloud as his lips first drank the nectar from her mouth, then moved to her throat and on down to the rosy peak that reached achingly out to receive his first kiss. The hot, moist tugging began, and she arched her throat with the thrill of the moment. She reached out to rake her fingers through the silk of his shoulder-length hair, loving the feel of the slippery texture and the weight that was like liquid gold pouring through her fingers. As he worked himself lower, she arched her hips, and when his talented lips found the velvet dip of her pelvis and planted erotic kisses there, she was writhing against him. Lower and lower his kisses went, until through a haze she saw him drawing her legs over his shoulders, and then his face disappeared from view.

A searing flame began in her face and moved swiftly down the length of her body until it settled in the velvet cleft of her womanhood, and the source of pleasure radiated from the spear of flesh invading her most secret places. His fingers spread her even more, until her head was tossing from side to side on the pillow. The firestorm of ecstasy began sweeping her up and away, and when he reached beneath her gently to take hold of her buttocks, Willow's fingers began a tormented, rhythmic massage across his shoulders. She was a moist flower budding in the heat of a fiery sun, spreading velvety petals ever outward, slowly swaying in a gentle, giant wind. Colors, clouds, shadows, all passed through her, and she hung for a moment bodiless, from underneath a fallen blossom. She yearned outward to the azure sky and met the amber sun there. Her body, swollen with tears, burst into a million ragged spumes and showering haloes, and away from the world she drifted, sinuously swimming through the stars and moon, expanding, exploding, amorously floating into space.

When Willow finally opened her eyes and realized she was a part of the human race, not just an amoeba constantly changing shape, she found herself staring up into the darkest jade-green eyes ever. He smiled warmly, muttering, "Welcome back, love."

She smiled back at him. "Was I gone that long?" She stretched sinuously beneath him.

"Long enough. I've been waiting for you; I've got a surprise that will send us both together into paradise." He kissed the rosy tip of her swollen breast and moved between her legs.

Willow cried out as the long silken length of him thrust within her. Sheathed by her velvet walls, Talon himself cried out, never realizing how desperately he'd needed to feel his flesh inside her own. His hands grasped her behind as he plunged deeper, feeling waves of ecstasy undulating through his groin. His body sprang to vibrant life, and it was as though a thousand tiny butteflies were beating against his manhood. Her golden sheath surrounded him and he felt himself being sucked deeper, deeper, into the honey-smoothness. The music of their senses blended, and then he found himself looking at Willow in another dimension. Here, the colors of mauve and pink swirled together, blond hair, streamers of mote-filled light; and they were surrounded by an enchanted paradise, a lover's paradise, and at the instant of greatest joy they touched the farthest limits of ecstasy. Shattering every cell of their beings, they became one in their exquisite union. He was deep inside her, filling her womb with the essence of new life, and Willow received the boundless love with all her heart and soul and body.

Just like that, they slept.

When Talon awoke the next morning and stretched to yawn wide, he found the once-warm place beside him empty. He came to his elbows, surveying the neatened room with curious glances here and there. The only spot that showed no sign of tidiness was the headboard behind him; his breeches had been draped over the deeply carved heart that decorated his four-poster. He frowned, wondering if she had read the names that linked the man and woman together in love. If she had, would she be angry? He had no time to think on it further, for the smell of bacon and eggs was luring him into the kitchen that was built at an angle off the side of the house.

Snatching his pants down from the headboard, he grinned one last time over his shoulder at the names and then stood to step into his ragged breeches. He had forgotten his sore leg, and as he was stepping into the tattered remnants that were his clothes he felt the sharp pain go lancing through his knee. Trying to keep his weight off the leg by hopping about on the good one, he soon went crashing to the floor. He landed on his butt hard, and Willow appeared at the open door with a hand clamped over her mouth to keep from giggling.

"Don't you dare laugh," he said crisply, shaking a long finger in her face as she stepped into the room, looking like a moppet angel in a borrowed overly large shirt that reached to the tops of her knees. He leaned back upon his arms, smiling roguishly at the slender length of her coltish legs, being afforded a very pleasant view from his grounded position. Finally he heard her giggle burst from her clamped lips. Her laugh was contagious, and he soon found himself joining her.

"I find you more down than up lately," she giggled through her words.

As the rosy morning light was spilling into the spacious chamber, Willow at once took notice that the heart could be read now if she chose to look that way. Following her line of vision, Talon watched her closely until her lashes swept downward and she was looking at his bare feet. She giggled again.

"Did anyone ever tell you what ugly feet you have?" She made quite a thing of it, gaping at his long appendage, his big toe. "Lordy, that's an ugly family of piggies," she said, slowly this time, counting to make sure all his toes were there.

When he snorted and growled like a huge, nasty bear, Willow squealed and jumped back out of his reach. But he was after her at once as she ran to the door, paused, stuck out her tongue, and then went padding along the hall barefoot.

"Ha! See if you can catch me!" She yelled back. "Bet you can't!" She went racing to the back gallery toward the lower stairs.

Limping over to the window, Talon stuck his good leg out. Once he was on the ground he pulled his sore leg out too. He hunkered close to the ground, staying near the wall as he limped over to the kitchen door. Hidden from view, he peeked out and saw her coming while she tossed glances over her shoulder now and again. Giggling like a happy little girl, she neared the door to the kitchen. She screamed then as he leapt out from his hiding place and reached for her, tottering with arms outstretched like a bogey man. She came to a screeching halt, swiftly changed course, and made to shoot past him. One leap on his good leg sent him crashing into her, and they toppled together into the moist grass.

"Gotcha now!" he growled, rolling over on top of her. His hands caressed her face, his fingertips meeting at the top of her disheveled head. He meant only to brush a soft kiss upon her lips.

When their mouths came together the hunger was renewed. It mattered not to them that they were lying on the wet ground; for it had rained the night before. As the blousy shirt she wore was convenient for what he had in mind, and she wore nothing underneath, he only had to loosen his breeches. It was an hour later when they rose from the ground, wet and shivering but happy, hugging each other close as they went inside to build a roaring fire. And it wasn't long before they built another fire outside the hearth. . . .

Chapter Twenty Six

While Talon's leg was on the mend, he spent glorious days in the winter sunshine walking with two gorgeous companions: One was his magnificent white stallion, the other his beautiful Aiyana. When she visited, which was quite often, and most times after school, she brought along a basket of goodies she had prepared for him, and they would have picnics in the misted woods flanking Strawberry Creek.

The air had grown chilly, though not uncomfortable. Talon breathed deeply of Willow's delicate, natural perfume. His eyes were closed, and a contented smile played about his well-shaped mouth. His hair was neatly combed back away from his face in the shoulder-length style Willow liked best, and she'd even told him his hair waved nicely when it was not so long. Rolling over on the blanket, she faced him now.

"You're not as pretty as you used to be," she mentioned playfully. "But . . . I think I'll get used to it." A thoughtful frown appeared between her eyes as she studied him where he suddenly loomed above her.

"Pretty?" He snorted softly through his flared nostrils. "Is that what you used to think of me, as being *pretty?* Be Jaysus! remind me never to wear my hair that long again."

Running a finger over his sensuously carved lips, she said, "I will, don't worry!"

"So." He tapped her mouth's cupid bow. "You didn't like me as a savage, hum? Is that what you're trying to say?"

"No . . . I just think men should wear their hair shorter. Leave the long hair to women."

Talon gathered the hank of her hair and brought it to his face, breathing deeply of the delicate perfume, the scent reminding him of a meadow in springtime's first glorious spread of color. Willow made him think nostalgically of magnolia and Texas mountain laurel, and the snowy and pink flowers of the lantana. And the irises.

"Iris."

She blinked up at him. "What did you say? And just who is Iris?"

"Azalea."

"What?"

"Anemone . . . windflower."

"Oh." She giggled. "Are you gathering flowers while ye may?"

Her head was turned aside and the tempting curve of her neck was displayed. He couldn't help but plant a kiss there, muttering, "Only one." His kiss went lower. "Aiyana, my only flower, *mi alma, mi fuego."*

"Muy bueno."

"What? How did you know the language?"

"Español?"

He threw back his head and laughed, saying, *"Si!* How many more surprises are there in you?"

"Muchísimos."

"Si, a great many . . . I believe you."

When he bent to kiss her, Willow's hand went to his chest trying to push him away. "How did you learn the love words? Did you . . . have many women who were Spanish or Mexican?"

What Carl had said about Talon Clay and his Mexican lover had come to her mind. The name was distant though something like Chiquita.

"Did you?" she persisted.

When he understood her jealousy, he laughed deep in his throat. "Just a few. But Conchita was every tomcat's girl."

"Tomcat?" she repeated, with a pretty pout. Conchita! That was the name of the woman Carl Tucker had mentioned, the very same one Talon was supposedly going to marry back then.

He sighed deeply, shaking his head and sending the silken waves of his hair into motion at the back of his head. "Willow please, let's not get into this same conversation again. I don't want to talk about my past flames anymore than you do." He tapped her pert nose. "You don't, you really don't, you know."

"So, they were your *flames."* She sat up in a huff. "Not more than a minute ago you were calling me your *fuego,* your flame," Willow pointed out ruefully.

"Lord, you are beautiful when your eyes spit golden fire and your cheeks turn to flaming cherries. You make me drunk with passion, Willow, more intoxicated than any strong drink ever can." He reached for her again, not suspecting his quarry was going to be so elusive.

"Flaming! There you go again mentioning your flames!" she exclaimed heatedly, golden fire shooting from her eyes.

"Willow," he murmured, looking at her with a disturbing frown, "I can't believe you are doing this to us." A chill wind whipped across the winter-blue creek, and Talon shivered with a premonition the likes of which he'd never known before. "Conchita meant nothing to me, honest to God, I swear it."

"I don't believe you!" She rose and pushed herself to her feet. "Carl Tucker told me you were planning to marry Conchita at one time—"

He flew to his feet, shouting, *"What?"* He studied the stubborn set of her chin and shook his head again. "Damn, you'd believe that no-good before me, wouldn't you?" He began to gather up the scattered items from the blanket, carelessly tossing them into the picnic basket. "I wonder if you will ever believe a word I say. This morning I told you I loved you . . . and what did you say?" He tossed a hunk of crusty bread into the hamper. "'Do you really mean that, Talon?' What kind of question is that, anyway? Haven't I shown you that I love you over and over the last week? What does it take for me to prove you will always be the only one for me, Willow Brandon? Why do other women always have to enter the picture? Damn, if you don't even put one ounce of trust in me, then how are we going to share the rest of our life in peace?"

Snapping the lid shut, Willow almost caught Talon's hand inside, but he was quick enough to pull it away before the damage could be done. His eyes spoke volumes as he stared into hers, telling her she was beginning to go too far in this.

"So you really believe I was planning to marry Conchita?" He stared upward into the leafy winter trees, then back to her. "How damn stupid can you get, Willow?"

She gritted her small pearly teeth, facing away from him as she gathered up the hamper, saying icily, "Stupid enough to bed down with you!" She prepared to mount Dust Devil, who had been rubbing long noses with Cloud, but was swiftly spun about to face Talon's glowering countenance.

"Oh, now you are really getting down dirty and where it hurts, aren't you love."

She slapped his hand away from her arm, blinking away the effulgence of the intruding sunbeam. "I am not your love, Talon Clay; you have too many women in your head, and I don't want to get mixed up with them and become just another one of your *stupid* conquests!"

"You are jealous!" he shouted up at her as the nervous mustang did a jig in the grass while she fought to control it.

"No, I am not jealous!" she yelled. "Why don't you go home and carve another name in that big heart you have carved in the headboard of your *Spanish* bed! I'd bet Conchita would like your bed—it's right in her class! I haven't looked, but I wonder if Garnet's name isn't even there!"

Tears burned in Talon's eyes as he slapped Dust Devil on the rump, and as the huge gray mustang shot into the air, Talon screamed at her head: "Damn you, Willow, damn you and your mother to hell!" When Dust Devil thundered from the misty glade, Talon leaned his head against a tree and pounded his fists upon the wood, conjuring a vision of the evil Garnet before his misting eyes. "Bitch . . . oh bitch, why did you ever have to come into my life!"

Sneaking through the stand of post-oaks, Carl Tucker watched with narrowed eye, his one good eye, as the delicate blonde played in the yard with a redheaded child toddling after her. A wicked red glow entered his eye. The Brandon child. A girl-child, with hair as bright as her mother's own, skin the same flawless ivory. A lovely child, if one could think of children in those terms. Runny-nosed brats, and this one was no different. The only difference was, this was Tanya and Ashe's own child. His greedy eyes shifted to the right, to Willow. She was a Brandon now, too. Too bad. He might have had some use for her, but now she was just as useless as the rest of them. Then again, he might just let her live and share her with his Apache friends now and then. The cracking of a twig alerted him, and he spun about to face his partner in crime.

"Is everything ready?" he said, saliva forming at the corners of his mouth. "I can't wait to get the show on the road."

"Everything's ready. I got the horses and the supplies stashed a ways on the other side of Emerald Creek." Harlyn Sawyer grinned proudly up at the huge bear of a man; it seemed each time he met up with Tucker, alias Randy Dalton, the man became uglier and heavier and meaner. "I can't wait either, to get the money you promised me so I can get back to the rancho. I'm goin' to buy my wife's relatives out, and show 'em who's boss!"

"Sure, Har, you do that." Tucker belched, passing his bottle to Sawyer, and that man took a swig of the fiery liquid and passed it back to Tucker. "Good stuff, eh? Never had better." He shoved the cork in the bottle and stuffed it in his coat. "Let's get goin', I'm anxious to set some wheels into motion. You got the gags ready for the girl and the child?"

"Yup."

"Let's move out, the time is right. Willow and the brat's playing in that same spot where no one can see them from the house. C'mon, let's take 'em!"

"Sarah . . . are you playing peekaboo with me again?" Willow stepped gingerly in the direction of the huge cottonwood she'd seen Sarah step behind. Walking closer to the line of trees where the wood began to grow dense, Willow stepped on a twig and it snapped ominously in the sudden silence all around her. "Sarah?" Willow's flesh began to crawl when the child did not answer, and the same feeling came over her again that she'd felt when she had ridden out alone to Emerald Creek. The hair stood on her arms then when she spied Sarah's pink-and-yellow-starred infant quilt, the piece of worn material she carried about in her chubby fist as she sucked her thumb at the same time. The quilt was lying forgotten in the carpet of dead leaves, lying there as if it had suddenly been tossed aside. Willow stood still, a sickening feeling churning in her belly.

Silence. All around her nothing but the dread silence.

"Sarah," Willow whispered frantically, her frightened mind imagining all kinds of horrors, monstrous beasts that could have dragged Sarah away in the blink of an eye.

The snapping of a twig. Willow whirled, thinking it was Sarah. A hand clamped over her mouth to keep her from screaming. She was being scooped up into bearlike arms, and then the monster was running, crashing through the woods, and Willow saw the canopy of the trees pass overhead in a dizzying blur . . . and then she saw no more. Before she passed into darkness there was the flicker of a name on her lips . . . *Sarah. . . .*

A gust of wind swooped across Sundance property sending the first leaves falling, and they fluttered like bright-winged birds to the ground beneath the giant trees. Ashe Brandòn watched his men combing the area, but his tormented gaze went more often and lingered the longest on the disturbing figure of his wife. Tanya stood by the rail surrounding the largest corral, her eyes staring blankly as she watched the men going in and out of the woods. She looked so helpless that it tore at Ashe's heart. His eyes shifted and he watched the leaves falling, mesmerized for a time, then wearily he pushed himself to his feet, rubbing his aching backside. He'd spent a whole day in the saddle searching for his child, Sarah, the light of his soul.

Tanya did not turn around when her senses told her someone approached from behind. Then her husband's warm arms enclosed her against his hard chest, while his lips merely brushed a tender caress upon her temple. No words were needed; together they shared their agony and the fear of never seeing Sarah or Willow alive again.

Softly Ashe said, “We’re leaving soon to go searching for them. I can’t tell you how long we’ll be gone . . . it all depends.”

“I know.” Tanya nodded. She sighed. “You haven’t had any sleep. . . .”

“Does it matter?” He answered his own question then, “Nothing matters . . . but finding them . . .” He was going to say “alive,” but he couldn’t bring himself to distress his wife anymore than she already was. He looked up then, seeing Talon and Cloud come thundering into the yard. “Talon’s here; we’ll be going as soon as the men return. They’ve seen Talon; they are coming now.” He turned Tanya in his arms. Looking down into her eyes, he could see that she had not yet broken down and cried. She’s kept all her sadness and anxiety locked up inside; he realized then that Tanya was in shock. “Miss Pekoe is coming, love—you let her take care of you.” He lifted her chin, muttering thickly, “Promise?”

“I . . . promise.” With all color drained from her lovely face, Tanya looked away from everything and everyone as Miss Pekoe came to fetch her to the house.

Dismounting and allowing the tired horse to roam at his will, Talon turned to reveal an ashen face and wildly frightened eyes. He seemed another man. Savagely he turned and smashed his fist into the rail, not seeing Tanya being led away by the sad-faced Miss Pekoe. This had happened to him once before . . . Carl. . . .

Talon's cheeks become enflamed as his fury rose. *"Tucker."* He turned his flaming green eyes on his brother.

"Tucker?" Ashe frowned, shaking his tawny head. "Tucker's most likely found his grave a dusty street after some shootout— What's wrong, Tal, why're you looking at me like that? Ahhh . . . Tucker's not dead? You have seen the bastard?"

"I have."

Clenching his fists at his sides, Ashe's face grew red and he growled, "Where?"

"I don't have time now, Ashe, but as soon as I have the chance I am going to tell you everything, even that Willow is . . . she's my wife, Ashe."

"So . . . now I understand both of your long absences from Sundance. I would congratulate you, brother, but we've a job to do. We've loved ones to find. Come on, let's talk while we round up the men, put Zeke in charge of them, while—"

"Ashe." Talon put a hand on his brother's arm. "We are going alone, you and I. No men, just the two of us."

"What are you saying?"

"I'm saying, it would be too easy for Tucker to spy us if there's too many."

"Of course, you're right." Ashe smiled a half-felt smile. "I'm supposed to be the Ranger, and look, here my younger brother's telling me how to run things. If that don't beat . . . what's that?" Gesturing toward Talon's Cloud, he said, "Cloud has something . . . it looks like . . . Sarah," he cried out, "it's Sarah's blanket!"

Flashing a glance toward the house to make certain Tanya was not watching, Talon swiftly met Cloud halfway across the greensward, and taking the bit of dainty cloth from the stallion's mouth, he hastily stuffed the blanket inside his buckskin jacket. Cloud nickered, tossing his white velvet face while Talon tried petting him. "You remember Sarah, don't you boy, let's go find her, what do you say?" He allowed Cloud to nuzzle the blanket peeping outside his jacket, and then he turned to Ashe and nodded. It was time to go in search of their loved ones.

Willow felt tears in her eyes as she looked over at Sarah's bright curls peeping out of Hurlyn's thick gray coat. She vowed to get them out of this danger if she had to murder both men herself, single-handed!

Determined she'd not let her fear get the better of her, Willow slanted her eyes upward and glared into Carl Tucker's face. He was ugly as sin. Though dark as night inside, Carl's outward appearance had not been all that hard to look upon when he was younger. She couldn't believe that Talon had grown up with this monster and not been influenced to such a degree that he'd become as evil as Tucker. Still, Talon had not entirely escaped Tucker's influence, for he'd become an outlaw right along with Tucker, who had turned him into one of the Wild Bunch. Talon had seen the light and had begun to reproach himself when Tucker had killed a man in cold blood while they had been robbing the stage.

"What did you say, missy?" Tucker bent his head as Willow's angry words came out in a muffled blur from beneath the gag. He chuckled deeply. "Suppose I kin take it off now; ain't no one going to hear you for miles around anyhow."

As soon as he untied the gag, Willow's heated words

spilled forth in a torrent of raging agony. "If you harm one hair on Sarah's head I'll carve your heart out, Carl Tucker!"

"Ahhh missy, ain't you being a little hard on poor ole me?"

"Huh, there's no one can be too hard on the likes of you, Carl Tucker!" she spat up at him, squirming in his bearlike hold. "What is it that you want from us?"

"Why don't you know, darlin'? I want me a pair of Brandon hearts to roast on the spit, and it's only the true Brandons I be speakin' of." He chuckled hoarsely. "Then again, it was Tanya what give me this bad leg and poked me in the eye, and that eye ain't no good to me a'tall anymore."

"You shot yourself!" Willow protested hotly. "And it was your own fault, too!"

Carl recalled the damaging moments as if it had happened just yesterday. . . .

Tanya had been coming along in her wagon and he had lain in ambush for her. He had urged her to pull her wagon off the road and up the hill, into the trees. She had done as she was told. They had argued over her horse that wouldn't keep still but tried to run. The horse Teychas had finally broken free, running down the small hill, swift as the wind. He had realized too late she'd worked at the traces to free the horse. He remembered Tanya's very words:

"Just look what you've done! Now she's run away!"

He had told her Teychas would head straight for home. *"But you won't be followin'. You're staying right here with me. Think he's goin' to be bringing back help for you, huh, little lady?"*

She'd said nothing.

He *had* hoped the horse would bring back help and he'd said as much. Meanwhile he was busy making plans for Ashe's inevitable arrival. He had watched her move closer to the wagon and had thought nothing of her gesture, seeing as there was no way she could escape his clutches. He had been dead wrong, almost dead, too. With her horsewhip in hand she'd moved quickly, before he could react to what she had in mind. He had armed himself then, lifting his rifle to warn her to back off. She'd slashed viciously at his eyes, and in that unguarded moment he'd stumbled back, clutching his face, and again he'd stumbled, this time over the draw bars. He'd reeled sideways, the rifle angling upward. Then, losing his balance, he'd released the rifle to catch himself, cursing every foul word he knew at Tanya's head. The butt of the rifle had struck the ground hard, setting off a thundering blast from the muzzle. He'd shot his damn fool self in the leg! . . . And who'd come along to save her, no one but the blasted half-breed himself, Talon Clay Brandon. He snorted now, squinting down at the blond head in front of him.

"Lakota."

Hearing her beloved's Indian name, Willow stiffened. "Why did you say that?" she asked Carl Tucker. Maybe if she played her cards right he might say something that would give her a clue as to how he planned to do away with the Brandon brothers. She had a feeling he also meant to include her in those plans . . . and then what would become of baby Sarah? Somehow she had to stay alive for the child and protect her as best she could, for she wouldn't put it past Carl Tucker to do away with Sarah, too.

"Heh! Like hearing the sound of your Injun lover's

name, do you?" Carl chuckled nastily. "Just wait till you see what I have in mind for him."

Now she knew Carl meant to lure the Brandon brothers by using her and Sarah as bait. He'd no doubt meant to accomplish the same evil deed when he'd abducted Tanya. But his plans had come to nothing; in fact it was he who had put himself in danger. He'd lost an eye. And he'd nearly lost a leg. She didn't care how he'd lost the finger on one of his hands, and she cared nothing about his losses—none of them. If he wasn't careful, Carl Tucker was going to lose more than a leg or an arm this time for messing with Brandon blood!

A day passed, and then another. They were headed north, that was all Willow could tell of their destination. Otherwise the scenery was pretty much the same as when she'd taken a similar route with Harlyn Sawyer on that fated journey into what had become bittersweet paradise to her. She would never forget her savage captivity. She and Talon had shared infinitely wonderful and precious moments together. He had been more than she had ever dreamed was possible. Never had she experienced such love, or such fear. How clearly she remembered his soft, teasing smiles, and his captivating touch. His beautiful eyes had reached down into her soul, her very being, and captured her heart. Often she'd melted into his arms with a sigh of pleasure, and deeper sighs of contentment afterward when they rested in the golden rapture. She sighed. Now everything was so different. She feared that Talon might think she truly hated him now. If she died, he might never know that he was the only love for her forever and ever. Her anger had been foolish; she saw that now. But he might never know how bad she felt.

Still, she was not the only one who needed to know that a part of loving was trusting to the fullest. Did Talon truly trust her? She thought not. No, how could he? Otherwise he would not have been so angry with her when she'd kept the secret that she was her mother's child. But was he still angry? And whose name was carved so tenderly with his inside the beautifully shaped heart?

"Missy, you better wake up now. We're goin' to camp here for the night. C'mon, you get your butt off the horse, I ain't helpin' you down. You can fend for yourself; just don't get no fancy ideas of trying to get away. I might have a bad leg, but I can catch you fast as a fox!"

Willow dropped to the ground, glaring up at Carl Tucker who sat his horse like a disheveled king. "I wasn't sleeping," she said, bringing a picture to mind of King Henry the Eighth that she'd seen in her history textbooks. Henry had been no less evil than Carl Tucker, killing off his women as fast as he took them to his bed. Only one thing was different. Carl was never going to take her, not as long as she was alive.

"Dreaming 'bout your Injun lover, wasn't you?"

"It's none of your business if I was," she told him, reaching for the child who had been whining continuously for the past hour. "Come to aunty now, Sarah. I am going to keep the big, bad men from hurting you."

Sarah went into Willow's arms and clung to her aunt like she'd never let her go. "She's cold," Willow protested. "So cold she's shivering—not to mention being terrified by the likes of you monsters!"

Carrying Sarah to a spot beneath a huge tree, she

tried to wrap the cloak more securely about the child's tiny frame. Fortunately, they had both been wearing wraps when the abduction had taken place, but the days were growing chillier, and Willow prayed constantly that the weather would warm up. Sometimes it did in December, sometimes not. But she wasn't even sure they were going to stay on the trail in Texas. One thing was certain; they were moving north, and it was always colder in the winter here, and most winters there was even snow on the ground. Willow automatically shivered. She hadn't seen snow in years!

Later that same night, while the woman and child were enveloped snugly in a bedroll together, sleeping soundly at last, Harlyn Sawyer moved closer to Tucker and sat down beside the man. Tucker cast a jaundiced eye at the man, then snorted rudely.

"What you want, Sawyer? If it's conversation, you better curl up with your bottle and talk to *it*. I ain't in any mood to be jawin' with you. Got my own problems to think about."

Taking a swig of the rotgut Carl had given him, Sawyer wiped his nose and mouth on the sleeve of his coat. With a look of disgust, Carl peered down at Sawyer, saying, "Don't you ever get enough of that stuff? You just about drunk up my whole liquor supply, and we're only three days into our jaunt. Can't hold your liquor, huh? You sure look like a pig's eye after two pulls on that bottle. Me? I can toss down two like that and never bat a bloodshot eye! Guess you're not a man, eh?" He nudged Sawyer hard in the bony framework of his ribs.

"Damn!" Sawyer swore. "That hurts, Tucker. What did you go and do that for?"

"Wake you up, that's what for. You always look like you're half in the bag or asleep on your feet. Think I'll just cut down your measure of booze, fella—we get attacked by the Brandons and you won't be in any condition to even do up your fly!"

"I'll just drink slower, Carl."

"You do that, Har."

Sawyer ducked his head sheepishly before he opened his mouth to speak again. "I been wondering about somethin', Carl, and I think we better talk about it now."

"Yeah?" Tucker sneered into Sawyer's face. "What's that?"

Sawyer backed off. "I-I just want to know what you plan to do with the . . . baby?"

In a low voice, Tucker snarled, "Why? What d'ya wanna know that for?"

"Well, I always wanted to have a kid of my own. My wife, God rest her soul—"

With a frightening roar, Tucker grabbed Sawyer by his coat lapels. "Don't ever mention God around me, hear? Him and I don't get along none, so keep Him out of our conversation!"

Sawyer gulped as he was finally released. "S-Sure, if you say so. I-I just wanted to know if I could maybe take the kid home with me. It's going to be kind of lonesome there and—and . . ."

"Take her, she's yours." Carl chuckled evilly. "Yeah, sure, the Brandons won't miss her anyhow; they're a cold bunch."

Chapter Twenty-Seven

The Guadalupe Mountains loomed above the rock-strewn earth in the distance. Willow had watched the sun set behind the escarpment for days while they plodded across tormented land of arroyos and sand dunes. Sand and more sand—and more arroyos. Now they were traveling west of the Pecos River, ever onward toward the rugged ridges. The countryside was made up of prickly pear, cane cactus, pincushion or strawberry cactus, melon cactus, button cactus, and turk's-head or fishhook cactus. Among the other desert plants were the Spanish dagger, yucca, sotol, bear-grass, century plant, mescal, goat bean, catclaw, and mesquite. Willow thought each strange and interesting, most of them very beautiful even when not in bloom. But her heart, naturally, was just not in harmony with everything.

Several more days passed and they were at the base of the mountains. Tucker had picked up a half-breed scout, *mingan,* Gray Wolf, and the Indian boasted he was descended from the Basket Makers, one of the earliest peoples in this area, more than two thousand years ago. He spoke English, and Gray Wolf told her his people had lived in the region from about the time of Jesus Christ until the year seven hundred. They were a long-headed people, with short and slender bodies, and he told her that they had lived in open caves, where later the great cliff houses were built. They'd made good baskets, which were used for many different household purposes, and, several hundred years later they had learned to make a plain gray pottery, which was used for cooking and carrying water. Then they had learned how to use the bow and arrow, and how to build strong houses. He pointed north, indicating by sign language and words that his people had settled there, several hundred miles away from this point of their origination.

"The Mescalero Apache have been here for century-moons, and they have held these highlands. We must be careful forever now."

With Sarah on the saddle before her, Willow reined her horse closer to Gray Wolf, speaking as low as she could and still be heard. "I know Tucker hired you on as a guide, Gray Wolf, but do you have any idea what is going—"

"Missy! Quit your jawin' else I'm going to have that horse back. She can be used for better uses than sightseeing," Tucker warned. "We picked up a lot of extra grub we're going to be needing . . . where we're going, and if you don't smarten up you'll be finding yourself riding front with me again." He guffawed loudly. "Don't think you care too much for that idea, neither."

Jerking her head around, she snapped, "I can't care

about anything but getting Sarah and my—"

"Missy," Carl warned, nudging his mount closer to hers. To Gray Wolf he said, "Scout on ahead will you, Wolf? I don't want to be runnin' blind into any of them murdering Mescaleros." He gave his attention back to Willow. "I'm gonna warn you again. That's it. If you try anything foolish, like trying to get Gray Wolf to help you escape, that there kid in front of you is going to be the one what suffers." His one eye narrowed ominously. "Wonder how she'd look with a few scars . . . here and there?"

Willow gasped, and then fell silent. She had nothing to say to Carl Tucker. He had already put Sarah and herself through a living hell going through the wild, rugged lands they'd so far traversed, fighting their way through the tough desert brush and tortured mountains of sand. They had been lucky on one account—that it was not the middle of summer. They would have been roasted alive!

Riding through the rugged foothills of the mountains was not so bad by day—tiring though it was—but at night Willow shivered in the blanket she'd borrowed from Gray Wolf, trying to lend some of her body heat to her poor darling Sarah. For the child's sake, she tried holding back her tears, but at night, while Sarah slept in the warm cocoon of her arms, the tears flowed freely. She fiercely loved this niece of hers, and she would do anything to keep her from harm. The only thing she seemed not to be capable of doing was escaping the one-eyed monster's clutches!

One day Carl brought his horse to a sudden halt, leaned forward, and studied a strange sight in the distance. Willow's mount slowed as the lead horse stopped, and she too stared: A giant column of black smoke seemed to be pouring out of the side of a mountain. It looked as though it was on fire. But that was impossible! A mountain on fire?

"Gray Wolf!" Tucker called back over his shoulder, watching the Indian riding smoothly up to him on his strong pony. "What the hell's going on here? Ain't that Badman's Cave up ahead?"

"It is."

Gray Wolf watched in silence for a few moments before he leaned forward and spoke in a solemn tone. "That smoke is alive."

"Alive?" Sawyer choked out as he came up alongside. "What do you mean?"

"Shut yer yap, Sawyer!"

The Indian went on. "They are winged creatures called bats."

"Bats!" Willow exclaimed, hugging Sarah closer. "Ugh! How awful, I hope we are not going that way!" She thought of nothing else but Sarah, not herself, not Talon Clay, only protecting the child at this time. Only at night did she allow her thoughts to roam to Talon, and then she prayed he would not be hurt in coming to rescue her and Sarah. For he surely would come, Carl Tucker had left enough "sign" behind them, and she knew he had done this intentionally.

The party struggled through the tangled brush that covered the gently sloping mountainside until they had come upon the edge of a large black pit leading into the earth. Mesmerized, Willow hung back, watching the moving stream of bats going down into the darkness of the pit below, and for what seemed like hours they listened to the soft beat of countless wings, millions of ugly bats swarming in the gathering twilight.

When they could see the bats no longer, Gray Wolf said, "The flight has ended. Like the bear in the north, they will sleep for many moons now. In the time of planting corn they will again begin to stir." He bent to pick up sticks for the fire he'd build.

Willow shivered, praying she would not be anywhere near at that time. She had watched them flying in a circle before entering the cave, rising above the rim, twisting and turning like dense smoke from a gigantic smokestack.

"What an ugly bird!" Sawyer exclaimed, peering into the pit of the cave.

"Bats are not birds," Gray Wolf instructed wisely. "They belong to the same group of animals we call cats, dogs, horses. Many animals. They do not have feathers, they have fur. But they can fly as well as most birds and better than some."

Now Harlyn Sawyer took a turn at shivering as Willow had. "Wh-What do they eat?" His brown eyes turned on the informative Indian.

As his long face swung about, Gray Wolf gave his answer. "Night insects. Beetles. Flies. Mosquitoes. These are the insects that are harmful to crops and woods. You see, the bats are our friends."

"Shoot!" Sawyer exclaimed. "Not my friends!"

Dismounting, Tucker said with an irritated growl, "Enough jawin' about them ugly creatures. Let's get those torches lit and get inside."

Sawyer backed off, his voice a mere squeak. "I ain't goin' in there! You must be plumb loco, man! Them flying monsters will eat us alive!"

With wide, staring eyes, Willow hugged Sarah to her

breast, trying to communicate to the child as best she could that no harm would come to her as long as Aunty Willow was here. She was getting worn out, however, with Sarah constantly hanging about her neck while she tried to soothe the child's fears. Now that madman Tucker wanted her to take Sarah inside a cave infested with horrible winged creatures—and God only knew what else!

"C'mon, I'd like to get some exploring done before we bed down," Tucker said.

"B-Bed down?" Sawyer pointed a shaky finger. "In there?"

"That's what I said," Tucker sang. "C'mon, missy, take your horse and follow us inside. Got those torches lit?" He whirled to ask Gray Wolf, seeing that the Indian was again one step ahead of him, leaning the third torch up against the entrance to the cave.

Carrying Sarah and leading her scrubby mustang, Willow began to recite from the Bible. "Yea, though I walk through the valley of the shadow of death I shall fear no evil . . . for Thou art with me—"

"Heyyy!" Tucker roared, waving his torch high in the air. "God ain't going to help you none, missy. It's Carl here what's going to protect you, so save your silly prayers for some other time when you'll really be needing 'em."

Gulping loudly, Willow followed close behind, her eyes ripe and wide as July's blackberries. She was startled suddenly by odd rock forms, which appeared out of nowhere like drooling monsters set to leap upon her and Sarah at any moment. As she walked further into the cave, the darkness closing in all around, she thought she heard strange noises, like sleigh bells . . .

windchimes, and one she couldn't name until Sawyer put it to words.

"Listen, s-sounds like s-someone's p-playin' a-a p-p-p-piano."

"Yeah," Sawyer said, captivated by the eerie tunes himself. "Hey, where's the Injun?"

"I am here," Gray Wolf said, his voice just as eerie as the sounds they were hearing.

"It's getting c-colder," Willow said, pressing her cheek against Sarah's.

"Co, weow, co," Sarah said, her eyes full of a child's inquisitiveness as they pressed downward to mysterious underground passages. "Mum . . . Poppy," she said in a tiny voice filled with great loneliness, making Willow's heart turn over in her breast.

"Oh God," Willow cried softly, "help us through this night!" Even as she said this, Willow began to gaze awestruck about her at the beauty and size of the halls and chambers they were passing through. Why weren't they suffocating? she wondered. Where did all the air come from, seeing as they were down beneath the earth? She did not feel breathless at all; in fact she felt an odd sort of exhilaration as they walked along a wide trail with graceful curves.

It was an easy grade leading down to the main corridor, but it seemed they had been walking forever and ever. When Sarah started to whine and she heard the child's stomach begin to growl of its hunger, Willow begged Carl to stop so that she could give Sarah a morsel to eat. "Please . . . besides I can't carry her another step. My arms and legs are aching, and I am famished, too."

Holding the pine torch high, Tucker turned about on

his heel and glanced down at the diminutive blond in her stained and dirty peach-striped dress, her shawl woefully short to afford her any sort of warmth. “Don’t want you catching your death,” Carl began, then turned to face the eerily ghostlike figure of Gray Wolf. “Suppose you could give her one of those ponchos you’re wearing?” He knew that Gray Wolf carried in his saddlebags various lengths of warmer clothing, but he usually dressed skimpily. Today was the exception. “Must be gonna get cooler, huh?” he asked the stone-faced Indian, who’d made a habit of studying the dainty blonde and the pretty child of late.

“There are rooms down here that are much warmer. But we have not come to them yet.” He pulled his poncho over his head and helped the shivering Willow on with it, lifting a heavy fold to tuck it about the darling cherub-faced girl. “I would have given it to you sooner had I known of your discomfort. You were shivering bad. Better now?”

“Yes.” Willow smiled at the concerned Indian. “Much better.”

“We will eat now,” Gray Wolf announced, tossing down a heavy pack he’d been carrying all along. He stuck his torch between two of the huge, solid piles of lime, being careful not to touch the tip with his fingers, for Indian rumor had it that by simply touching a formation with a finger, a person might remove enough limestone to destroy a whole year’s growth on the stalagmite.

“I’ll be the one to say when we should take a rest,” Tucker growled, nevertheless tossing down his own packs and sticking his torch carelessly into a beautifully colored formation that crumbled at the fragile lacelike tip. He tapped another lightly with his fingernail and grinned stupidly when the formation gave off a musical sound; he explored the formation further. "Ouch!" He jerked his hand back and sucked at two of his fingers. "Damn stuff bit me!"

"They only bite certain people," Gray Wolf informed him with a smiling gleam in his black eyes.

"Bet you never got bit," Tucker snorted.

"Have you not said that you have been in here before?" Gray Wolf questioned Tucker, watching him closely.

"Yeah—but not this far in!"

Hoisting two torches, Harlyn Sawyer walked about in wide circles, turning this way and that illuminating the chamber, causing the beautiful rock formations to become even more lovely as the soft yellow light shone upon them. Just then it seemed each formation resounded with a different note, from a diminutive tinkle down to a deep bass, strange and ghostly music.

Tucker's head shot up and he spun about as if he were about to be attacked from behind. "What's that?" He gulped, making his adam's apple bounce.

"Father Wind plays games with us, nothing more." Gray Wolf grinned hugely, his woodenlike countenance bronzed darkly by the many torches he had lit to illuminate the chamber.

"Well—" Tucker pulled an ugly face. "Tell him to stop. I ain't in no mood for music." He grabbed several sticks of jerked meat and joined Sawyer. "What're you doing, Har, looking for a jug of firewater some Injun might've stashed in here long ago?" He chuckled. "All you're going to find is some more of them stupid baskets then Injuns made hundreds of years ago."

Awestruck, Willow was staring upward at the gleaming draperylike formations, some of them hanging straight down to the floor. Some of them looked folded back or partly raised, as if a play were about to begin on some unseen stage. Gray Wolf hunkered down beside Willow, smiling at the child, who was falling asleep with a hunk of moistened bread held loosely in her hand. Willow was surprised when the Indian reached a gentle hand to the child's brow and tenderly brushed back a shining red curl. Feeling as if she could trust the Indian now, Willow again looked up, interested in the strange, wild beauty of the cave.

"They are like . . . curtains," she said. "They look so much like cloth that it is hard to believe that they are only fashioned of cold, hard stone."

Gray Wolf pulled his torch out of the sand where he'd stuck it and stood, holding the light behind a formation, smiling when the young beauty's eyes widened. "Oh, some are so delicate that when you put the light behind them it brings out soft hues of pink and rose."

"There is more," Gray Wolf softly said, taking his torch with him over to a darkened area.

Checking to see that Sarah was sound asleep in the Indian blanket, Willow stood to walk over to where Gray Wolf stood, his torch held high over something. She breathed in surprise, looking down into a small green pool beside the trail.

"How did I miss it?" she wondered out loud.

"This enchanted place goes on forever and ever," he told her. Then, leaning closer, he asked her: "What is wrong, little woman? You have trouble, I can see. This man is not your husband as he says, I think."

"He said that?" Willow paled then when she saw Tucker over Gray Wolf's shoulder. Tucker was bearing down on them like a stampeding bull buffalo, the torches lighting up his gruesome face in shades of angry red and shadowing it black as thunder. "Oh . . . say no more," she warned the Indian. Then: "Oh yes, the pool is very lovely." She moved past the two men, who were staring each other down. "I think I'll turn in," she announced cheerfully, though she doubted she'd even sleep a wink!

The sun had slid down the Guadalupe Mountain range and the white clouds had turned to rose. Now they were changed abruptly to a fiery vermilion. On the lower slopes of the Chihuahuan Desert the plants and animals flourished, even at this cooler time of the year, like the yucca and many species of cacti. Piñon pine and junipers dotted the slopes midway at the foot of the mountains, while oaks and maples grew in protected canyons. Sturdy specimens of ponderosa pine, limber pine, and Douglas fir covered the highlands. Wild animals roamed abundantly. Mule deer, jackrabbits, ring-tailed cats, bobcats, porcupines, skunks, foxes, and especially mustangs congregated in the canyons near water. This was the time of the year for mustangs.

Suddenly the rhythmic thud of flying hoofs filled the air, and then puffs of dust rose from the scrubby bushes and sand. A huge white horse came to a pounding halt and shook his velvety head. This magnificent one was alone, but off in the distance galloped the herd of mares. The wild mares saw the white one transformed to a glowing vermilion and stood motionless, until they broke and ran toward the stallion. Like a strong wind they came. Blacks, bays, whites, spotted, tans, their long manes and tails streaming wild and free.

Cloud curvetted from a leap into a long, easy lope across the rock-and-brush-strewn earth. The sweet fragrance of burning wood blew over him, drawing Cloud to the place where the humans had built their campfires.

The moon, crowning the mountain, cast enchantment's glow down upon the pine-flanked area where the men had made their camp; it lightened the face of the man sitting there. There was a tired, sad cast to his face. He sat motionless, lost in thought, a reflection of the man beside him.

"Lakota." Ashe shook his head, rubbing his two weeks' growth of beard. He stared at his brother, a half-breed, long and hard. *Half-breed.* My brother's half an Indian. "That makes our mother a whore," Ashe said to Talon, looking at him as if he were nothing but a stranger. "Why didn't you tell me this . . . long ago?"

"First, our mother was not what you called her. She was in love . . . with Nightwalker, Kijika."

"Martha, my dear mother? In love with a—a redskin, an Indian? Hah, someone has been feeding you a line, dear brother! So, who was it?" Ashe rolled his eyes, then stared at Talon hard. "It was Almanzo, wasn't it? And this Nightwalker . . . he's your father. That makes you and Almanzo brothers, right?"

"Wrong." Talon's face felt red and moist, his eyes hot and stinging. He licked his lips before he went on. "Damn, Ashe, I *know* Nightwalker is my father. He gave me a medallion; it is pounded gold with the face of the sun in the center."

"Where is it, then?"

Talon shrugged and heaved a deep sigh. "I gave it to Willow to wear around her neck last time I saw her. She was fascinated by it . . . she loves trinkets like that." Suddenly he smiled as he envisioned her sweet, mischievous imp of a grin as she took the medallion from him and hung the heavy thing between her perfect breasts. He licked his lips again, wiping the perspiration dots of his upper lip with the back of his hand. "She's my wife, Ashe, remember I told you? We were married in the village, Black Fox's Indian camp, and—" He looked down at the hand that had clamped about his wrist, and up into cat-hazel eyes.

"Did you force her to marry you?"

"Yeah, I guess I did." He looked down at Ashe's hand, then up again. His eyes narrowed. "I think Willow loves me, Ashe."

"You think!" Ashe snorted, shoving Talon's hand away. "God . . ." He ran his hand through his sandy mane of hair. He stiffened then, his voice grinding out, "Does Tanya know about this?"

"If she does, it was not I who told her."

"Willow."

"Maybe," was all Talon could say.

Slanting a sideways look at his brother, Ashe thought he detected a look of sadness, a brow burdened with pain. Ashe cleared his throat, saying, "Have you . . . forgotten her yet?"

Heaving a deep sigh, Talon looked up. "Garnet?" He looked at Ashe then, smiling. "I think she's fled my memory, Ashe."

"Let me tell you my story, how Tanya rid me of Garnet Haywood Brandon."

Talon laughed. "Hayes, you mean."

"Well, I got rid of Haywood, you get rid of Hayes—once and for all!" He slapped Talon Clay on the back, none too gently, and Talon coughed.

"Jaysus!" Talon pointed. "Look . . . it's Cloud!" He jumped up, pulling his brother up by the hand and dancing around with him whether he wanted to or not. Zeke and Roberto came running, seeing the white stallion, and they too started dancing a jig. Ashe had thought it the wiser decision to bring along two more men, and so he had won that argument with his younger brother. "I knew it; Cloud has been trailing them too! He found them before we did."

"Whoa, whoa," Ashe tried calming his excited brother. "How do you know Cloud has been trailing our loved ones?" He was the one to point now, up in the moon-balanced shadows where the herd of wild mustangs stood eyeing them from above on the rocky ledge. "Aren't those mares?"

Zeke craned his neck, then, after taking a good look, said, "Sure looks like mares to me, sure does. A nice brood at that."

Talon squeaked in a high voice, "You mean we have been trailing the scent of mares in their *heat?*"

"Sheesh!" Zeke exclaimed, sitting down hard on the ground.

"I'll be a uncle's monkey," Roberto said, then spun off into a spate of rapid-fire Mexican no one could understand. He reverted to English again. "We find thee trail to Emeralds Creeks and then we follow thee white one, and all the time he is coming to mate with thee wild ones? Aiy, aiy, aiy! *Increible!*"

But the two brothers could only stand together and

stare into the flames, each lost in his own torment and particular kind of hell.

Bathed in limestone-green light, Carl Tucker cast a jaundiced eye every now and again at the woman and child snuggled close in their sleep over by the farthest wall of stalagmites. He breathed deeply. He couldn't understand it. The air was pure and fresh, but how this natural ventilation system of the caves worked, he couldn't say. Actually, he didn't care. All he wanted was the Brandon men. Carl stared into the fire Gray Wolf had built.

He decided he'd have to keep a closer eye on Willow. Of course, she wasn't going anywhere. She was smart enough to know she and the child couldn't survive without supplies and without the Indian as guide. She wouldn't get very far, and she'd be attacked by the Apaches without an Indian scouting ahead of her.

Sawyer finished chewing a piece of the jerked meat and wiped his mouth on the back of his sleeve. "What are you planning to do once you get the Brandon brothers here?"

Tucker looked over at the pathetic sight that was supposed to be a man, seeing nothing but a drunken fool who would never make a mark in life for himself. Now, Tucker—he himself had plans to become one of the richest Texas ranchers—like one of the King ranchers, that was what! All he had to do was manipulate the fools working under Ashe Brandon, get Tanya under his thumb, tell her a sob story about how some Indians had murdered Ashe and his brother Talon in cold blood, tell her he was really sorry for what he'd done in the past—and take over Sundance for himself. Join Saw Grass with Sundance; that'd always been his goal anyhow. Wouldn't his poor mama be happy. She deserved better, always having to grub at Ashe's feet to borrow a little money to see her through the year. But suddenly Ashe had stopped lending Janice Ranae the cash she'd needed to get by. It had probably been his own fault back then, for first kidnapping Tanya . . . he didn't want to hurt her. He'd only wanted her to lead both brothers to him so he could murder them both at the same time. Sure, there'd been times when he could have picked them both off, but that was too close to home, and he'd been a fool that other time.

Carl Tucker chuckled to himself. When he had gunned Butch down in the street, a few of the guys thought Talon Clay had done it, 'cause the lousy half-breed had been riding out of town almost the same time Butch had met his end in that hot, dusty street. Yeah, he had gotten rid of a few of the others in the Wild Bunch, too. He wasn't going to let them turn themselves in like that fool Talon Clay had when he had gone along with his brother to Austin—and turned in all their loot, too! Talon had no right—damn fool.

Sawyer tried again to get an answer out of Tucker. "The older Brandon was a Ranger once upon a time not too long ago. Do you think we can fight him off? And his brother, who's a half-breed? Lakota won't be an easy one to cut down, either."

"Here's my plan." Tucker started off by unloading from his person all the weapons he'd been carrying all this time. He chuckled as Sawyer's eyes widened over the various-sized guns, daggers, bullets—Carl Tucker was a walking arsenal!

"This is going to settle an old score," Tucker said. "An eye for an eye."

Harlyn Sawyer shivered disgustedly when Tucker slapped his knee after pointing at his one good eye and laughing out loud.

"They will kill you, Tucker," Sawyer declared, watching the humorless smile play over Carl's lips as he studied the weapons spread out on the sand before him. "Why did you want to get them so far from home just to kill them, when you could've done it right out on the range, or on the road? Those two is always traveling."

The torches flared and grew brighter for a second, and Sawyer stared as the light struck the colored formations. They sparkled and shone, resembling church steeples hanging upside down in gorgeous colors of blue, pink, pastel green, jade, soft plum, like magical jewels in a giant fairyland. Tucker's one eagle-eye studied this stunning play for a few minutes before he went back to cleaning and polishing his many weapons. Sawyer stared at them all, fascinated. The weapons included Toledo steel knives, dirks, stilettos with razor-sharp points, single-barreled guns, double-barreled, horse-pistol, and six-shooter. Besides all kinds of live shot.

Tucker gave Sawyer a wintry smile, saying, "Don't think they'll have much of a chance, do you?" With the swift efficiency of one who knew his weapons, Tucker primed and loaded a long-barreled rifle.

Shakily, Sawyer asked, "Where'd that one come from?"

"Had it attached to my saddle all the time; you just

didn't see it, fella."

"Well . . . point it some other way, huh?"

"Sure, Har, sure." Laying it aside, still loaded, Carl reached for another.

"You ain't gonna load all those, are you?"

"Sure . . . why not? We'll be ready when they come, and you can take your pick . . . but don't touch the rifle. That one's mine."

"You didn't answer my question, Carl."

"Why didn't I pick 'em off closer to home? I'll tell you." He stared around for a moment, then formed his answer. "This place makes a better burial ground, the sand is deep, and there's pits all over a person could toss a body into." He chuckled slowly. "Two bodies. That way none of Ashe's Ranger friends will find the bodies, and I'll stay away for a while until the storm blows over and Tanya Brandon finds herself a lonely, miserable widow with no one to run her ranch for her." He slowly rubbed down the barrel of a pistol with an oiled rag. "Till Tucker comes along, and like I said, if she's going to make things rough for me, I'll make 'em tougher for her."

"What about the blonde?" he asked, jerking his head toward the sleeping figures. Willow's arms made a protective circle about the cherub-faced child, whose red curls peeked out from the Indian blanket. "You said I could take Sarah, but Willow ain't gonna let her go without a fight, and I don't think I want that high-spirited filly around trying to run things at my *rancho,* know what I mean? She's not hard to look at, I'll say that for her, but I'm afraid you kill that half-breed and *he's* gonna come haunting the both of us. If she's anywhere near, like if I took her home with me, I'm afraid Lakota's ghost ain't going to give me a moment's peace. I don't want that kind of trouble, I'm going to have enough to handle just trying to get my *rancho* back. By the way, Tucker, when are you going to give me those bank notes you said you'd give me?"

"Told ya, once the job's over. Are you good with a gun? I ain't gonna fight them off all by myself, not if they brought some men with them. We'll pick off the others, then I want the Brandon men to myself, want to watch them die slow if I can."

As sure as the hawk had its mate, Lakota would come for his; Harlyn Sawyer knew this for a fact. All the weapons in hell couldn't help. There would be no stopping that one!

Sarah was awake before Willow the next morning, but it didn't take Willow long to awaken herself once she began to grow uncomfortable and realize the front of her was soaking wet!

"Weow . . ." Sarah tugged playfully on the long, silken ends of Willow's hair.

When Willow realized where they were, she came upright in a flash, having forgotten that she and Sarah had spent the entire night sleeping in a mysterious cave infested with bats! How she could have slept even a wink amazed her. She must have been exhausted, and Sarah, too. Working quickly now, she removed Sarah's damp clothing and wrapped the child in Gray Wolf's poncho. Her eyes encountered Harlyn Sawyer across the way; he had been watching them all the while, she discovered. Gray Wolf and Tucker were not in sight, but she wasted no time wondering where they could be, for she only had one thing in mind now, to find a place to wash Sarah and herself in privacy. When she came to her feet, Sawyer did the same, and she saw that he was carrying a long-nosed horse pistol.

"You can put that away," Willow said, gesturing with her free hand toward the gun. "I don't think we are in any position to go tiptoeing from the cave and out into the wilderness to fend for ourselves. Go on, put it away." Sarah began to whine. "See, you are frightening her with that gun, can't you see that? Why are you staring like that, Harlyn Sawyer?"

"You," Harlyn began, pointing the gun downward now. "How come you're not crying your eyes out, or tearing your hair out in fright? What're you made of . . . stone?" He stared about at the stalagmites and stalactites. "Just like this spooky place—you could be made out of stone too."

Laughing lightly, Willow said, "I assure you, Sawyer, I am not made out of stone. You just don't see what is on the inside; I don't think you ever will where other people are concerned. Then again, there still might be some hope for you. Now, tell me where I can find a place where Sarah and I might bathe."

"What for?"

Willow shook her head at Harlyn's stupidity. "To get clean, what else! Besides, I'm sure you haven't forgotten the many times we had to bathe along the trail. Sarah's clothes have to be changed often . . . she's a baby." She looked down woefully at her torn skirts. "And there's not much left of my dress and pettis after making baby clothes for Sarah! Do you think you can manage to help me find a place where I can wash us up *and* our clothes?"

Stowing his gun and grumpily snatching up a torch, Sawyer led the way.

With Harlyn looking the other way, Willow sat on a stone lily pad and washed herself and Sarah as best she could. There wasn't any soap, of course, but she thanked God for the white stalactites hanging above that supplied the fountains with cool, clear water. When she was done washing Sarah, she called Harlyn over, as she had on many occasions on the trail, and asked him to hold her while she kept herself wrapped squawlike in a blanket to wash the rags that were supposed to be their clothes. As it was warmer in this big room with all its fountain basins, Willow hung the clothes carefully to dry on the shorter limestone formations. Then Willow joined Sawyer, taking Sarah from his arms as he turned about.

"She sure is a good child," Harlyn mentioned, his mind seeming to be elsewhere than on the object of his compliment.

"Could we go back to the other room and eat now? Sarah is hungry."

"Gray Wolf came and went this morning already. He brought some food and something fresh to drink. It's some kind of milk, but don't ask me where it came from."

"Milk!" Willow exclaimed, hugging Sarah happily. When she sobered as they stepped back into the room with the green pool in it. "Is it safe to drink?" she asked, concerned about Sarah's drinking an unknown beverage.

"Gray Wolf said it is better than cow's milk. It's in one of those Tarahumara Indian pots, and Gray Wolf said it's clean too, not to worry. He is also bringing in more firewood."

"Oh, bless his heart!" Willow said with unrestrained exuberance. She hugged Sarah, and the child rewarded her with a happy giggle, never knowing that her Poppy's ultimate misfortune was being planned at that very moment by a devious, maniacal mind.

Chapter Twenty-Eight

Wild and grand, Talon's Cloud moved against the sky; then he was gone.

Willow's hackles rose when she stepped from the big room with the many fountains, the dry rags over her arm. The items slipped from her hold as she stared awestruck at the white stallion. There was something about him, an almost ghostly appearance there in the cave illuminated by the many torches set about. His leonine beauty and wildness struck Willow—as if he was half-horse and half-lion. Talon's Cloud, she was sure of it. But, where was he . . . *Talon.* It had to be . . . Talon had come for her!

Feeling panic, looking over to check and see if Sarah was sleeping, she thought quickly of what would happen should Tucker come now and see the white horse. She was sure he'd recognize the white stallion as being Talon's own. Working swiftly, Willow reached inside the bodice of her dress, pulled out the sun medallion that belonged to Talon, and drew it over her head, moving smoothly so as not to frighten Cloud.

"Come boy," she urged softly. "Come, I've something for you to wear, my beauty, to take back to your master. Hurry now, we haven't much time." Her heart pounded furiously as she shot a glance up the slope to see if she could make out any torches coming, but there was only a dark void that way. She stepped closer to the once-wild stallion, and he tossed his leonine head as she approached. When he stepped back out of reach, she moaned. "Oh no, come back please. We haven't much time . . . please, come and wear your master's medallion."

What happened next amazed Willow. Cloud came toward her so swiftly she thought he was about to trample her under his flashing silver hoofs. He made quite a thing of frightening her, and then he brought his long, velvety face in a downward swoop, and when he straightened he was wearing the medallion about the upper part of his neck. He stayed still as she leaned forward to place the thing behind his ears . . . now he was stepping away from her. When she blinked twice Cloud had vanished.

Willow went at once to sink down onto the blanket, her legs quivering so badly she doubted she'd be able to stand back up if she had to. She rubbed her eyes and shook her head. Had she been imagining things? Was Cloud only a figment of her overworked imagination? She'd been dreaming of Talon rescuing her, as he had once before in the camp occupied by the Apaches and Carl Tucker. To make sure she had not been daydreaming, Willow reached inside her bodice and searched for the sun medallion. It was surely gone. She could only wait now. Stroking Sarah's red curls as the child slept on peacefully for now, sucking her thumb in her sleep, Willow tried to breathe normally as she stared long and hard, with eyes moist and afire, toward the black void that marked the trail that was the only way out.

Willow was so weary of the wait that two hours later she was lying across a corner of the blanket she'd slowly gravitated toward, her body gaining over her will to remain awake.

Carl Tucker was just returning to the entrance of the cave when he saw the white stallion running up the grade straight for him, the eyes flashing wickedly, silver hoofs churning up the sandy loam. Before the horse reached him, Tucker had his whip down from his saddle, and, trying to keep himself from coming to harm by staying near his horse, he lashed out with his whip and caught the white beauty across the neck. A long red welt appeared in the snow-white coat, but the horse kept on running, something gold shining dully around his neck as it turned and spun at his velvet throat. When all he could see was the rear of the horse, the streaming white tail standing almost straight as the magnificent stallion ran, Tucker lifted a hand to stroke his chin in thought.

"That there horse looks familiar." Then he gawked in the direction the horse had come from. "Heyyy, he was just inside the cave . . . what the . . . Gray Wolf." The man appeared as if from nowhere at his side. "Where've you been? I almost get trampled by a wild stallion and you get lost. You give me the creeps, Injun, stop sneaking up on me like that! You stay here, I'm going down to check on the . . . on Willow and the kid."

"I will stay close by. But I must gather more pine for the torches. I will not be far."

"Yeah, and watch out for that stallion, he just about killed me. He comes around again, you shoot at him, hear? Maybe we'll have some mustang meat for supper."

"That magnificent one was not full-blood mustang. He has the Arabian blood of the great beauties of horses. You will not eat that one, he will kill you before you get close."

"Yeah, well he can't shoot a gun." To prove his point, Tucker hoisted his rifle in the air and gave it a shake. "If it's gotta be me or him what gets it, it'll damn sure be him first. I ain't about to be kicking the bucket just yet, got too much livin' to do. And I got me some Brandon men to kill."

At length Talon noticed how all the sharp ridges or ends of slopes to his left ran about a hundred yards and then sheered down quite suddenly. Here then, was the main canyon through which the trail ran . . . the trail he'd seen Cloud vanish into as if the horse had been nothing but a wisp of smoke descending.

"The trail," he called back softly to Ashe. "I found it." He waited for his brother to catch up, leading their mounts. "Where did Zeke and Roberto go just when we need them?"

"Look!" Ashe pointed. "They are already down there. Looks like they found something. Let's get going; it will take a long time to get where they're at. They look like ants." He spun around then. "Talon, watch out! Cloud is coming up at an angle—I don't think he sees you!"

Talon stepped back just in time, and then it seemed Cloud was flying up over the ridge like a winged horse. "Whoa!" he shouted, and the horse veered before crashing into the spotted mustang Ashe was holding by the reins. "He looks crazy, Ashe, what's wrong with him?"

Cloud came to a shivering halt, his sides going in and out like a bellows gone wild. The medallion caught the sharp rays of the nooning sun and sent beams of light striking every which way. Blinded for an instant, Talon lifted his arm, and when he lowered it he got a clear picture of the magnificent stallion wearing his own sun medallion, the very same one he'd let Willow wear four, no five, maybe six weeks before.

The brothers stared, both too speechless to mutter a single word, stared too at the blood staining the white coat.

Gray Wolf watched the two men dismounting. They had not spotted Gray Wolf just yet. These must be the men Tucker had warned him about that morning. They were hunting for the girl and the child, these men, and they meant to kill her. Tucker had said that the girl knew something about a stagecoach murder, and she was going to turn these men in. Tucker had helped the girl escape with her child, and then had married her on the way, to protect her, "in a way," Tucker had told Gray Wolf. But this Indian did not yet know whether to believe Tucker about the marrying part; there just was not time to find anything out. But now these men were after the lovely girl and the babe, and he meant to see they didn't get to her. He couldn't kill them both with one shot; he'd have to lure them into the cave. . . .

The two men spotted the Indian walking about and then disappearing into what appeared to be a black pit. They followed the Indian, trying not to get too close to him. Looking down, they made out several sets of horse prints in the sand, going in and out, and some of the impressions appeared to belong to a smaller person, like a woman. They had found the cave, and they guessed that this was where they would find Willow and Sarah. Carefully, stealthily, they entered the cave, keeping close to the ruddy walls. But it was dark, so dark . . . was that a light way up ahead?

Down below, Gray Wolf emerged from the dark. At first Tucker was a little startled by the sudden appearance of the wild-eyed Indian. Something was wrong; Tucker could tell.

"They're coming, right?" was all Tucker said in the way of a question. He received a nod at once. "Good." He seemed to vibrate from head to foot then, blood lust shining evilly in his eye. "Where's Sawyer?" When the man stepped out from the shadows, Tucker grunted at the man just doing up his fly. "You stay with the girl and the kid. Come on, Gray Wolf, let's get 'em before they know what hit 'em!"

At the sound of all the excited voices, Willow rose from the blanket, baby Sarah in her arms and clinging like a pretty monkey around Willow's neck. "What is it, Sawyer?" Willow shivered. "Is someone coming?" Her eyes looked fearful and hopeful at the same time. "Yes, you don't have to speak, I can see that it is about to begin." She eyed the gun he held shivering in his hands. "Sawyer . . . why don't you let me have that? I know how to use it; I'm a good shot."

"Yeah, and who'd you shoot, Miss Willow?"

"Well," she began with a captivating smile, "we both know the answer to that, don't we. Give it up, Sawyer, Tucker will never pay you." She watched the flickering in his bloodshot eyes. "That's it; I thought so. He *was* going to pay you for helping him do away with the Brandon men, wasn't he?" She waited to see him nod before she went on. "He will never give you a thing, Sawyer. He'll kill you first. There is nothing but hate in Carl Tucker. Do you know he tried to rape me once? That's right, and he tried killing the Brandons once before, when he took my sister Tanya's wagon and forced her off the road. He wasn't going to rape her like many thought; he was using her for bait just like he's used me this time. And he's using you, too, Sawyer; you don't mean a thing to him, neither does your life. You are only another means to an end. He's used you all along." She stepped closer, keeping her eye trained on the gun. "Are you a man or a mouse? Come on, Sawyer, stand up to Tucker!" she hissed softly. "Please, do it for me, and especially for yourself."

"H-He'll kill me." He reached out to stroke the soft red curls nestling all about the child's round, cherubic head. "She's beautiful. I always wanted a child of my own, but my wife never gave me one. She was barren, see." He jerked away from the hand that reached out for the gun. "No! I ain't going to let this chance to get my rancho back slip by me. Keep away from this gun, Willow Brandon!"

"Harlyn," she cajoled in a sweet voice, directing Sawyer's eyes to the child as she stroked the baby's head. "This beautiful girl has a mommy who loves her so much she'd die of a broken heart if she never got her back. You know Tanya; you met her. You know Ashe, too. Their world centers on Sarah, and without her their life would be meaningless." Her eyes were brown and wide, the gold torches swimming in their depths. "Can you imagine what your life would be like if you'd had a child and it was suddenly and cruelly snatched from you? Could you live with the horrible thoughts that would run through your head, wondering if you would ever see your darling babe ever again? To never hold it close to you? To watch it grow? Never again, that's what it would be like for Tanya and Ashe if you allow that monster to take their loved one from them."

Harlyn Sawyer was thinking hard, his hand shaking worse than before. "No," he finally ground out, "No, I don't care about no one else; they never cared about me. And Talon, that half-breed, and his brother, they treated me like I was white trash. I ain't white trash, I ain't. Folks' been calling me that since I was a small boy."

"Harlyn, you have it all wrong. Ashe and Talon did not treat you like white trash. You didn't give them a chance to show you how kind they could really be, you were always frustrated and bitter toward them, ever since . . . you first met Talon Clay at the Indian village, and then Ashe at Sundance . . . what's that?"

When Harlyn spun about to meet the imaginary intruder, Willow's hand shot out and knocked the weapon from Sawyer's grasp, sending it to the soft sand below their feet. When Sawyer made a lunge for the fallen piece, Willow stepped out and covered it with the hem of her skirts, kicking it aside with the toe of her shoe. He scuffled in the sand, while Willow kept right on kicking the gun, until one last shove sent it behind a fat group of stalagmites. Before Sawyer could argue with her about the gun's whereabouts, running footsteps were coming toward them.

Then it all happened so fast. Several shots were fired, and as Willow stared into the fringe of torchlight, two bodies slumped to the earth right in front of her. She waited, every nerve in her body taut as a bowstring. Then, before her shock-widened eyes, Tucker and Gray Wolf stepped into the orange glow of the light.

"We got 'em," Carl whooped and hollered. "We got the Brandon bastards!"

Her heart banging in her throat, Willow stared down at the two bodies lying side-by-side, blood seeping into the pale sand, the long fingers of both men curled around the still smoking pistols. Tucker's gun was smoking, too. His was a six-shooter. He'd done all the killing himself. Two shots each for the fallen men who lay dead. And one shot, only one, had gone into the air. In his ill-disposed triumph, Carl didn't realize that only one more shot now remained in his six-shooter.

Crumpling to the sand, Willow's arms automatically released Sarah. She didn't even notice that the child was standing there by herself staring down at the dead men, and then she said two new words that did not register in Willow's anguished brain, but Tucker heard them; he heard them well, and he stared at the precious darling who had spoken them out loud; to Carl Tucker it was as if Sarah Brandon had suddenly grown two monstrous heads.

"Zik." She directed a pudgy finger at the first man; then the second, "'Bertoo."

Gray Wolf stared down at the dead men. It was as if a great, foreboding wind blew across his soul just then, and he looked up expecting to see the spirits of his dead ancestors coming to swoop down over them with claws outstretched like dreadful talons. He stared around at the four people, the two strangely-behaving men, the young, courageous woman who had suddenly crumpled to a pluckless heap, and the poor wee babe. His head jerked up again as the eerie notes, like someone playing an organ, a eulogy put to music for the deceased, floated along the air currents in the cave. Gray Wolf knew he didn't intend to die in here along with some of the tormented spirits; he was going to do everything in his power to stay alive. That meant killing Carl Tucker—who was clearly insane and full of hate—if he had to.

Blindly, wiping her nose on the end of her sleeve, Willow groped for Sarah, and the child went willingly into her aunt's arms, her round blue eyes staring down at the men in horrible fascination. Sarah shook a baby hand toward the men, wondering why they wouldn't wake up. When Willow opened her vacantly staring eyes she received her second shock of the day, but this was the most traumatic shock she'd ever received in her entire life. There, across from them, their tall forms half in shadow, half in torchlight, stood Ashe and Talon Clay partly concealed behind the huge stand of stalagmites!

No one was the wiser when Willow's eyes visibly widened and she stared down at the two men lying dead in the wheaten sand. Though she mourned the two who had always been friends when she needed them, the moment was stirringly beautiful as she gazed across the way and found a pair of amazingly green eyes speaking to her in the language of love. An intoxicating warmth filled her. After a moment Talon's mouth tightened and she realized he'd been warning her . . . she looked swiftly down again and then up, right into Carl Tucker's wary eye. Watching her closely, Tucker nudged the bodies until they lay face up, their eyes closed in death.

Tucker's eye narrowed over Willow's face, which, if he thought about it, seemed to wear a look of mild surprise. Too mild, Tucker was thinking to himself. "Too bad it ain't your Injun lover, missy." His eye flared for an instant before he went on. "Somethin's wrong, I can feel it in my bones." He whirled about, thrusting his gun out, but the Brandons, planning their best course of action, pulled back into the deepest shadows. "No one there . . . guess I'm just being jumpy." Facing the young woman abruptly, he stared at the child hard, wondering why she was staring up into Willow's face with such curiosity. "What's wrong with her?"

"Sh-She's wondering why I was crying . . . that's all."

"Well," Carl said, relaxing his guard, "let's get these bodies out of here." He gestured to Gray Wolf and Sawyer, indicating they were to do the dirty work. "Take 'em in a back chamber; we'll bury them later. Seeing as they ain't the Brandons, we'll give 'em a decent burial." With a terrible expression, he stared at the torches, saying, "I've got a much better idea for burying the Brandons." Uncognizant, he turned his back on those he'd just mentioned.

Now, only several moments before the action began, Talon's eyes went to Willow, as well as his heart. She had been looking so woeful and miserable, until he'd caught her attention with a dull flash from his Colt revolver. She had only broken down once, when she'd thought the bodies on the ground to be his and Ashe's. Her courage shone through, especially when she had looked for the child. He respected her for her courage and for the very precious love and protectiveness directed toward little Sarah.

Respect. This was a new word to Talon Clay, and he liked the way it made him feel inside, all rich and glowing, like a halo round his heart. He'd never known a woman he could respect. That one word chased away all the somber ghosts of the other women he'd known but never loved. Lust only made one feel empty. It cannot give, only take. Love is giving of one's whole self. Deep within himself, Talon now understood why he'd fought against loving her so completely.

Feeling into the buckskin pouch hanging from his waist, he lovingly caressed the lock of golden hair he'd snipped off when Willow had slept in their tepee, before she'd run away from him. With her, she'd taken his heart. Willow was beautiful inside as well as outside. He loved Willow Margaret Brandon with all his heart and soul. He loved her with a fire in his blood. He loved her with his mind.

And he respected her!

"Willow, Willow, I love you darling Aiyana." His heart spoke volumes, and just then Willow glanced up sharply as Harlyn stepped between her and Carl Tucker.

Then all hell broke loose!

"Hold it . . . right there!"

Gray Wolf saw the brothers first, heard the one man's voice warn him to stay where he was. At the same time Carl Tucker whirled about, Gray Wolf's gun came up . . . but he was too late. Talon Clay stepped out then, his gun held ramrod straight pointed at the Indian. Tucker heard the shot, then watched as Gray Wolf's head began to sprout a red stream of blood. His gun spun loosely in his hand, and then Gray Wolf slumped forward dead before he hit the ground. Wild-eyed and frantic, Tucker lifted his own gun a second later, and, aiming it at Willow and the child, he called out a warning to the Brandon brothers.

"Throw down your guns or she and the kid get it!"

Ashe and Talon froze, not moving a muscle.

Just as the shot was squeezed off, Willow ducked and shielded Sarah with her body. At the same time, Harlyn stepped again in front of Willow and took the shot in his chest as he turned to Carl Tucker, the meaning clear in his eyes. In horrible fascination, Tucker stared down at his smoking six-shooter, his look saying he had not meant for it to go off just then, not yet; it was too soon. But a reflex action had spurred Tucker into action. Hate and fear flared in his eye.

Willow, still shielding Sarah, turned her head to see who had taken the shot, and found herself eye-to-eye with Harlyn Sawyer. Willow's brain seemed to be clogged. She was seeing Harlyn . . . but was this really the Harlyn Sawyer she knew? This man whose eyes seemed to be pleading for mercy . . . from her? He'd taken the shot meant for her and Sarah . . . she knew it. The truth was there in Sawyer's eyes. As he slumped to the sand, Willow realized that Harlyn Sawyer had died a hero, not the coward everyone had thought him to be. She looked up again, meeting Talon's eyes, then she caught the movement to her left.

"Talon!" she screamed.

"Now it's the both of you!" Tucker snarled, lifting his six-shooter to take first Talon down and then his brother.

An empty click sounded; it was loud as thunder in their ears.

In stupefaction, Carl Tucker stared down at his empty six-shooter, realizing too late that he'd shot five rounds off beforehand, and given Harlyn Sawyer the sixth! With an insane glaze in his eyes, he pulled a long-bladed dagger from out of nowhere and went for the nearest man. The torch flared on his crazed face as he lunged forward, and it was then that Talon squeezed the trigger. Amazingly, his shot ricocheted off the stalagmites, making an eerie dancing melody that resounded with the shot in the huge, winding corridor. He blinked his eyes wide. There was no one there to receive his bullet, nothing but open space. . . .

"Ahh . . ."

Ashe, too, had been about to pull his trigger when Carl lunged for Talon, but the man with the clumsy leg was overhasty in his desire to murder, and he tripped on a new growth of stalagmites near an open pit. He stumbled, reached for nothing but air, and then fell headlong into the pit, which was infested with the hibernating bats clinging to the ceiling upside down. Ashe took down a torch, and holding it over the stinking pit he looked down at Carl Tucker and shook his head, sucking his teeth with his lips. Talon, wrapping his arm about Willow's waist, joined his brother at the edge of the bat hole.

From out of Carl Tucker's belly protruded a gigantic, razor-sharp stalagmite. He was lying impaled there, almost in midair, his sightless eyes staring up at the live ceiling above him, staring as they would for possibly hundreds of years to come. . . .

"Good riddance," said Talon Clay Brandon, taking a shiny gold locket from out of his pocket and tossing it, too, into the pit, never hearing it reach the bottom, "Good riddance . . . to both of you."

SUNDANCE, three weeks later.

The New Year had come and been long gone before the weary riders ever reached Sundance. It was a glorious, sunny day in February now, and one and all, even little Sarah, had recuperated from their long ordeal. Christmas had been celebrated shortly after their return, Tanya wanting it that way, and Ashe agreeing wholeheartedly. Gifts had been exchanged, too. Today everyone was enjoying those gifts: Ashe, a new leather saddle that Tanya had had put away for a long time; Sarah, all her new toys and cute little clothes; Tanya, a new sewing machine she'd been longing for; Clem; Samson; the drovers; the mustangers; Miss Pekoe; and the other housemaids . . . and special prayers had been said for the deceased, Roberto and Zeke. Talon had been saving his present especially for this sunshiny day when he and Willow could walk in the woods and spend some time away from everyone.

And so did Willow have a surprise for Talon Clay.

Talon turned to pull Willow beneath the spreading arms of a huge cottonwood. It was nice and cozy where they stood, with rays of pale yellow sunshine finding them and wrapping them in a delicious blanket of warmth.

"I have something for you," Talon murmured against Willow's forehead. He kept his eyes trained on her face as he brought his hand up with a brown-wrapped package.

With a tinkling laugh, she said, "I've been wondering what you have been carrying in your hand all this time." She slanted a flirtatious look up at him from beneath her long, tawny lashes.

"Well." He tapped her hand when she hesitated. "Go ahead, open it."

"First," she softly said, laying it aside to reach up and wrap her arms about his neck, "I want a kiss. I've been dying to have you kiss me, Talon Clay."

He murmured deep in his throat, and, moving closer, much closer, he said, "I'd be more than happy to oblige you, sweet Pussywillow."

When their lips made contact, it was like thousands of tiny shock waves ran through their flesh. The breath-robbing kiss deepened, and then he placed scalding kisses tenderly across her face, down her throat—and then her bodice was being opened with a swift hand that shook. He returned to her lips, and the sun-warmed kiss went on forever, so sweet and wild that it shook the very ground they stood on. Hungry for more, Willow pressed her soft body nearer to his, feeling with delight his hand slip beneath her skirts and then across her belly. He gasped then and tore his lips from her bruised ones. Powerful currents of desire were pulsing through his loins.

"Willow . . . please, I have to have you . . . now."

He gave her no time to answer, for next he was peeling her dress off over her head and pulling her gently down with him to the grass. Talon kissed Willow until she was weak with desire, so weak that when he penetrated her the force of his entry triggered a huge explosion inside of her. His manhood reached like tongues of fire deep into her womanhood. The joy of ultimate ecstasy burst over them, imprinting itself forever and ever on both their hearts. She joined with him so quickly this time that Talon could hardly believe it was happening, for he'd thought she would never keep up with his ardent passion.

When it was over Talon cupped her fine chin in his big hand, his eyes like huge, sparkling emeralds, framed by soft brown lashes that were unbelievably long for a man. Their faces were mere inches apart when he slid his hand across her damp belly. He smiled into her eyes, saying:

"What is your present to me?" As he said this, his hand rested on the tiny, rounded lump beneath her belly button. "Can I guess?" While he asked her this, his hand gently massaged her. She nodded, her eyes growing larger. "Let me see . . . you have been sick most every morning for the last three weeks, ah, give or take a few days. Ah . . . you have strange cravings in the middle of the night . . . your sister has told me about that one. I wouldn't know, because you have been recuperating at *her* house." Lovingly he gazed into her eyes, "When will you come and live with me and . . ."

Be my love? Was this what he'd been about to say to her? He must love her . . . he just had to! There was only one way she could find out . . . if he wasn't going to tell her.

When he finally let her go, she gathered her clothes and began to dress, hurrying now that she had to go and see something for herself. When she realized he was still sitting there naked as the day he was born, she knew the truth had to come from her own lips. But he knew it already!

"I am having our baby!" she stood, whirling around to announce it to the whole world.

"I knew it," Talon said with a gasp, dragging his pants up as he stood, then jerking them on and racing along with her. She seemed to have a single purpose in mind, was already breaking out in a run up the hill from Strawberry Creek. "Wait! Willow . . . what the heck . . . where are you going. Damn . . . woman, wait till I get my pants up!"

When Talon finally caught up with her, she was standing in the doorway of the bedroom in Le Petit Sundance, and then as he came up behind her and she detected his presence, she broke away and ran to the bed. Kneeling on the mattress, she pressed her hand to the beautifully executed carving on the headboard, tracing the names imprisoned there forever in the huge, curving heart. Happy tears came to her eyes as she stared until her eyes burned.

"You forgot something," Talon said tenderly from the doorway. Willow turned and looked down at the unopened package, then, thinking the shape of the package looked somewhat familiar. She looked over to the dresser, and her heart leapt when she saw that the lovely tortoiseshell comb and brush set was missing. Her gaze slid over and met Talon's. He held the package out, smiling sheepishly.

Once more Willow turned to admire the lovely heart, and when she turned about, her sweet face was a wreath of happy smiles as he shouted the heart's message at the top of his lungs. Willow went running into Talon's open, waiting arms. Holding her close, his eyes went to the carved heart . . . already knowing in *his* heart what was forever engraved there. . . .

Talon Clay

Loves

Willow Margaret

THE ECSTASY SERIES
by Janelle Taylor

SAVAGE ECSTASY (Pub. date 8/1/81) (0824, $3.50)

DEFIANT ECSTASY (Pub. date 2/1/82) (0931, $3.50)

FORBIDDEN ECSTASY (Pub. date 7/1/82) (1014, $3.50)

BRAZEN ECSTASY (Pub. date 3/1/83) (1133, $3.50)

TENDER ECSTASY (Pub. date 6/1/83) (1212, $3.75)

STOLEN ECSTASY (Pub. date 9/1/85) (1621, $3.95)

Plus other bestsellers by Janelle:

GOLDEN TORMENT (Pub. date 2/1/84) (1323, $3.75)

LOVE ME WITH FURY (Pub. date 9/1/83) (1248, $3.75)

FIRST LOVE, WILD LOVE
(Pub. date 10/1/84) (1431, $3.75)

SAVAGE CONQUEST (Pub. date 2/1/85) (1533, $3.75)

DESTINY'S TEMPTRESS
(Pub. date 2/1/86) (1761, $3.95)

SWEET SAVAGE HEART
(Pub. date 10/1/86) (1900, $3.95)

Available wherever paperbacks are sold, or order direct from the Publisher. Send cover price plus 50¢ per copy for mailing and handling to Zebra Books, Dept. 1923, 475 Park Avenue South, New York, N.Y. 10016. Residents of New York, New Jersey and Pennsylvania must include sales tax. DO NOT SEND CASH.